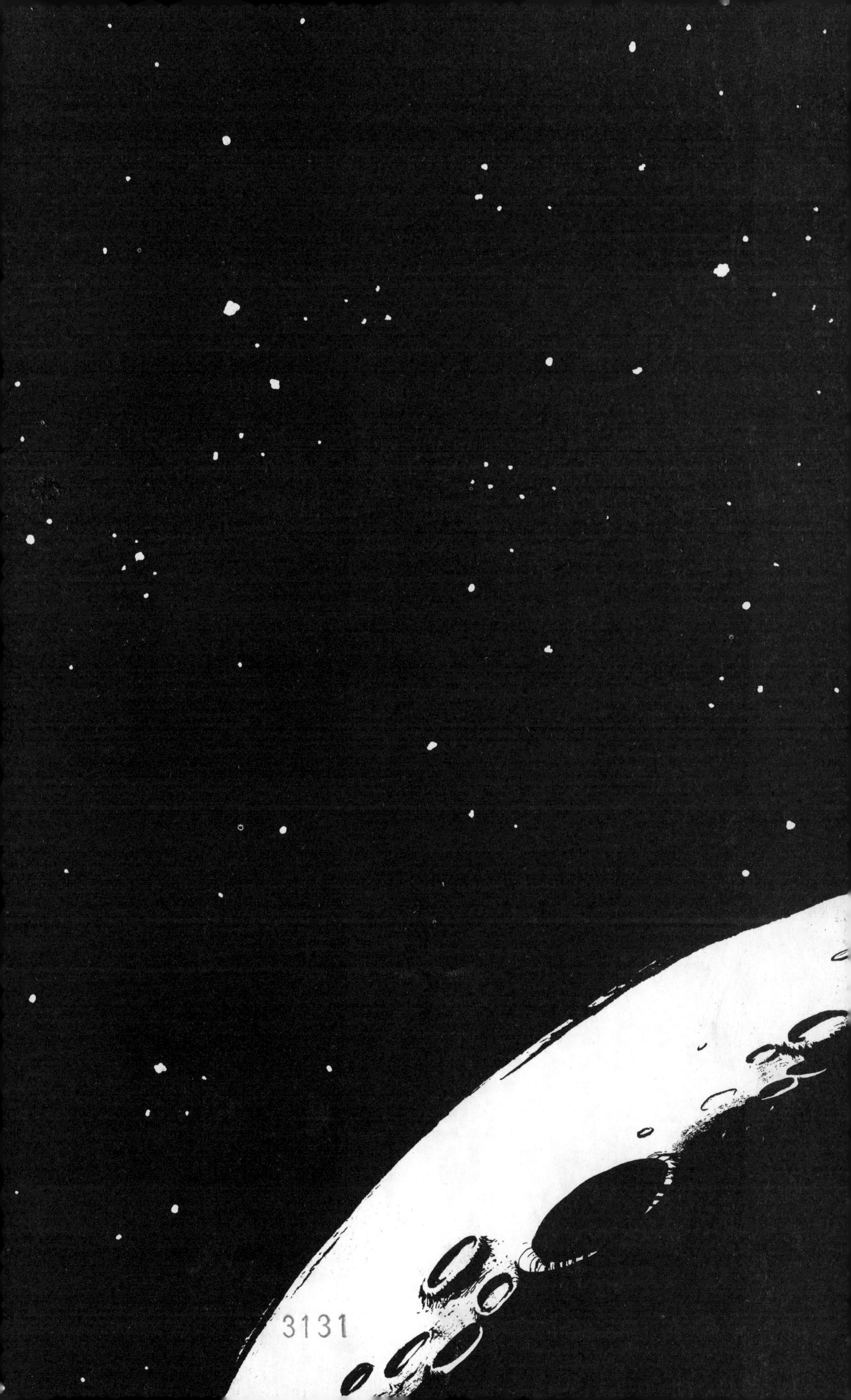

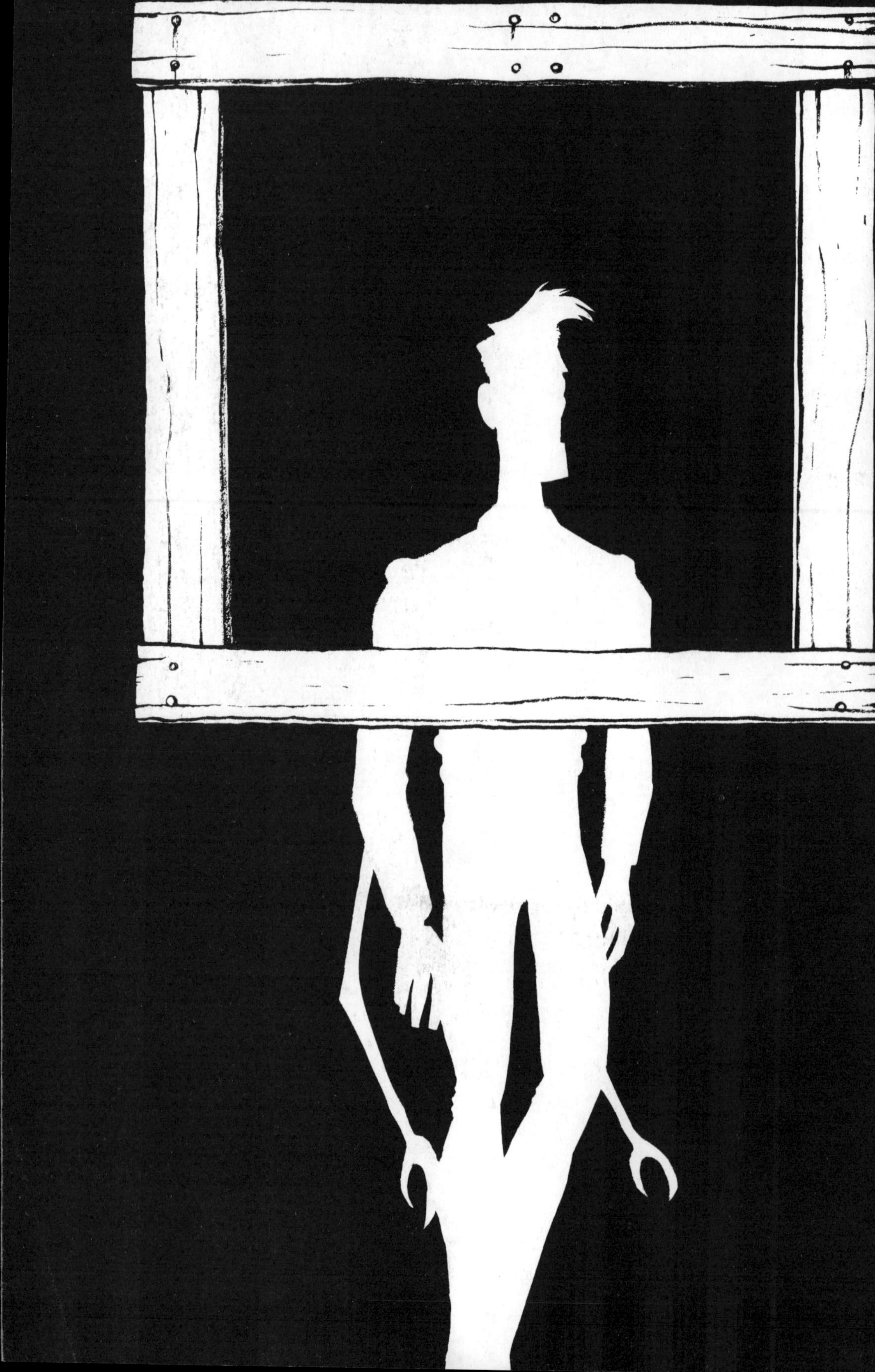

Creature Tech

by
**Doug
TenNapel**

Lettered by Digital Chameleon

Edited by Chris Staros

Editing Assistance by Rob Venditti-Kramer

Art Direction by Brett Warnock

Published by Top Shelf Productions

www.tennapel.com

Doug wishes to thank: Creative consultant: Philip Simon. Tech consultants: Joe Potter, Brian Godawa, Greg Egland. Reference crew: Edward Schofield, Don Rossiter, Dave Schmidli, Hugh Speed, Randy Whittaker, Ellis Goodson. Family and friends: Angie, baby Ahmi, Mom and Dad, Charlie G., Gill H. Counsel: Jeff Rose. Inspiration: Koukl, Behe, Prager, Dembski, Lewis, Dr. Johnson.

Creature Tech © 2002, 2003 by Doug TenNapel

Top Shelf Productions, Inc. PO Box 1282, Marietta, Ga 30061-1282. www.topshelfcomix.com. Published by Top Shelf Productions, Inc. Top Shelf Productions and the Top Shelf logo are ™ and © by Top Shelf Productions, Inc. All rights reserved. No part of the contents of this book may be reproduced without the written permission of the publisher, except for small excerpts for purposes of review. Second printing: February 2003.
Printed in Canada

ISBN: 1-891830-34-1
1. Graphic Novels
2. Science Fiction

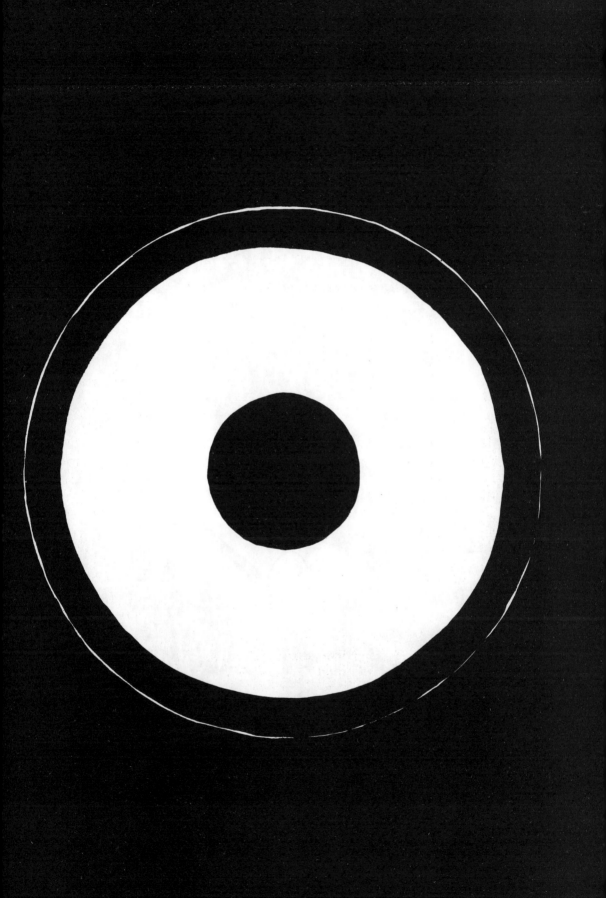

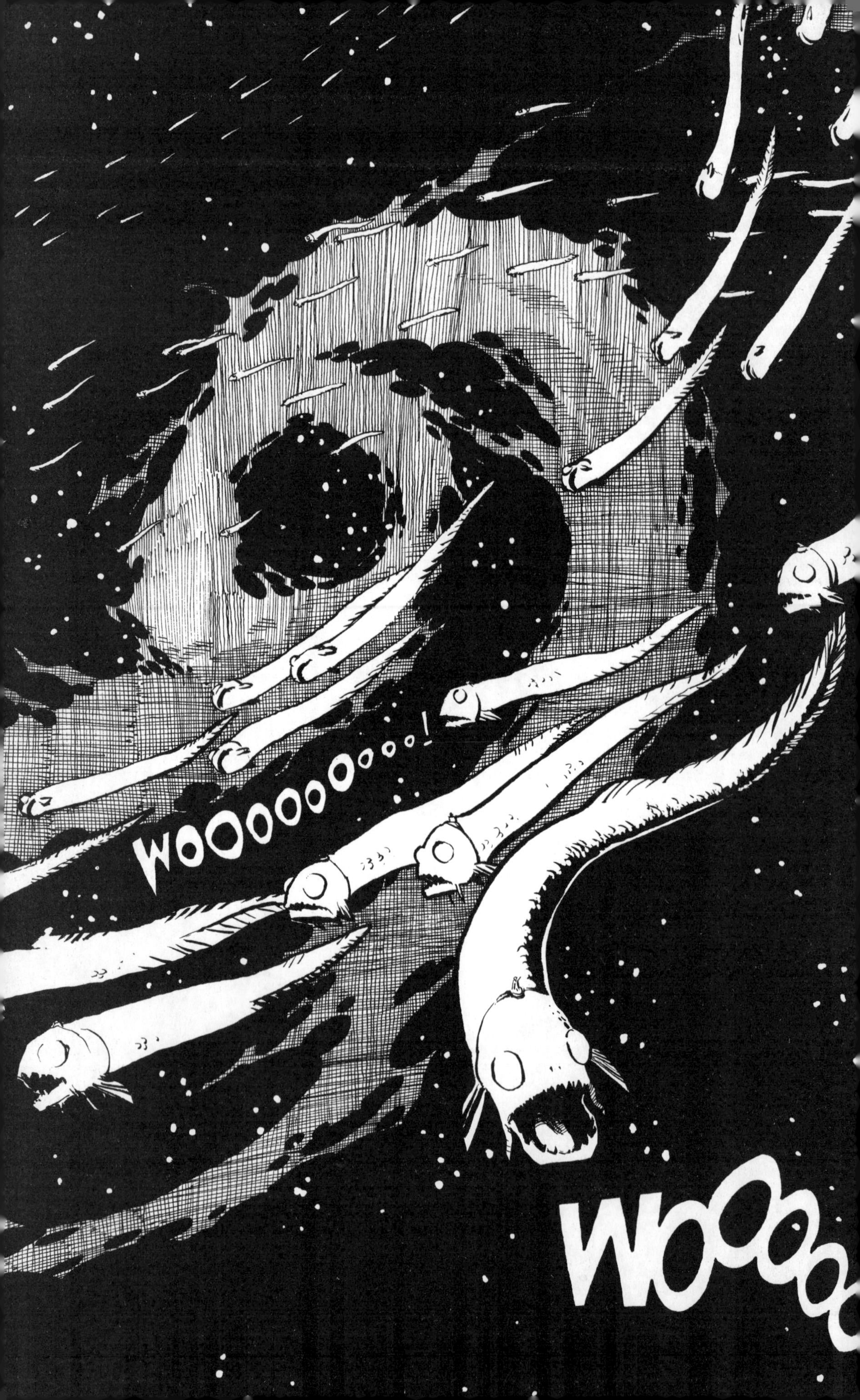
WOOOOOOooo!
WOOOOO

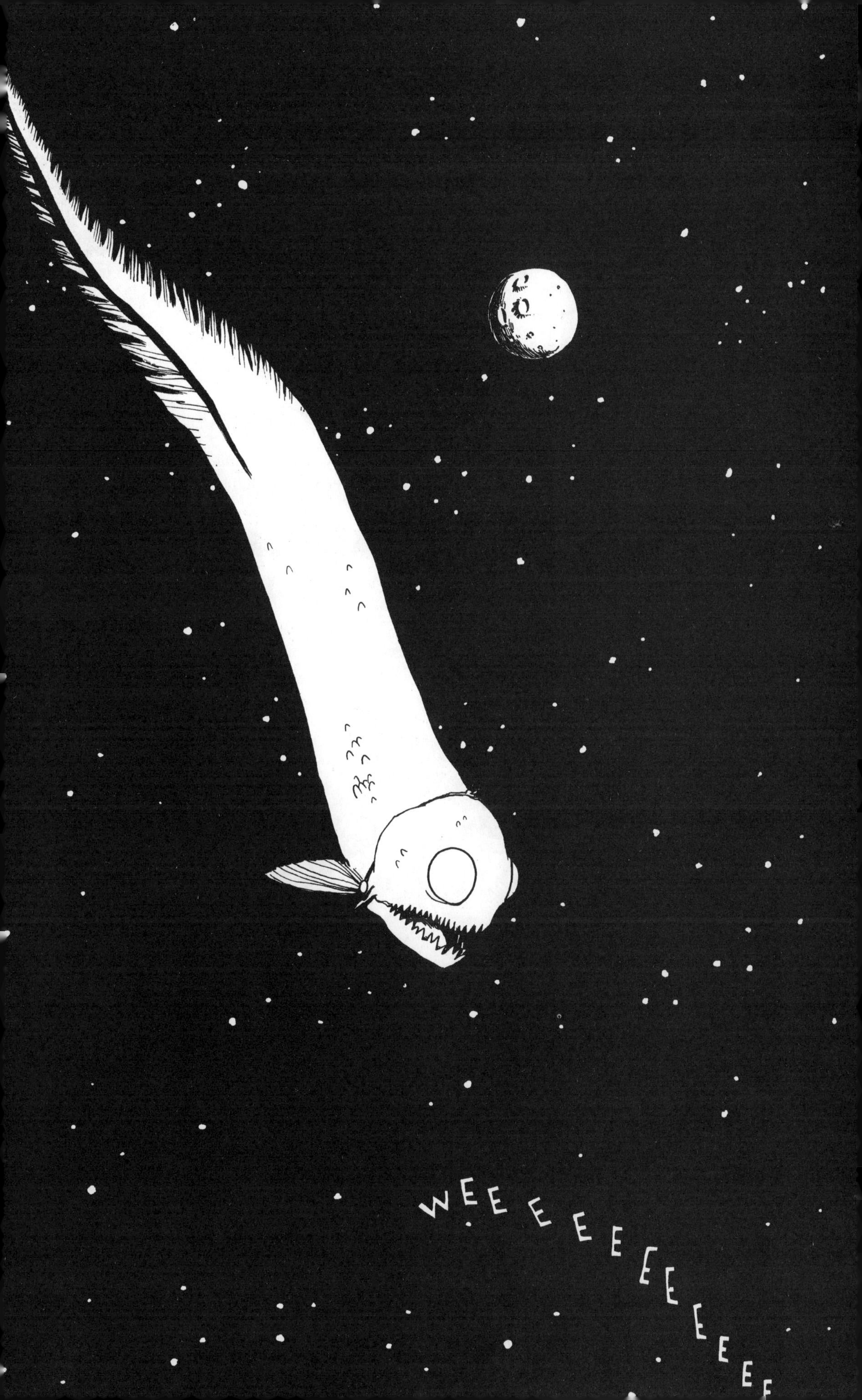
WEEEEEEEEEE

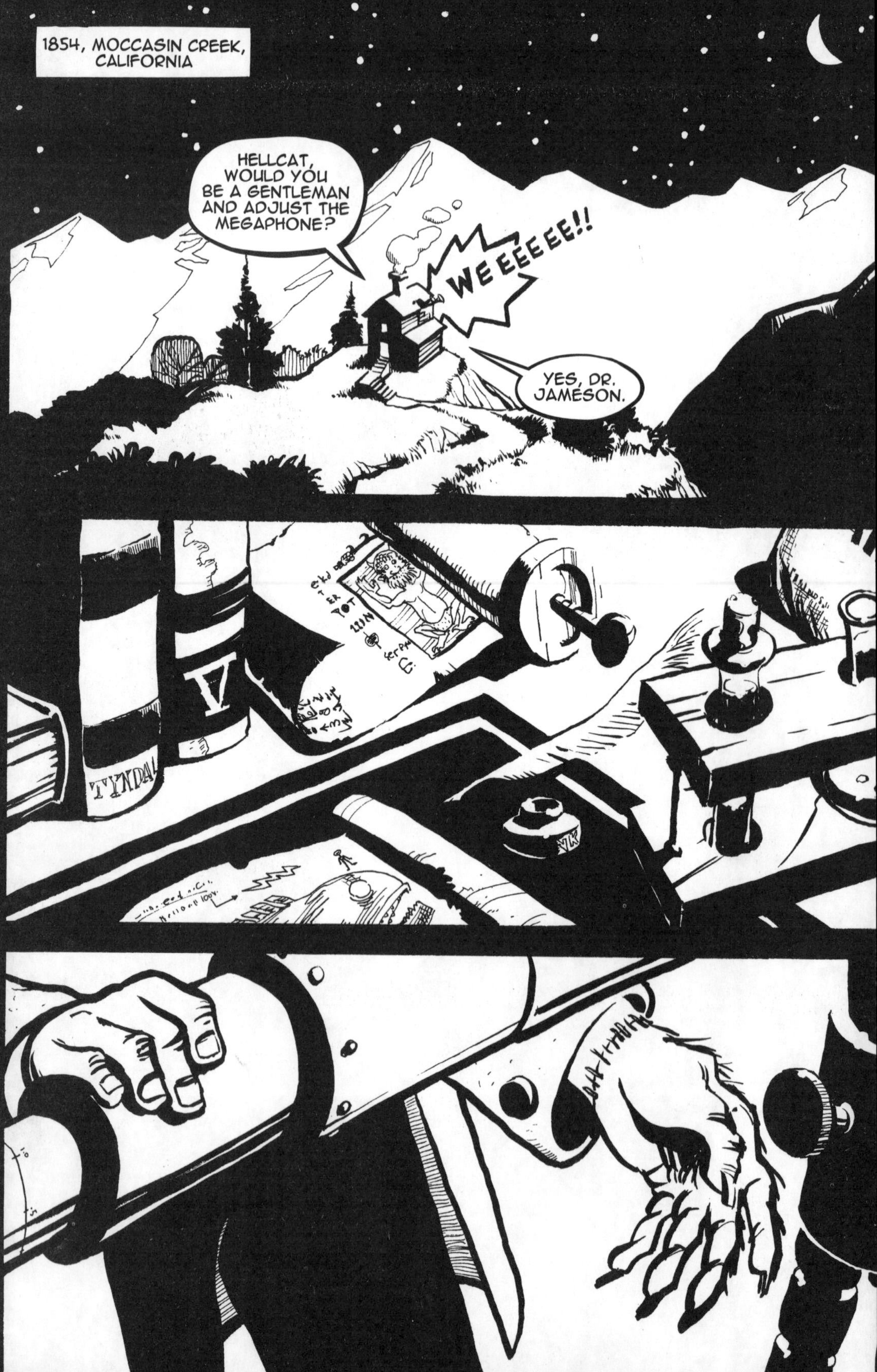
1854, MOCCASIN CREEK, CALIFORNIA
HELLCAT, WOULD YOU BE A GENTLEMAN AND ADJUST THE MEGAPHONE?
WEEEEEE!!
YES, DR. JAMESON.

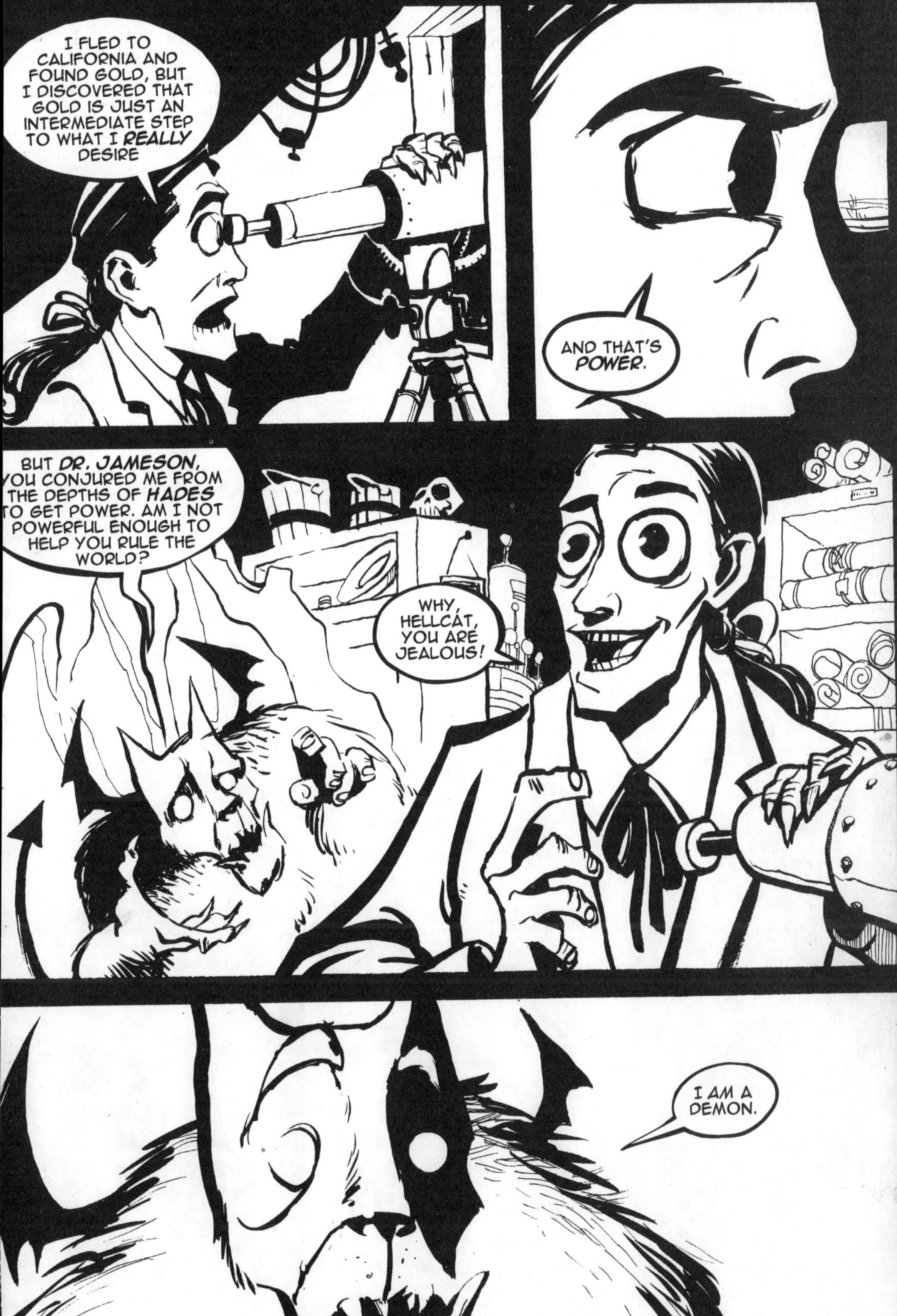
I FLED TO CALIFORNIA AND FOUND GOLD, BUT I DISCOVERED THAT GOLD IS JUST AN INTERMEDIATE STEP TO WHAT I *REALLY* DESIRE
AND THAT'S *POWER*.
BUT *DR. JAMESON*, YOU CONJURED ME FROM THE DEPTHS OF *HADES* TO GET POWER. AM I NOT POWERFUL ENOUGH TO HELP YOU RULE THE WORLD?
WHY, HELLCAT, YOU ARE JEALOUS!
I AM A DEMON.

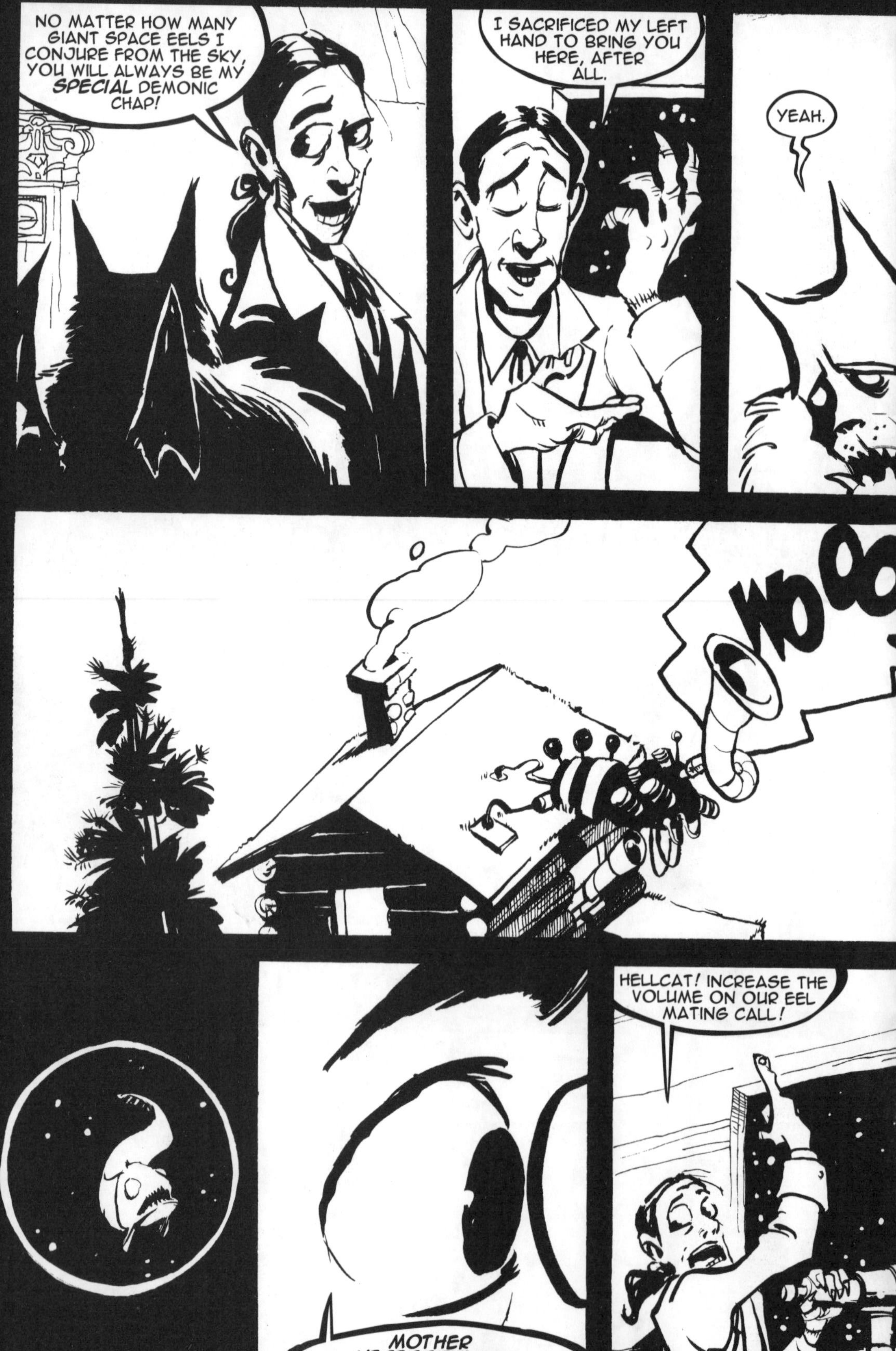
NO MATTER HOW MANY GIANT SPACE EELS I CONJURE FROM THE SKY, YOU WILL ALWAYS BE MY SPECIAL DEMONIC CHAP!
I SACRIFICED MY LEFT HAND TO BRING YOU HERE, AFTER ALL.
YEAH.
MOTHER NECESSITY! THE GIANT SPACE EEL APPROACHES! AT LAST MY PLAN FOR VENGEANCE COMES TO FRUITION!
HELLCAT! INCREASE THE VOLUME ON OUR EEL MATING CALL!

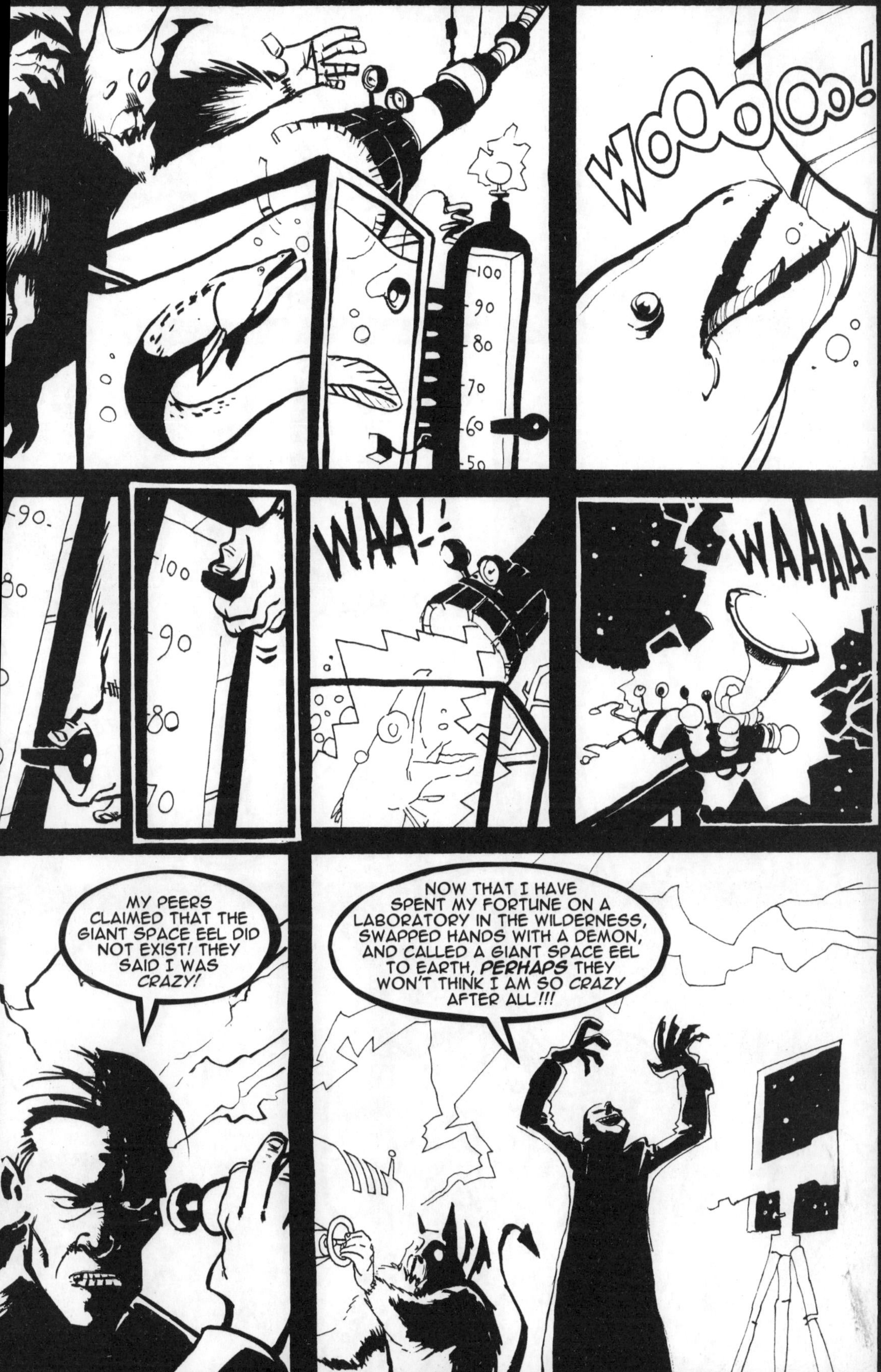
100
90
80
70
60
50
WOOOOO!
90
80
100
90
80
70
WAA!!
WAAAA-
MY PEERS CLAIMED THAT THE GIANT SPACE EEL DID NOT EXIST! THEY SAID I WAS *CRAZY!*
NOW THAT I HAVE SPENT MY FORTUNE ON A LABORATORY IN THE WILDERNESS, SWAPPED HANDS WITH A DEMON, AND CALLED A GIANT SPACE EEL TO EARTH, ***PERHAPS*** THEY WON'T THINK I AM SO *CRAZY* AFTER ALL!!!

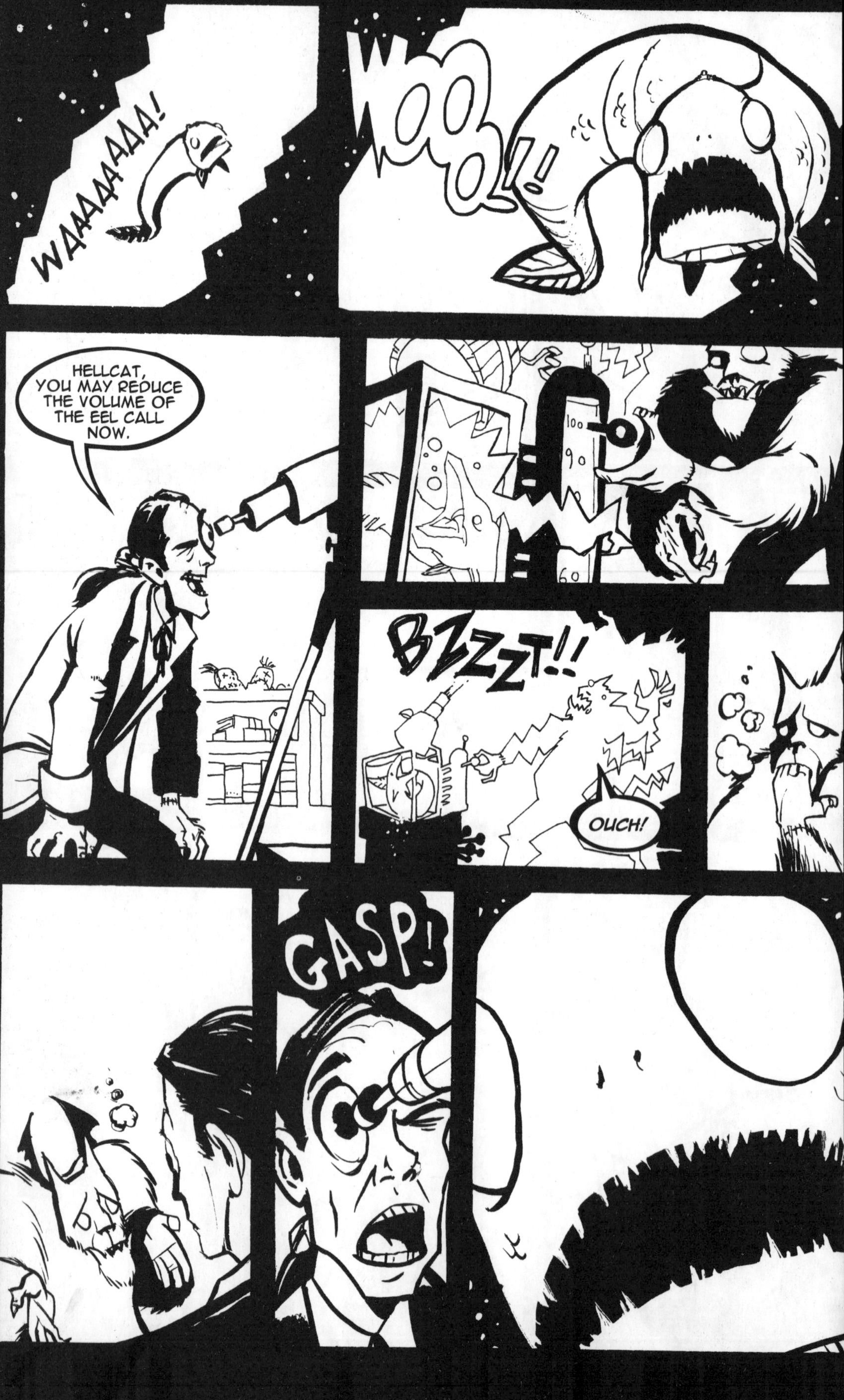
WAAAAAAAA!
WOOOO!!
HELLCAT, YOU MAY REDUCE THE VOLUME OF THE EEL CALL NOW.
BZZZT!!
OUCH!
GASP!

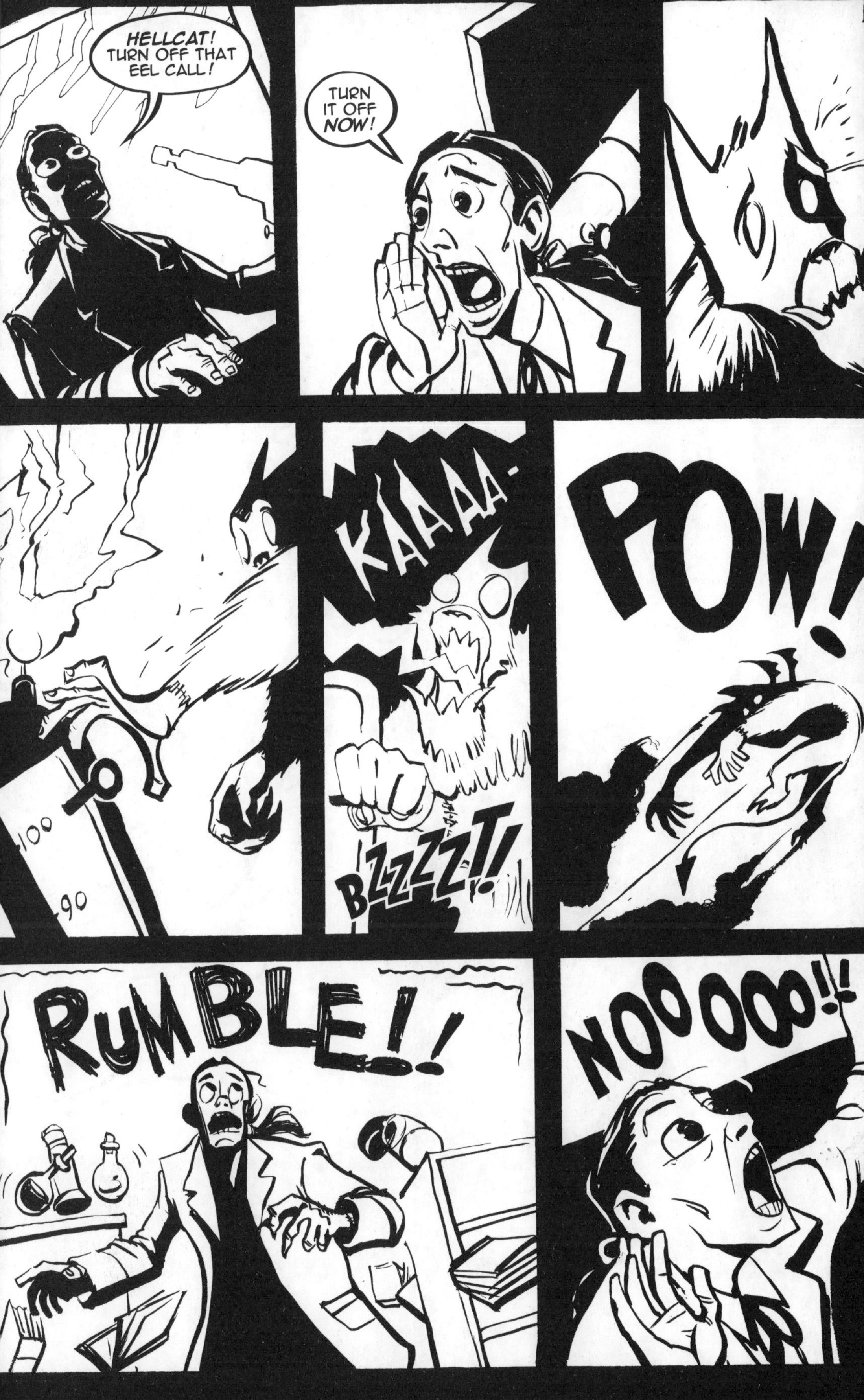
HELLCAT! TURN OFF THAT EEL CALL!
TURN IT OFF NOW!
KAAAA-
BZZZZT!!
POW!!
100
90
RUMBLE!!
NOOOOO!!

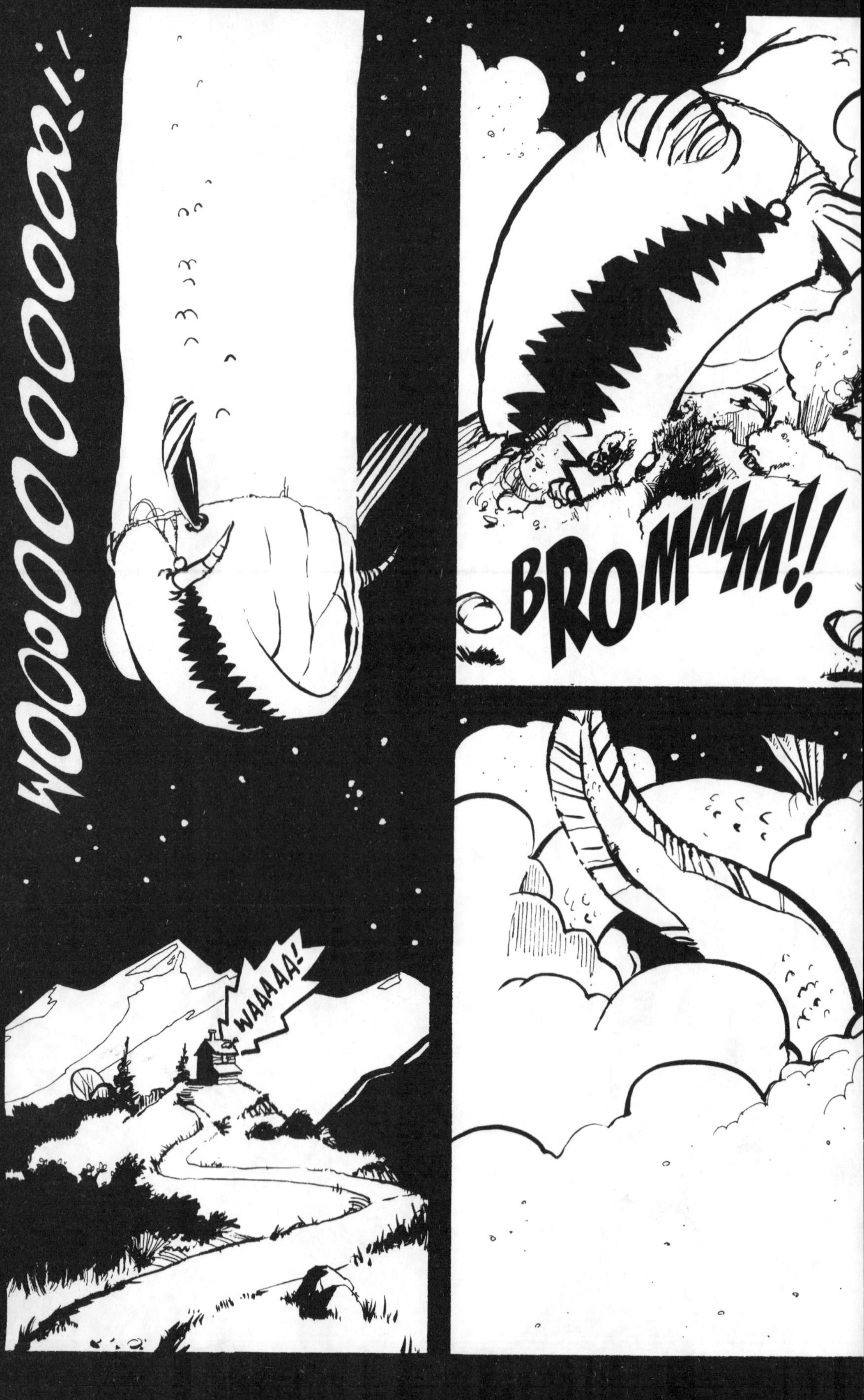
WOOOOOOOOOOM!!
WAAAAA!
BROMMMM!!

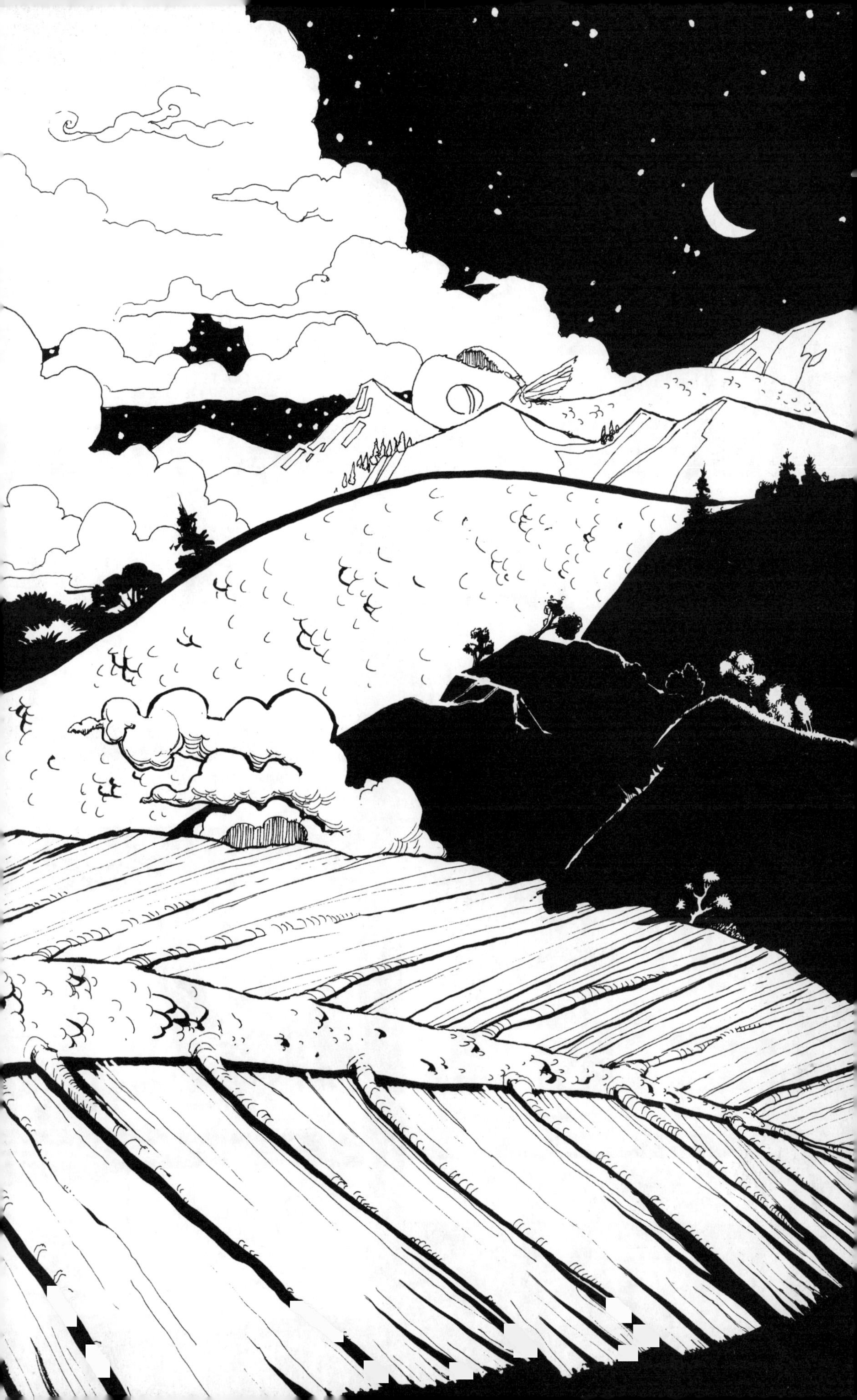

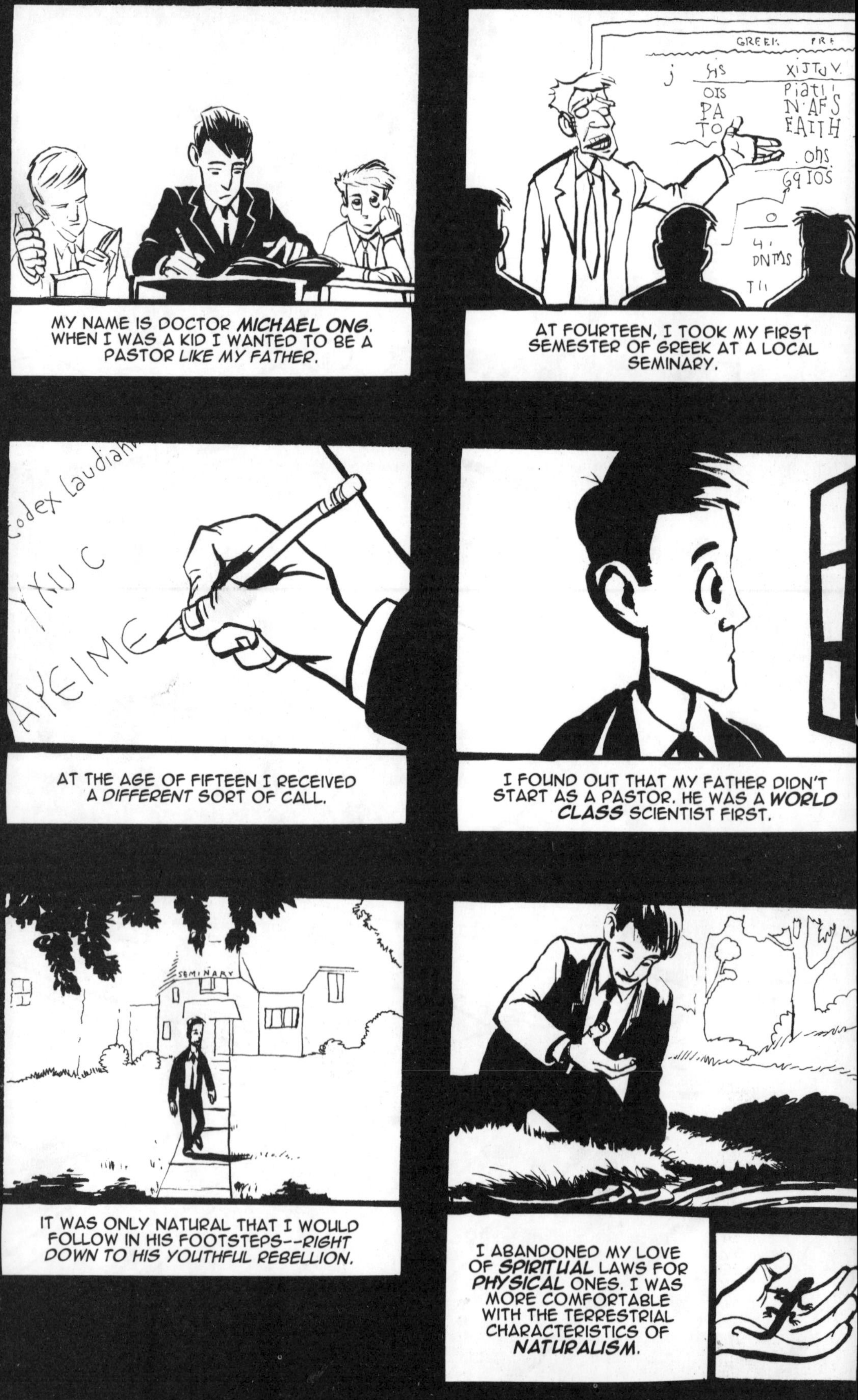
MY NAME IS DOCTOR MICHAEL ONG. WHEN I WAS A KID I WANTED TO BE A PASTOR LIKE MY FATHER.
AT FOURTEEN, I TOOK MY FIRST SEMESTER OF GREEK AT A LOCAL SEMINARY.
AT THE AGE OF FIFTEEN I RECEIVED A DIFFERENT SORT OF CALL.
I FOUND OUT THAT MY FATHER DIDN'T START AS A PASTOR. HE WAS A WORLD CLASS SCIENTIST FIRST.
SEMINARY
IT WAS ONLY NATURAL THAT I WOULD FOLLOW IN HIS FOOTSTEPS--RIGHT DOWN TO HIS YOUTHFUL REBELLION.
I ABANDONED MY LOVE OF SPIRITUAL LAWS FOR PHYSICAL ONES. I WAS MORE COMFORTABLE WITH THE TERRESTRIAL CHARACTERISTICS OF NATURALISM.

WHEN I GRADUATED HIGH SCHOOL AT SIXTEEN, I WENT AS FAR AWAY FROM MY HOMETOWN OF *TURLOCK* AS POSSIBLE.

AT 19 I BECAME THE YOUNGEST WINNER OF THE NOBEL PRIZE FOR SCIENCE.

RRRRING!

I LIVED IN LOS ANGELES PURSUING MONEY AND FAME AS A KIND OF CELEBRITY WITHIN THE EDUCATED ELITE. THEN I GOT A DIFFERENT SORT OF CALL.

THERE MUST BE SOME KIND OF *MISTAKE*.

IT WAS THE *U.S. GOVERNMENT*.

SORRY, *DR. ONG*, YOU'LL BE BRIEFED UPON ARRIVAL.

WELL, *WHERE* WILL I BE RELOCATED?

UNCLE SAM WAS IMPRESSED WITH MY SCIENCE AS WELL AS MY BACKGROUND IN THEOLOGY. HE ENLISTED ME TO CONDUCT STUDIES AT A LOW-PROFILE FACILITY CALLED *RESEARCH TECHNICAL INSTITUTE* (R.T.I.).

TURLOCK.

I'M *NOT* MOVING BACK TO *TURLOCK*!

BUT LIKE EVERY GOOD SCIENTIST, CURIOSITY GOT THE BEST OF ME.

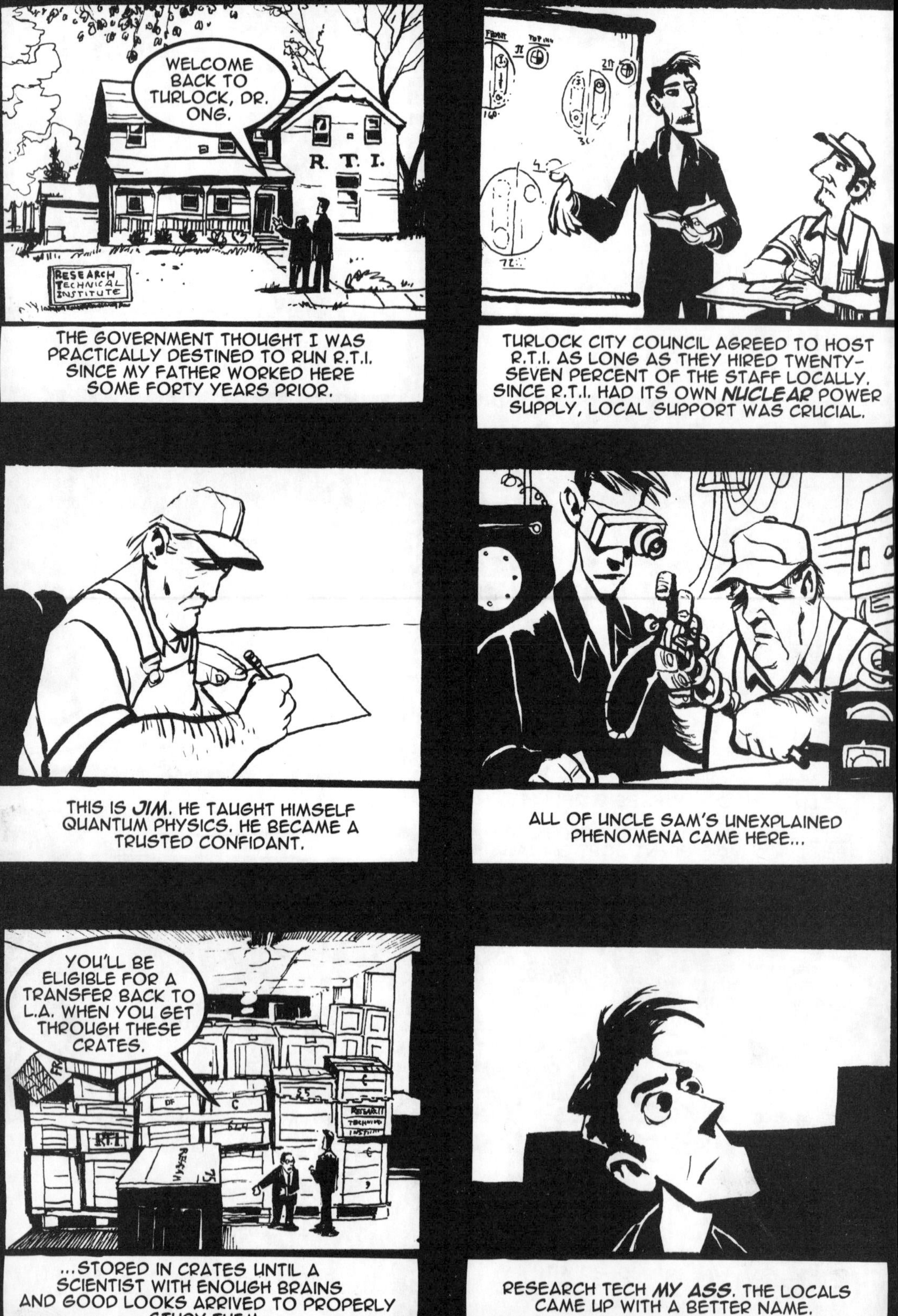
WELCOME BACK TO TURLOCK, DR. ONG.
R. T. I.
RESEARCH TECHNICAL INSTITUTE
THE GOVERNMENT THOUGHT I WAS PRACTICALLY DESTINED TO RUN R.T.I. SINCE MY FATHER WORKED HERE SOME FORTY YEARS PRIOR.
TURLOCK CITY COUNCIL AGREED TO HOST R.T.I. AS LONG AS THEY HIRED TWENTY-SEVEN PERCENT OF THE STAFF LOCALLY. SINCE R.T.I. HAD ITS OWN *NUCLEAR* POWER SUPPLY, LOCAL SUPPORT WAS CRUCIAL.
THIS IS *JIM*. HE TAUGHT HIMSELF QUANTUM PHYSICS. HE BECAME A TRUSTED CONFIDANT.
ALL OF UNCLE SAM'S UNEXPLAINED PHENOMENA CAME HERE...
YOU'LL BE ELIGIBLE FOR A TRANSFER BACK TO L.A. WHEN YOU GET THROUGH THESE CRATES.
R.T.I.
...STORED IN CRATES UNTIL A SCIENTIST WITH ENOUGH BRAINS AND GOOD LOOKS ARRIVED TO PROPERLY STUDY THEM.
RESEARCH TECH *MY ASS*. THE LOCALS CAME UP WITH A BETTER NAME.

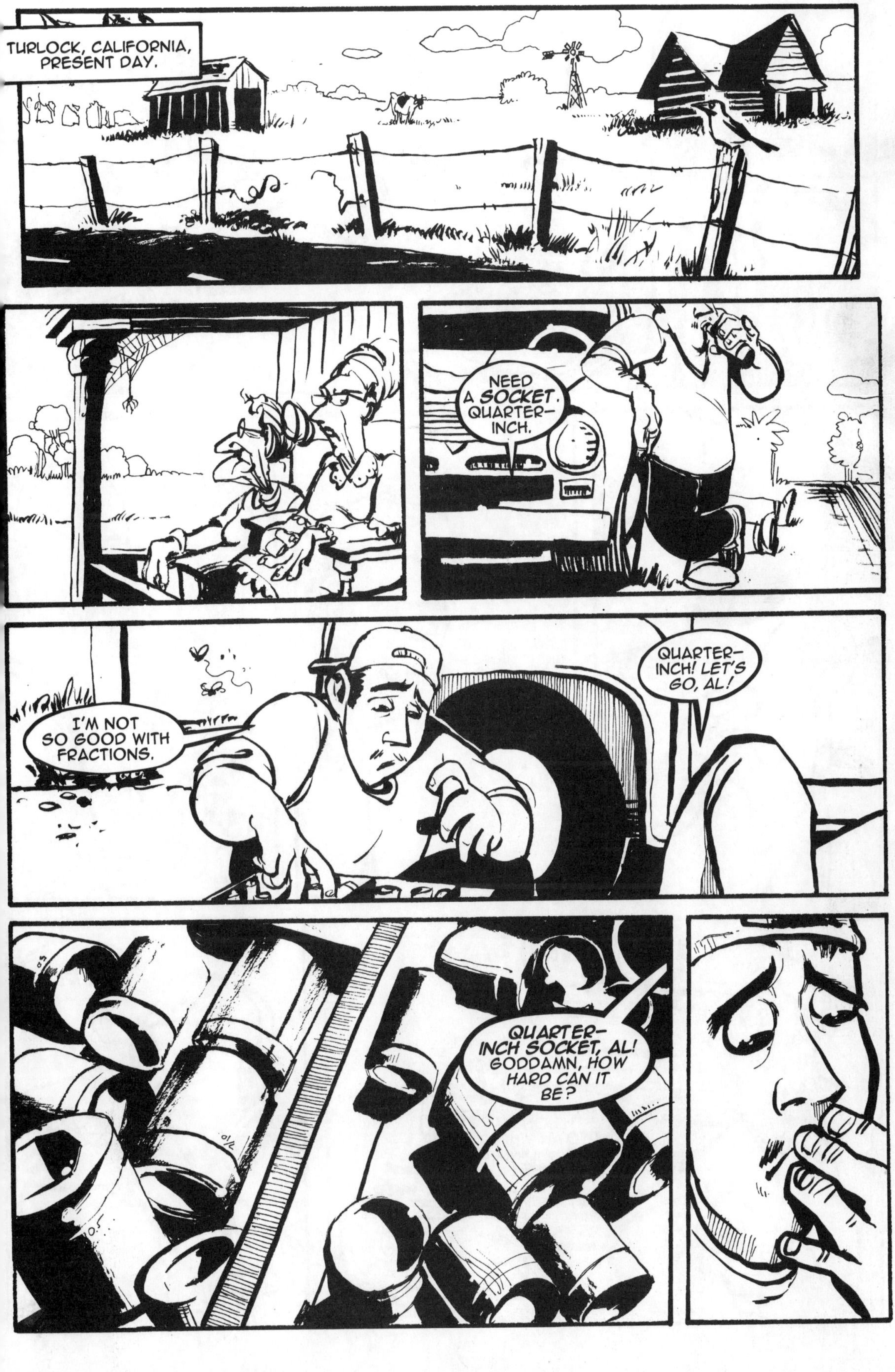
TURLOCK, CALIFORNIA, PRESENT DAY.
NEED A SOCKET. QUARTER-INCH.
I'M NOT SO GOOD WITH FRACTIONS.
QUARTER-INCH! LET'S GO, AL!
QUARTER-INCH SOCKET, AL! GODDAMN, HOW HARD CAN IT BE?

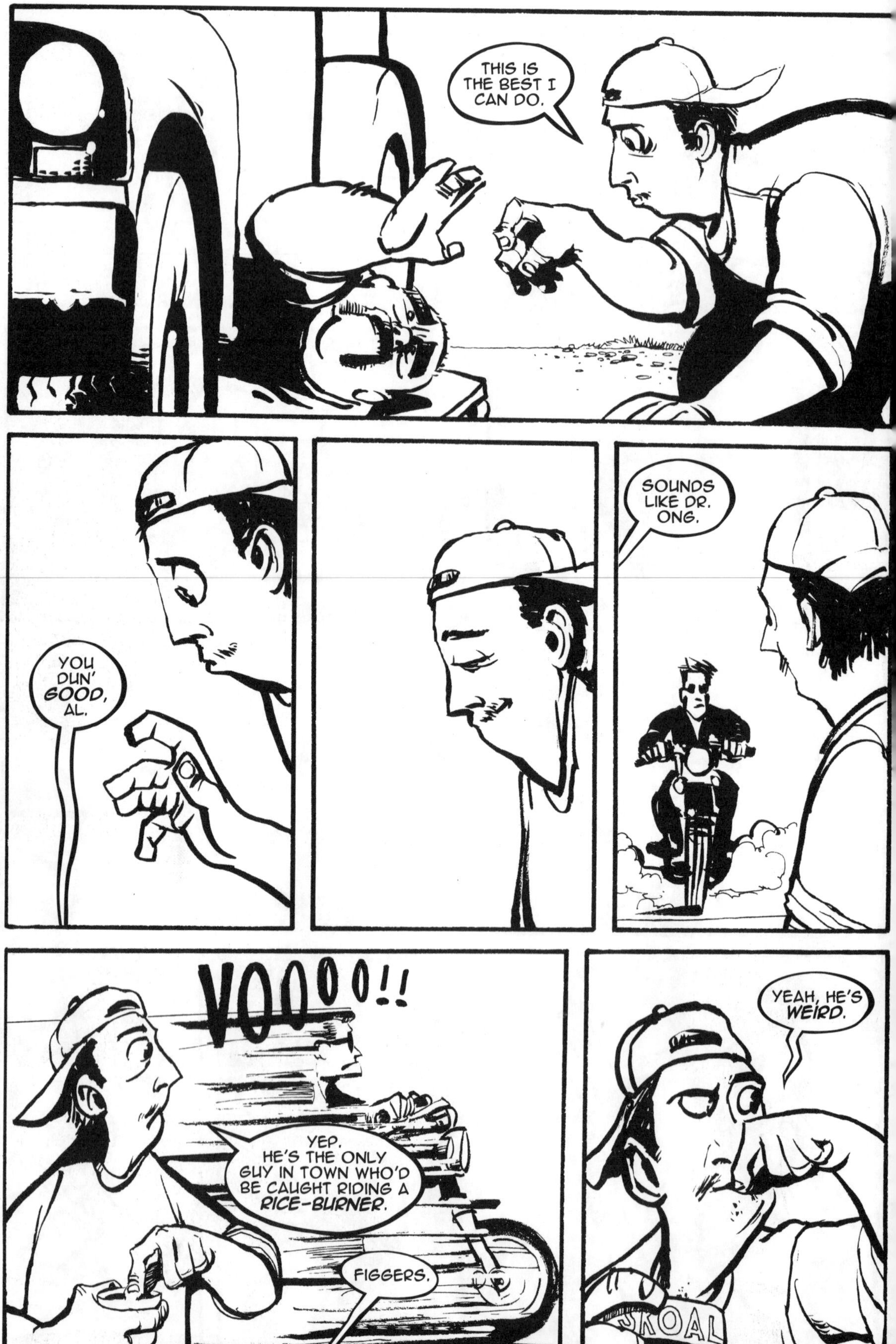
THIS IS THE BEST I CAN DO.
YOU DUN' GOOD, AL.
SOUNDS LIKE DR. ONG.
VOOOO!!
YEP. HE'S THE ONLY GUY IN TOWN WHO'D BE CAUGHT RIDING A RICE-BURNER.
FIGGERS.
YEAH, HE'S WEIRD.
SKOAL

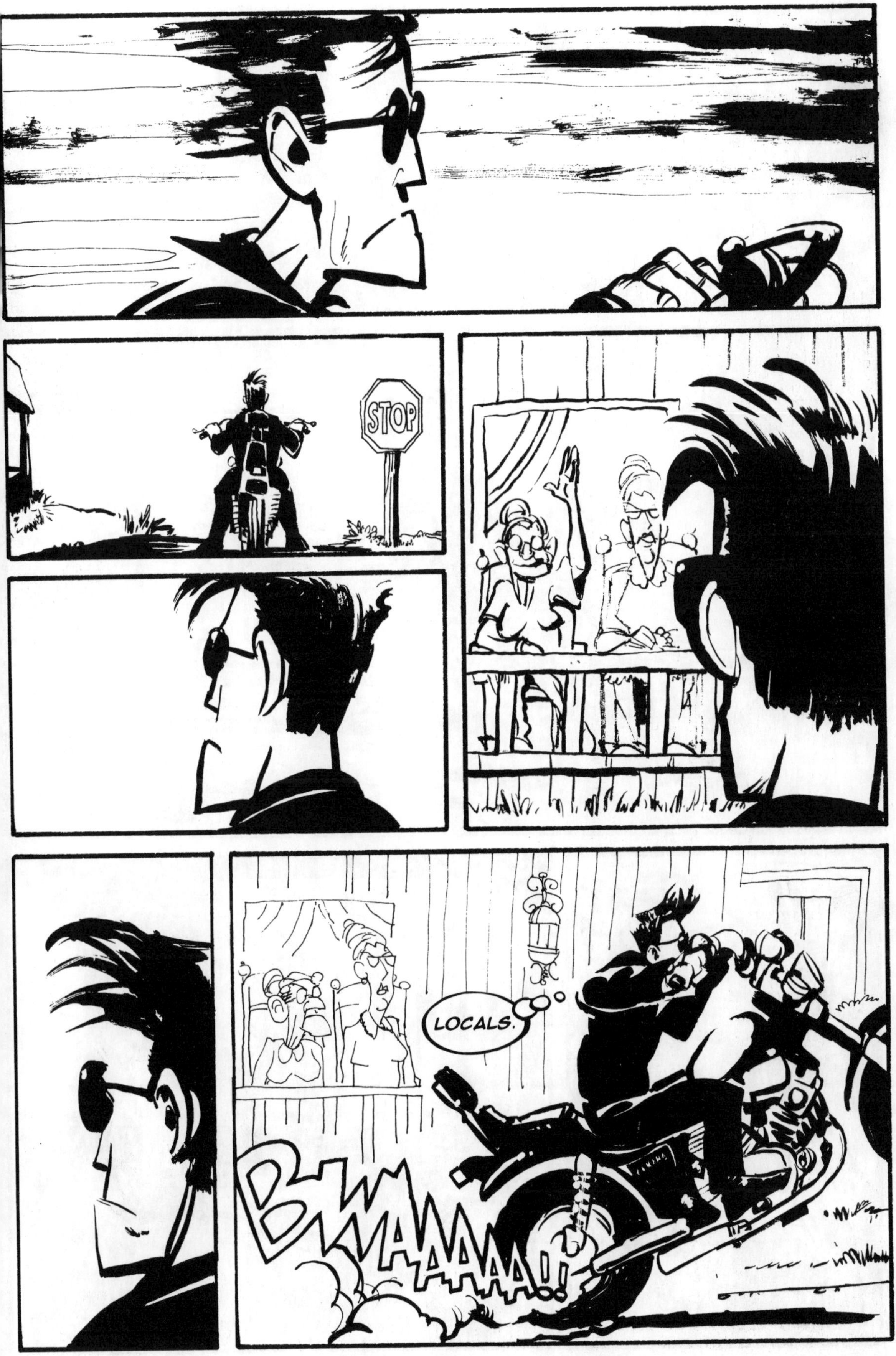
STOP
LOCALS.
BWAAAAAA!!

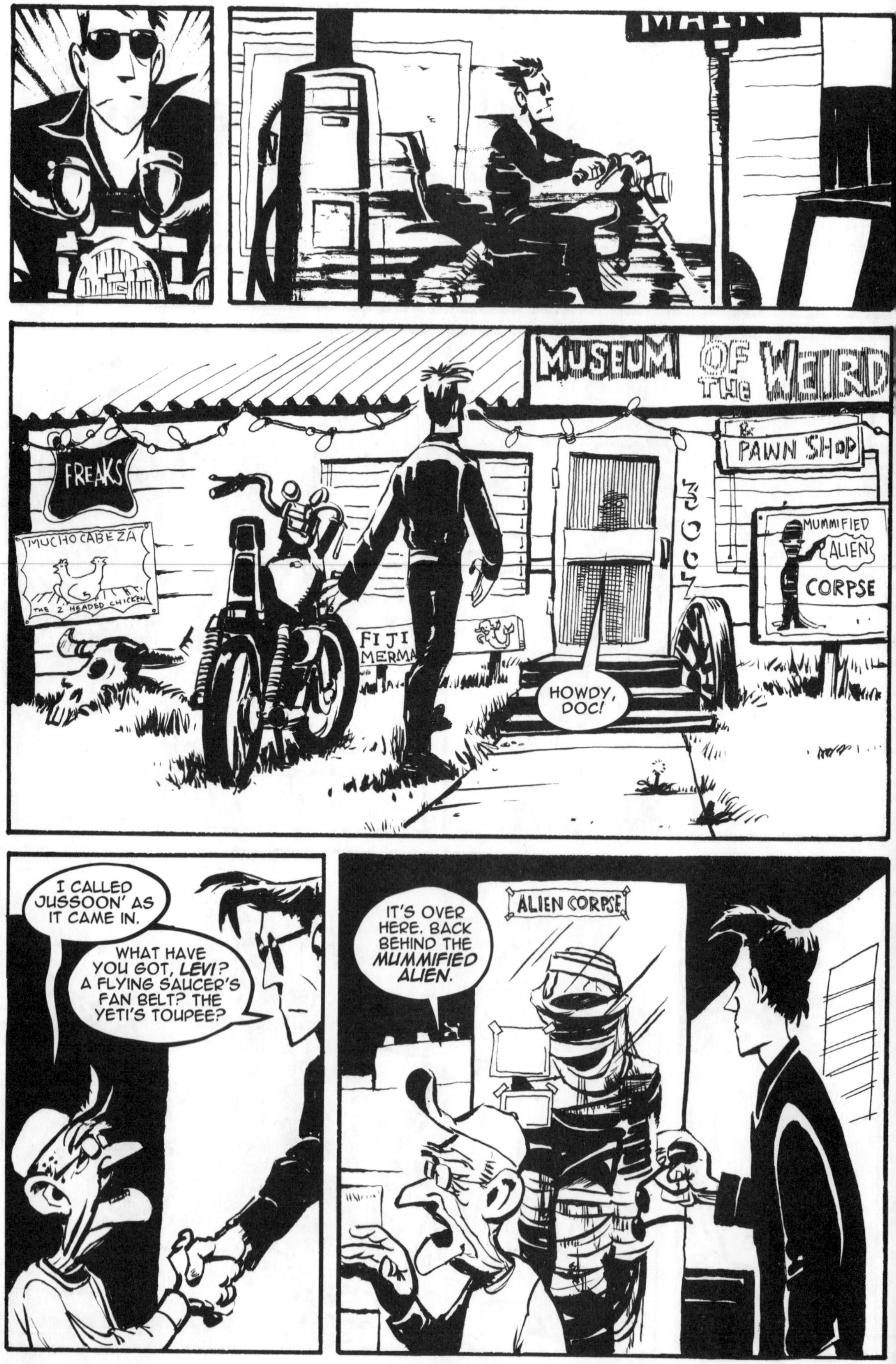
MUSEUM OF THE WEIRD
FREAKS
MUCHO CABEZA
THE 2 HEADED CHICKEN
PAWN SHOP
MUMMIFIED ALIEN CORPSE
FIJI MERMA
HOWDY, DOC!
I CALLED JUSSOON' AS IT CAME IN.
WHAT HAVE YOU GOT, *LEVI*? A FLYING SAUCER'S FAN BELT? THE YETI'S TOUPEE?
ALIEN CORPSE
IT'S OVER HERE. BACK BEHIND THE *MUMMIFIED ALIEN*.

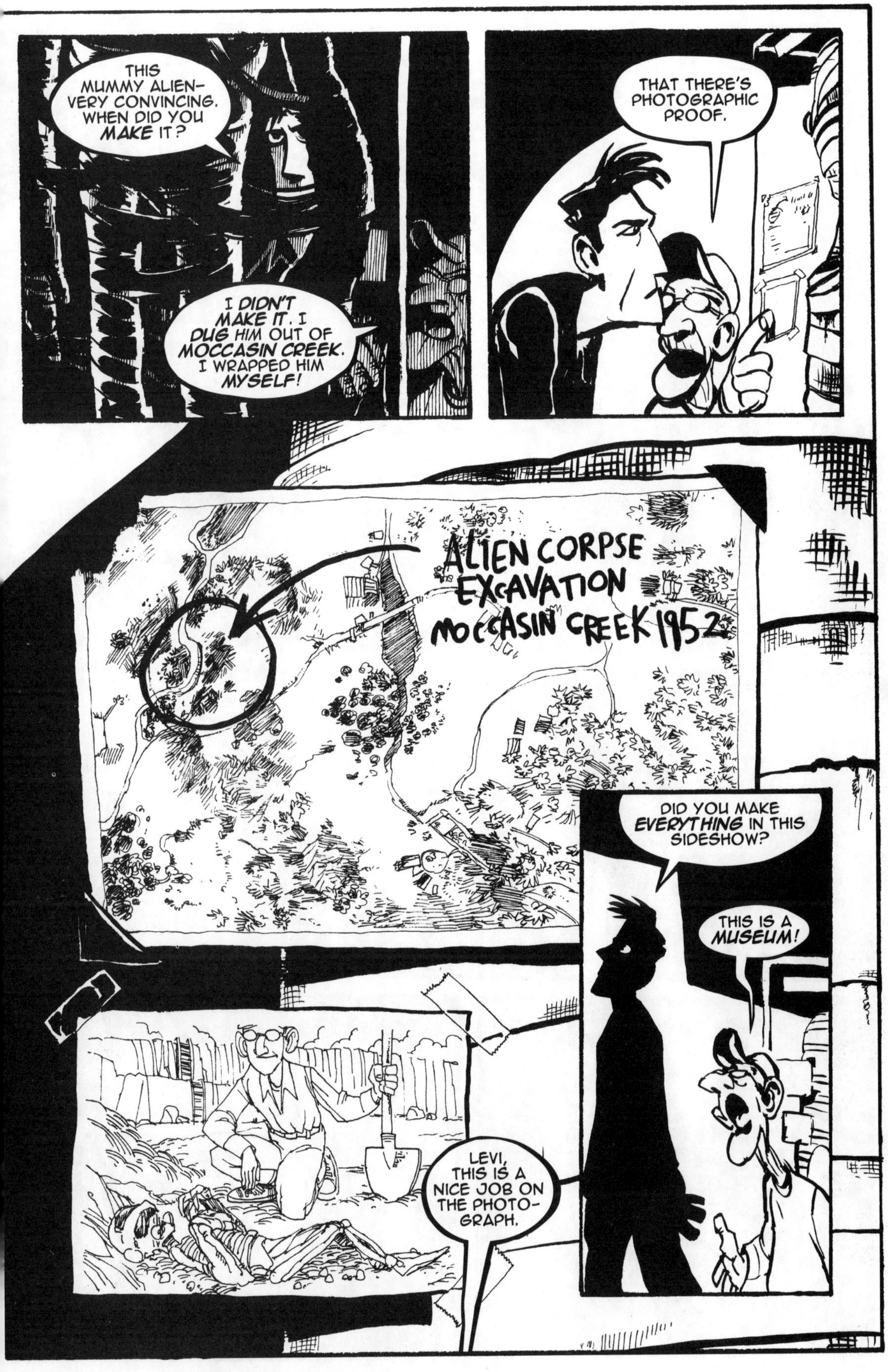

THIS MUMMY ALIEN- VERY CONVINCING. WHEN DID YOU MAKE IT?
I DIDN'T MAKE IT. I DUG HIM OUT OF MOCCASIN CREEK. I WRAPPED HIM MYSELF!
THAT THERE'S PHOTOGRAPHIC PROOF.
ALIEN CORPSE EXCAVATION MOCCASIN CREEK 1952
DID YOU MAKE EVERYTHING IN THIS SIDESHOW?
THIS IS A MUSEUM!
LEVI, THIS IS A NICE JOB ON THE PHOTO- GRAPH.

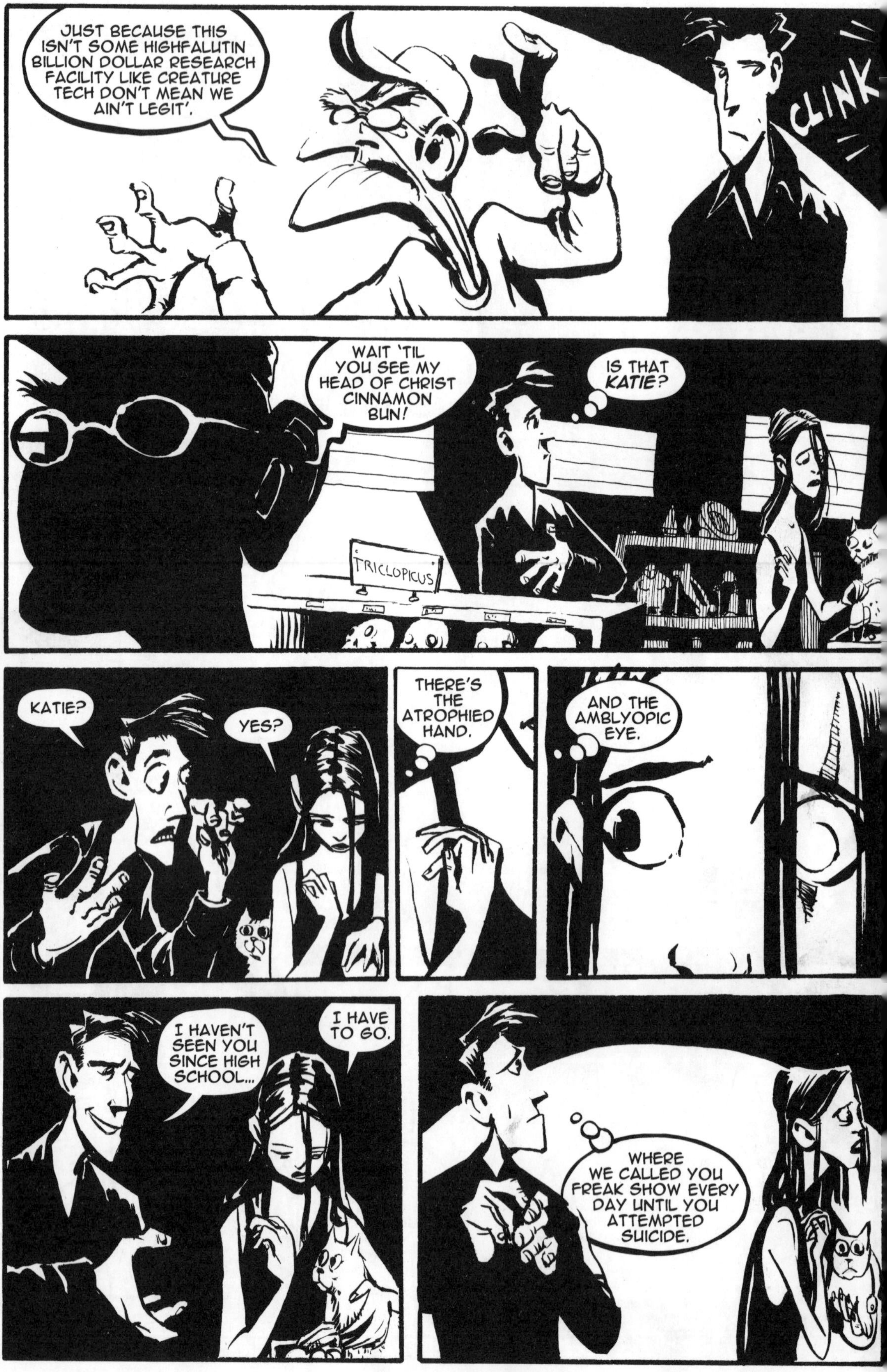
JUST BECAUSE THIS ISN'T SOME HIGHFALUTIN BILLION DOLLAR RESEARCH FACILITY LIKE CREATURE TECH DON'T MEAN WE AIN'T LEGIT'.
CLINK
WAIT 'TIL YOU SEE MY HEAD OF CHRIST CINNAMON BUN!
IS THAT *KATIE*?
TRICLOPICUS
KATIE?
YES?
THERE'S THE ATROPHIED HAND.
AND THE AMBLYOPIC EYE.
I HAVEN'T SEEN YOU SINCE HIGH SCHOOL...
I HAVE TO GO.
WHERE WE CALLED YOU FREAK SHOW EVERY DAY UNTIL YOU ATTEMPTED SUICIDE.

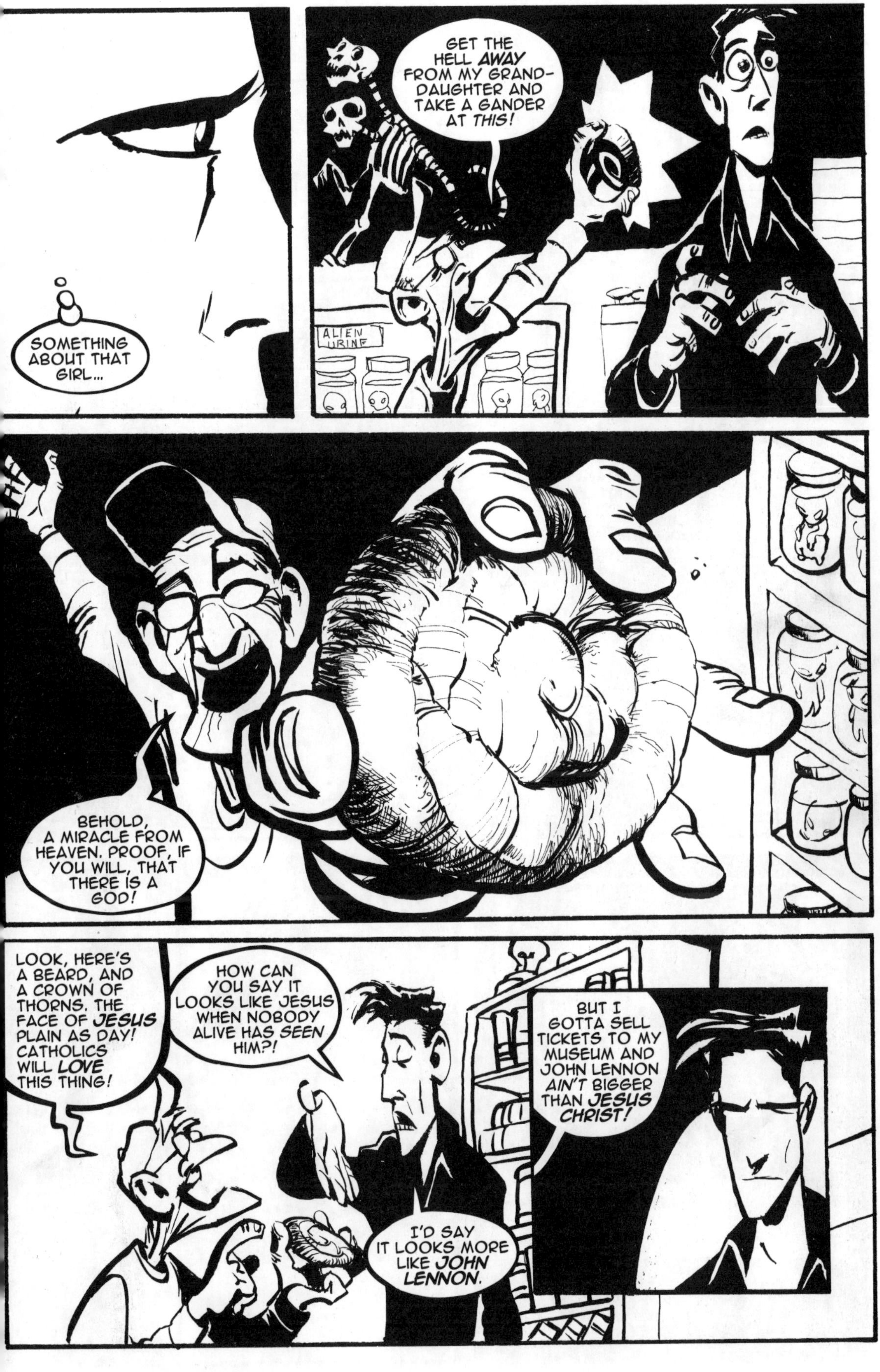
SOMETHING ABOUT THAT GIRL...
GET THE HELL *AWAY* FROM MY GRAND-DAUGHTER AND TAKE A GANDER AT *THIS!*
ALIEN URINE
BEHOLD, A MIRACLE FROM HEAVEN. PROOF, IF YOU WILL, THAT THERE IS A GOD!
LOOK, HERE'S A BEARD, AND A CROWN OF THORNS. THE FACE OF *JESUS* PLAIN AS DAY! CATHOLICS WILL *LOVE* THIS THING!
HOW CAN YOU SAY IT LOOKS LIKE JESUS WHEN NOBODY ALIVE HAS *SEEN* HIM?!
I'D SAY IT LOOKS MORE LIKE *JOHN LENNON*.
BUT I GOTTA SELL TICKETS TO MY MUSEUM AND JOHN LENNON *AIN'T* BIGGER THAN *JESUS CHRIST!*

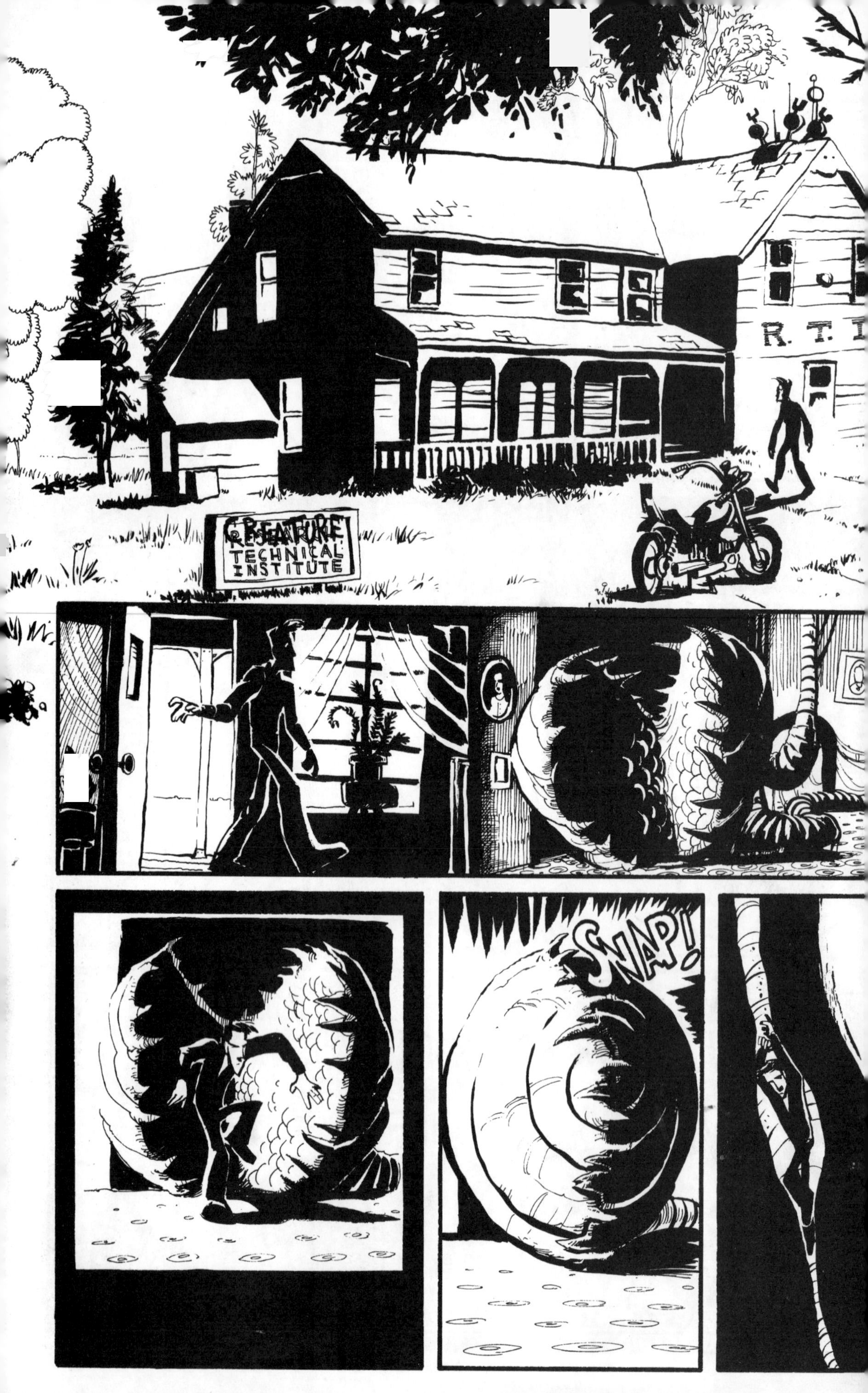
R. T. I
CREATURE
TECHNICAL
INSTITUTE
SNAP!

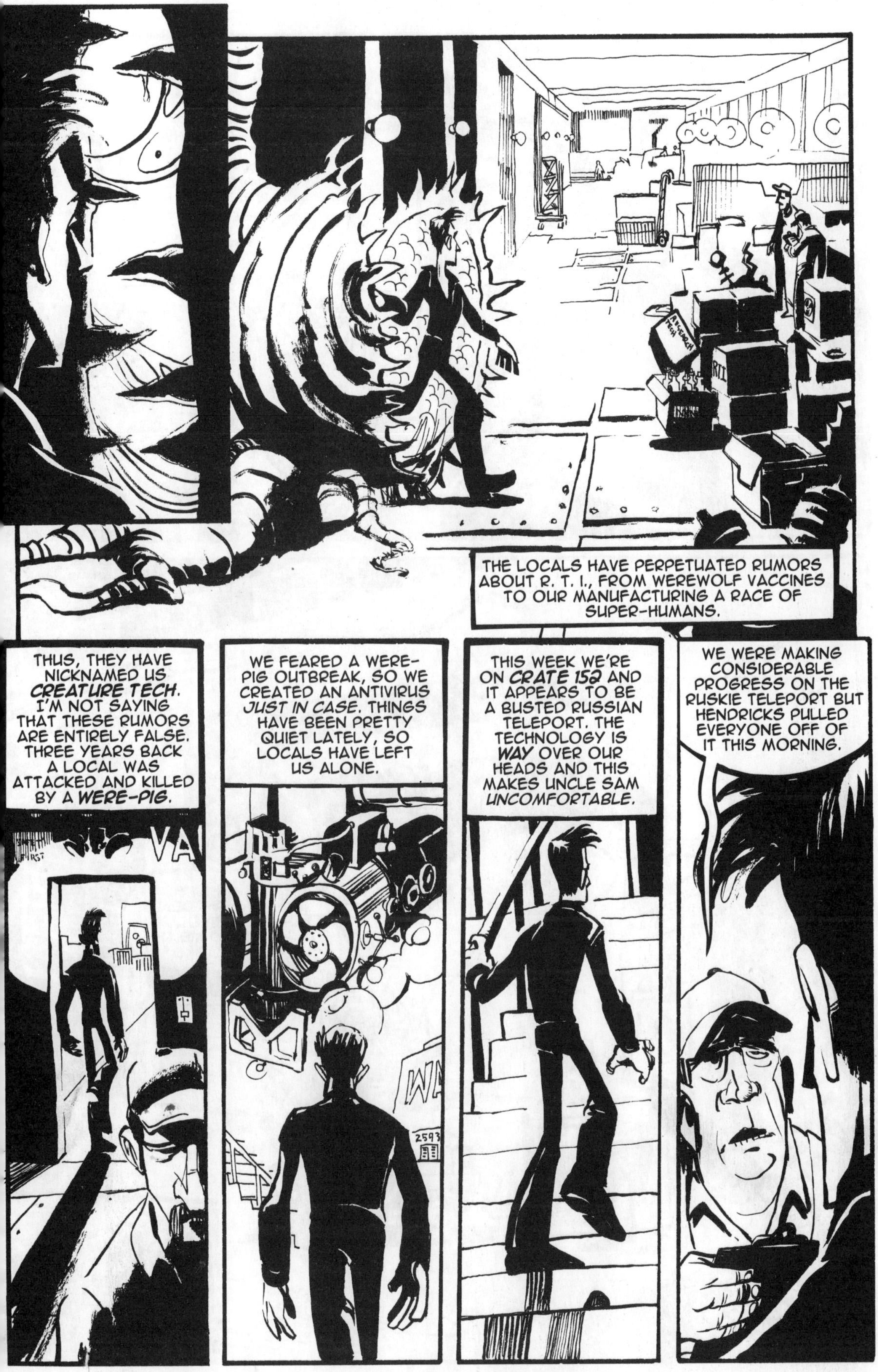
THE LOCALS HAVE PERPETUATED RUMORS ABOUT R. T. I., FROM WEREWOLF VACCINES TO OUR MANUFACTURING A RACE OF SUPER-HUMANS.
THUS, THEY HAVE NICKNAMED US *CREATURE TECH*. I'M NOT SAYING THAT THESE RUMORS ARE ENTIRELY FALSE. THREE YEARS BACK A LOCAL WAS ATTACKED AND KILLED BY A *WERE-PIG*.
WE FEARED A WERE-PIG OUTBREAK, SO WE CREATED AN ANTIVIRUS *JUST IN CASE*. THINGS HAVE BEEN PRETTY QUIET LATELY, SO LOCALS HAVE LEFT US ALONE.
THIS WEEK WE'RE ON *CRATE 152* AND IT APPEARS TO BE A BUSTED RUSSIAN TELEPORT. THE TECHNOLOGY IS *WAY* OVER OUR HEADS AND THIS MAKES UNCLE SAM *UNCOMFORTABLE*.
WE WERE MAKING CONSIDERABLE PROGRESS ON THE RUSKIE TELEPORT BUT HENDRICKS PULLED EVERYONE OFF OF IT THIS MORNING.

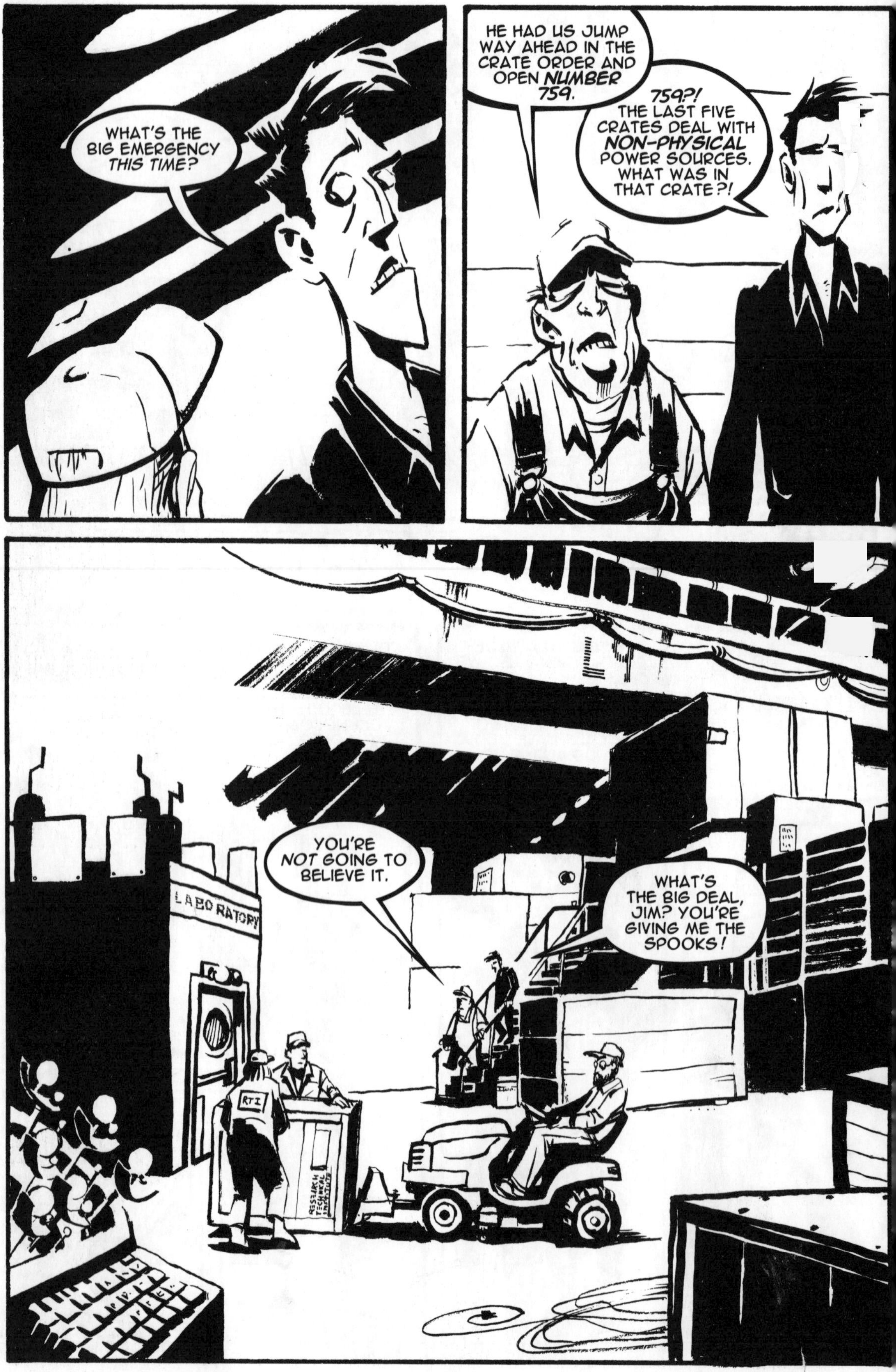
WHAT'S THE BIG EMERGENCY *THIS TIME?*
HE HAD US JUMP WAY AHEAD IN THE CRATE ORDER AND OPEN ***NUMBER 759.***
759?! THE LAST FIVE CRATES DEAL WITH ***NON-PHYSICAL*** POWER SOURCES. WHAT WAS IN THAT CRATE?!
LABORATORY
YOU'RE *NOT* GOING TO BELIEVE IT.
WHAT'S THE BIG DEAL, JIM? YOU'RE GIVING ME THE SPOOKS!
RTI

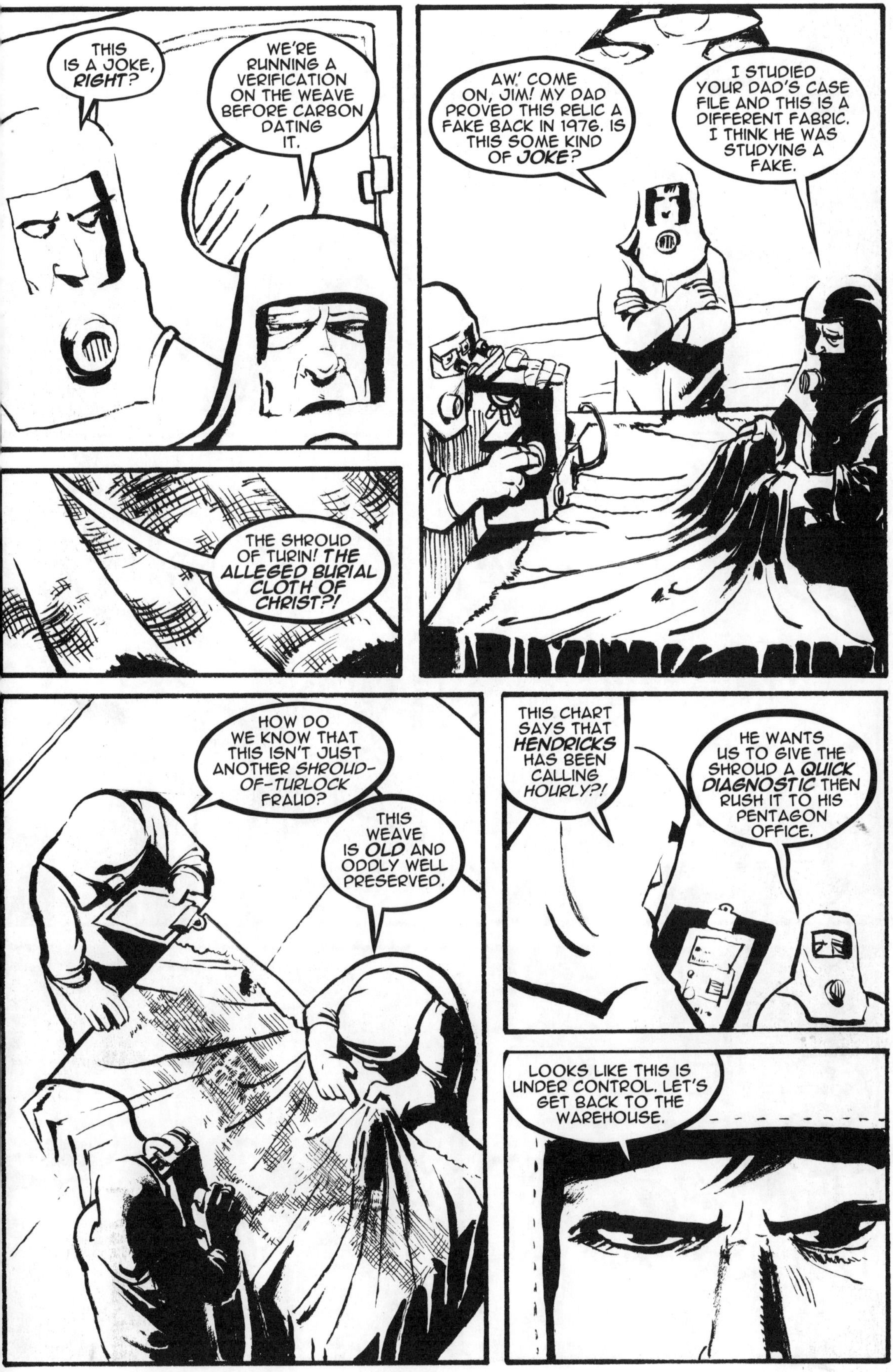

THIS IS A JOKE, RIGHT?
WE'RE RUNNING A VERIFICATION ON THE WEAVE BEFORE CARBON DATING IT.
THE SHROUD OF TURIN! THE ALLEGED BURIAL CLOTH OF CHRIST?!
AW! COME ON, JIM! MY DAD PROVED THIS RELIC A FAKE BACK IN 1976. IS THIS SOME KIND OF JOKE?
I STUDIED YOUR DAD'S CASE FILE AND THIS IS A DIFFERENT FABRIC. I THINK HE WAS STUDYING A FAKE.
HOW DO WE KNOW THAT THIS ISN'T JUST ANOTHER SHROUD-OF-TURLOCK FRAUD?
THIS WEAVE IS OLD AND ODDLY WELL PRESERVED.
THIS CHART SAYS THAT HENDRICKS HAS BEEN CALLING HOURLY?!
HE WANTS US TO GIVE THE SHROUD A QUICK DIAGNOSTIC THEN RUSH IT TO HIS PENTAGON OFFICE.
LOOKS LIKE THIS IS UNDER CONTROL. LET'S GET BACK TO THE WAREHOUSE.

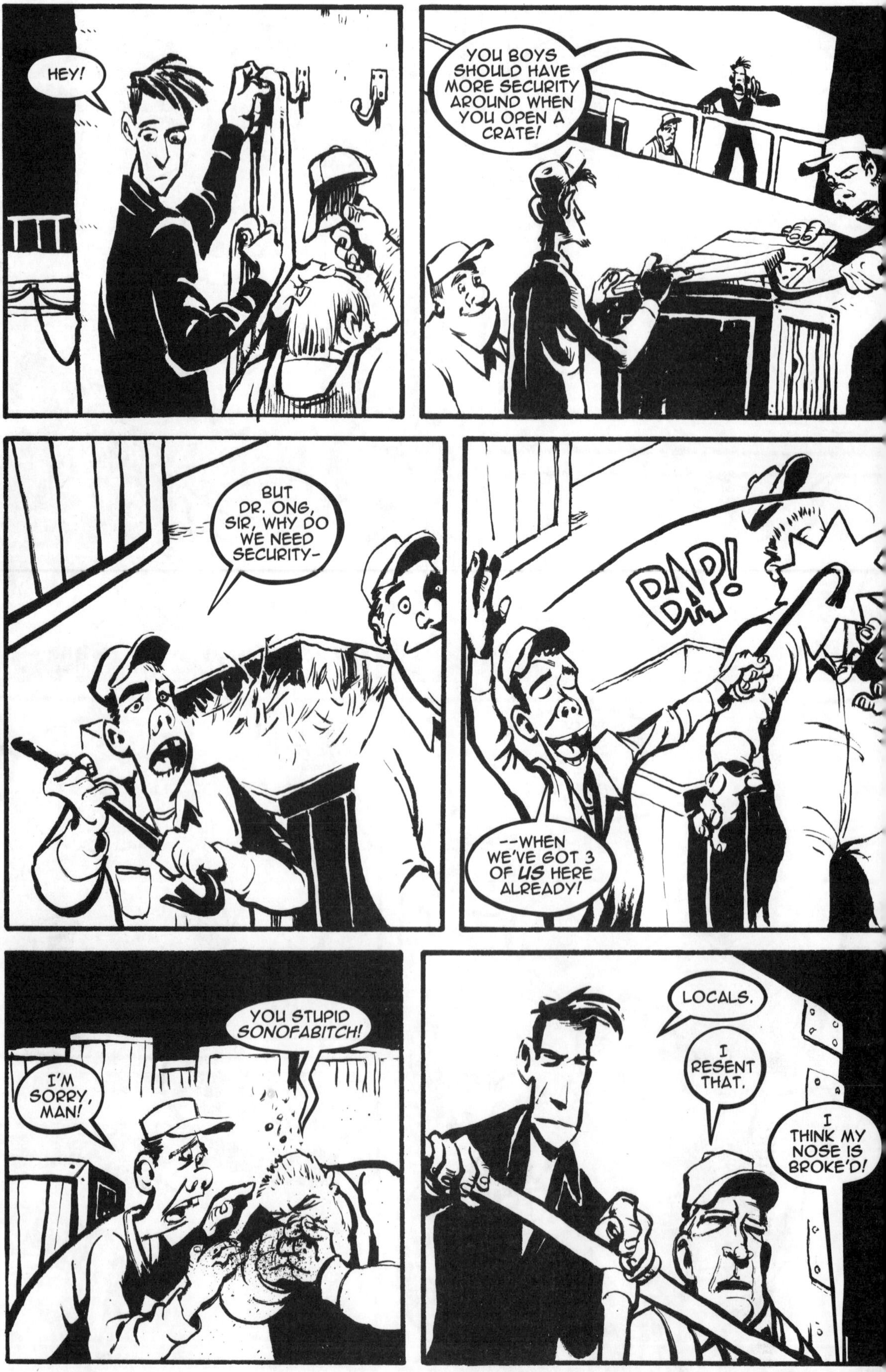
HEY!
YOU BOYS SHOULD HAVE MORE SECURITY AROUND WHEN YOU OPEN A CRATE!
BUT DR. ONG, SIR, WHY DO WE NEED SECURITY-
DAP!
--WHEN WE'VE GOT 3 OF US HERE ALREADY!
I'M SORRY, MAN!
YOU STUPID SONOFABITCH!
LOCALS.
I RESENT THAT.
I THINK MY NOSE IS BROKE'D!

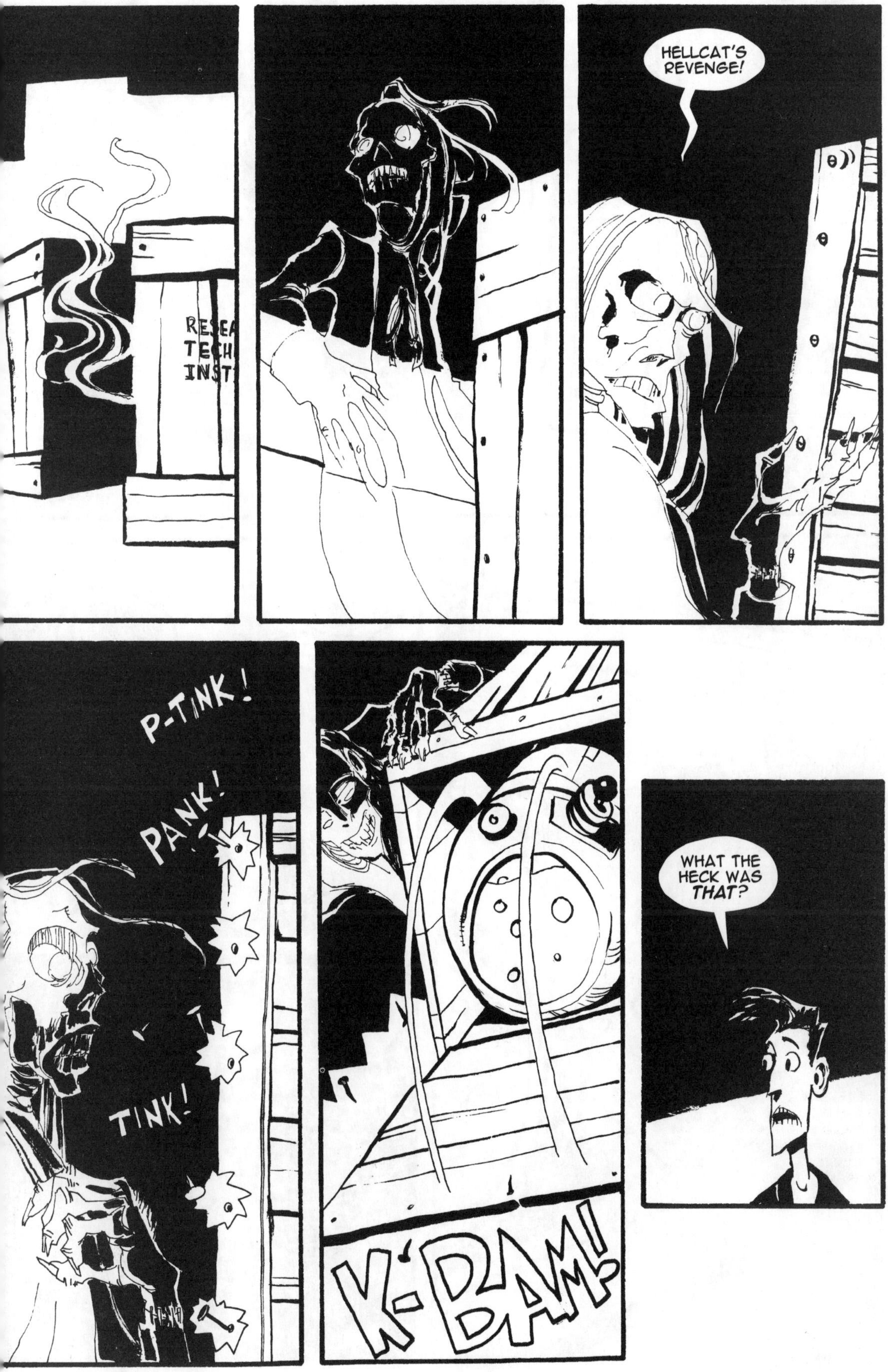
RESEA
TECH
INST
HELLCAT'S REVENGE!
P-TINK!
PANK!
TINK!
K-BAM!
WHAT THE HECK WAS *THAT*?

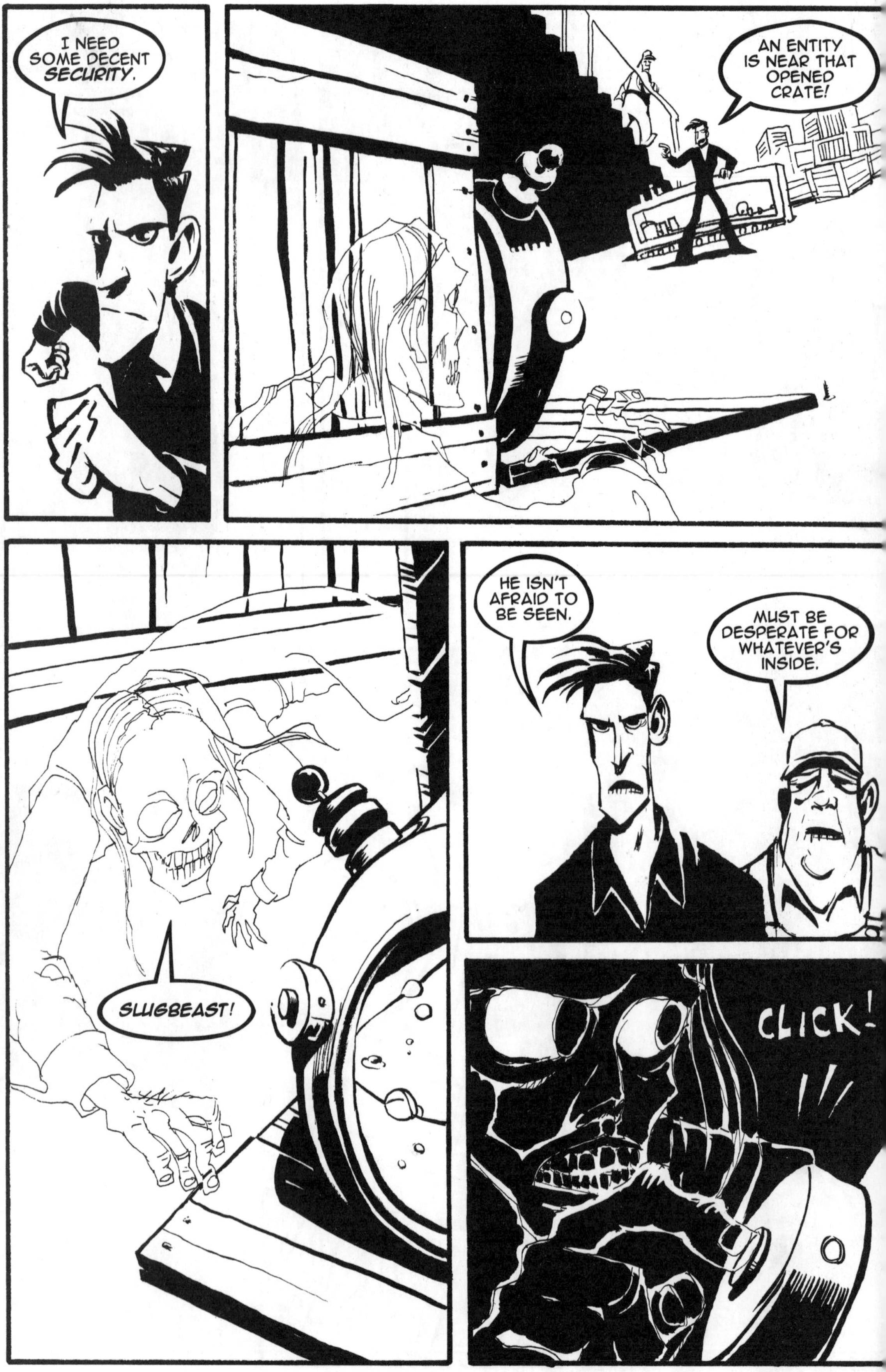

I NEED SOME DECENT *SECURITY*.
AN ENTITY IS NEAR THAT OPENED CRATE!
SLUGBEAST!
HE ISN'T AFRAID TO BE SEEN.
MUST BE DESPERATE FOR WHATEVER'S INSIDE.
CLICK!

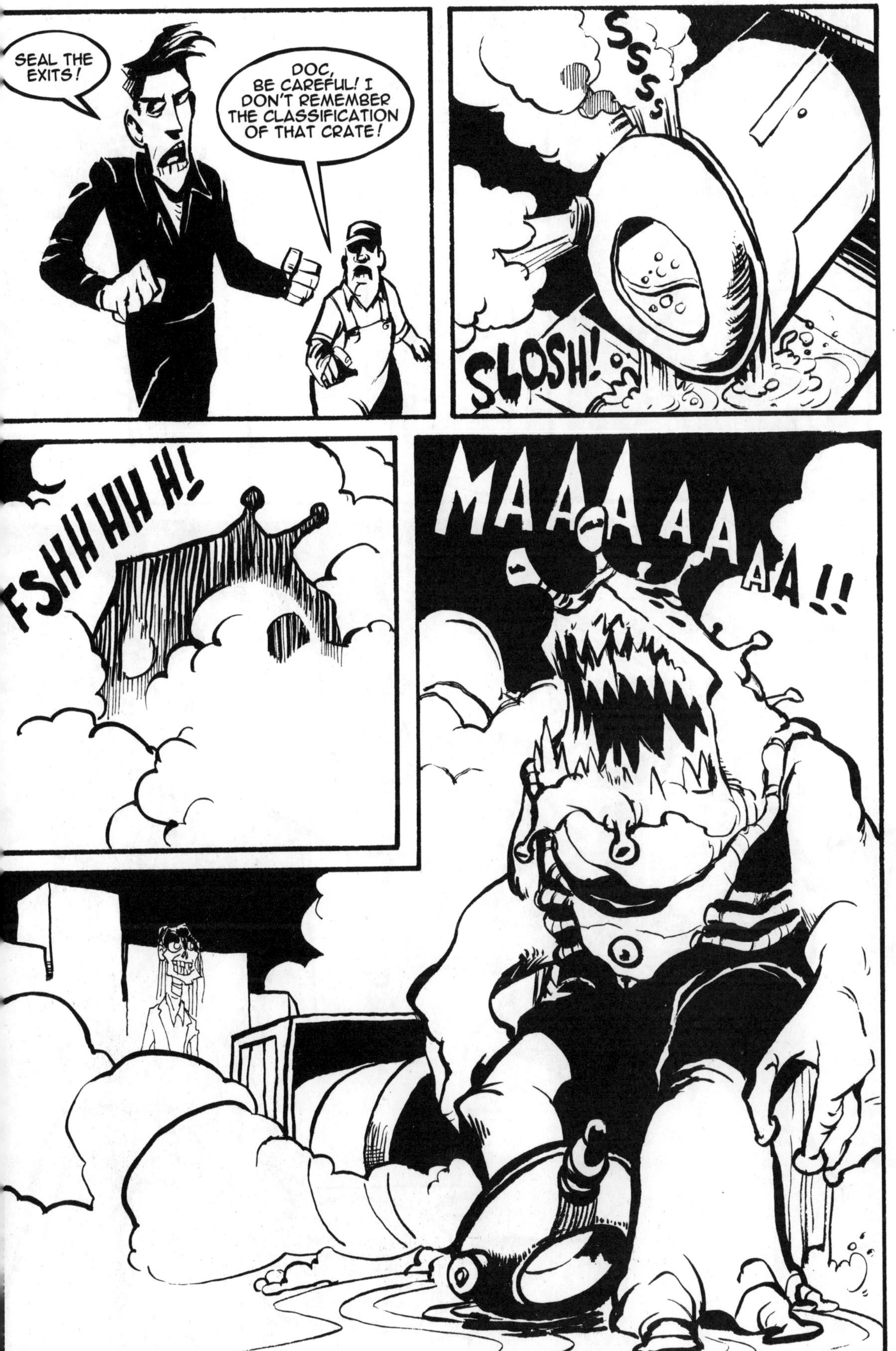

SEAL THE EXITS!
DOC, BE CAREFUL! I DON'T REMEMBER THE CLASSIFICATION OF THAT CRATE!
SSSS
SLOSH!
FSHHHH H!
MAAAAAAAA!!

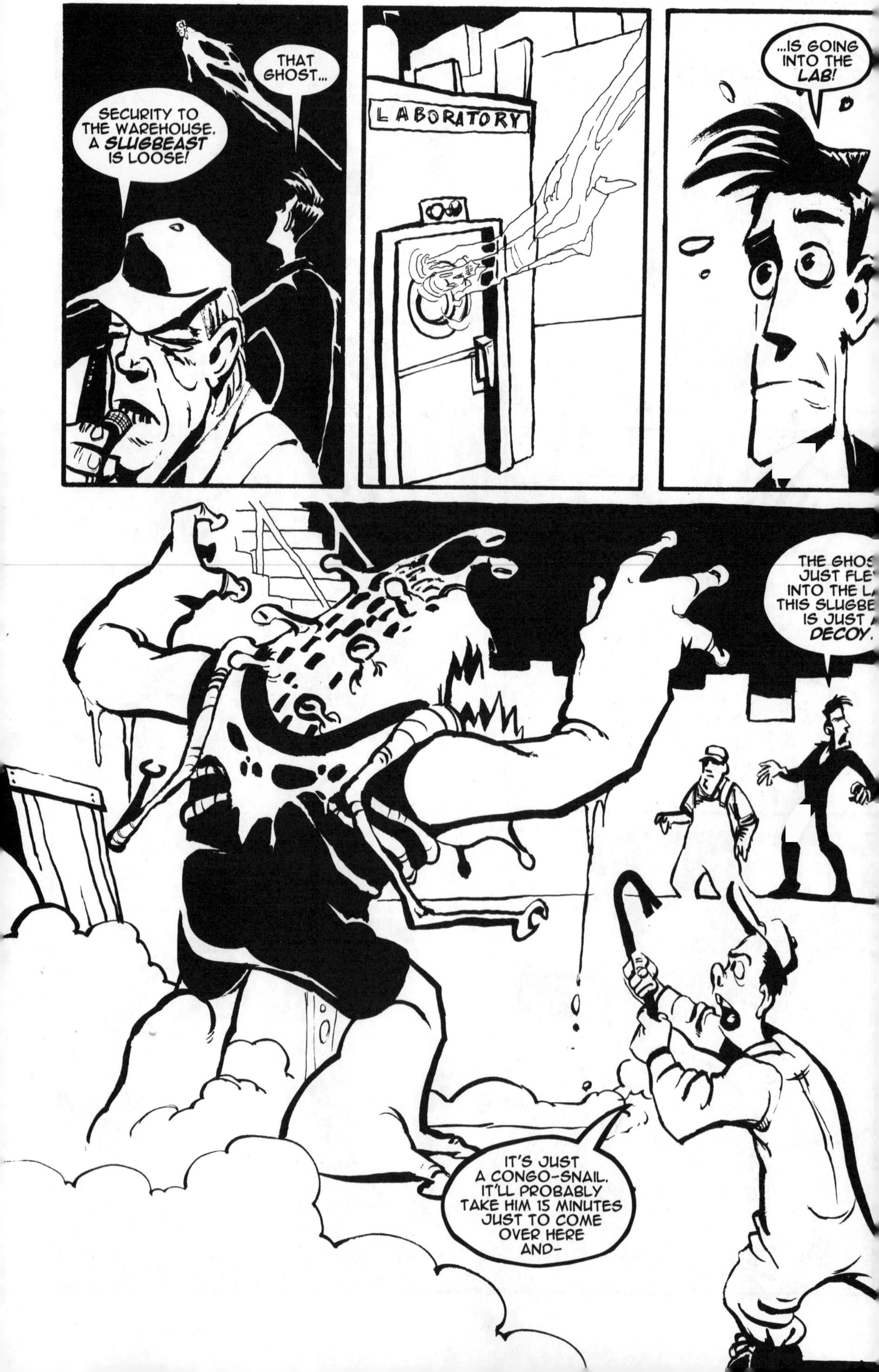
SECURITY TO THE WAREHOUSE. A SLUGBEAST IS LOOSE!
THAT GHOST...
LABORATORY
...IS GOING INTO THE LAB!
THE GHOS JUST FLE INTO THE L THIS SLUGBE IS JUST DECOY.
IT'S JUST A CONGO-SNAIL. IT'LL PROBABLY TAKE HIM 15 MINUTES JUST TO COME OVER HERE AND-

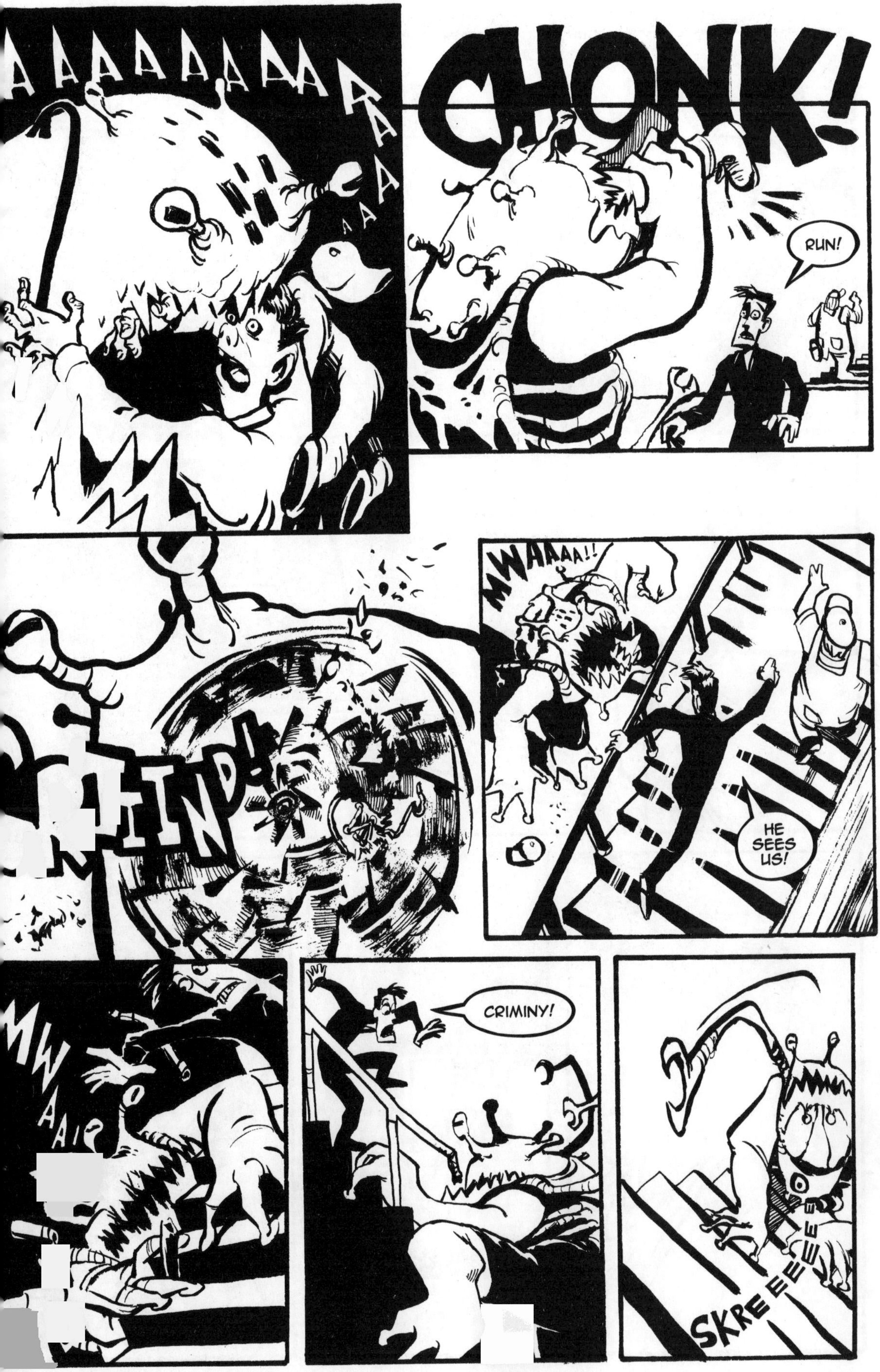
AAAAAAAARAAA
CHONK!
RUN!
MWAAAA!!
HE SEES US!
MWAA!
CRIMINY!
SKREEEEEEE

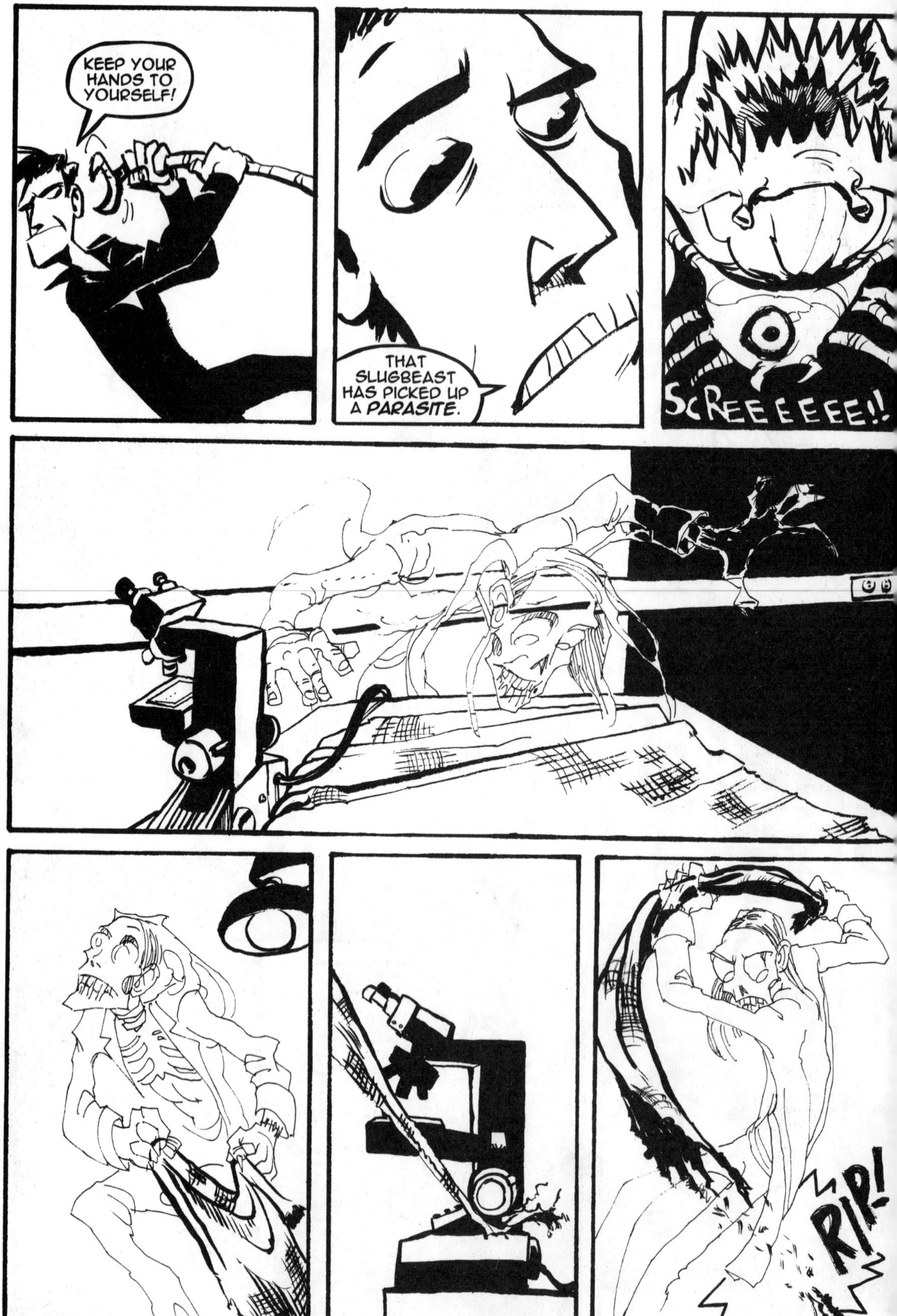
KEEP YOUR HANDS TO YOURSELF!
THAT SLUGBEAST HAS PICKED UP A *PARASITE*.
SCREEEEEEE!!
RIP!

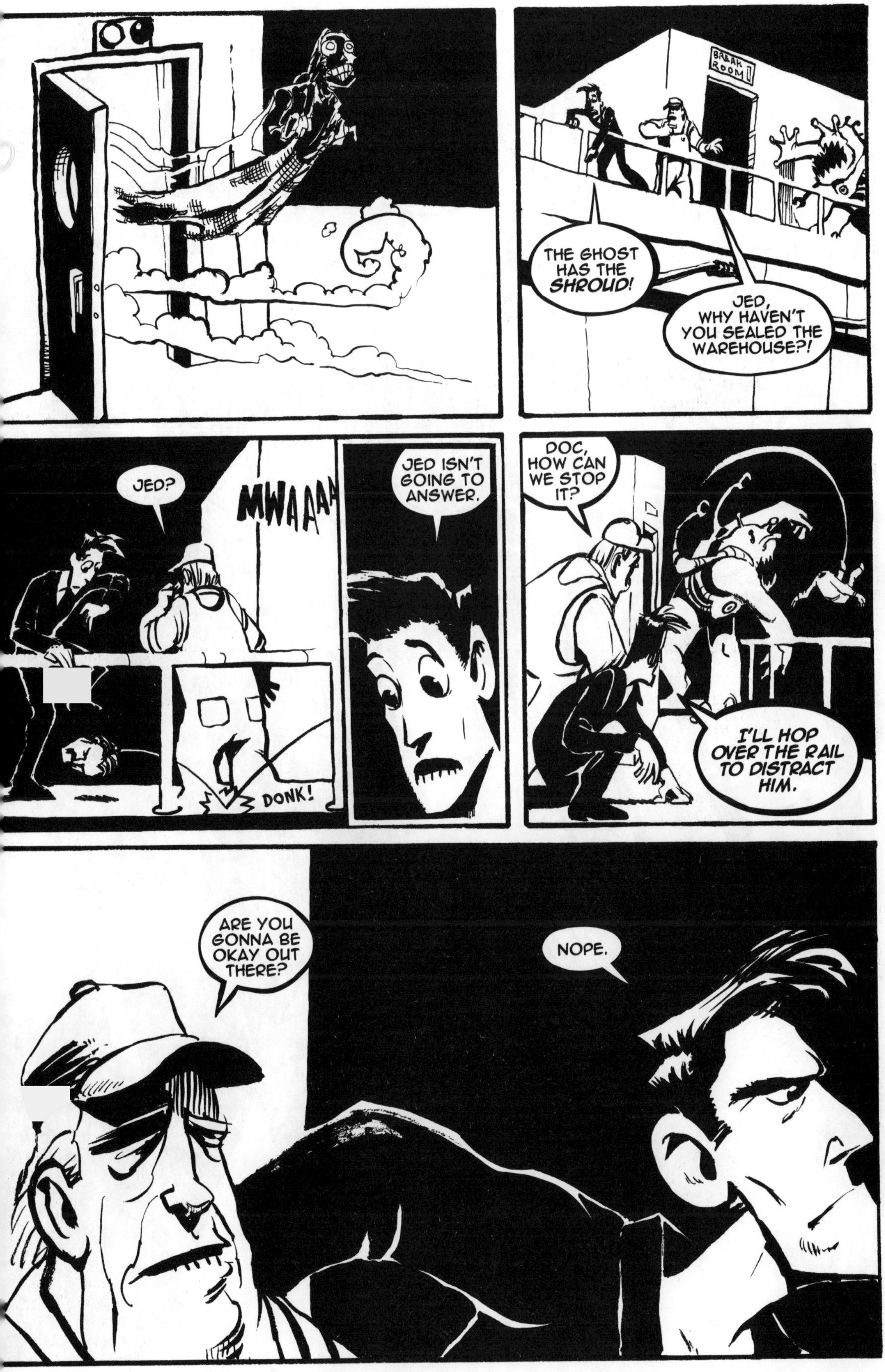
BREAK ROOM
THE GHOST HAS THE SHROUD!
JED, WHY HAVEN'T YOU SEALED THE WAREHOUSE?!
JED?
MWAAAA
DONK!
JED ISN'T GOING TO ANSWER.
DOC, HOW CAN WE STOP IT?
I'LL HOP OVER THE RAIL TO DISTRACT HIM.
ARE YOU GONNA BE OKAY OUT THERE?
NOPE.

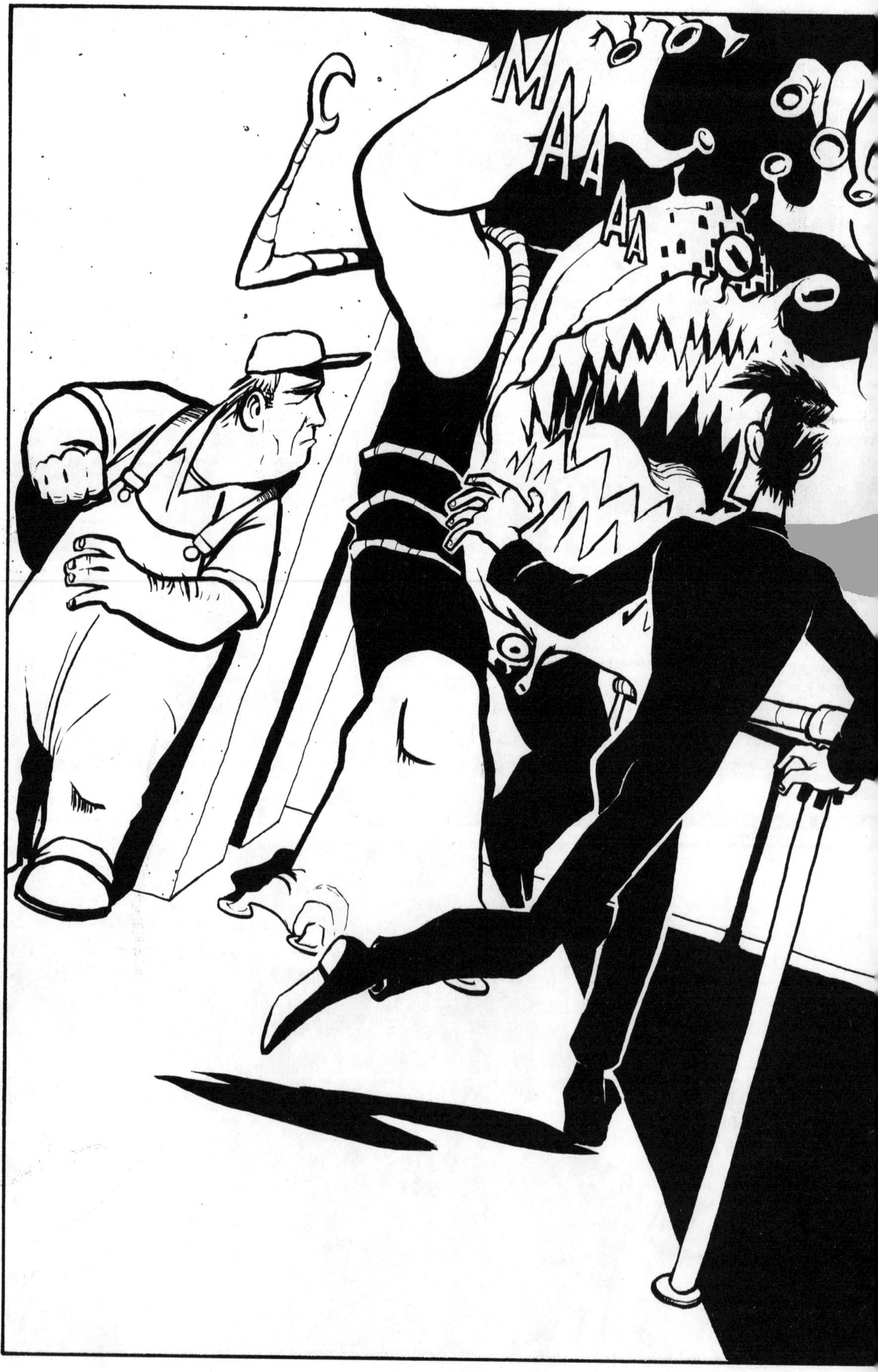
MAAAAAA

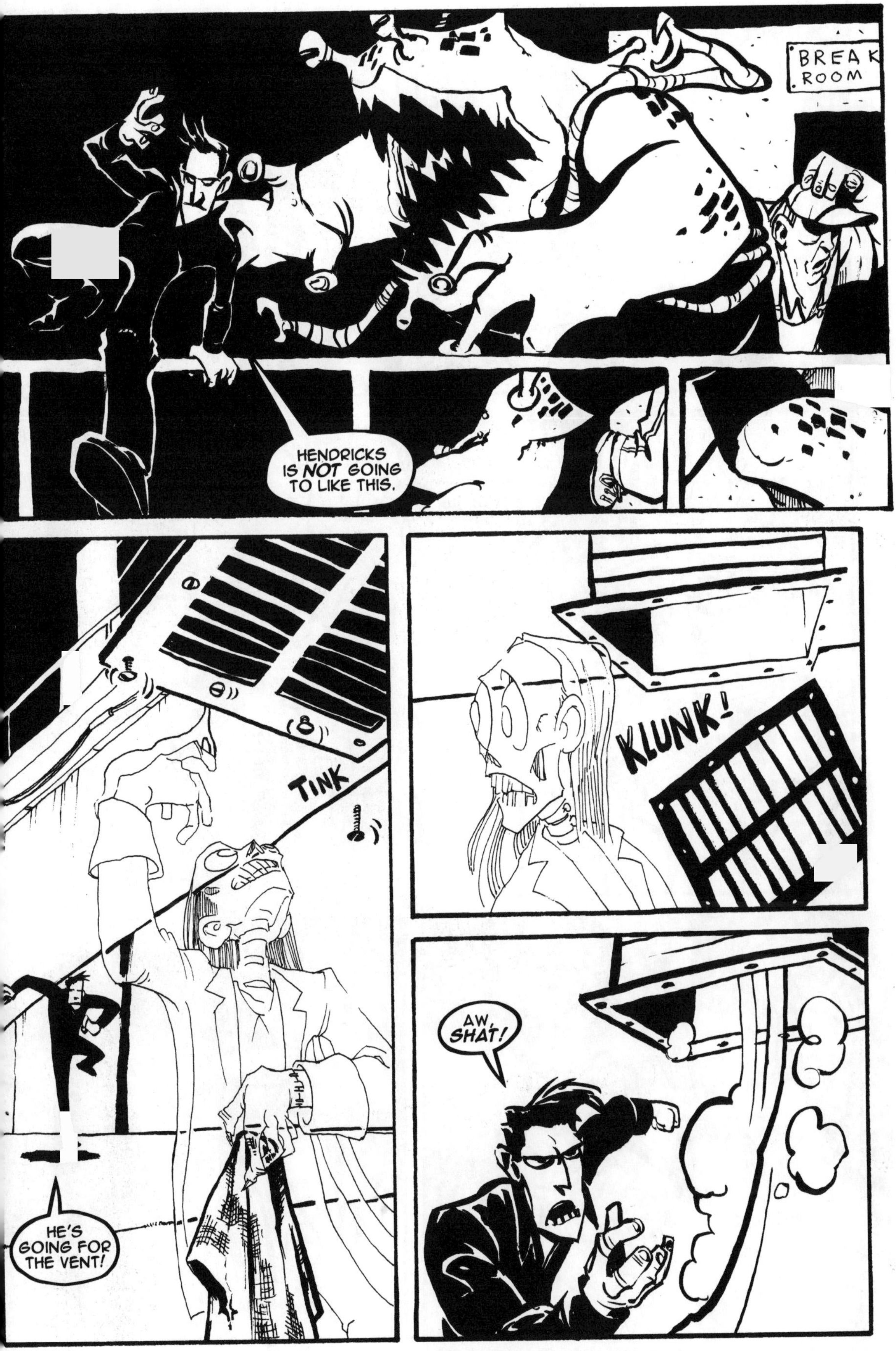
BREAK ROOM
HENDRICKS IS NOT GOING TO LIKE THIS.
TINK
HE'S GOING FOR THE VENT!
KLUNK!
AW, SHAT!

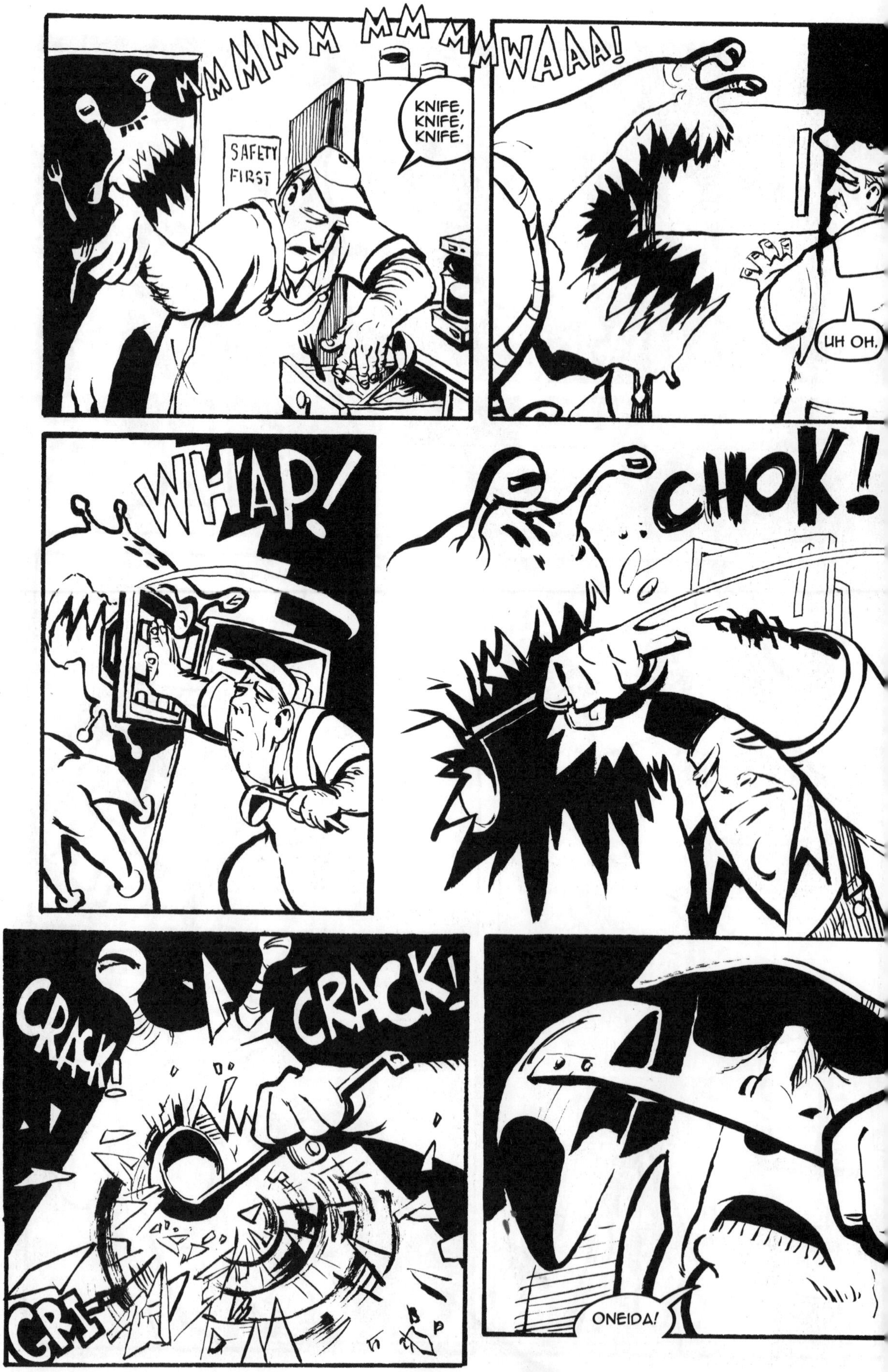
MMMMMM MMM MMWAAA!
SAFETY FIRST
KNIFE, KNIFE, KNIFE.
UH OH.
WHAP!
CHOK!
CRACK!
CRACK!
GRI-
ONEIDA!

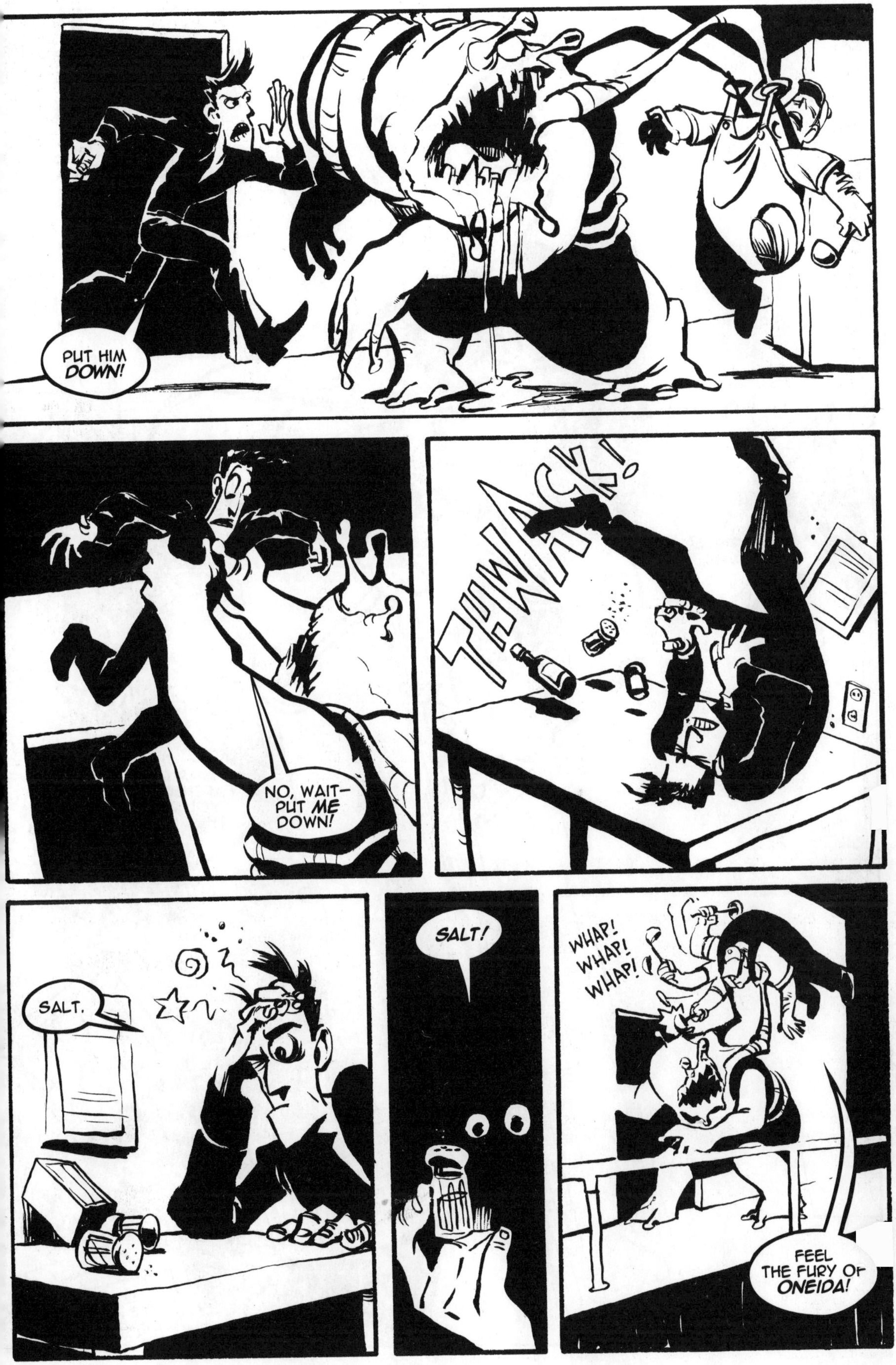
PUT HIM DOWN!
NO, WAIT– PUT ME DOWN!
THWACK!
SALT.
SALT!
WHAP! WHAP! WHAP!
FEEL THE FURY OF ONEIDA!

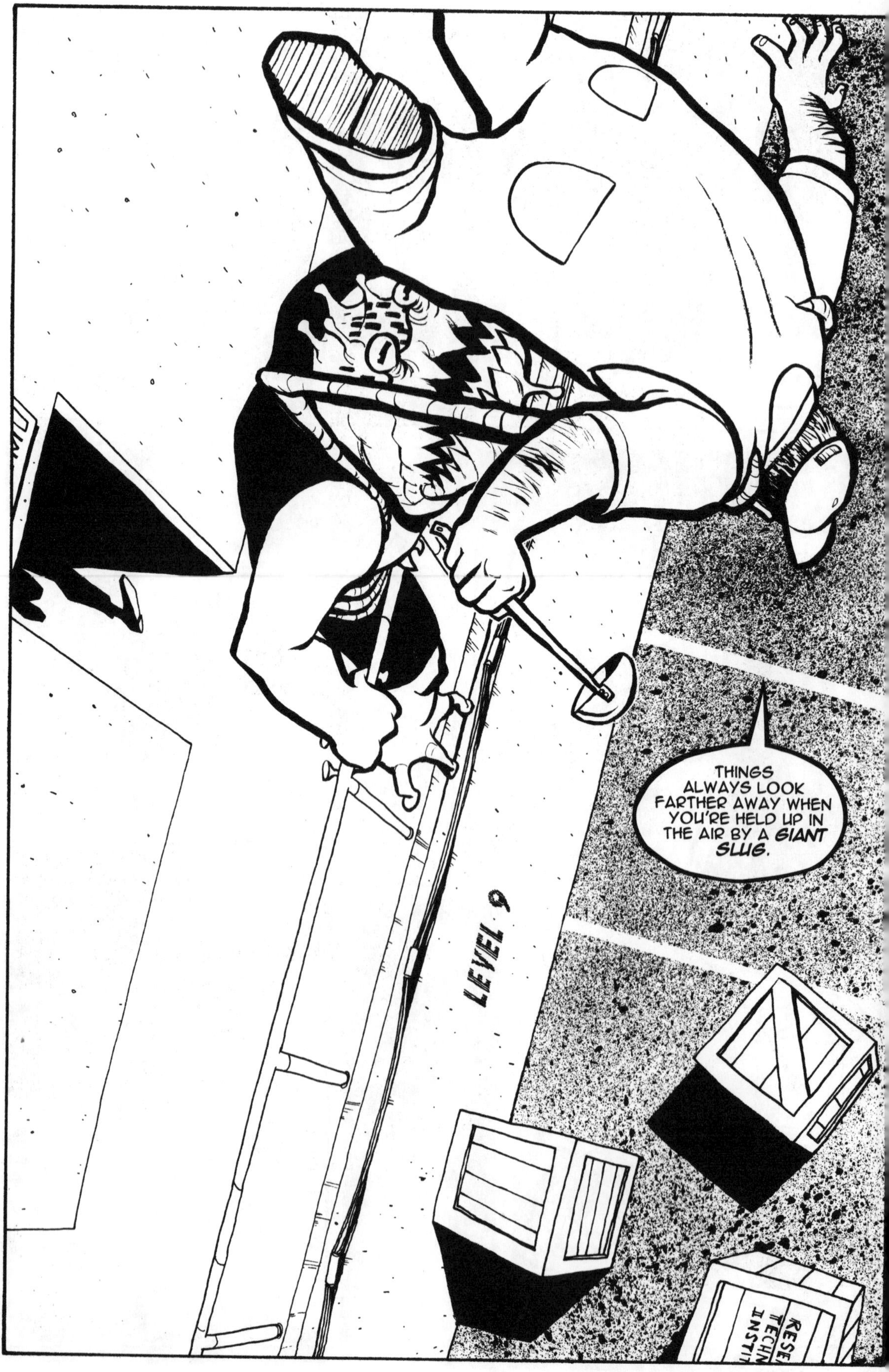
THINGS ALWAYS LOOK FARTHER AWAY WHEN YOU'RE HELD UP IN THE AIR BY A *GIANT SLUG*.
LEVEL 9

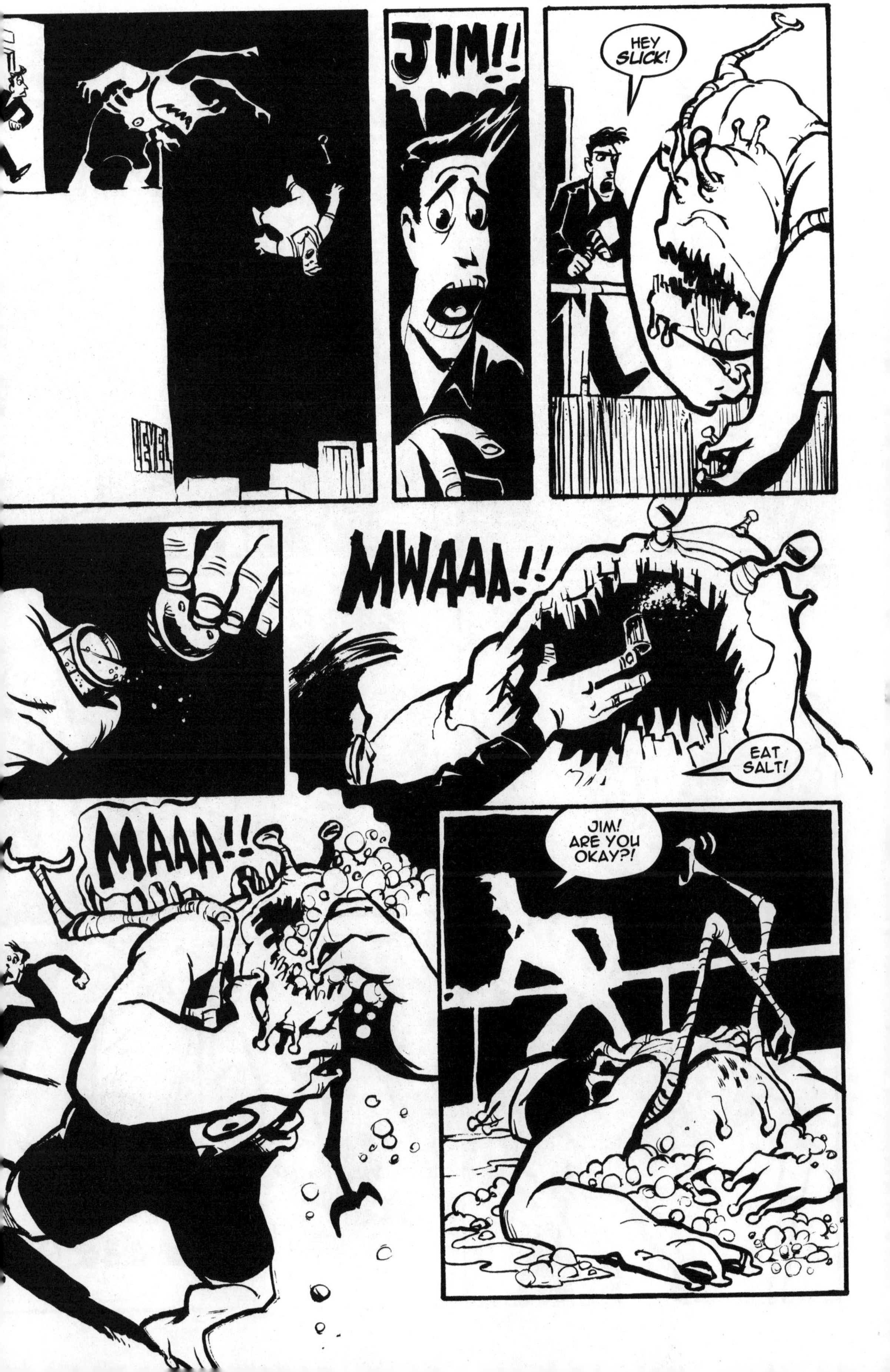
LEVEL
JIM!!
HEY SLICK!
MWAAA!!
EAT SALT!
MAAA!!
JIM! ARE YOU OKAY?!

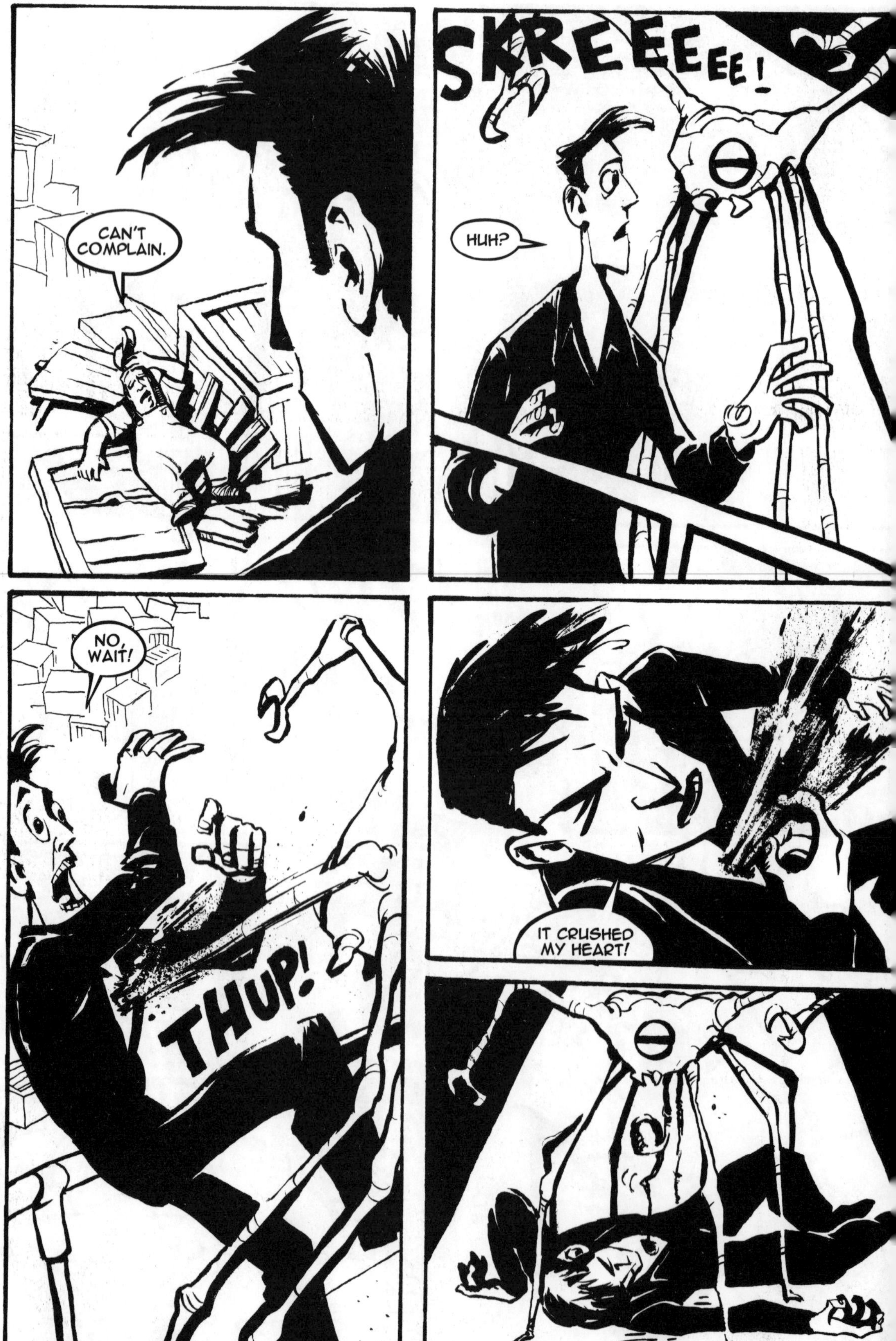
CAN'T COMPLAIN.
SKREEEEEE!
HUH?
NO, WAIT!
THUP!
IT CRUSHED MY HEART!

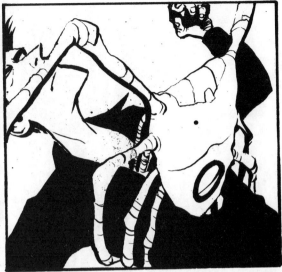

SKREEEEEE

GASP!

WHA?!

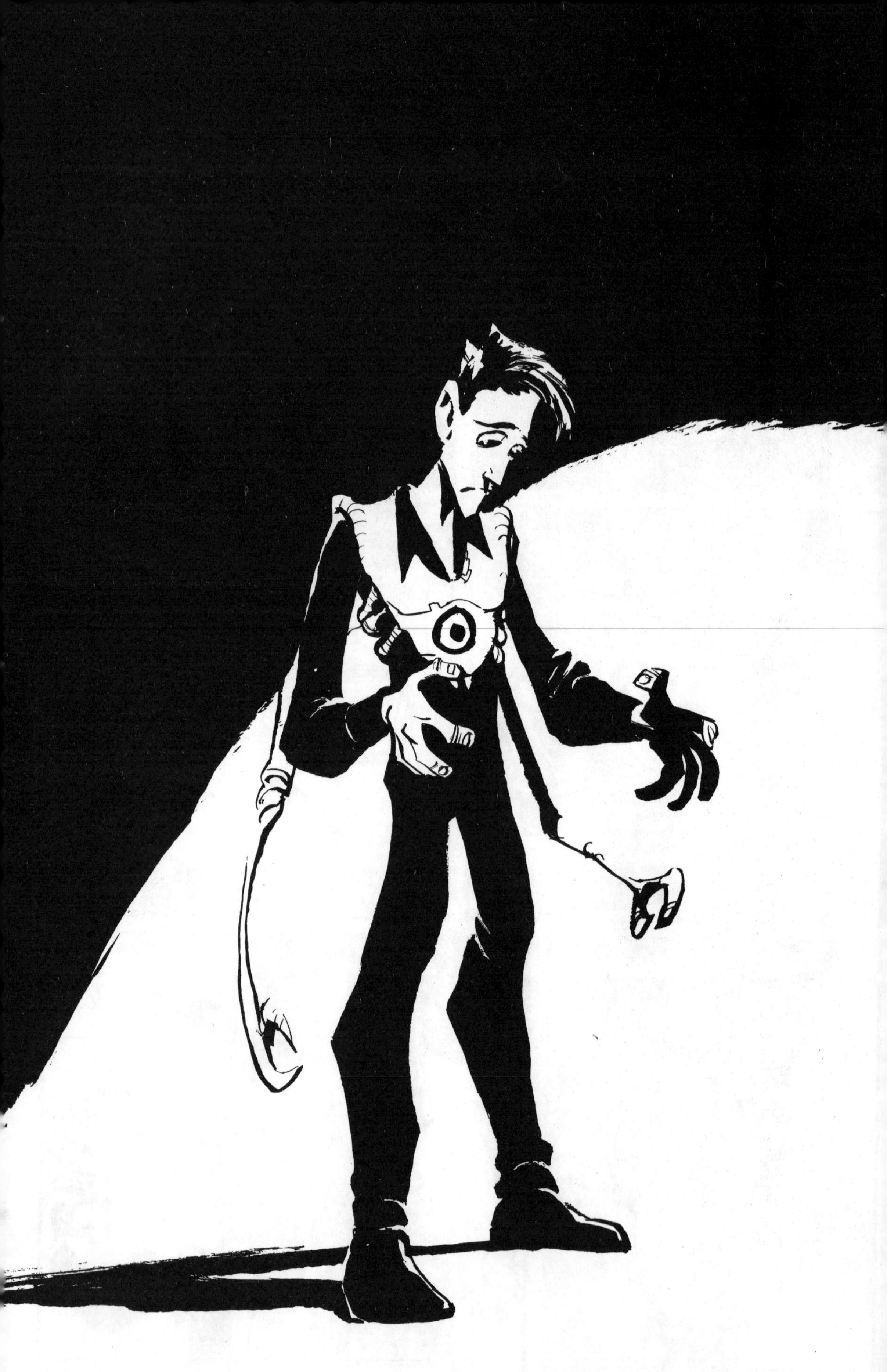

THIS IS A LATERAL PROJECTION. A CLUSTER OF THE ORGANISM'S TENDRILS ENTERED INTO THE *THORACIC CAVITY* AND HAS ATTACHED ITSELF TO THE *AORTIC ARCH.*

IT DESTROYED YOUR HEART THEN PROVIDED ITS *OWN* BLOOD PUMPING ABILITY. IT FORCED YOU INTO A *SYMBIOTIC RELATIONSHIP.*

THE CREATURE HAS GRAFTED A *NERVE NET* THROUGH THE DURA MATTER OF YOUR SECOND AND FOURTH CERVICAL VERTEBRAE.

IT MUST BE INTERCEPTING SOME OF MY BRAIN SIGNALS. *CAN WE CUT IT OFF?*

TOO DANGEROUS. IT CHOOSES WHICH SIGNALS IT WILL CARRY OUT AND WHICH SIGNALS IT WILL LET YOU CARRY OUT.

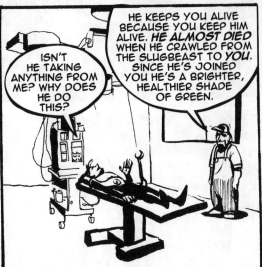

ISN'T HE TAKING ANYTHING FROM ME? WHY DOES HE DO THIS?

HE KEEPS YOU ALIVE BECAUSE YOU KEEP HIM ALIVE. *HE ALMOST DIED* WHEN HE CRAWLED FROM THE SLUGBEAST TO *YOU.* SINCE HE'S JOINED YOU HE'S A BRIGHTER, HEALTHIER SHADE OF GREEN.

SO IT'S A *SYMBIOTIC RELATIONSHIP.* WE LIVE OFF EACH OTHER. LIKE A SEA ANEMONE AND A CLOWN FISH! LIKE APHIDS AND ANTS!

LIKE BO AND LUKE DUKE.

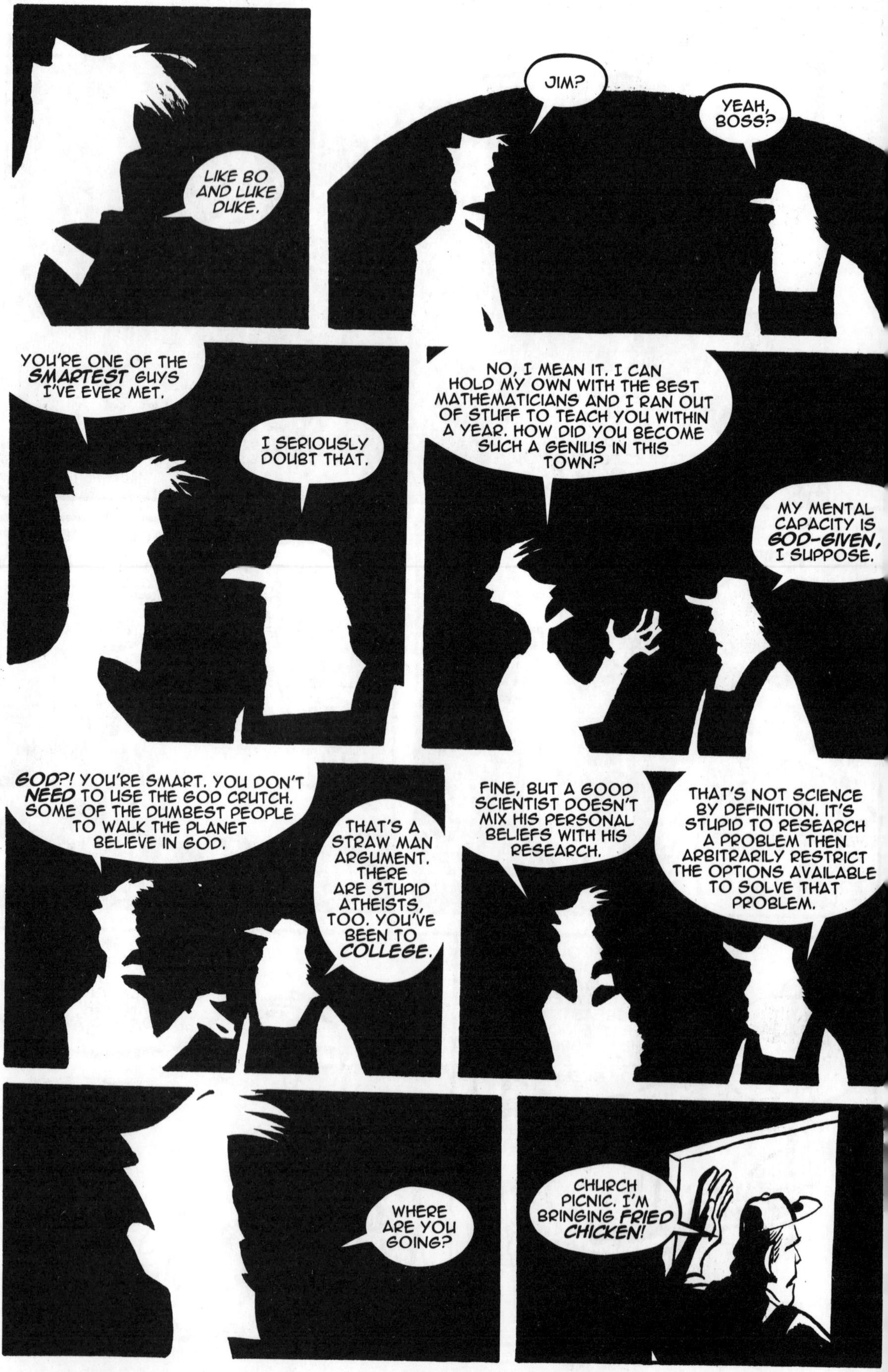
LIKE BO AND LUKE DUKE.
JIM?
YEAH, BOSS?
YOU'RE ONE OF THE SMARTEST GUYS I'VE EVER MET.
I SERIOUSLY DOUBT THAT.
NO, I MEAN IT. I CAN HOLD MY OWN WITH THE BEST MATHEMATICIANS AND I RAN OUT OF STUFF TO TEACH YOU WITHIN A YEAR. HOW DID YOU BECOME SUCH A GENIUS IN THIS TOWN?
MY MENTAL CAPACITY IS GOD-GIVEN, I SUPPOSE.
GOD?! YOU'RE SMART. YOU DON'T NEED TO USE THE GOD CRUTCH. SOME OF THE DUMBEST PEOPLE TO WALK THE PLANET BELIEVE IN GOD.
THAT'S A STRAW MAN ARGUMENT. THERE ARE STUPID ATHEISTS, TOO. YOU'VE BEEN TO COLLEGE.
FINE, BUT A GOOD SCIENTIST DOESN'T MIX HIS PERSONAL BELIEFS WITH HIS RESEARCH.
THAT'S NOT SCIENCE BY DEFINITION. IT'S STUPID TO RESEARCH A PROBLEM THEN ARBITRARILY RESTRICT THE OPTIONS AVAILABLE TO SOLVE THAT PROBLEM.
WHERE ARE YOU GOING?
CHURCH PICNIC. I'M BRINGING FRIED CHICKEN!

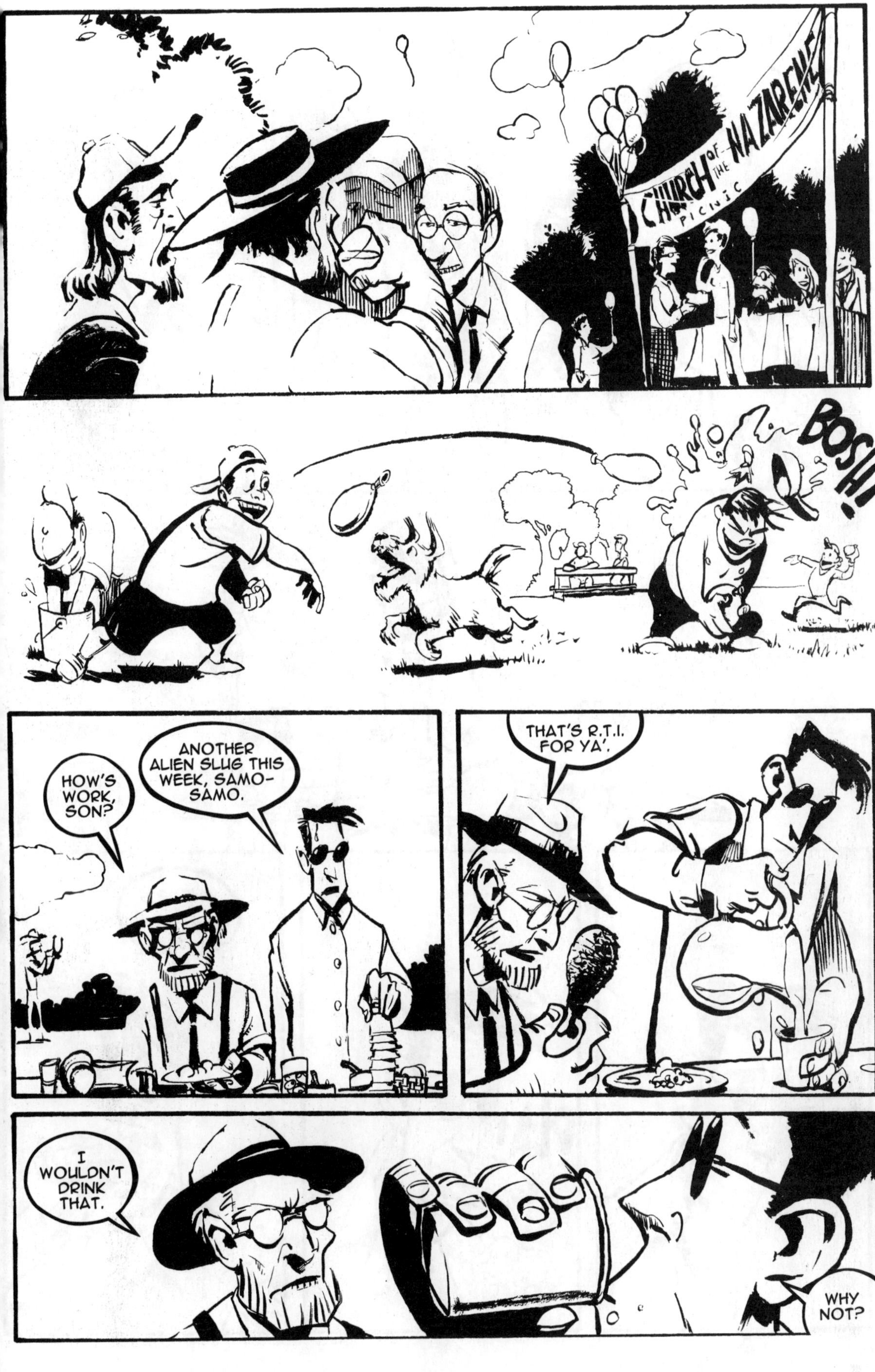
CHURCH OF THE NAZARENE
PICNIC
BOSH!!
HOW'S WORK, SON?
ANOTHER ALIEN SLUG THIS WEEK, SAMO-SAMO.
THAT'S R.T.I. FOR YA'.
I WOULDN'T DRINK THAT.
WHY NOT?

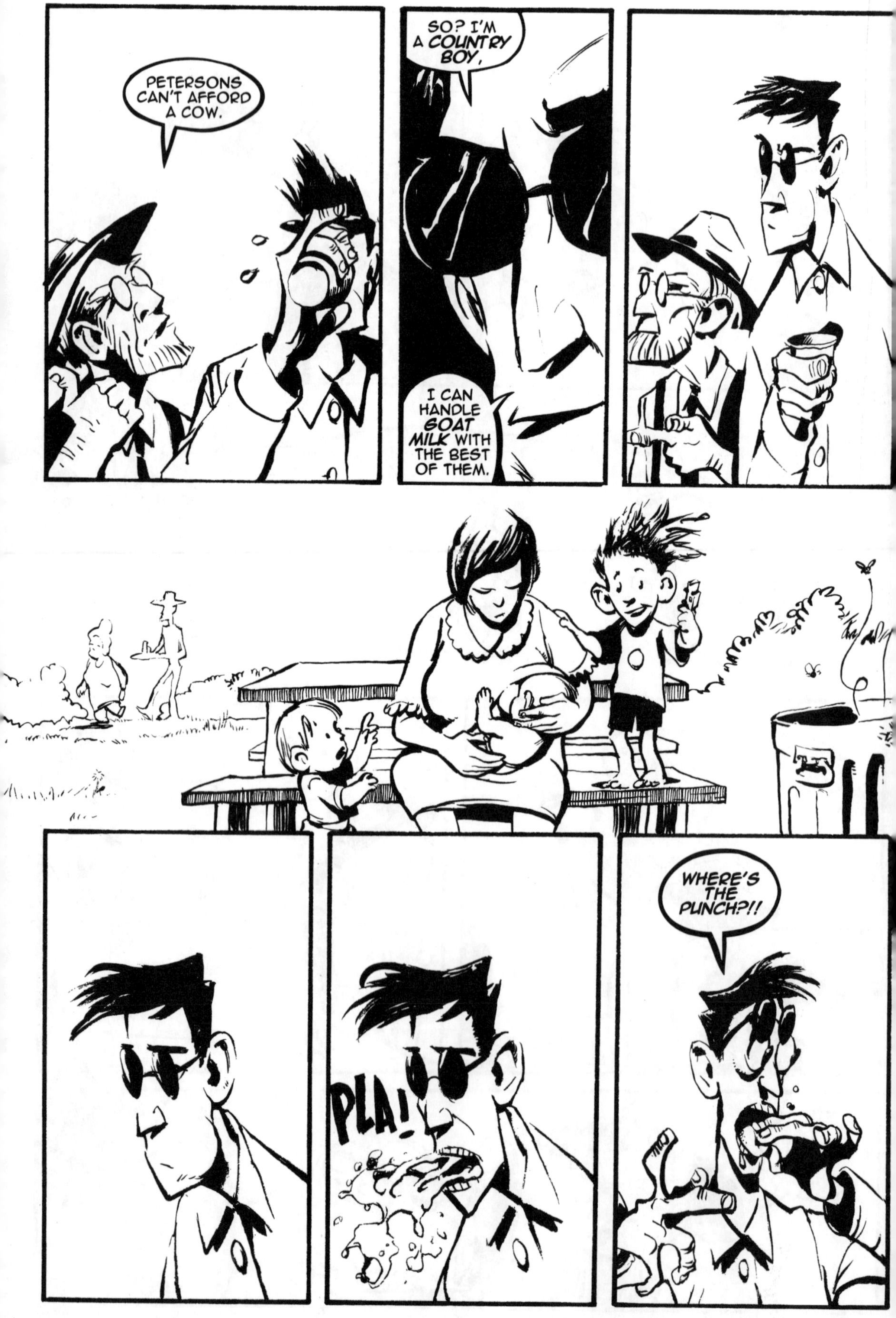
PETERSONS CAN'T AFFORD A COW.
SO? I'M A COUNTRY BOY,
I CAN HANDLE GOAT MILK WITH THE BEST OF THEM.
PLA!
WHERE'S THE PUNCH?!!

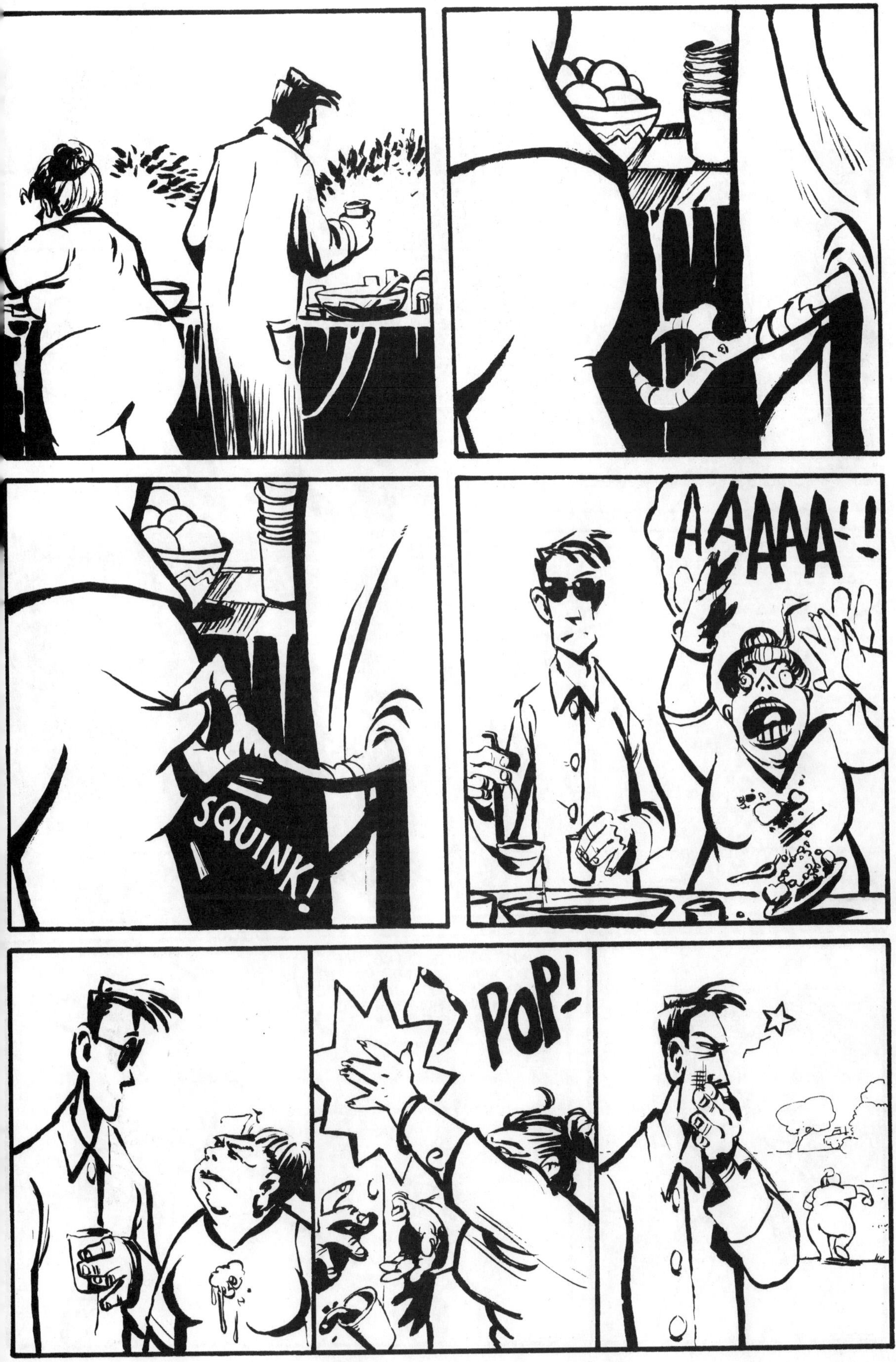
SQUINK!
AAAAA!!
POP!

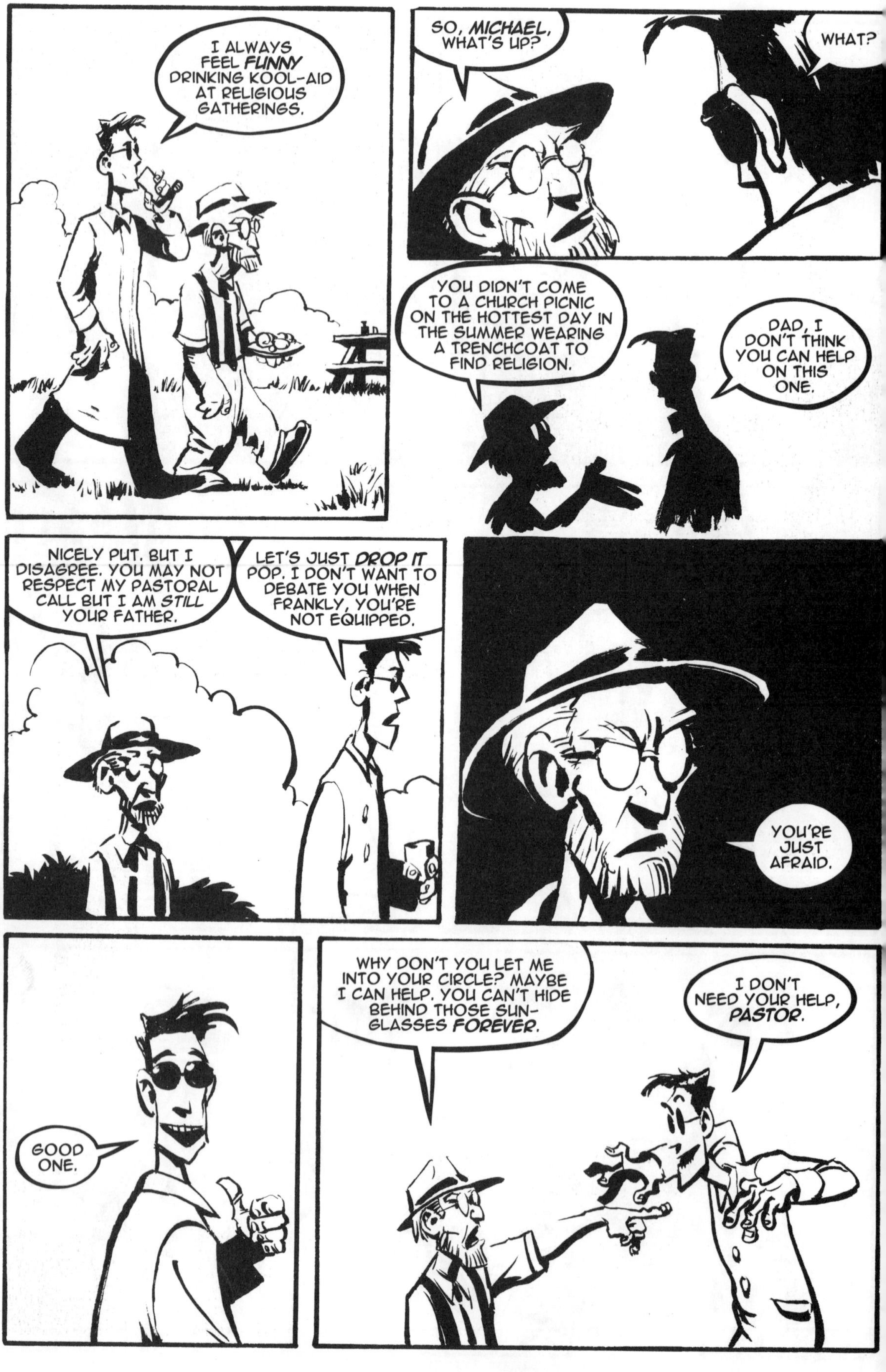
I ALWAYS FEEL FUNNY DRINKING KOOL-AID AT RELIGIOUS GATHERINGS.
SO, MICHAEL, WHAT'S UP?
WHAT?
YOU DIDN'T COME TO A CHURCH PICNIC ON THE HOTTEST DAY IN THE SUMMER WEARING A TRENCHCOAT TO FIND RELIGION.
DAD, I DON'T THINK YOU CAN HELP ON THIS ONE.
NICELY PUT. BUT I DISAGREE. YOU MAY NOT RESPECT MY PASTORAL CALL BUT I AM STILL YOUR FATHER.
LET'S JUST DROP IT POP. I DON'T WANT TO DEBATE YOU WHEN FRANKLY, YOU'RE NOT EQUIPPED.
YOU'RE JUST AFRAID.
GOOD ONE.
WHY DON'T YOU LET ME INTO YOUR CIRCLE? MAYBE I CAN HELP. YOU CAN'T HIDE BEHIND THOSE SUN-GLASSES FOREVER.
I DON'T NEED YOUR HELP, PASTOR.

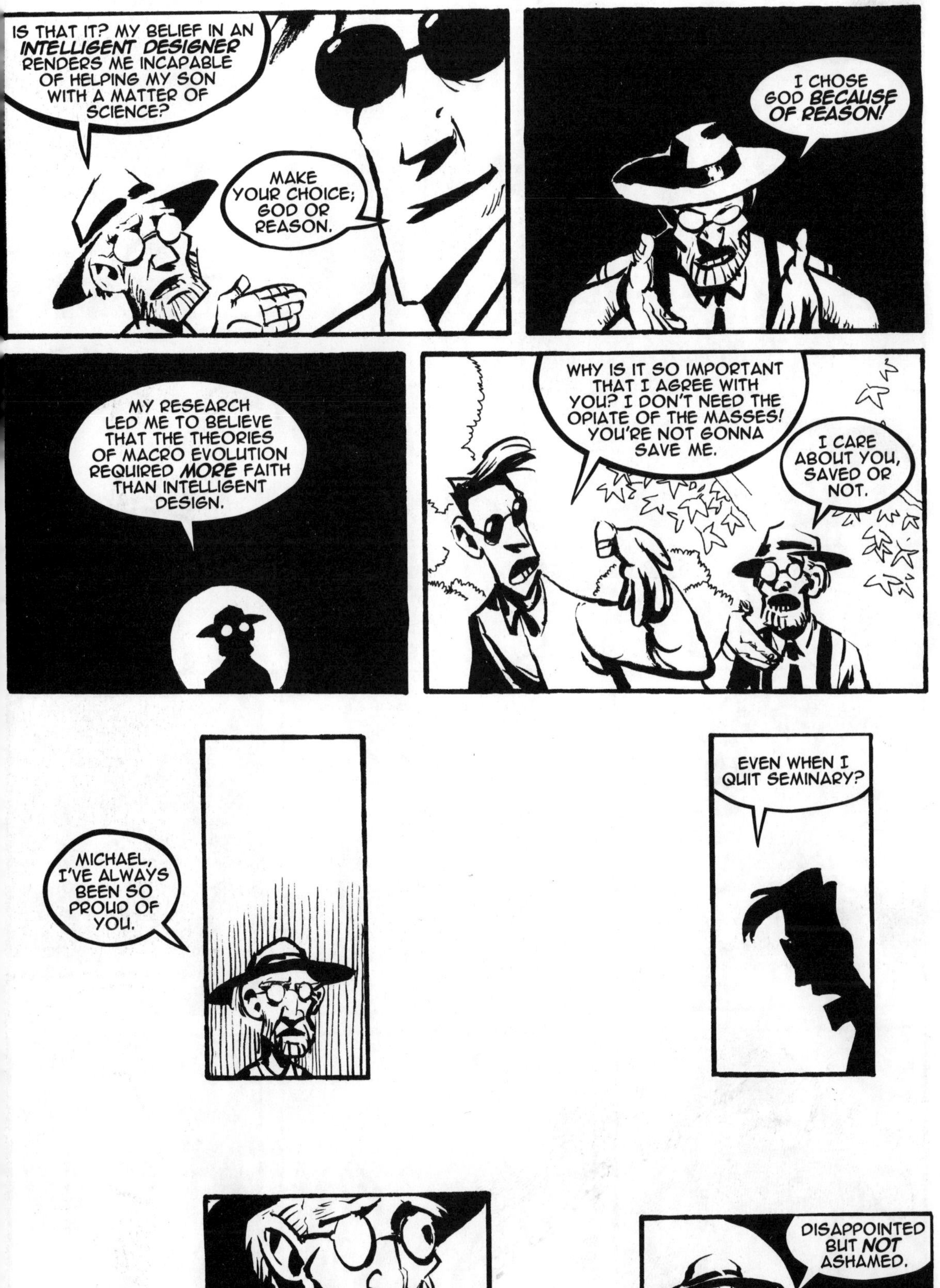
IS THAT IT? MY BELIEF IN AN *INTELLIGENT DESIGNER* RENDERS ME INCAPABLE OF HELPING MY SON WITH A MATTER OF SCIENCE?
MAKE YOUR CHOICE; GOD OR REASON.
I CHOSE GOD *BECAUSE OF REASON!*
MY RESEARCH LED ME TO BELIEVE THAT THE THEORIES OF MACRO EVOLUTION REQUIRED *MORE* FAITH THAN INTELLIGENT DESIGN.
WHY IS IT SO IMPORTANT THAT I AGREE WITH YOU? I DON'T NEED THE OPIATE OF THE MASSES! YOU'RE NOT GONNA SAVE ME.
I CARE ABOUT YOU, SAVED OR NOT.
MICHAEL, I'VE ALWAYS BEEN SO PROUD OF YOU.
EVEN WHEN I QUIT SEMINARY?
DISAPPOINTED BUT *NOT* ASHAMED.

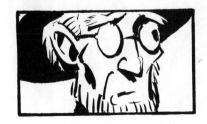

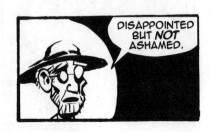

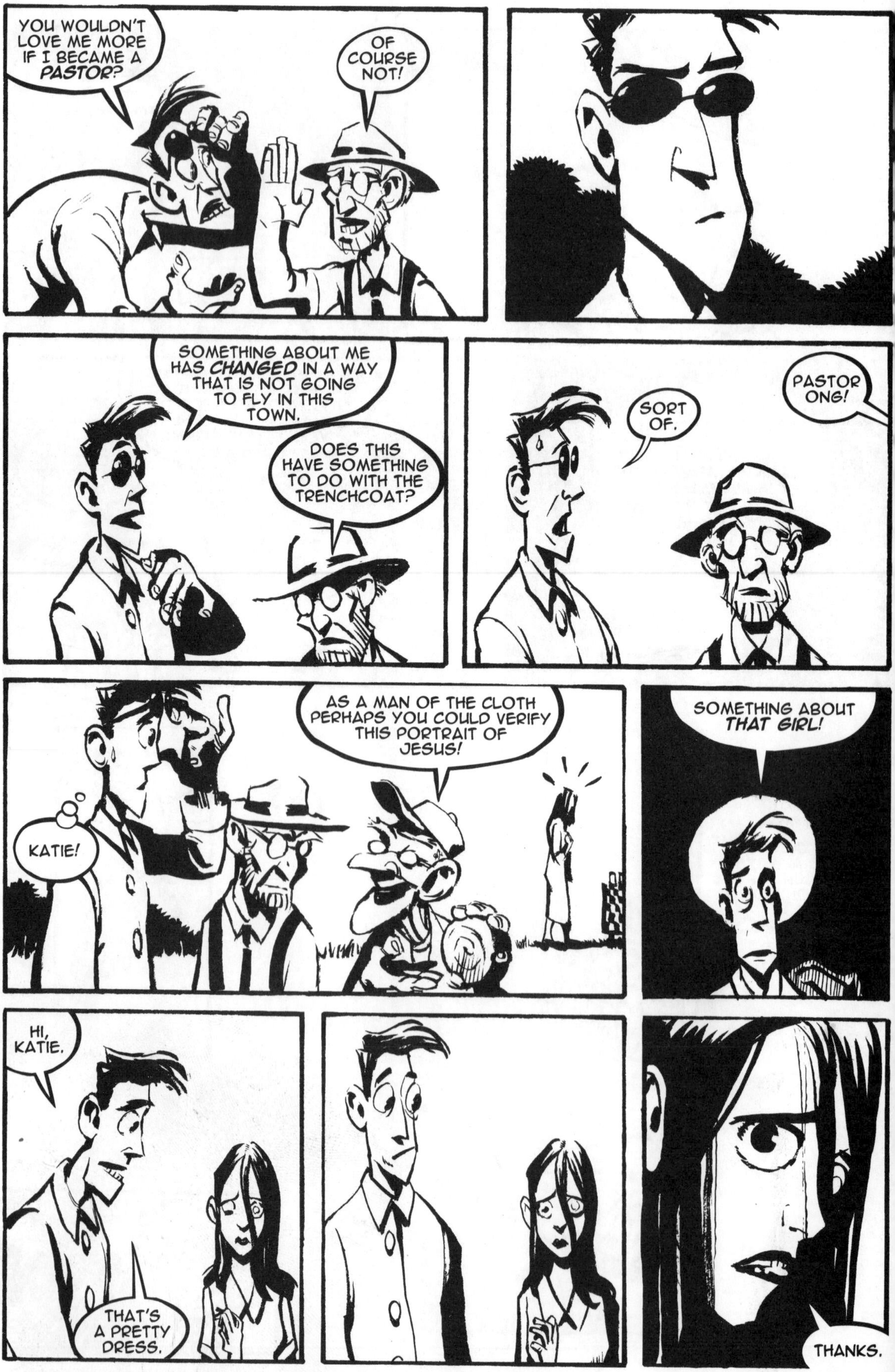
YOU WOULDN'T LOVE ME MORE IF I BECAME A PASTOR?
OF COURSE NOT!
SOMETHING ABOUT ME HAS CHANGED IN A WAY THAT IS NOT GOING TO FLY IN THIS TOWN.
DOES THIS HAVE SOMETHING TO DO WITH THE TRENCHCOAT?
SORT OF.
PASTOR ONG!
AS A MAN OF THE CLOTH PERHAPS YOU COULD VERIFY THIS PORTRAIT OF JESUS!
KATIE!
SOMETHING ABOUT THAT GIRL!
HI, KATIE.
THAT'S A PRETTY DRESS.
THANKS.

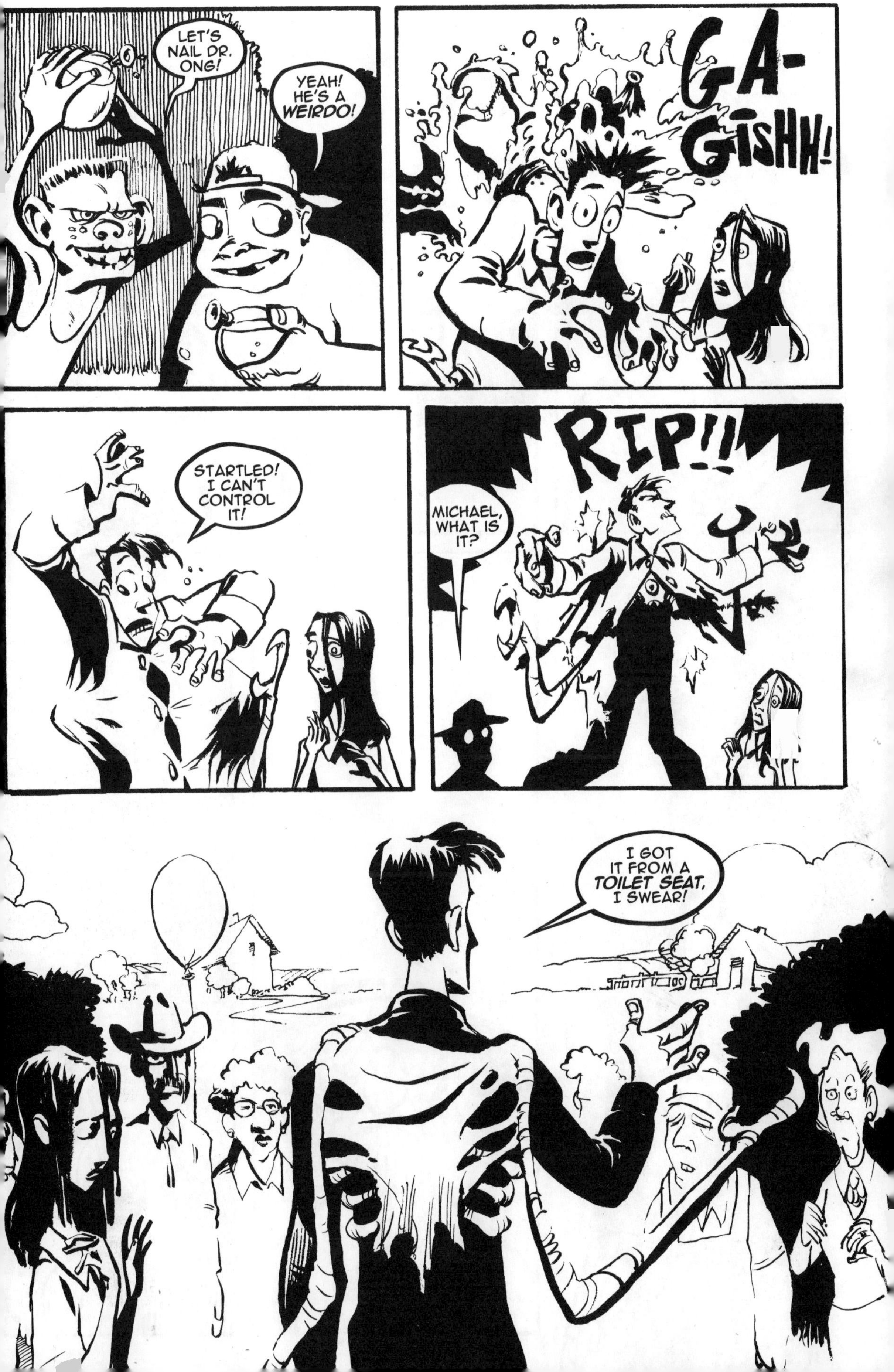
LET'S NAIL DR. ONG!
YEAH! HE'S A WEIRDO!
GA-GISHH!
STARTLED! I CAN'T CONTROL IT!
RIP!!!
MICHAEL, WHAT IS IT?
I GOT IT FROM A TOILET SEAT, I SWEAR!

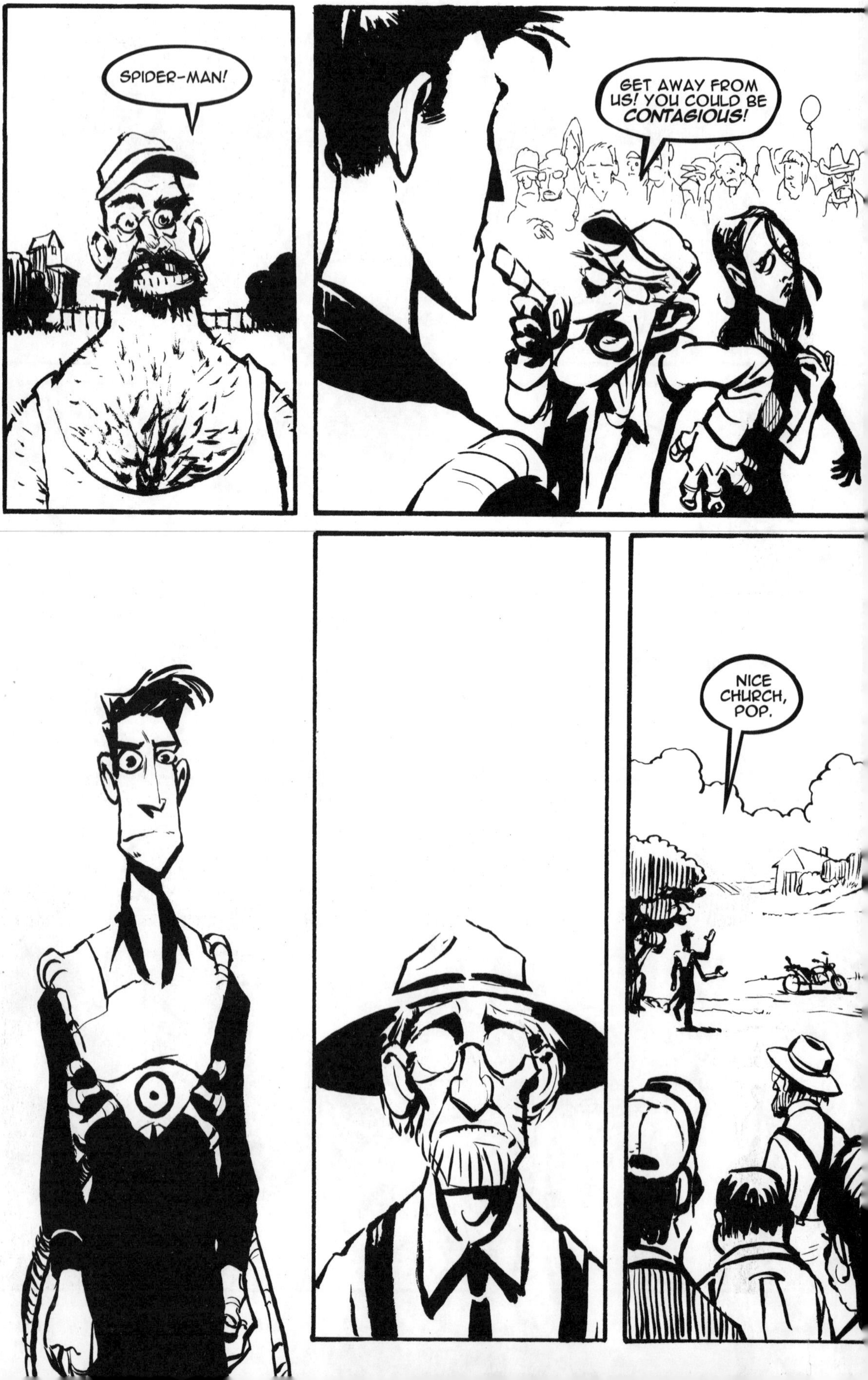
SPIDER-MAN!
GET AWAY FROM US! YOU COULD BE CONTAGIOUS!
NICE CHURCH, POP.

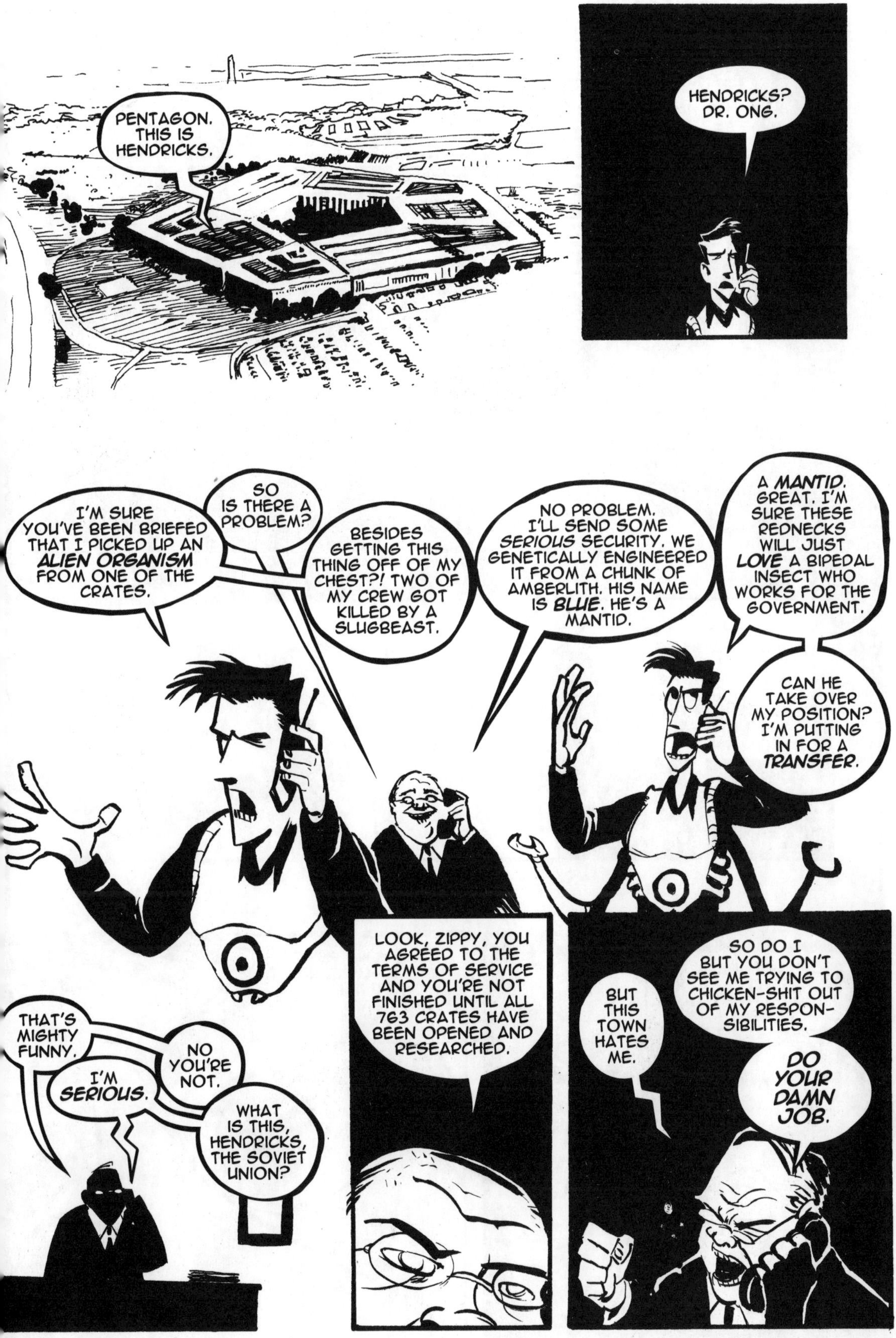
PENTAGON. THIS IS HENDRICKS.
HENDRICKS? DR. ONG.
I'M SURE YOU'VE BEEN BRIEFED THAT I PICKED UP AN ALIEN ORGANISM FROM ONE OF THE CRATES.
SO IS THERE A PROBLEM?
BESIDES GETTING THIS THING OFF OF MY CHEST?! TWO OF MY CREW GOT KILLED BY A SLUGBEAST.
NO PROBLEM. I'LL SEND SOME SERIOUS SECURITY. WE GENETICALLY ENGINEERED IT FROM A CHUNK OF AMBERLITH. HIS NAME IS BLUE. HE'S A MANTID.
A MANTID. GREAT. I'M SURE THESE REDNECKS WILL JUST LOVE A BIPEDAL INSECT WHO WORKS FOR THE GOVERNMENT.
CAN HE TAKE OVER MY POSITION? I'M PUTTING IN FOR A TRANSFER.
THAT'S MIGHTY FUNNY.
NO YOU'RE NOT.
I'M SERIOUS.
WHAT IS THIS, HENDRICKS, THE SOVIET UNION?
LOOK, ZIPPY, YOU AGREED TO THE TERMS OF SERVICE AND YOU'RE NOT FINISHED UNTIL ALL 763 CRATES HAVE BEEN OPENED AND RESEARCHED.
BUT THIS TOWN HATES ME.
SO DO I BUT YOU DON'T SEE ME TRYING TO CHICKEN-SHIT OUT OF MY RESPON-SIBILITIES.
DO YOUR DAMN JOB.

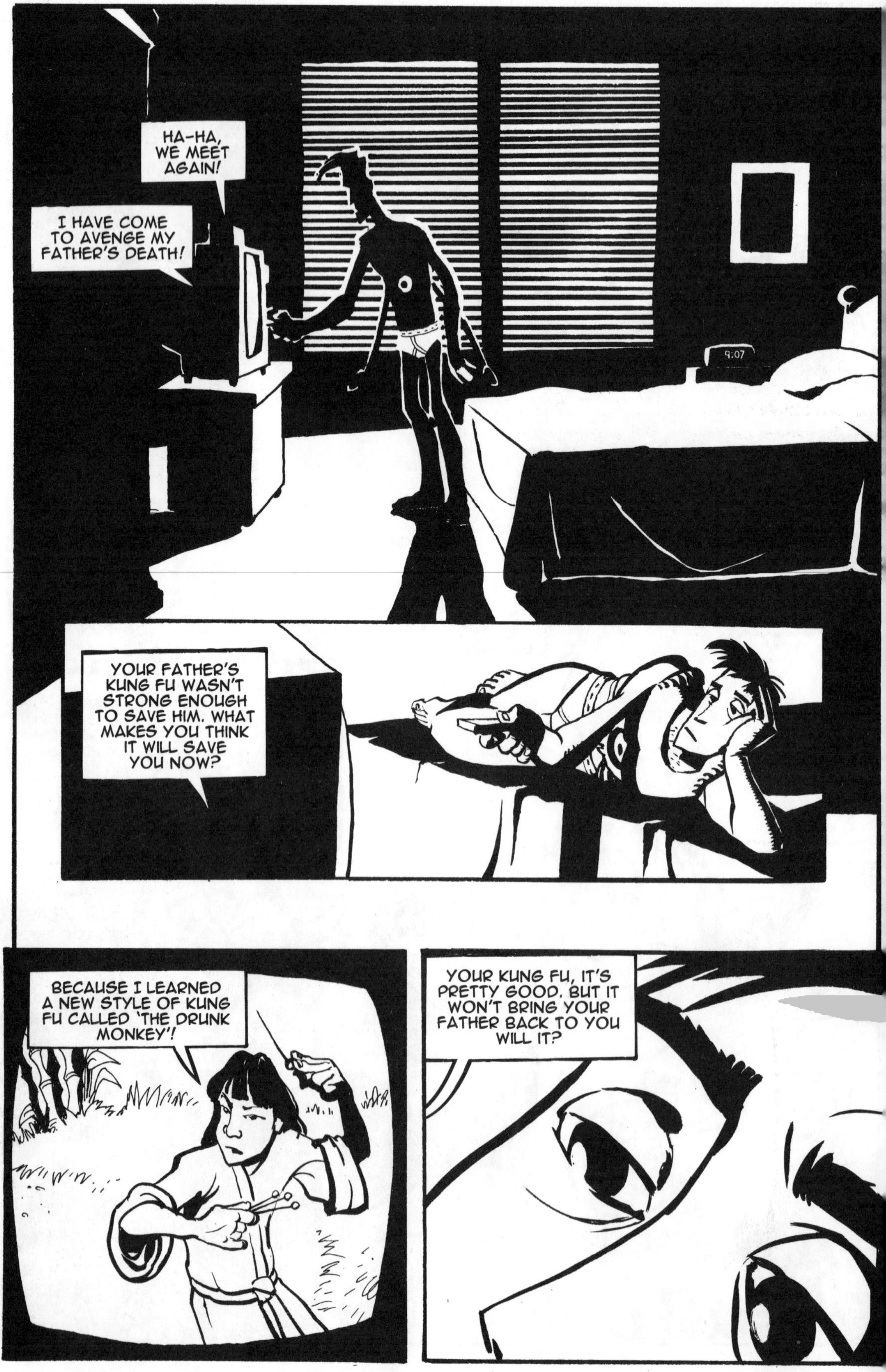
HA-HA, WE MEET AGAIN!
I HAVE COME TO AVENGE MY FATHER'S DEATH!
9:07
YOUR FATHER'S KUNG FU WASN'T STRONG ENOUGH TO SAVE HIM. WHAT MAKES YOU THINK IT WILL SAVE YOU NOW?
BECAUSE I LEARNED A NEW STYLE OF KUNG FU CALLED 'THE DRUNK MONKEY'!
YOUR KUNG FU, IT'S PRETTY GOOD. BUT IT WON'T BRING YOUR FATHER BACK TO YOU WILL IT?

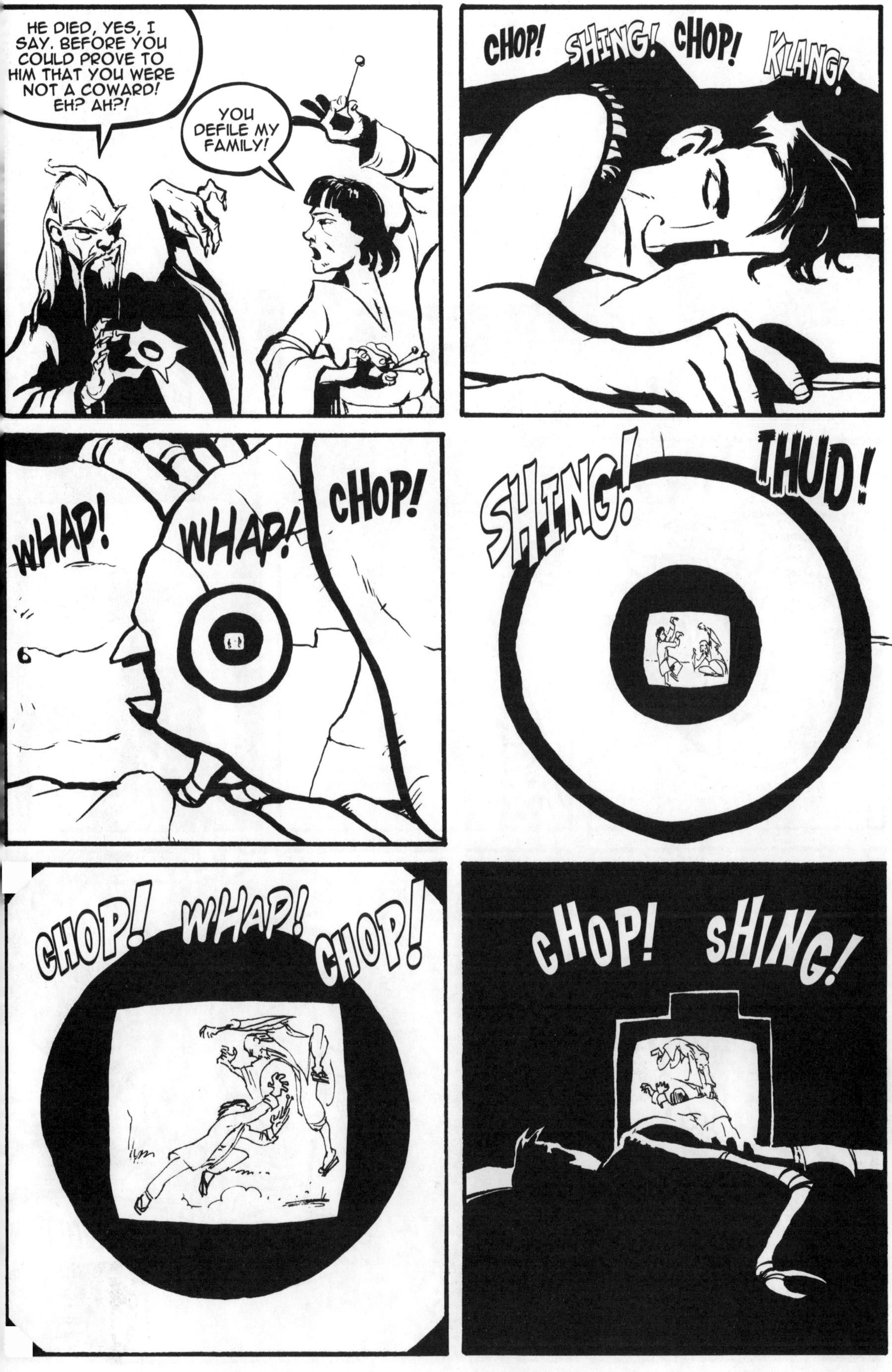
HE DIED, YES, I SAY. BEFORE YOU COULD PROVE TO HIM THAT YOU WERE NOT A COWARD! EH? AH?!
YOU DEFILE MY FAMILY!
CHOP! SHING! CHOP! KLANG!
WHAP! WHAP! CHOP!
SHING! THUD!
CHOP! WHAP! CHOP!
CHOP! SHING!

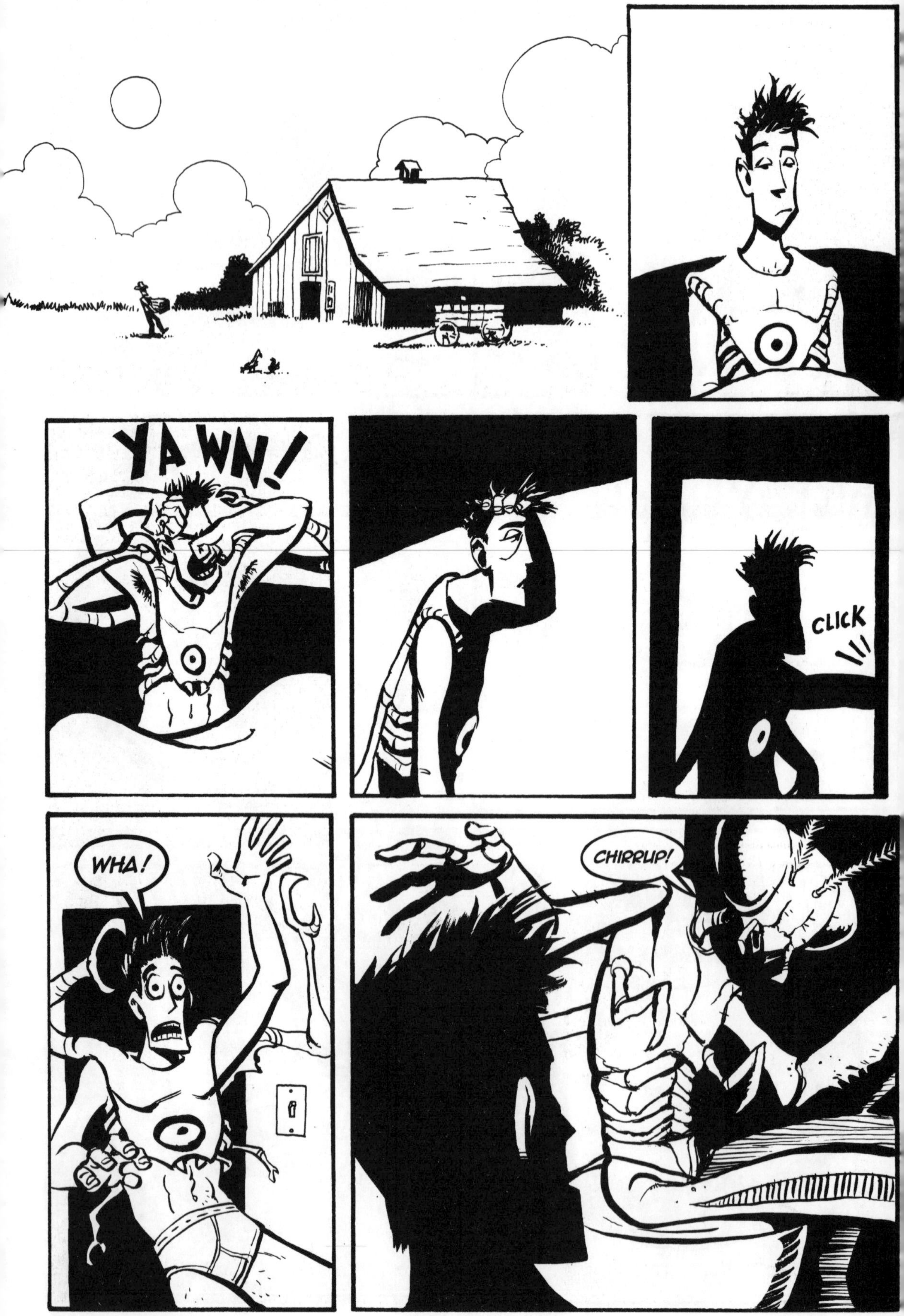
YAWN!
CLICK
WHA!
CHIRRUP!

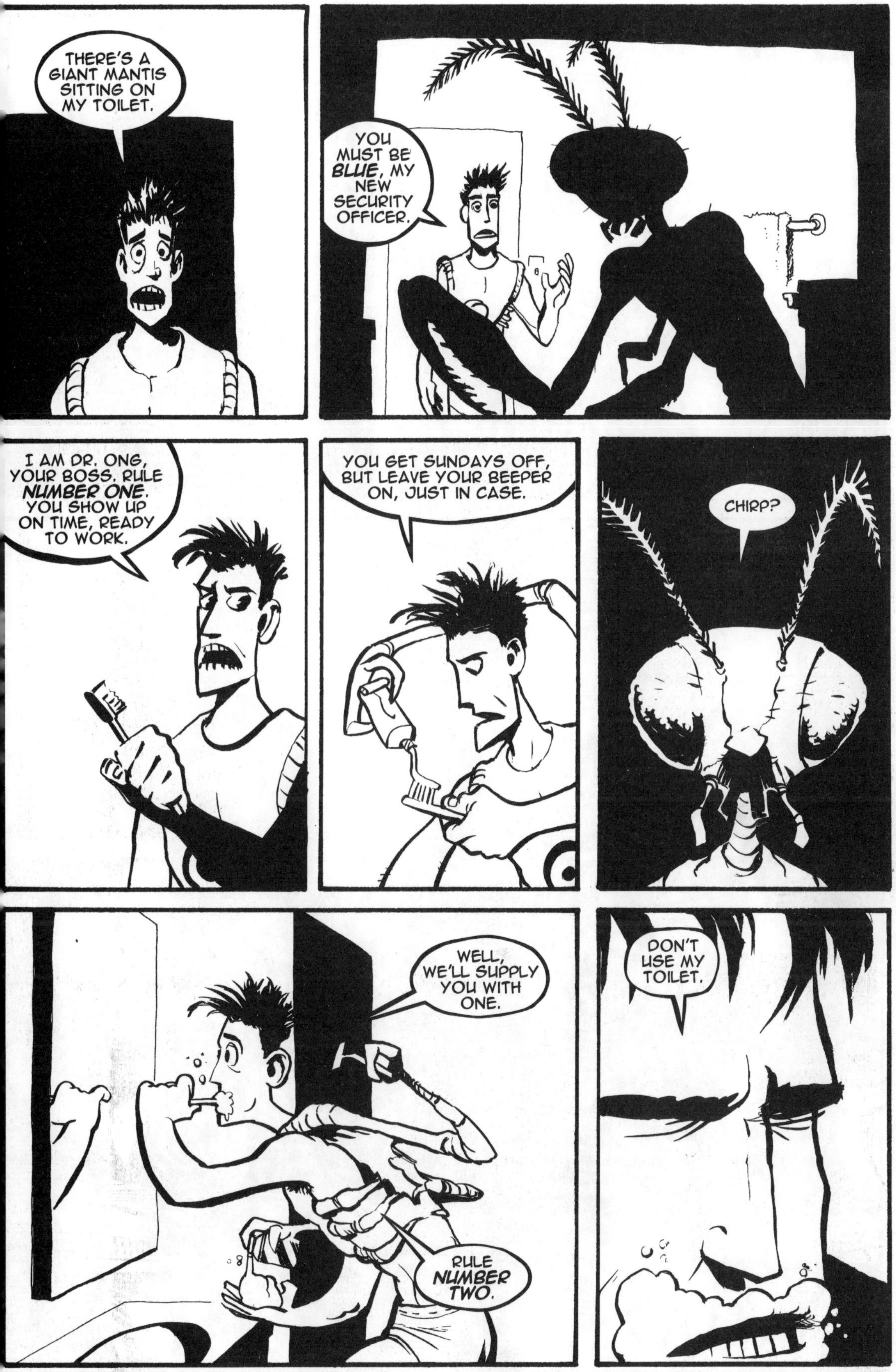
THERE'S A GIANT MANTIS SITTING ON MY TOILET.
YOU MUST BE BLUE, MY NEW SECURITY OFFICER.
I AM DR. ONG, YOUR BOSS. RULE NUMBER ONE. YOU SHOW UP ON TIME, READY TO WORK.
YOU GET SUNDAYS OFF, BUT LEAVE YOUR BEEPER ON, JUST IN CASE.
CHIRP?
WELL, WE'LL SUPPLY YOU WITH ONE.
RULE NUMBER TWO.
DON'T USE MY TOILET.

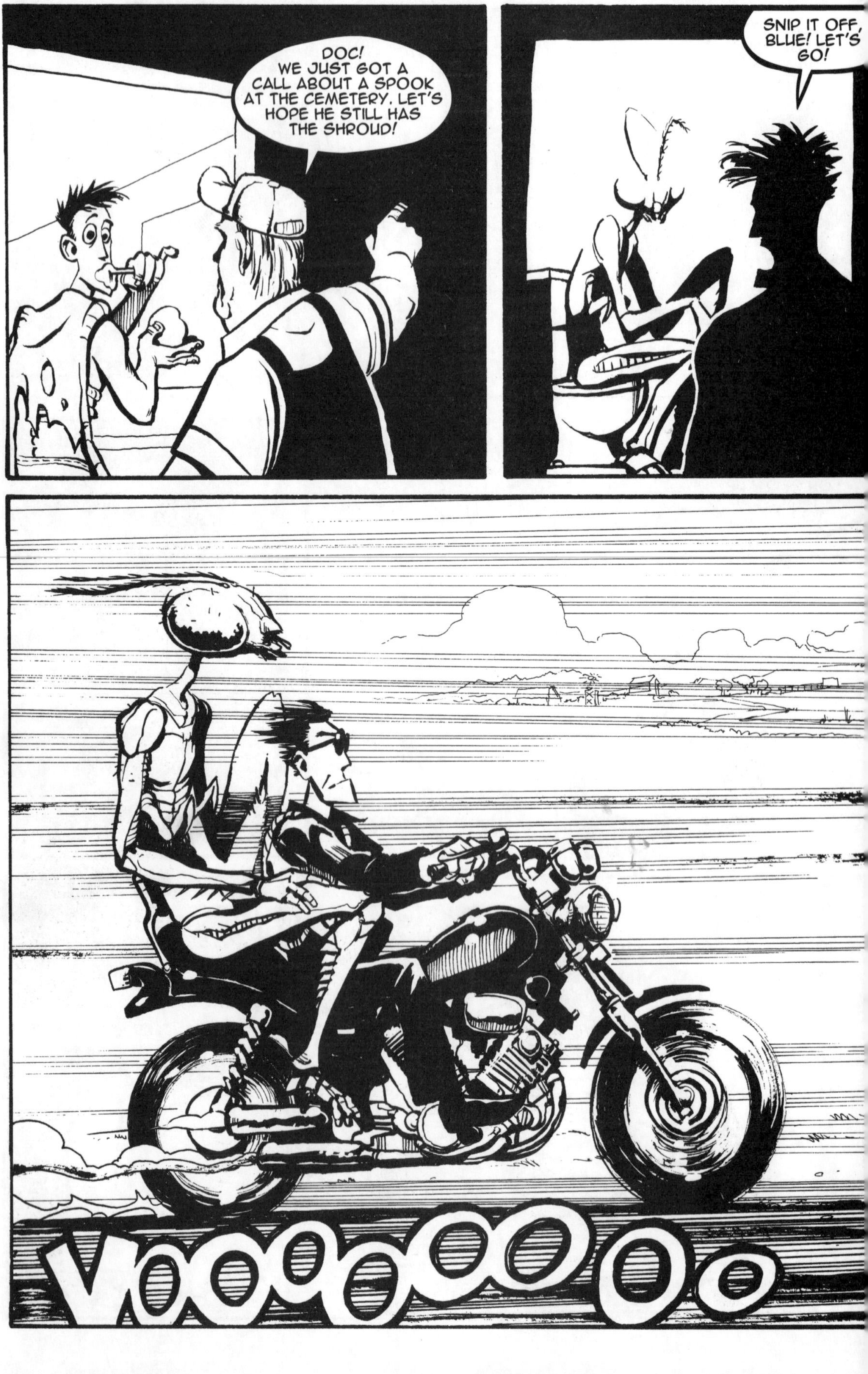
DOC! WE JUST GOT A CALL ABOUT A SPOOK AT THE CEMETERY. LET'S HOPE HE STILL HAS THE SHROUD!
SNIP IT OFF, BLUE! LET'S GO!
VOOOOOOOO

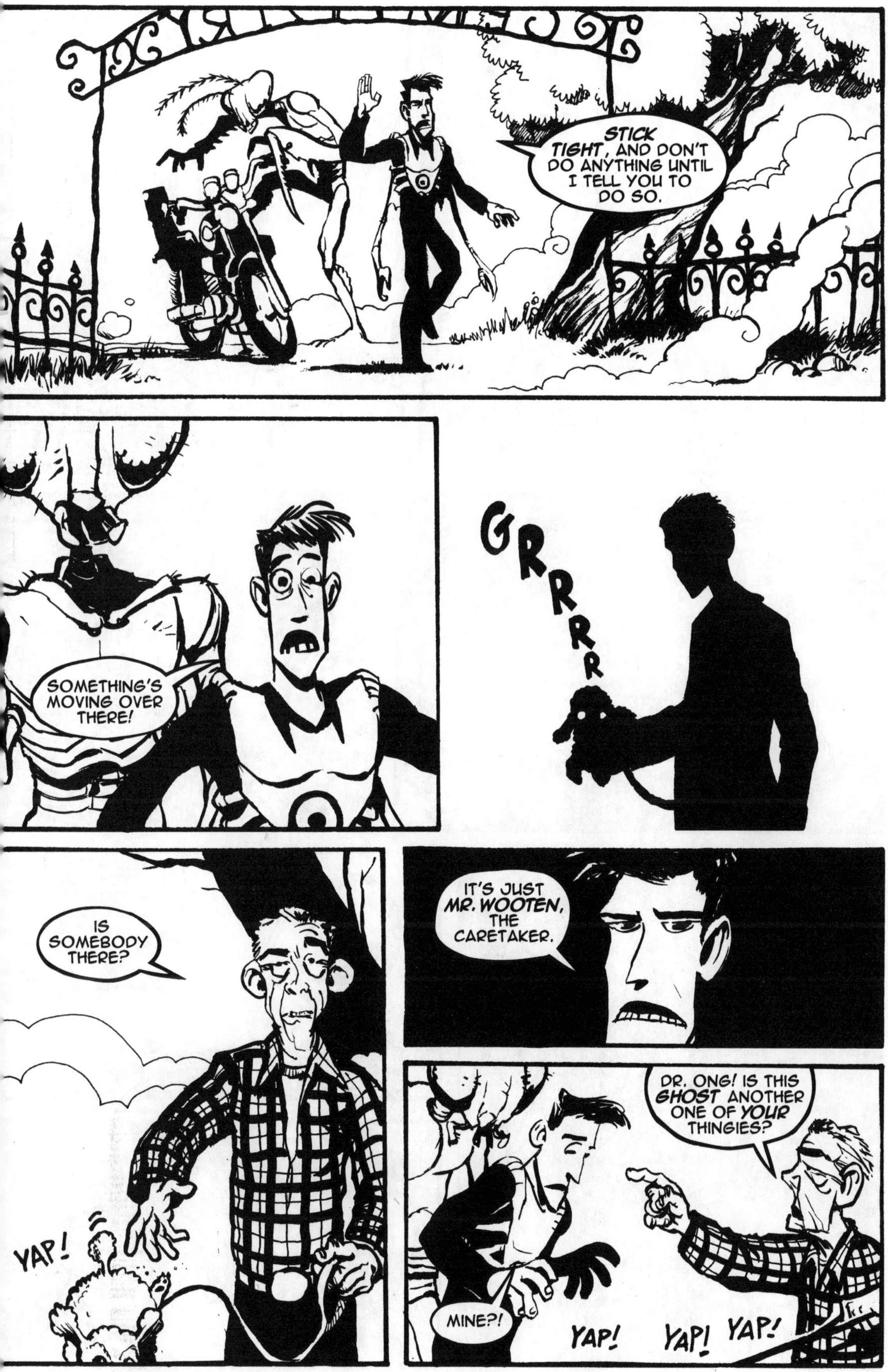

STICK TIGHT, AND DON'T DO ANYTHING UNTIL I TELL YOU TO DO SO.
SOMETHING'S MOVING OVER THERE!
GRRRRR
IS SOMEBODY THERE?
YAP!
IT'S JUST MR. WOOTEN, THE CARETAKER.
DR. ONG! IS THIS GHOST ANOTHER ONE OF YOUR THINGIES?
MINE?!
YAP! YAP! YAP!

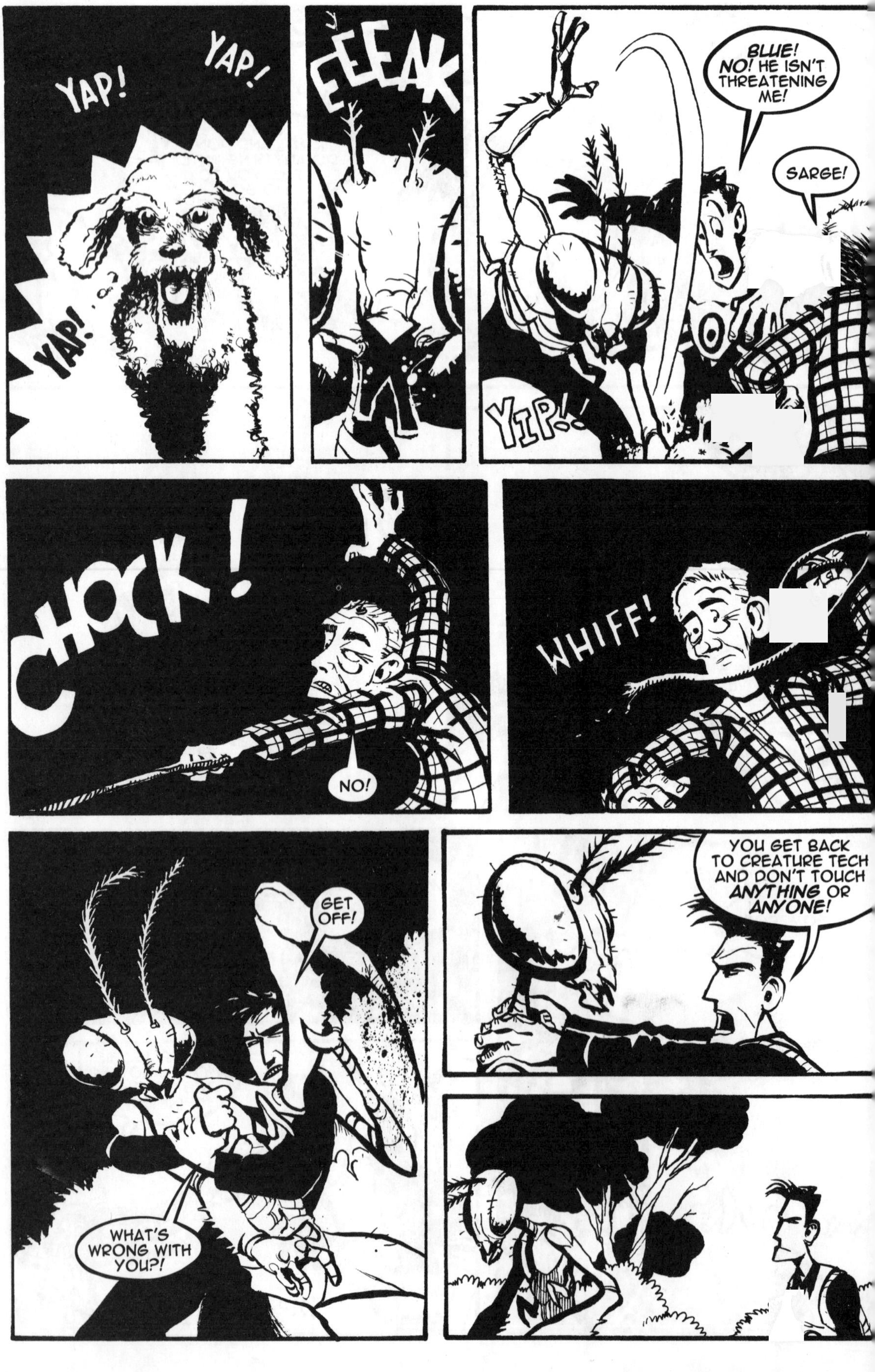
YAP!
YAP!
YAP!
EEEEAK
YIP!!
BLUE! NO! HE ISN'T THREATENING ME!
SARGE!
CHOCK!
NO!
WHIFF!
GET OFF!
WHAT'S WRONG WITH YOU?!
YOU GET BACK TO CREATURE TECH AND DON'T TOUCH ANYTHING OR ANYONE!

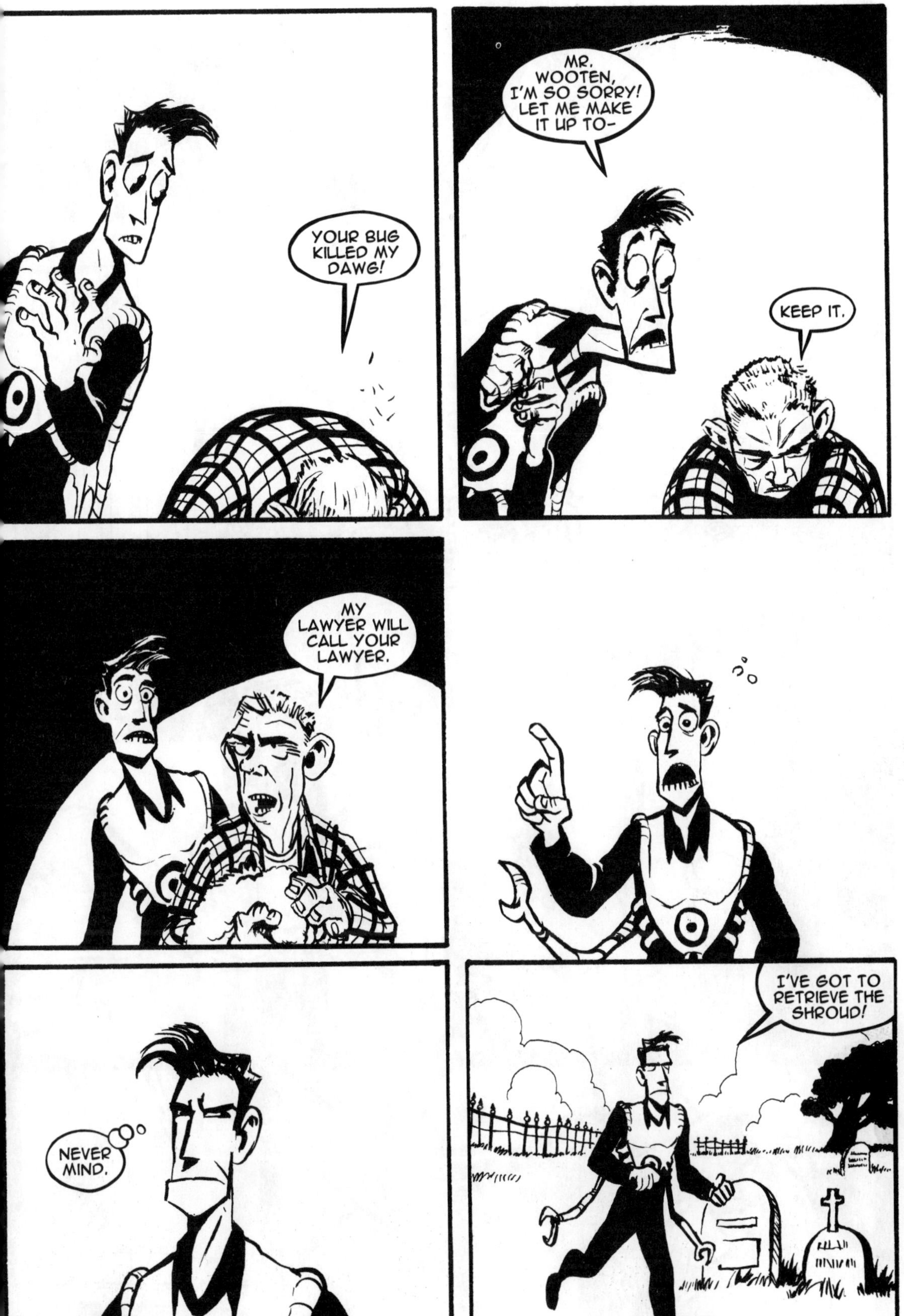
YOUR BUG KILLED MY DAWG!
MR. WOOTEN, I'M SO SORRY! LET ME MAKE IT UP TO-
KEEP IT.
MY LAWYER WILL CALL YOUR LAWYER.
NEVER MIND.
I'VE GOT TO RETRIEVE THE SHROUD!

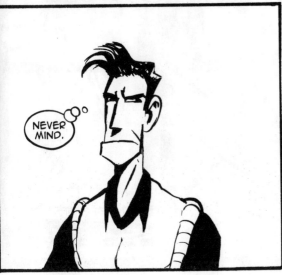

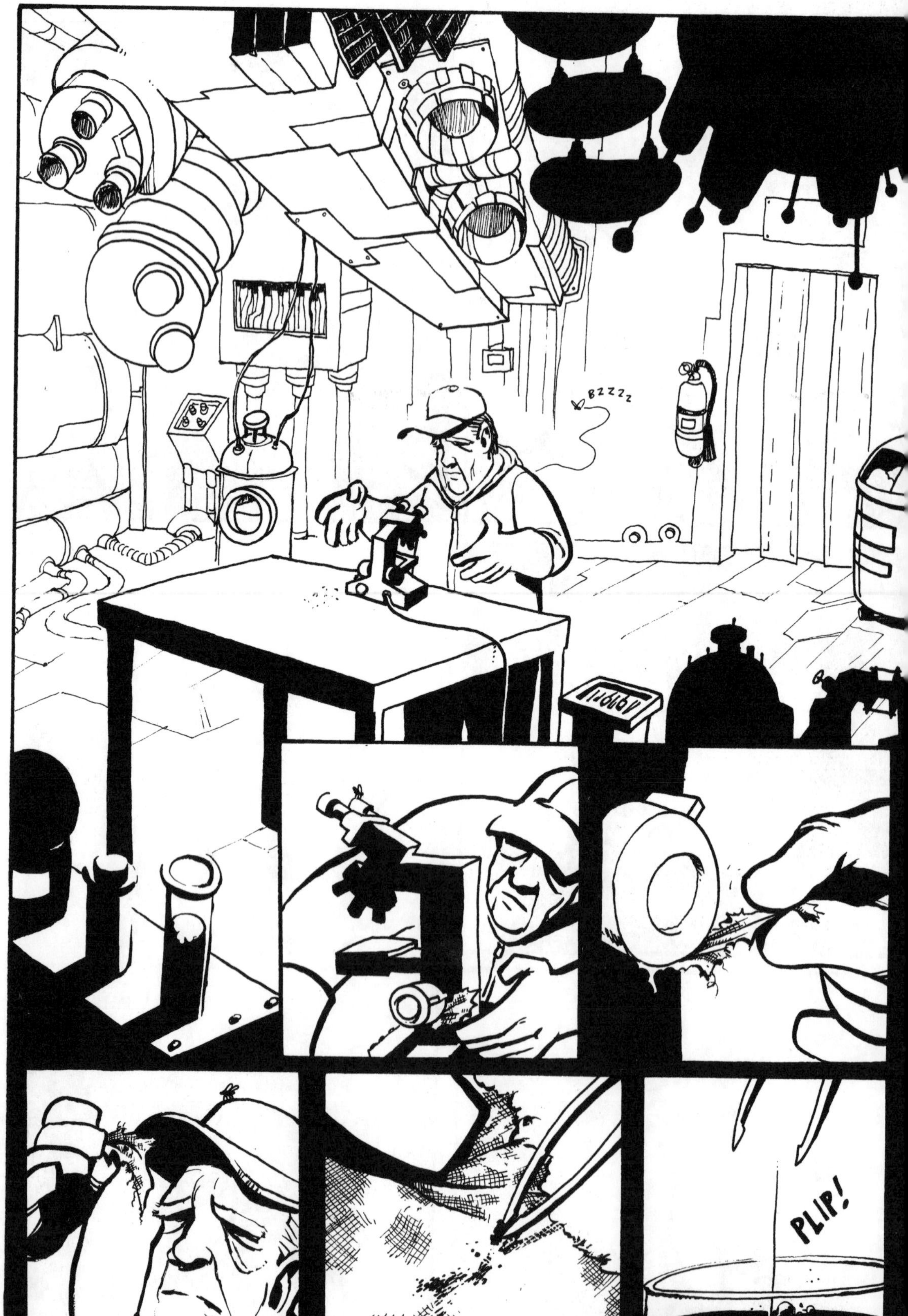
BZZZZ
PLIP!

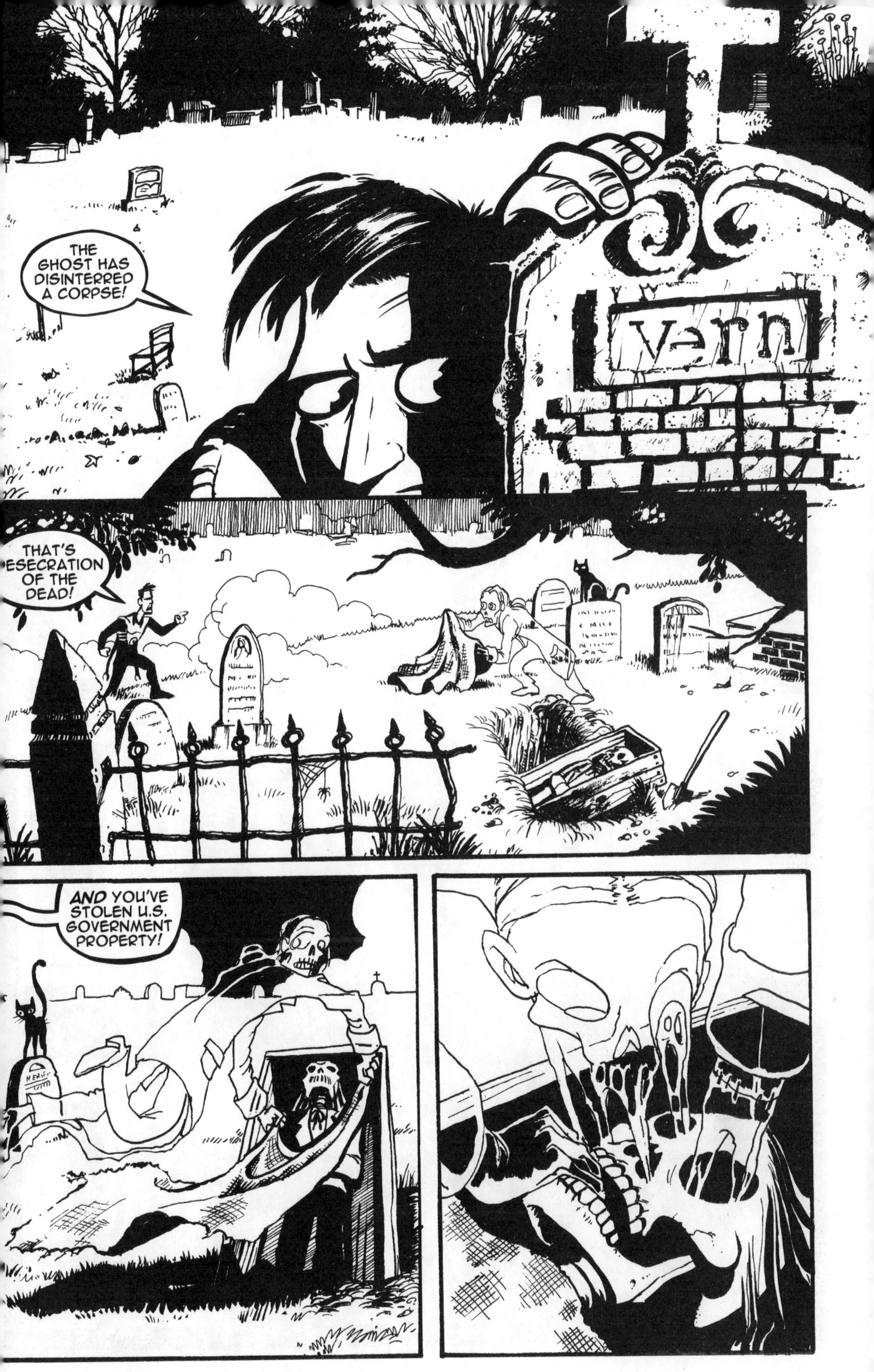
THE GHOST HAS DISINTERRED A CORPSE!
THAT'S ESECRATION OF THE DEAD!
AND YOU'VE STOLEN U.S. GOVERNMENT PROPERTY!

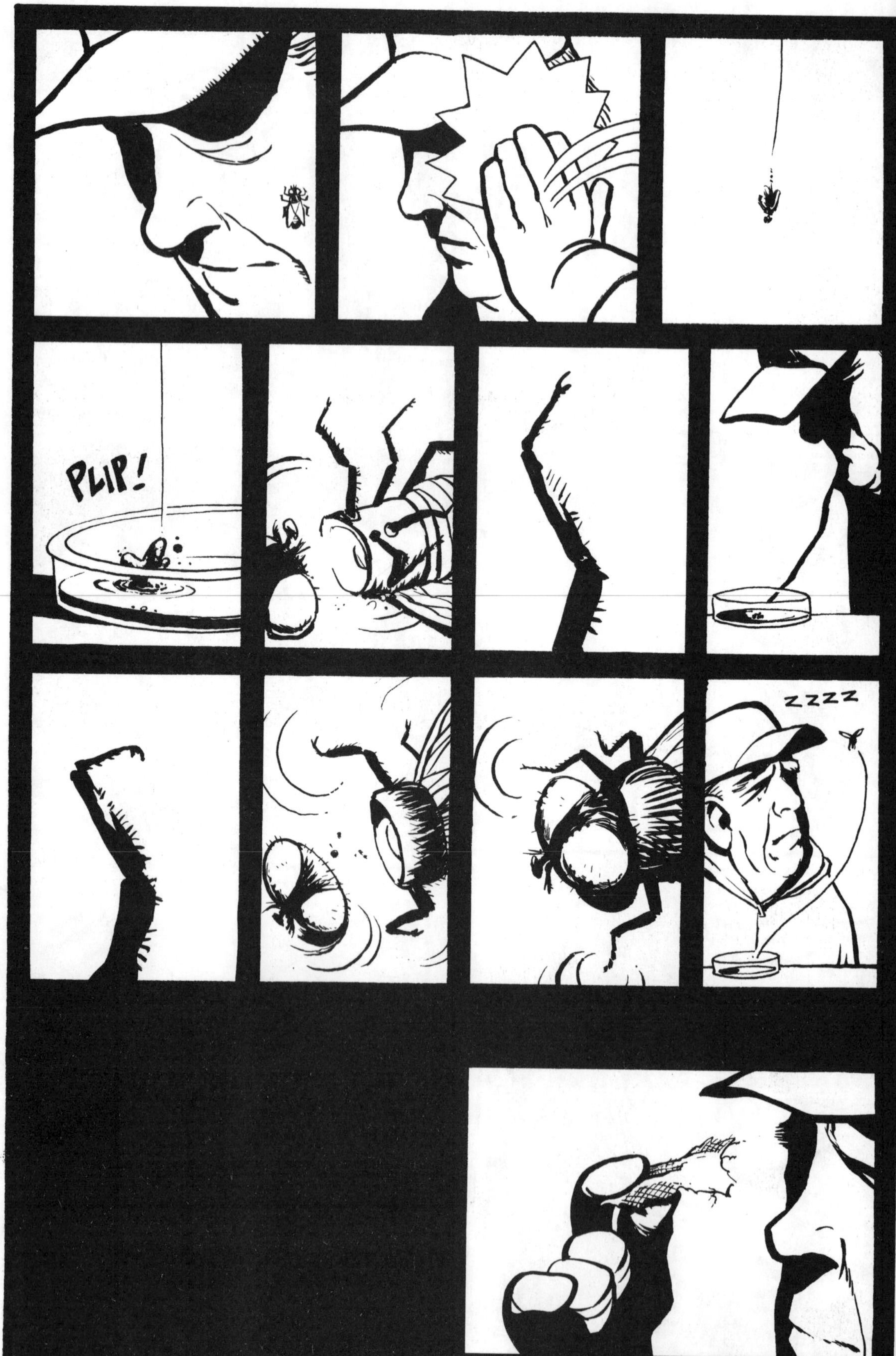
PLIP!
ZZZZ

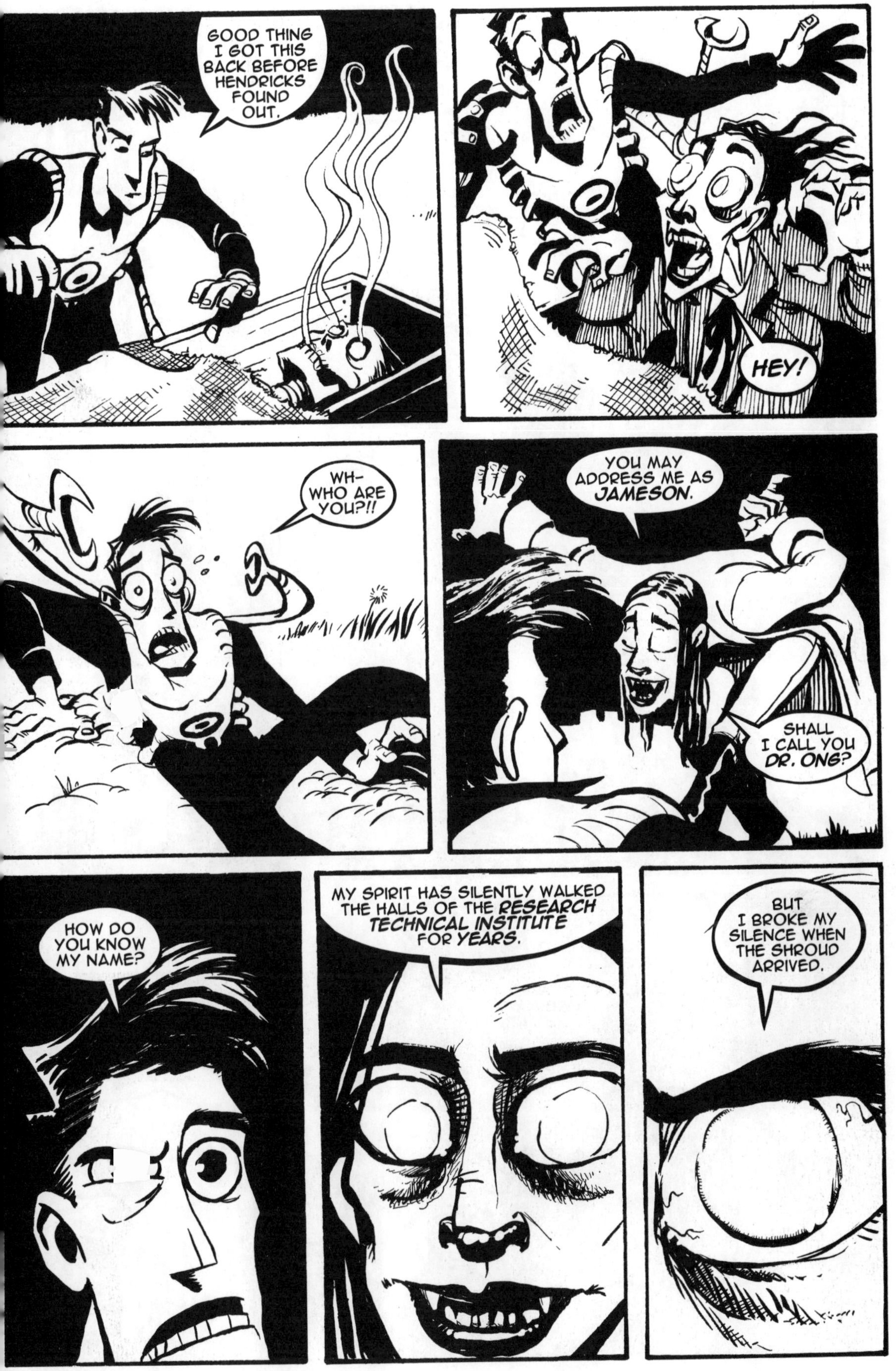
GOOD THING I GOT THIS BACK BEFORE HENDRICKS FOUND OUT.
HEY!
WH- WHO ARE YOU?!!
YOU MAY ADDRESS ME AS JAMESON.
SHALL I CALL YOU DR. ONG?
HOW DO YOU KNOW MY NAME?
MY SPIRIT HAS SILENTLY WALKED THE HALLS OF THE RESEARCH TECHNICAL INSTITUTE FOR YEARS.
BUT I BROKE MY SILENCE WHEN THE SHROUD ARRIVED.

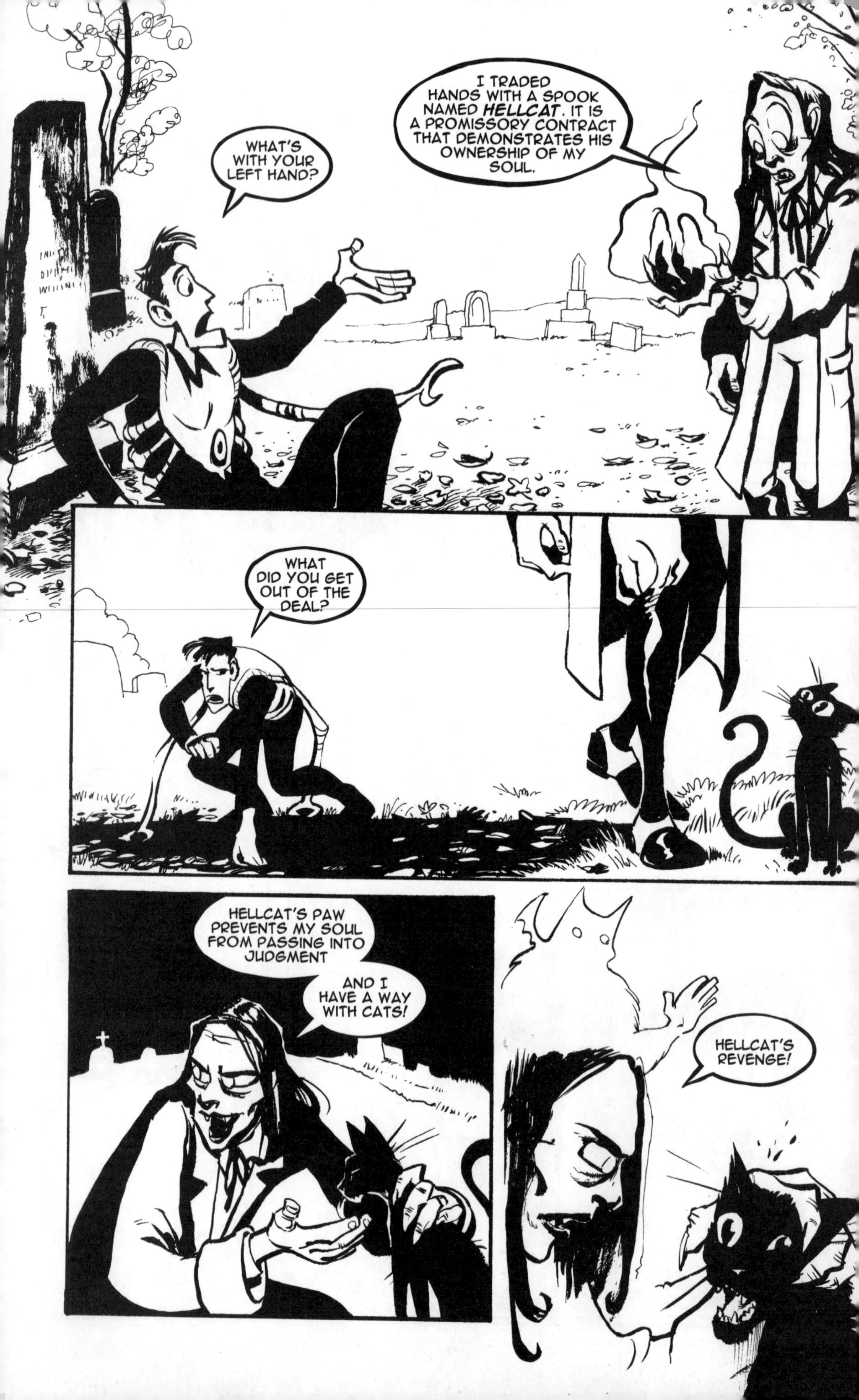

WHAT'S WITH YOUR LEFT HAND?
I TRADED HANDS WITH A SPOOK NAMED HELLCAT. IT IS A PROMISSORY CONTRACT THAT DEMONSTRATES HIS OWNERSHIP OF MY SOUL.
WHAT DID YOU GET OUT OF THE DEAL?
HELLCAT'S PAW PREVENTS MY SOUL FROM PASSING INTO JUDGMENT
AND I HAVE A WAY WITH CATS!
HELLCAT'S REVENGE!

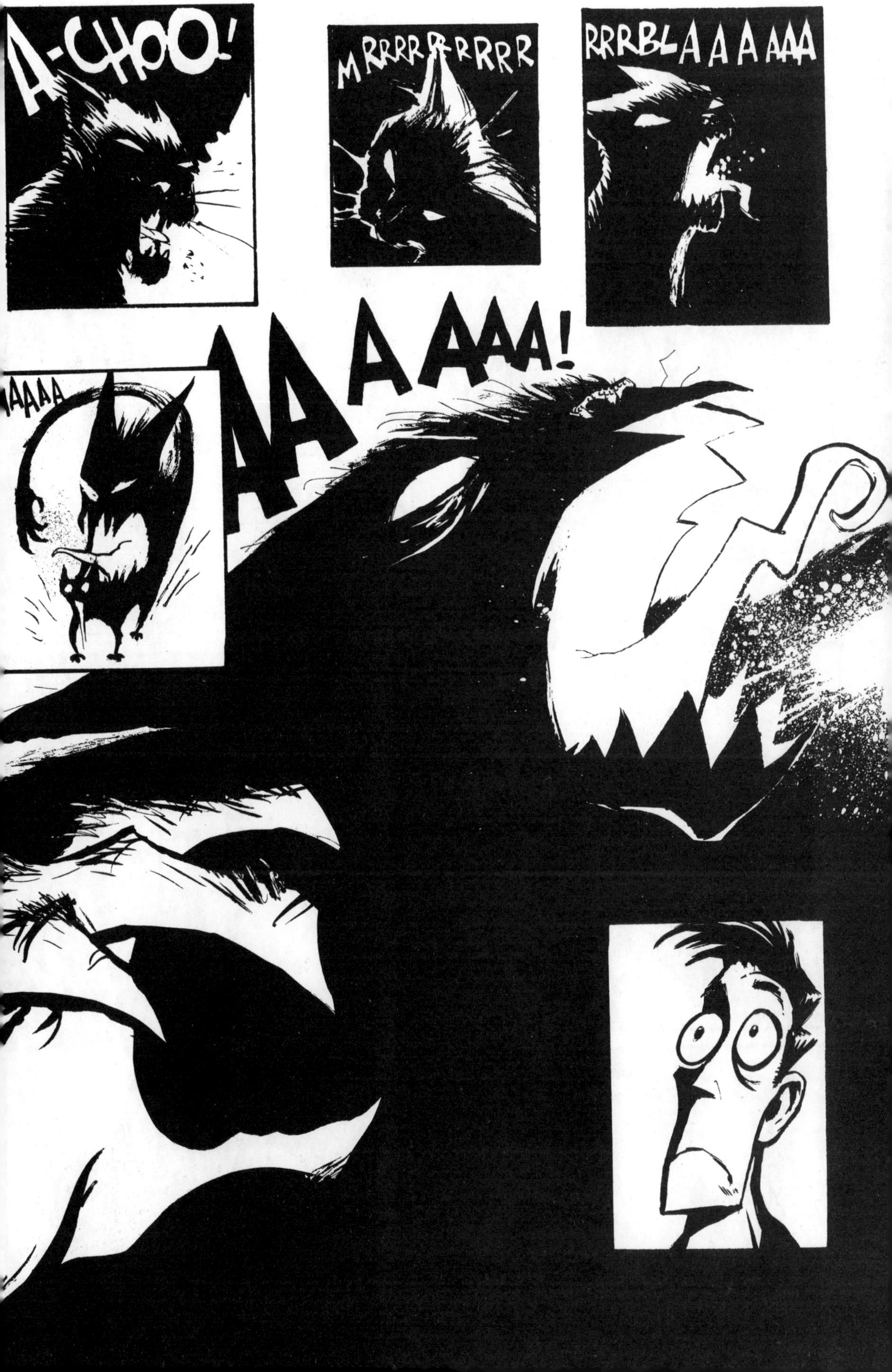
A-CHOO!
MRRRRRRRRRR
RRRBLAAAAAA
AAAA
AAAAAAA!

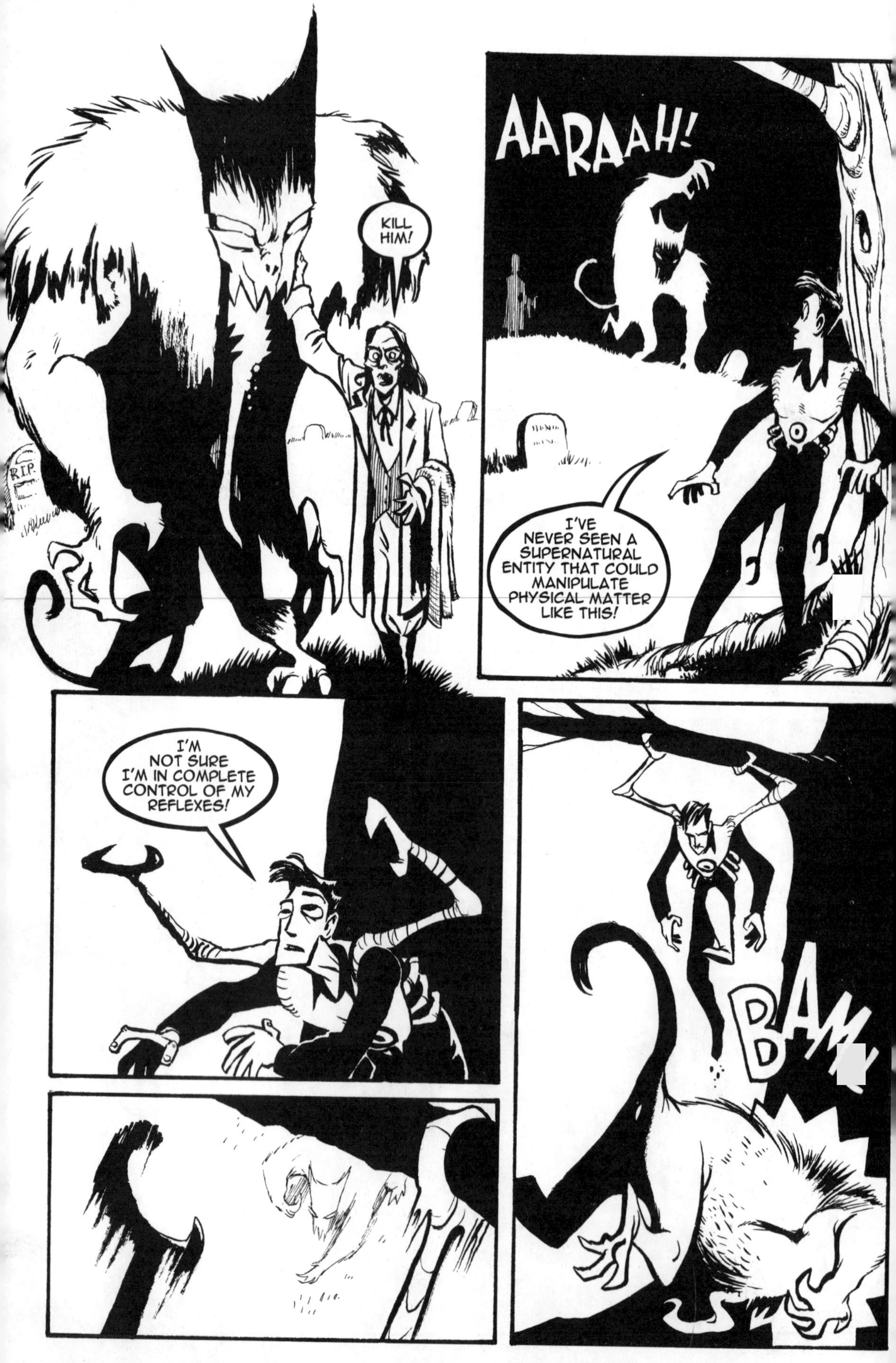
KILL HIM!
AARAAH!
I'VE NEVER SEEN A SUPERNATURAL ENTITY THAT COULD MANIPULATE PHYSICAL MATTER LIKE THIS!
I'M NOT SURE I'M IN COMPLETE CONTROL OF MY REFLEXES!
BAM

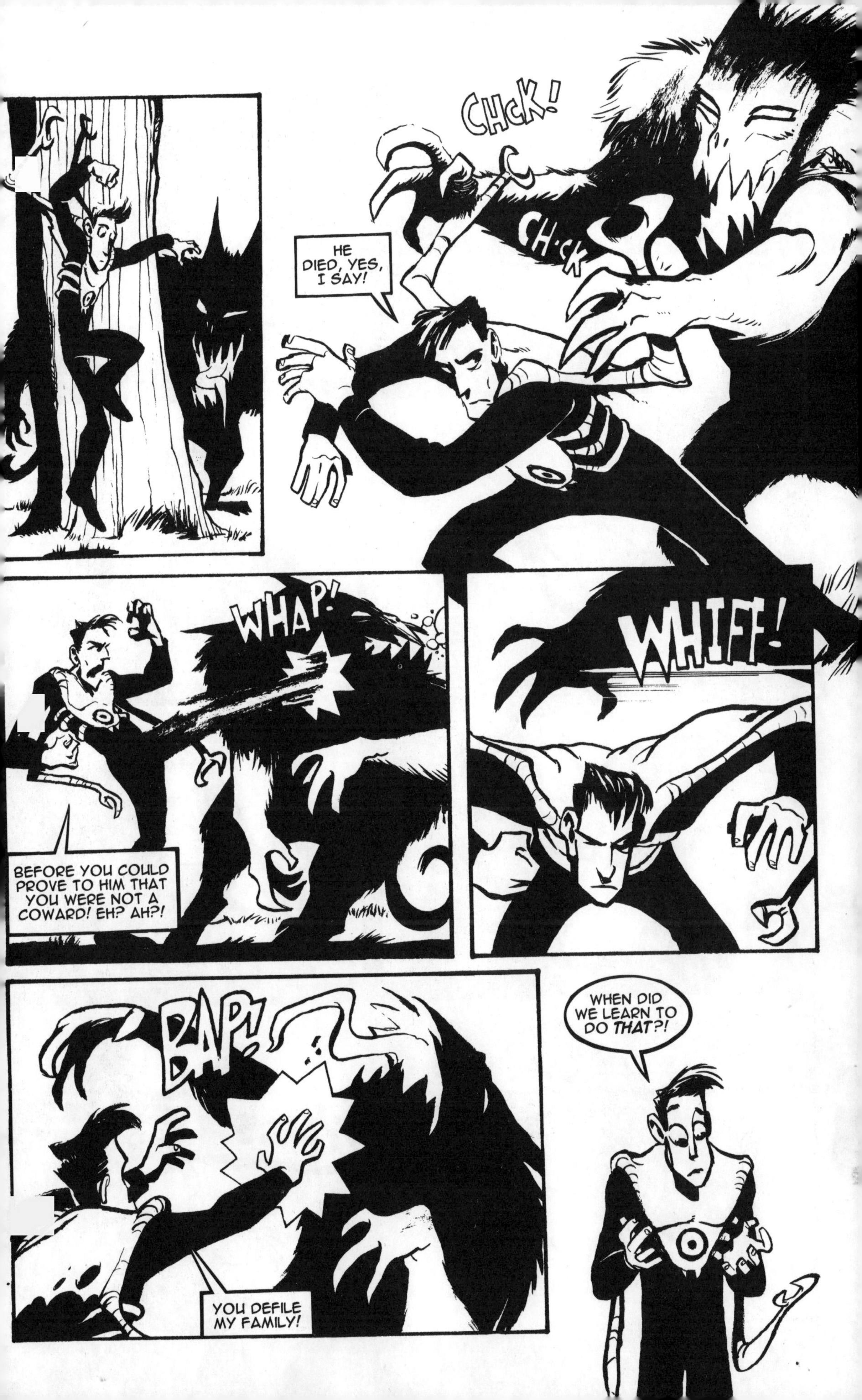
CHCK!
CH-CK
HE DIED, YES, I SAY!
WHAP!
BEFORE YOU COULD PROVE TO HIM THAT YOU WERE NOT A COWARD! EH? AH?!
WHIFF!
BAP!
YOU DEFILE MY FAMILY!
WHEN DID WE LEARN TO DO *THAT*?!

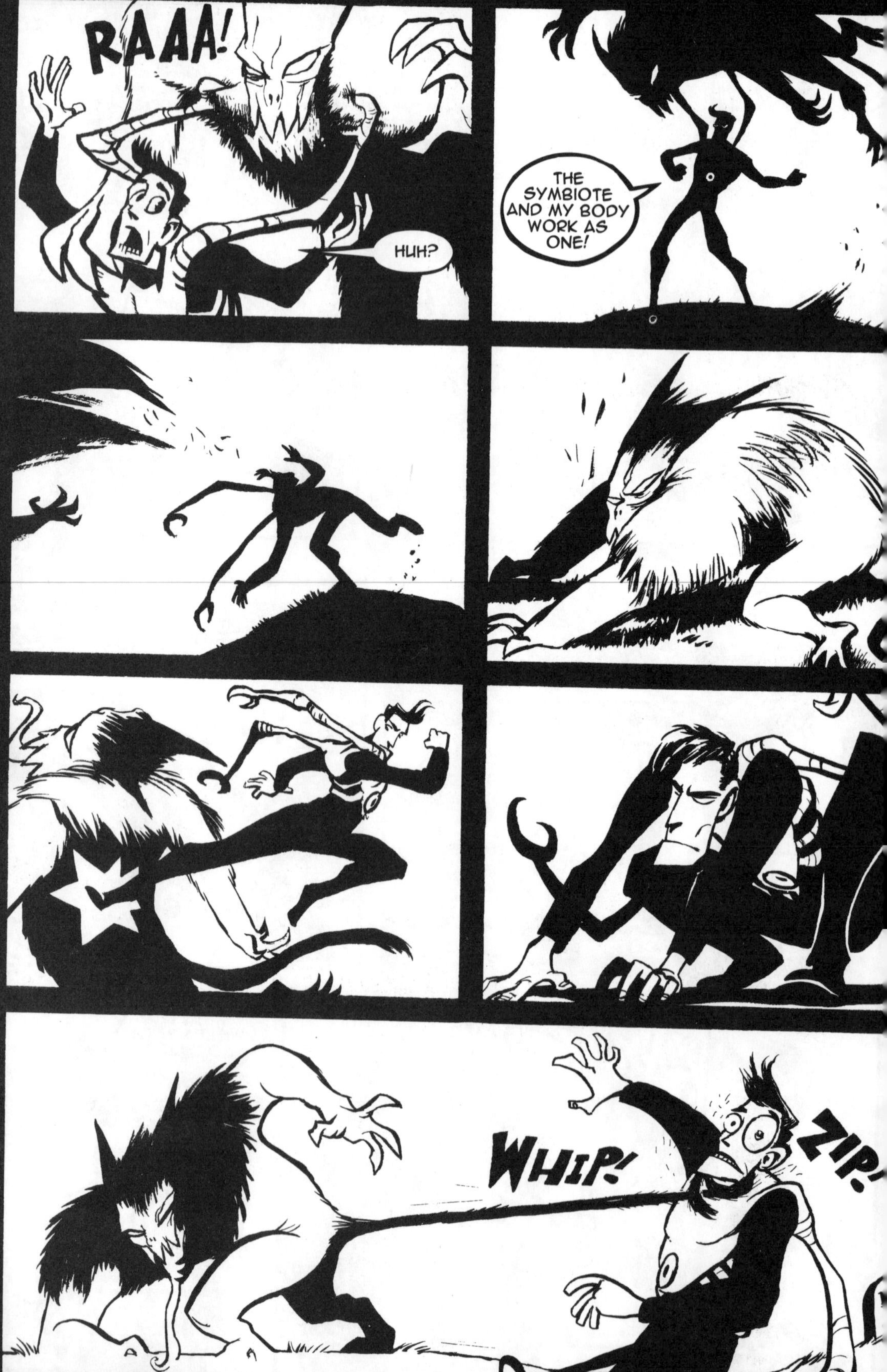
RAAA!
HUH?
THE SYMBIOTE AND MY BODY WORK AS ONE!
WHIP!
ZIP!

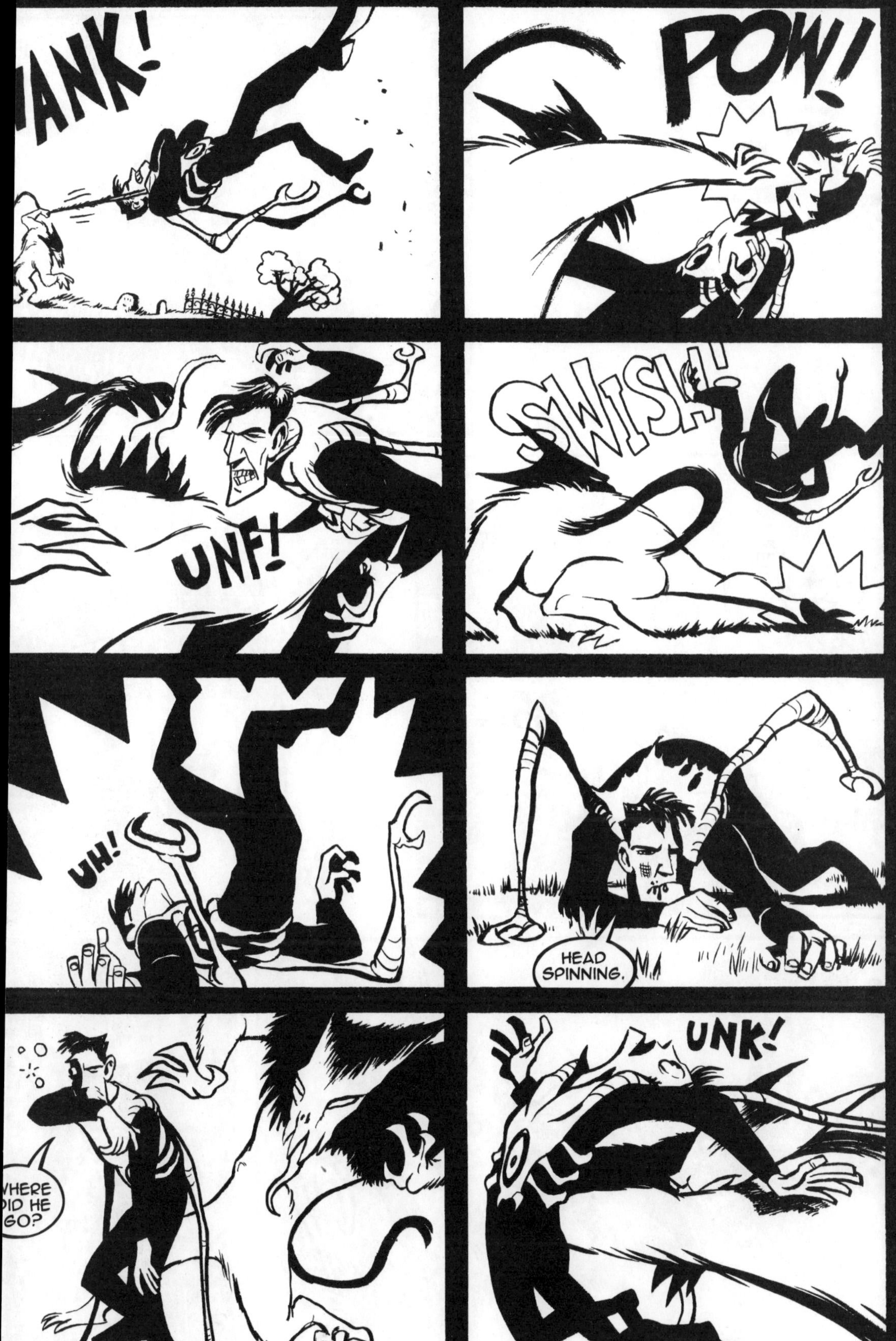

ANK!
POW!
UNF!
SWISH!
UH!
HEAD SPINNING.
WHERE DID HE GO?
UNK!

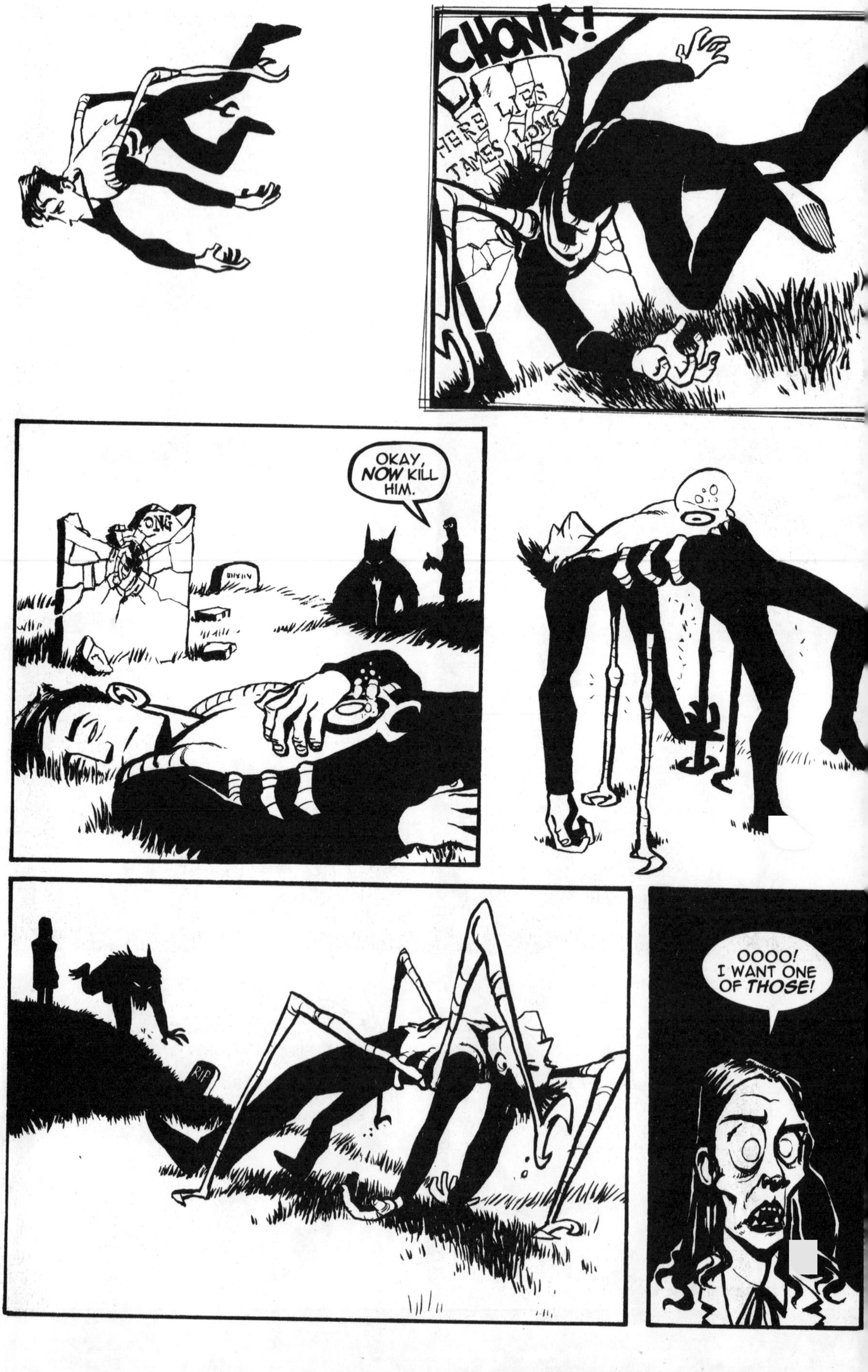
CHONK!
OKAY, *NOW* KILL HIM.
RIP
OOOO! I WANT ONE OF *THOSE!*

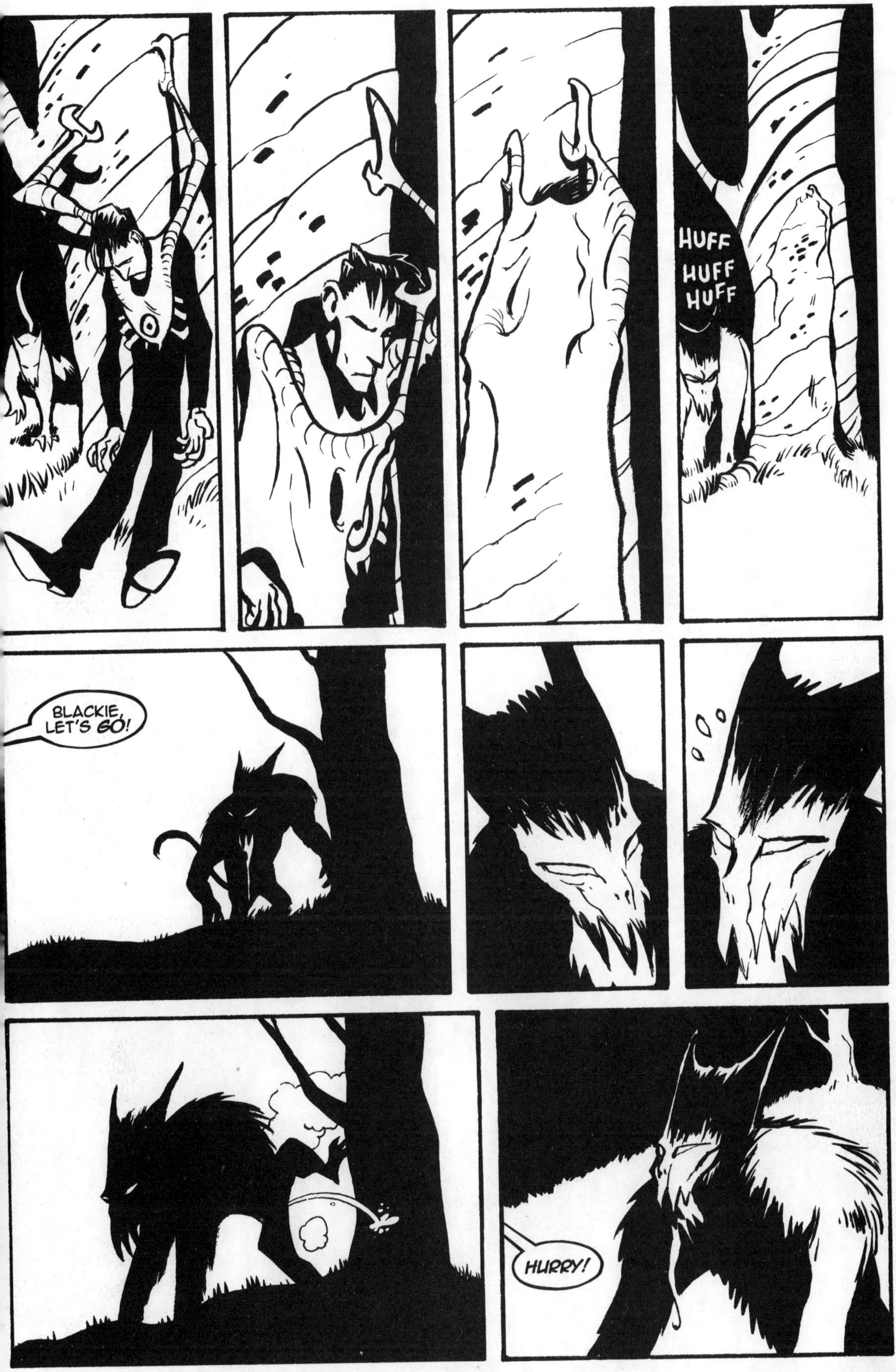
HUFF
HUFF
HUFF
BLACKIE, LET'S GO!
HURRY!

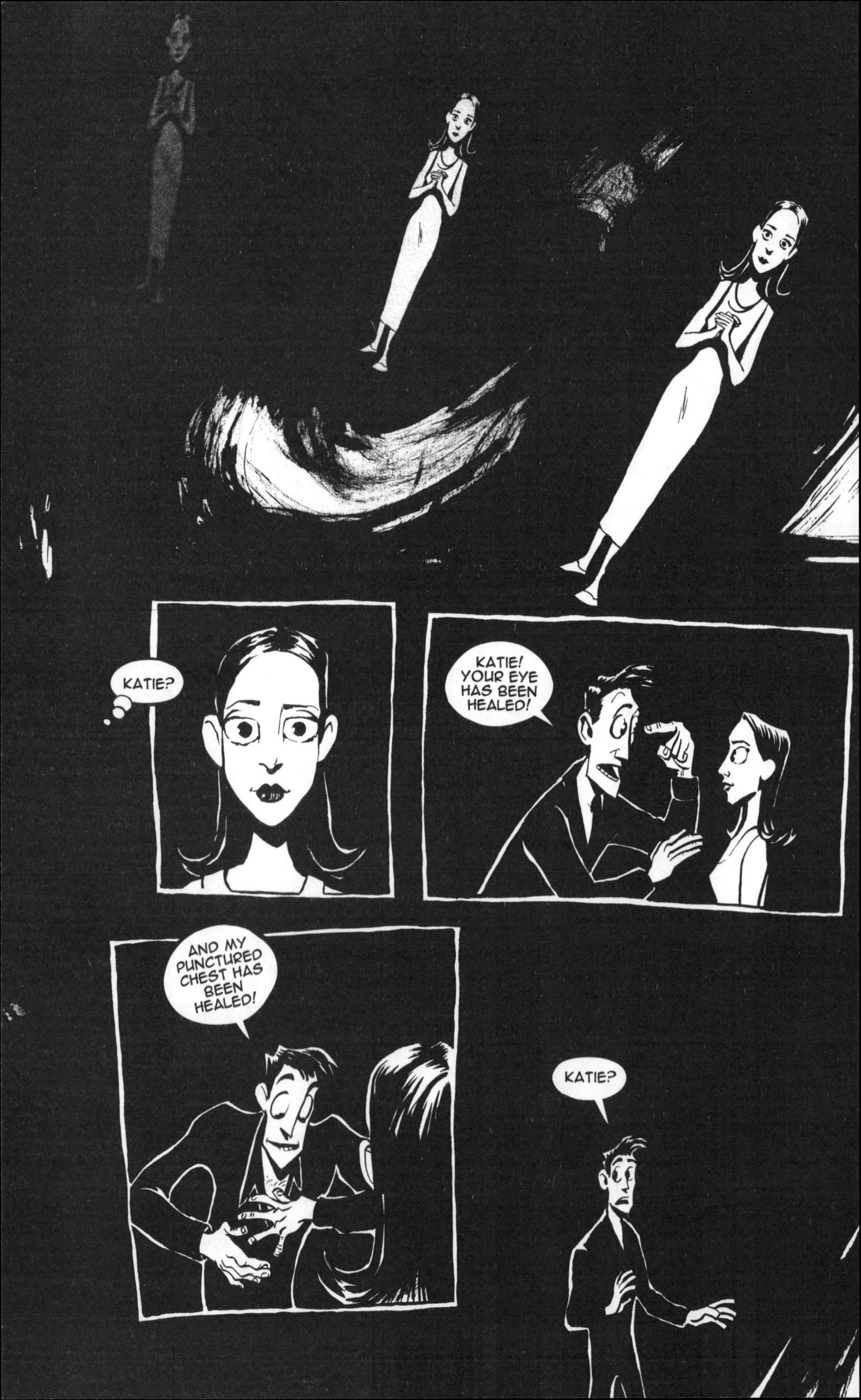
KATIE?
KATIE! YOUR EYE HAS BEEN HEALED!
AND MY PUNCTURED CHEST HAS BEEN HEALED!
KATIE?

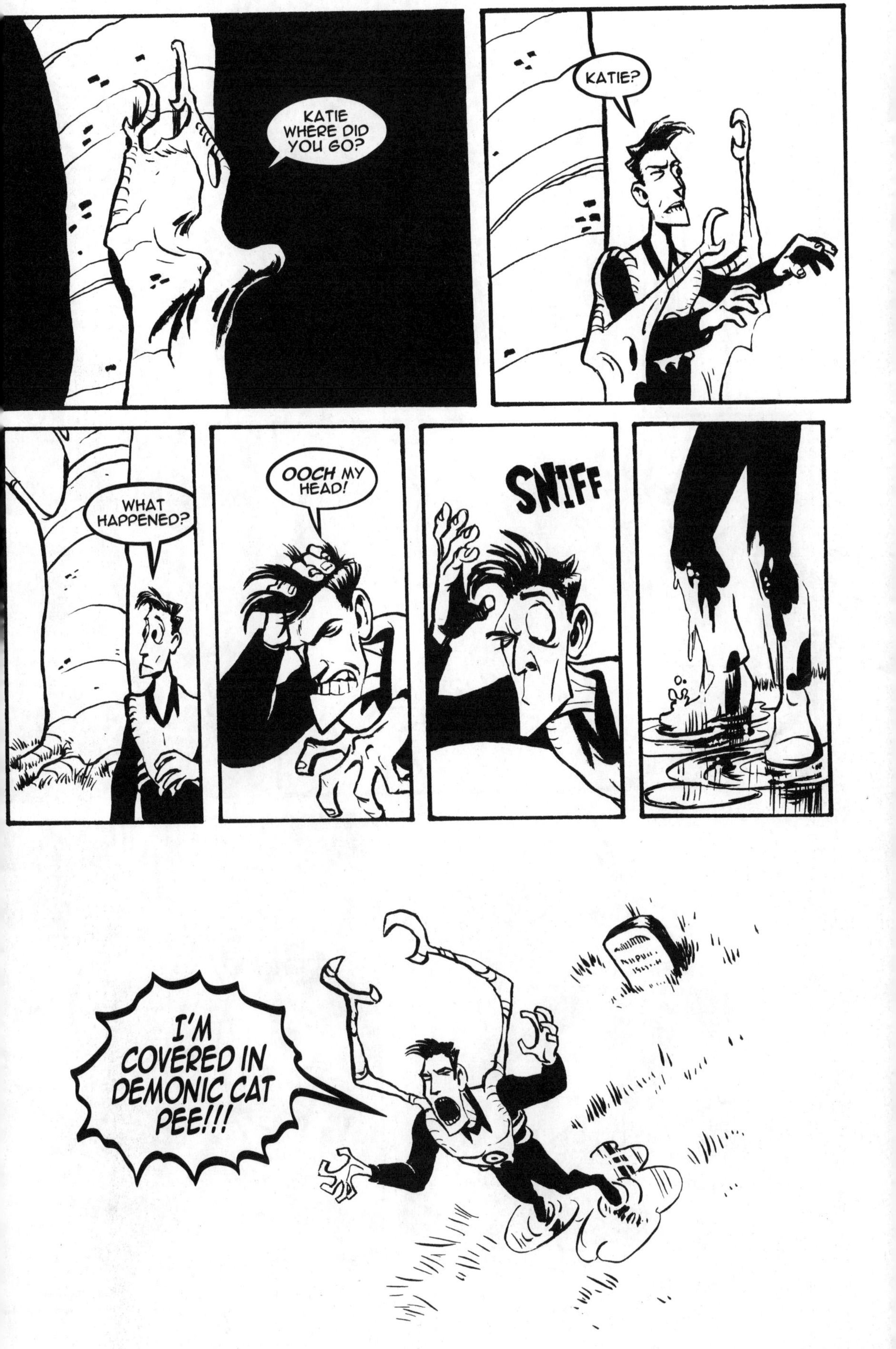
KATIE WHERE DID YOU GO?
KATIE?
WHAT HAPPENED?
OOCH MY HEAD!
SNIFF
I'M COVERED IN DEMONIC CAT PEE!!!

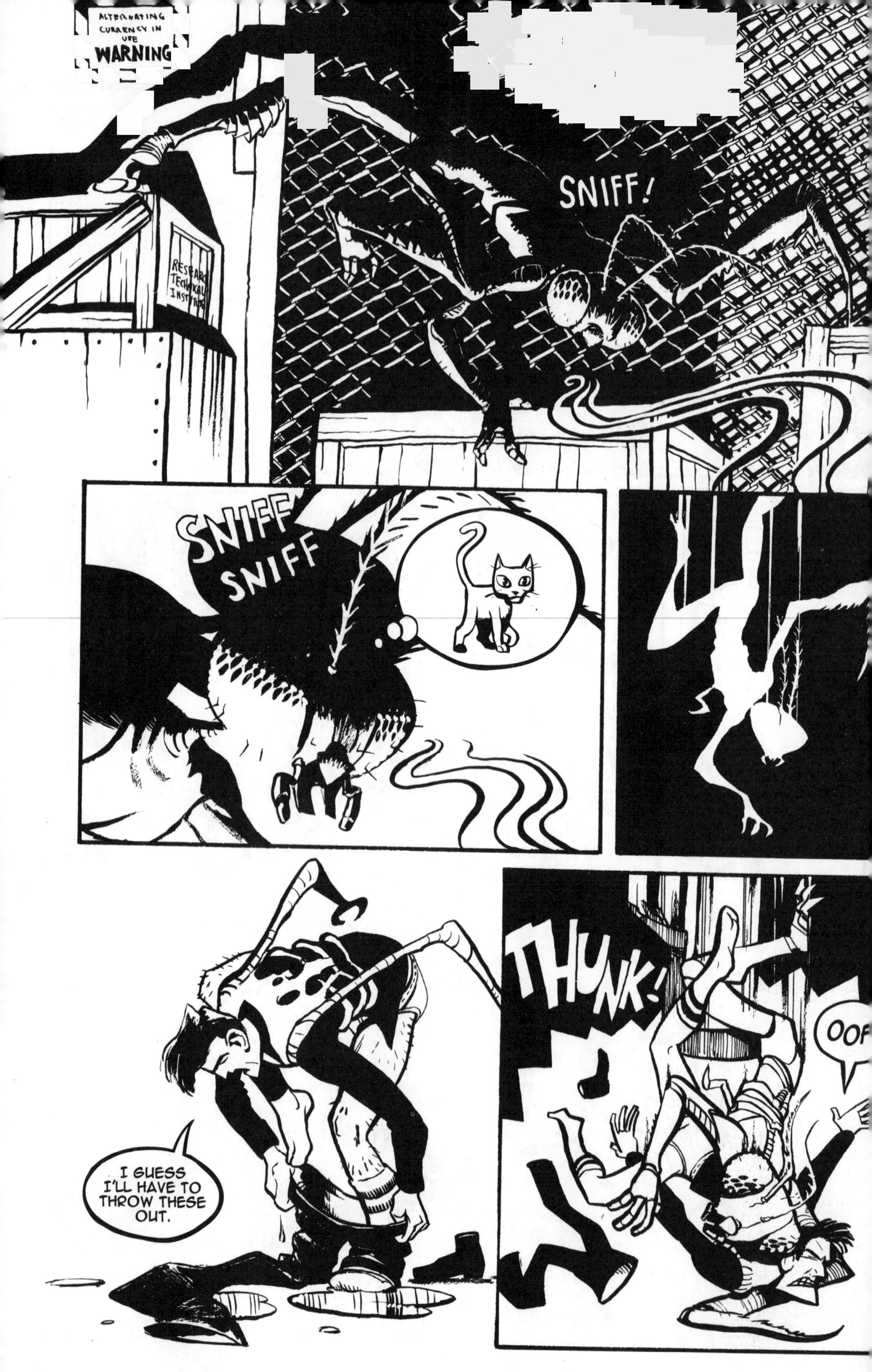
ALTERNATING CURRENCY IN USE
WARNING
SNIFF!
SNIFF
SNIFF
I GUESS I'LL HAVE TO THROW THESE OUT.
THUNK!
OOF

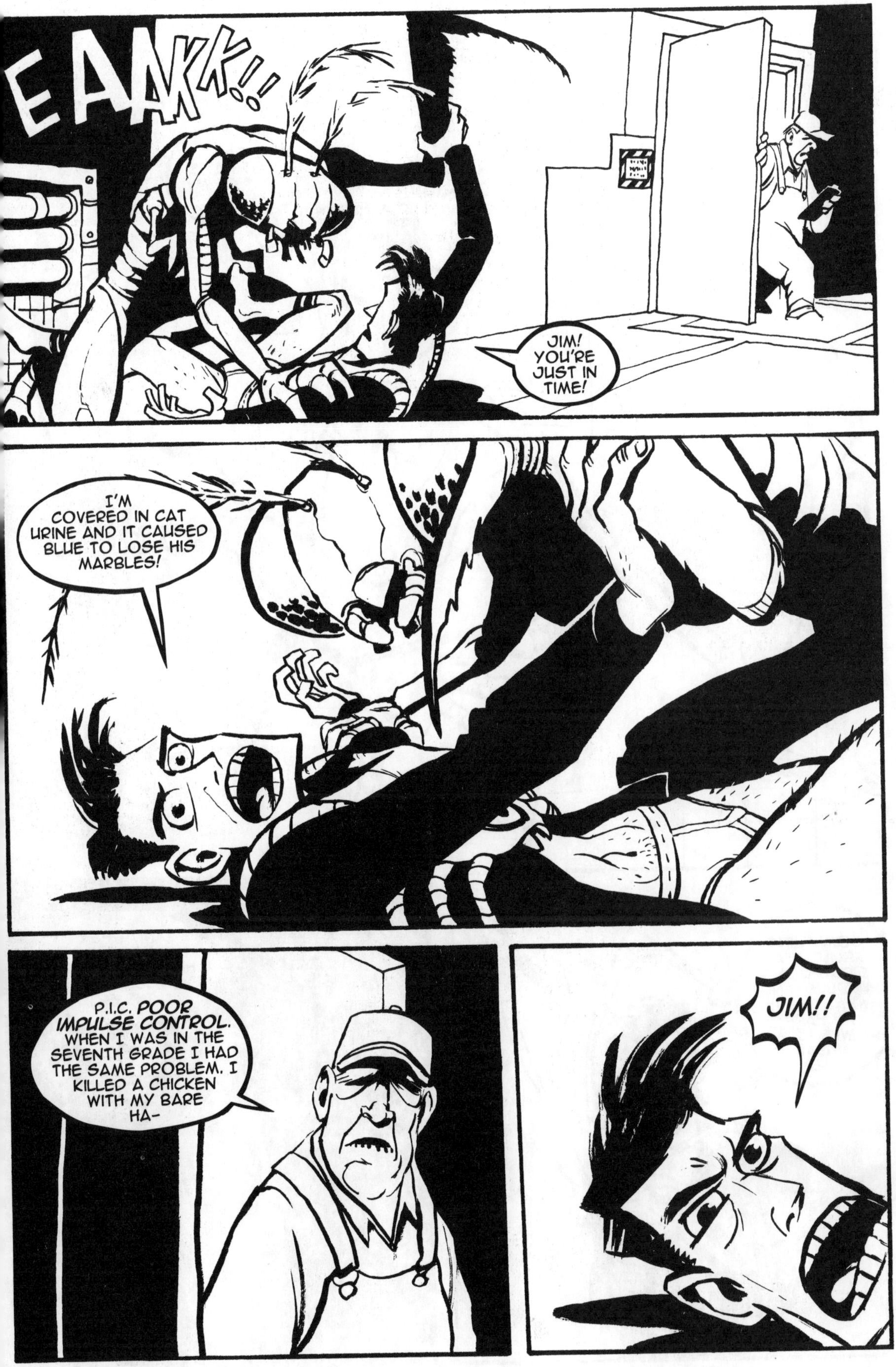
EAAKK!!
JIM! YOU'RE JUST IN TIME!
I'M COVERED IN CAT URINE AND IT CAUSED BLUE TO LOSE HIS MARBLES!
P.I.C. POOR IMPULSE CONTROL. WHEN I WAS IN THE SEVENTH GRADE I HAD THE SAME PROBLEM. I KILLED A CHICKEN WITH MY BARE HA-
JIM!!

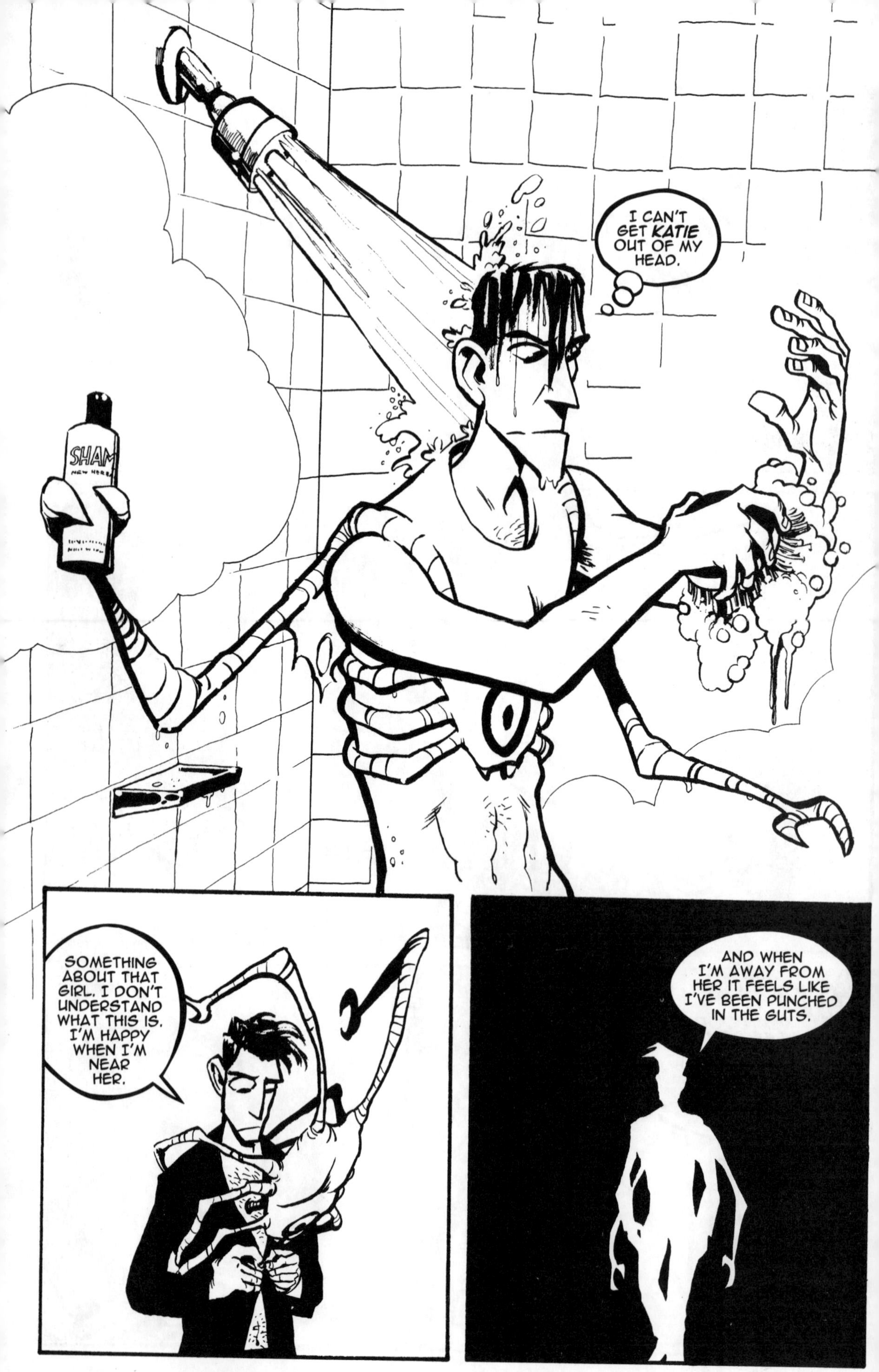

I CAN'T GET KATIE OUT OF MY HEAD.
SHAM
NEW HERB
SOMETHING ABOUT THAT GIRL. I DON'T UNDERSTAND WHAT THIS IS. I'M HAPPY WHEN I'M NEAR HER.
AND WHEN I'M AWAY FROM HER IT FEELS LIKE I'VE BEEN PUNCHED IN THE GUTS.

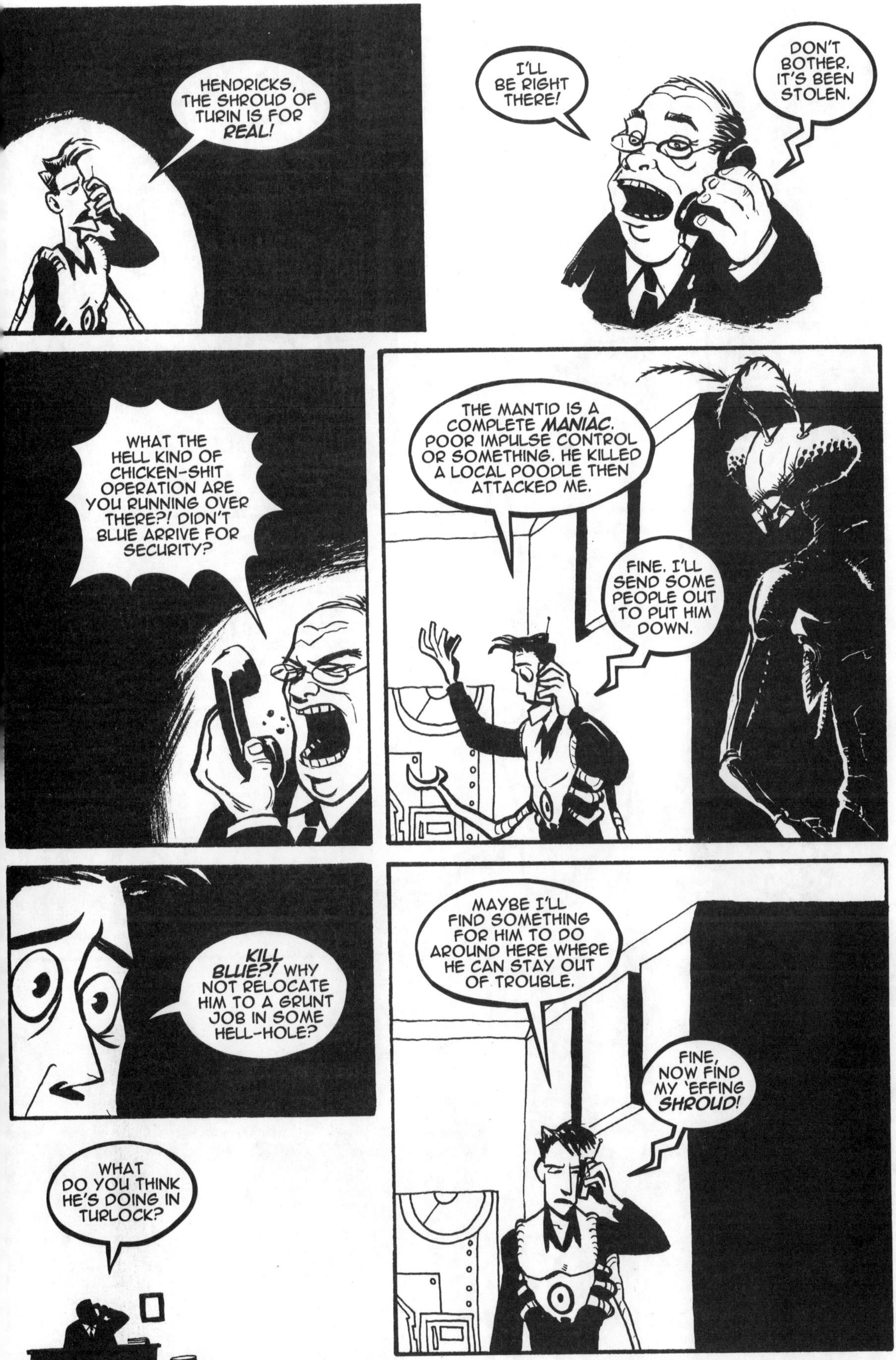
HENDRICKS, THE SHROUD OF TURIN IS FOR *REAL!*
I'LL BE RIGHT THERE!
DON'T BOTHER. IT'S BEEN STOLEN.
WHAT THE HELL KIND OF CHICKEN-SHIT OPERATION ARE YOU RUNNING OVER THERE?! DIDN'T BLUE ARRIVE FOR SECURITY?
THE MANTID IS A COMPLETE *MANIAC*. POOR IMPULSE CONTROL OR SOMETHING. HE KILLED A LOCAL POODLE THEN ATTACKED ME.
FINE. I'LL SEND SOME PEOPLE OUT TO PUT HIM DOWN.
KILL BLUE?! WHY NOT RELOCATE HIM TO A GRUNT JOB IN SOME HELL-HOLE?
WHAT DO YOU THINK HE'S DOING IN TURLOCK?
MAYBE I'LL FIND SOMETHING FOR HIM TO DO AROUND HERE WHERE HE CAN STAY OUT OF TROUBLE.
FINE, NOW FIND MY 'EFFING *SHROUD!*

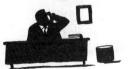

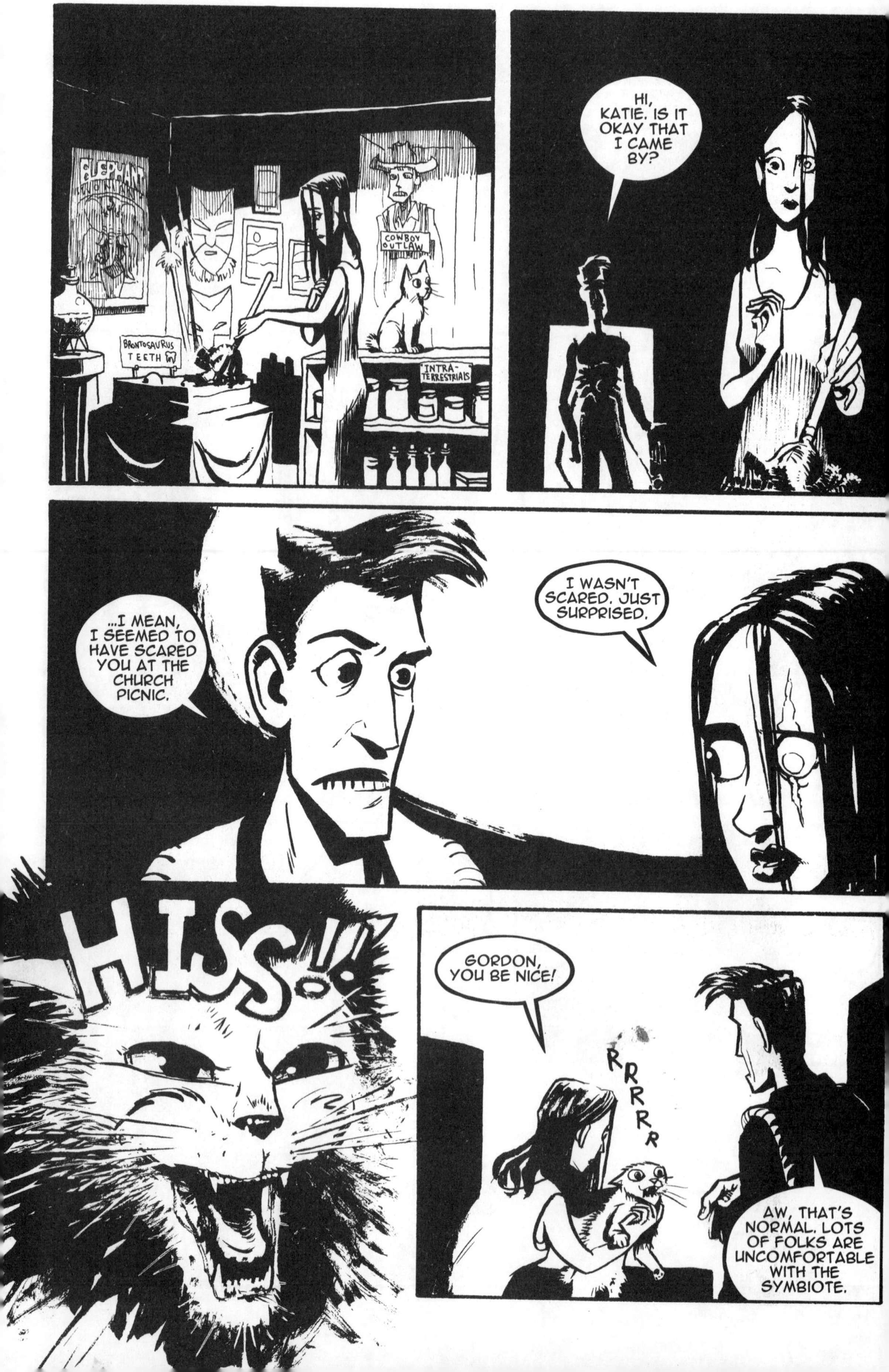
ELEPHANT
BRONTOSAURUS TEETH
COWBOY OUTLAW
INTRA-TERRESTRIALS
HI, KATIE. IS IT OKAY THAT I CAME BY?
...I MEAN, I SEEMED TO HAVE SCARED YOU AT THE CHURCH PICNIC.
I WASN'T SCARED. JUST SURPRISED.
HISS!!
GORDON, YOU BE NICE!
RRRRR
AW, THAT'S NORMAL. LOTS OF FOLKS ARE UNCOMFORTABLE WITH THE SYMBIOTE.

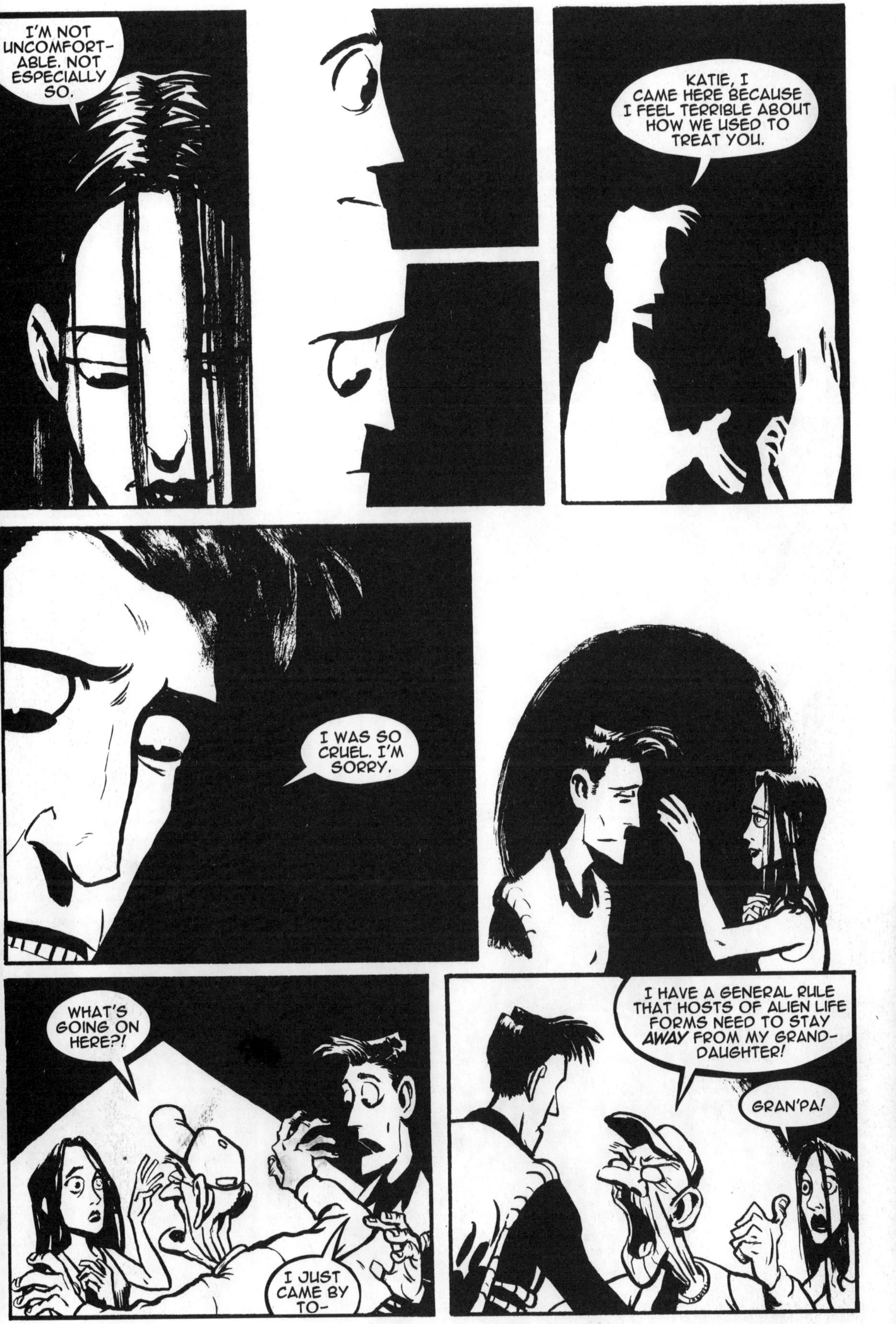
I'M NOT UNCOMFORTABLE. NOT ESPECIALLY SO.
KATIE, I CAME HERE BECAUSE I FEEL TERRIBLE ABOUT HOW WE USED TO TREAT YOU.
I WAS SO CRUEL. I'M SORRY.
WHAT'S GOING ON HERE?!
I JUST CAME BY TO-
I HAVE A GENERAL RULE THAT HOSTS OF ALIEN LIFE FORMS NEED TO STAY *AWAY* FROM MY GRAND-DAUGHTER!
GRAN'PA!

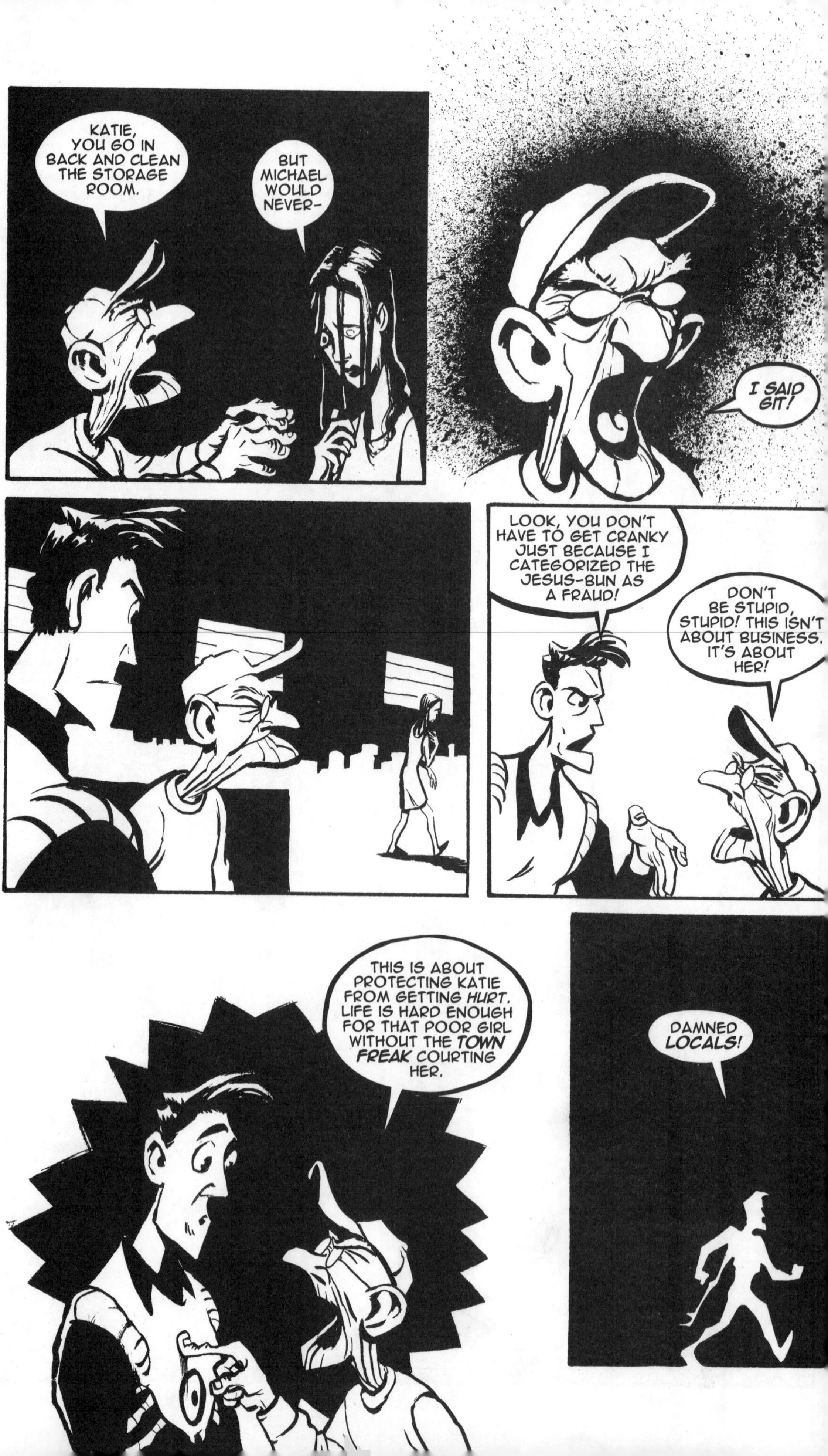
KATIE, YOU GO IN BACK AND CLEAN THE STORAGE ROOM.
BUT MICHAEL WOULD NEVER-
I SAID GIT!
LOOK, YOU DON'T HAVE TO GET CRANKY JUST BECAUSE I CATEGORIZED THE JESUS-BUN AS A FRAUD!
DON'T BE STUPID, STUPID! THIS ISN'T ABOUT BUSINESS. IT'S ABOUT HER!
THIS IS ABOUT PROTECTING KATIE FROM GETTING HURT. LIFE IS HARD ENOUGH FOR THAT POOR GIRL WITHOUT THE TOWN FREAK COURTING HER.
DAMNED LOCALS!

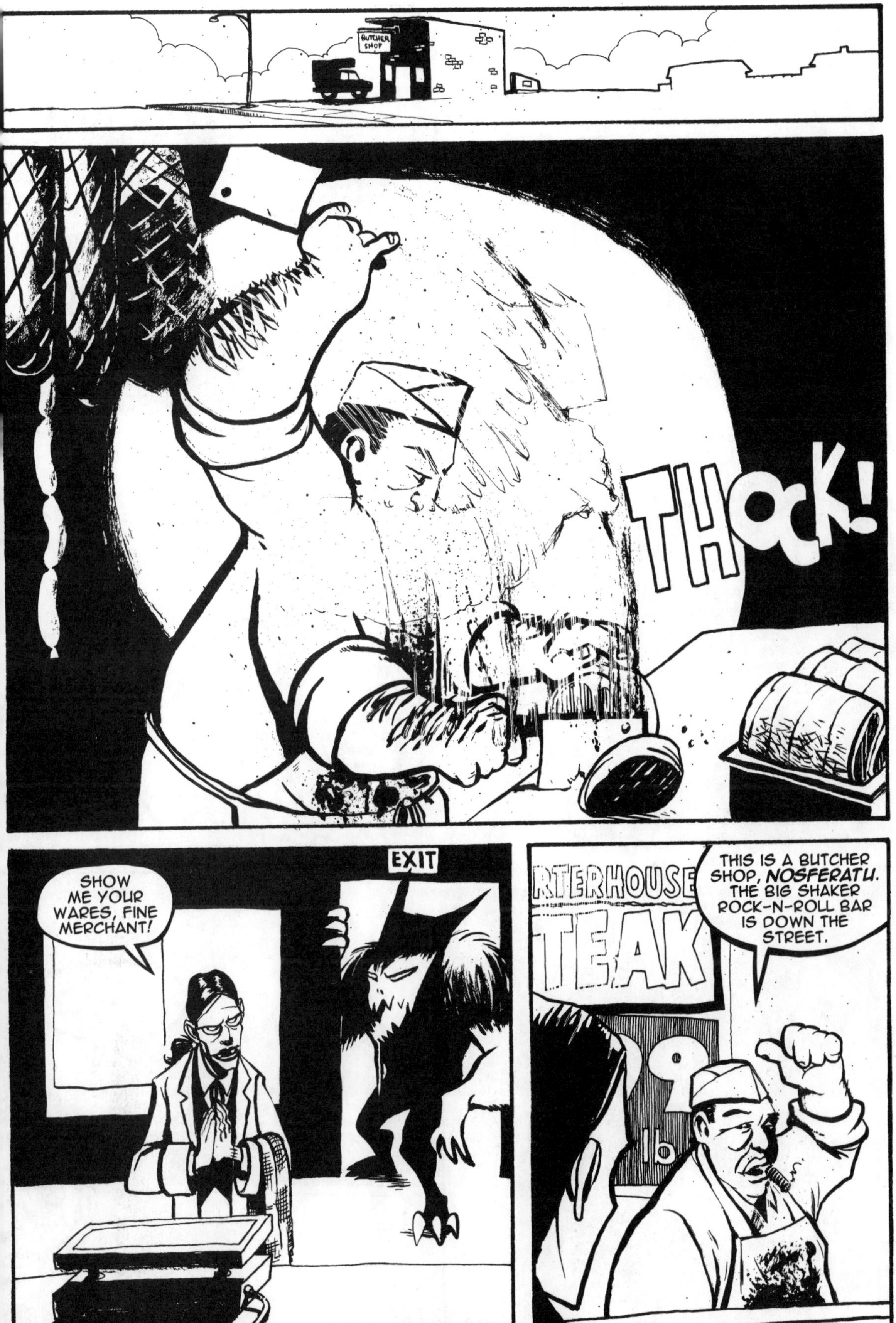

BUTCHER SHOP
THOCK!
SHOW ME YOUR WARES, FINE MERCHANT!
EXIT
RTERHOUSE
TEAK
THIS IS A BUTCHER SHOP, NOSFERATU. THE BIG SHAKER ROCK-N-ROLL BAR IS DOWN THE STREET.

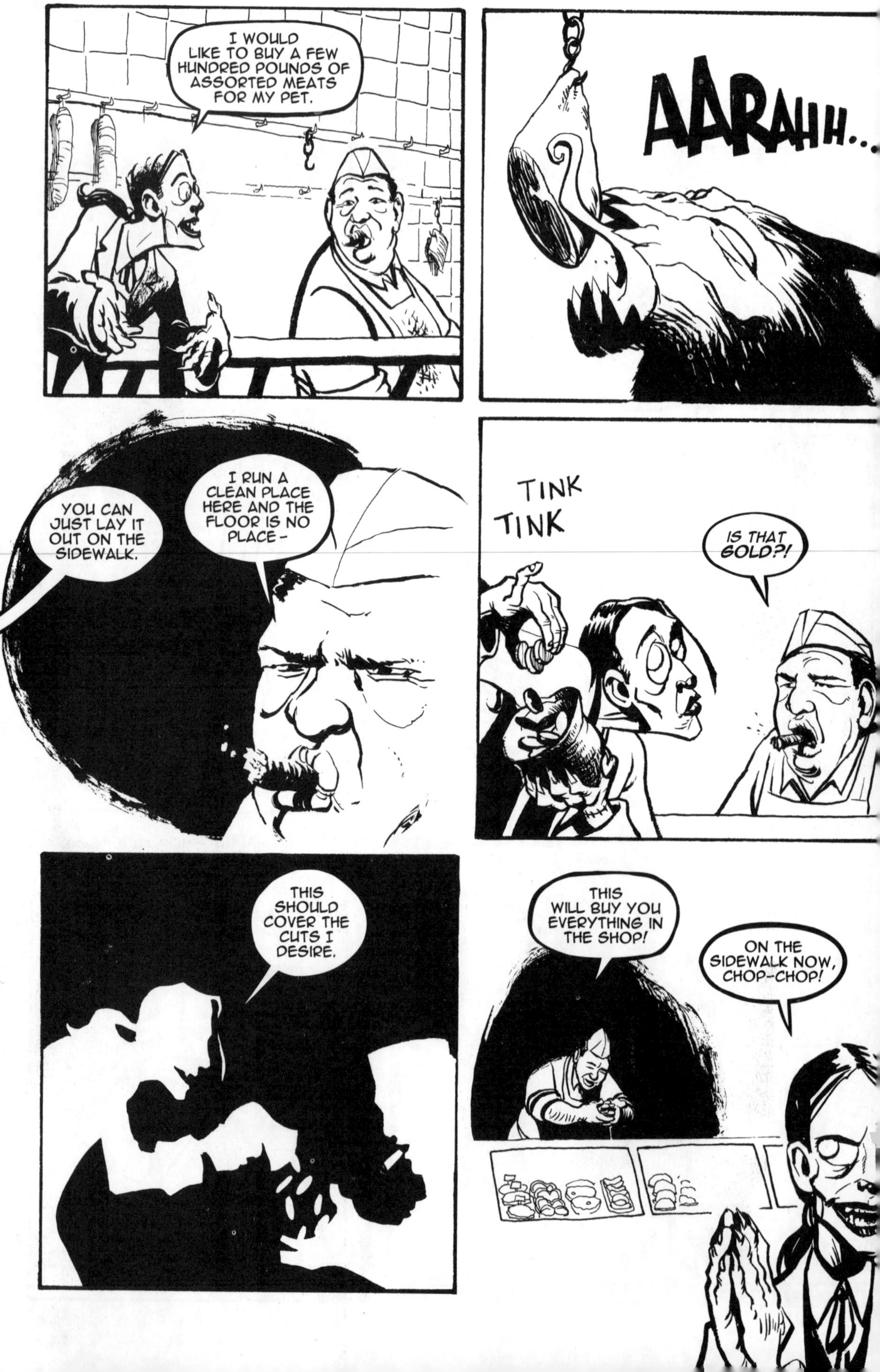
I WOULD LIKE TO BUY A FEW HUNDRED POUNDS OF ASSORTED MEATS FOR MY PET.
AARAHH...
YOU CAN JUST LAY IT OUT ON THE SIDEWALK.
I RUN A CLEAN PLACE HERE AND THE FLOOR IS NO PLACE-
TINK
TINK
IS THAT GOLD?!
THIS SHOULD COVER THE CUTS I DESIRE.
THIS WILL BUY YOU EVERYTHING IN THE SHOP!
ON THE SIDEWALK NOW, CHOP-CHOP!

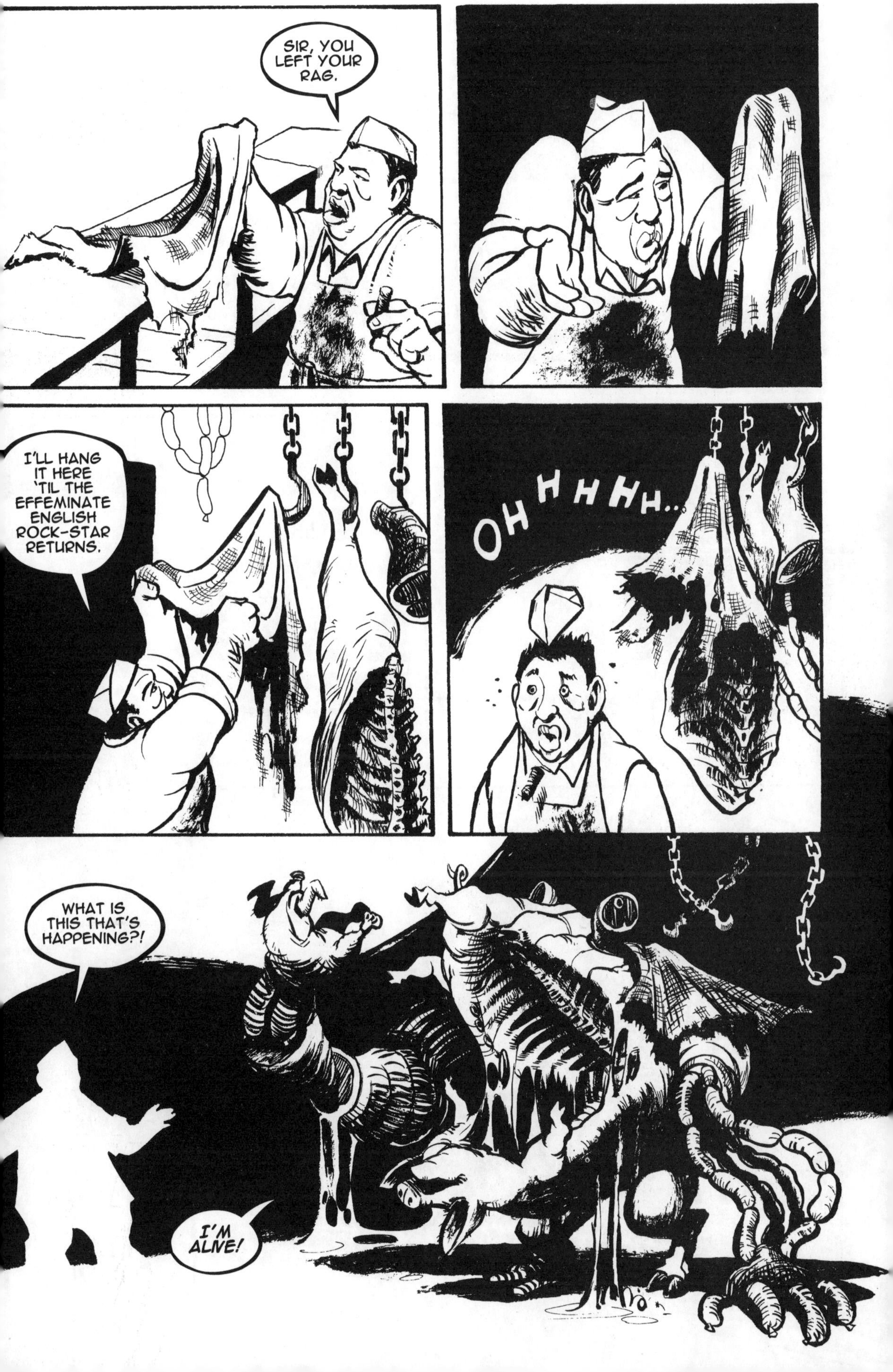
SIR, YOU LEFT YOUR RAG.
I'LL HANG IT HERE 'TIL THE EFFEMINATE ENGLISH ROCK-STAR RETURNS.
OHHHHHH...
WHAT IS THIS THAT'S HAPPENING?!
I'M ALIVE!

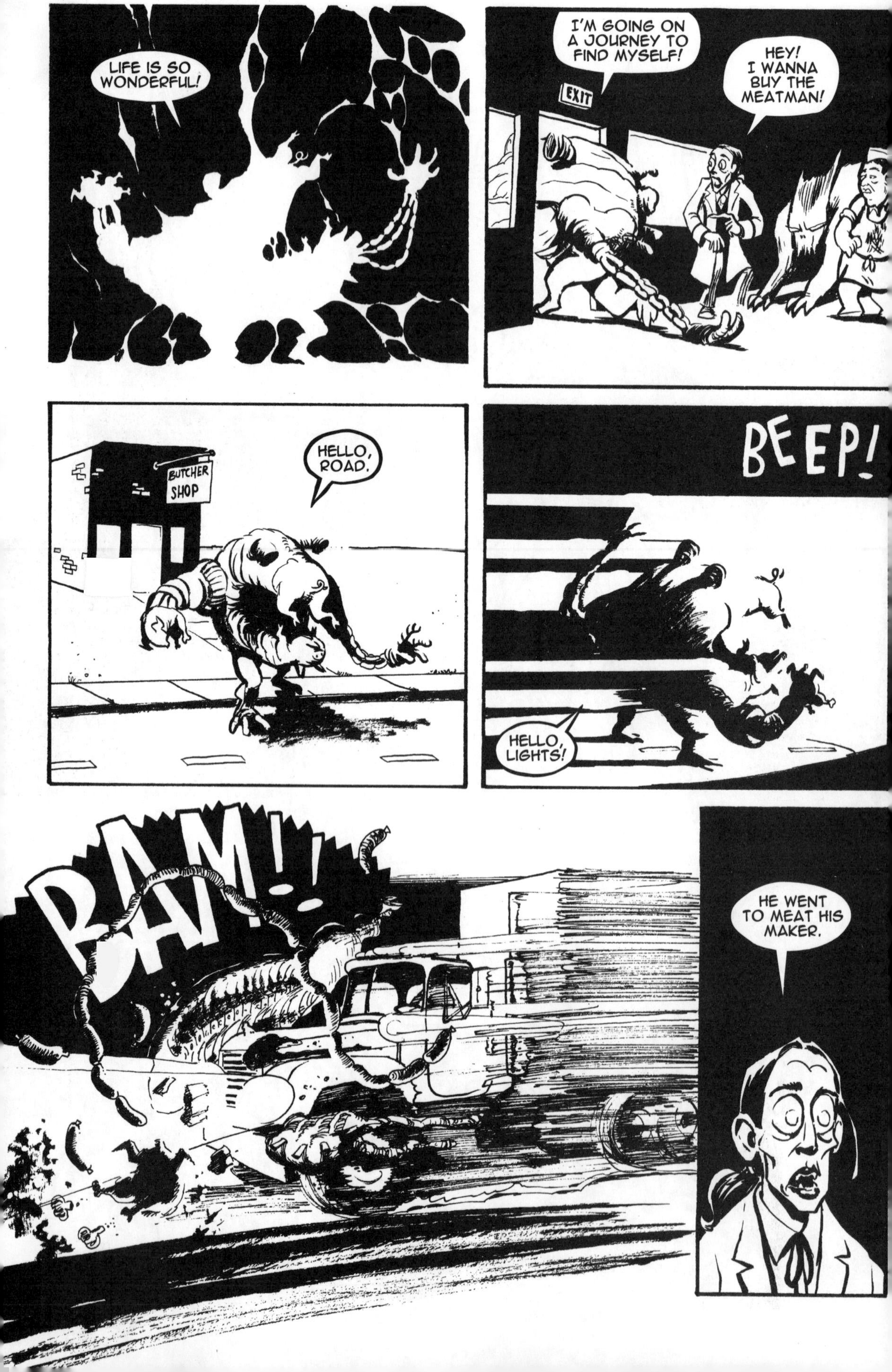
LIFE IS SO WONDERFUL!
I'M GOING ON A JOURNEY TO FIND MYSELF!
EXIT
HEY! I WANNA BUY THE MEATMAN!
BUTCHER SHOP
HELLO, ROAD.
BEEP!
HELLO, LIGHTS!
BAM!!
HE WENT TO MEAT HIS MAKER.

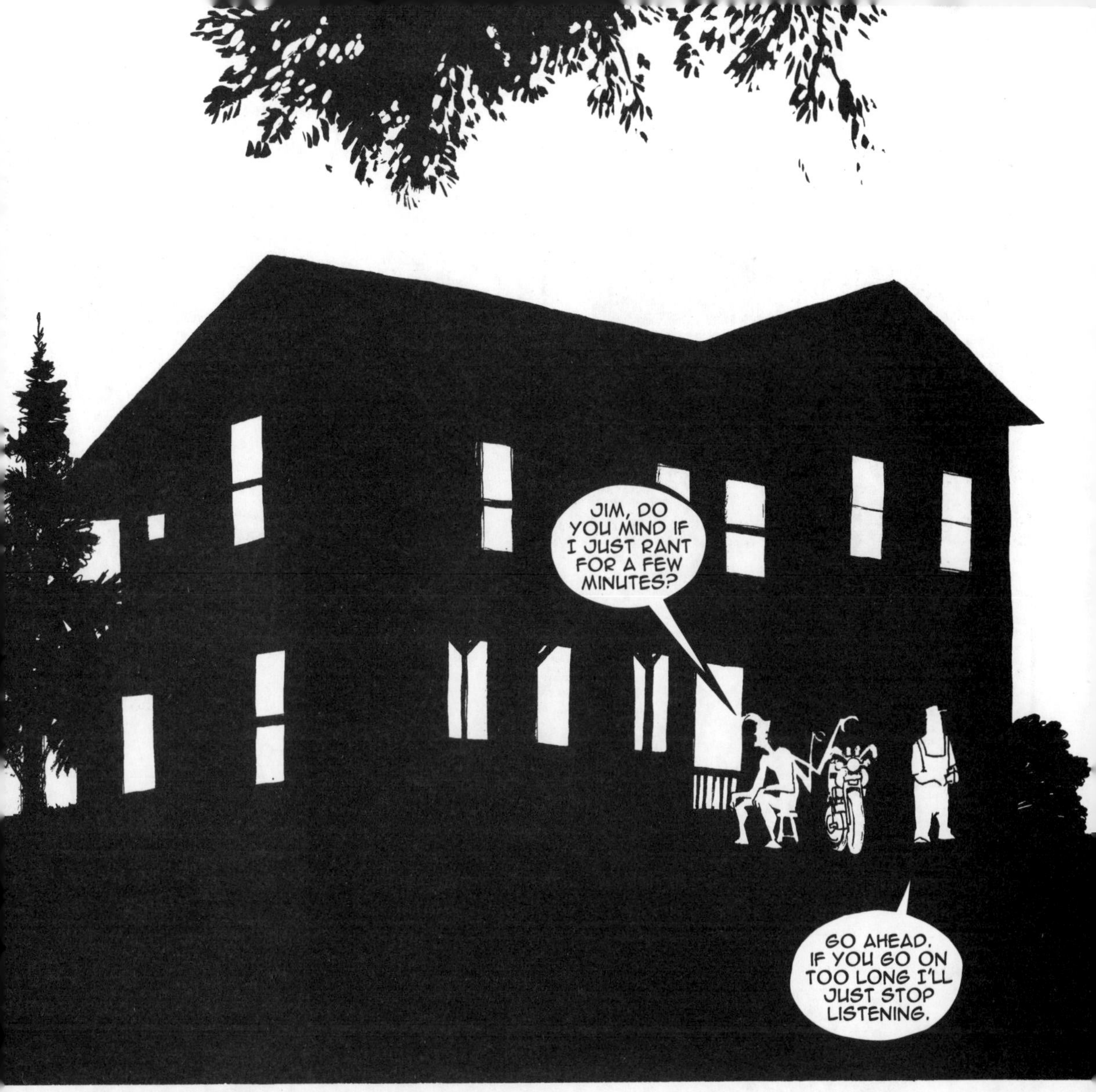
JIM, DO YOU MIND IF I JUST RANT FOR A FEW MINUTES?
GO AHEAD. IF YOU GO ON TOO LONG I'LL JUST STOP LISTENING.

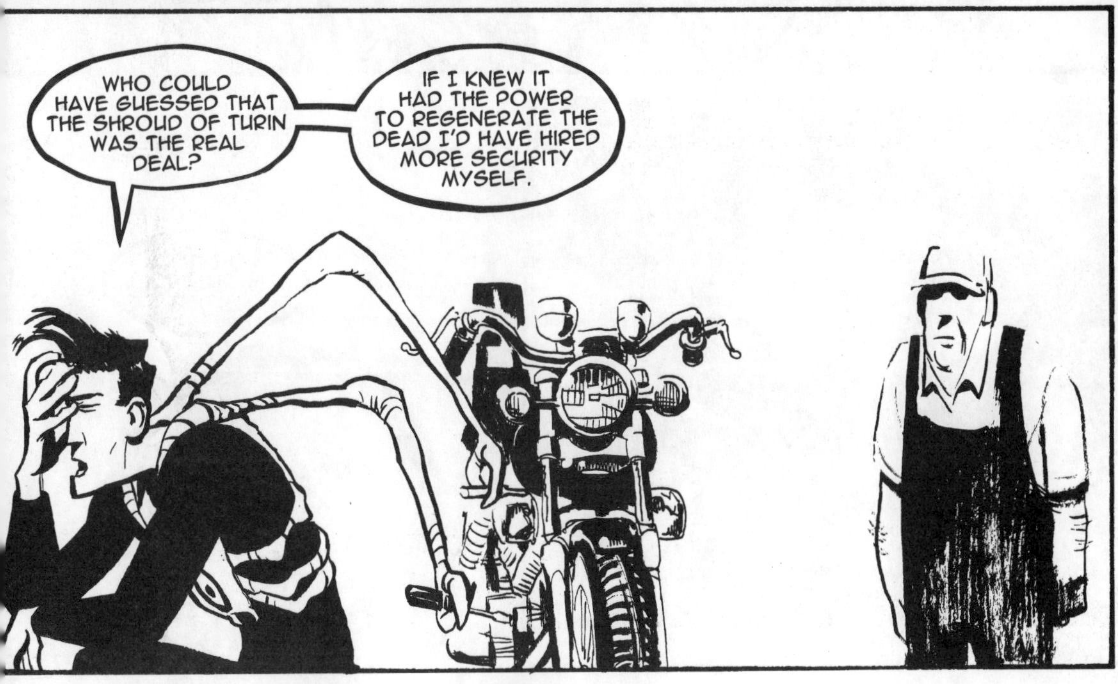
WHO COULD HAVE GUESSED THAT THE SHROUD OF TURIN WAS THE REAL DEAL?
IF I KNEW IT HAD THE POWER TO REGENERATE THE DEAD I'D HAVE HIRED MORE SECURITY MYSELF.

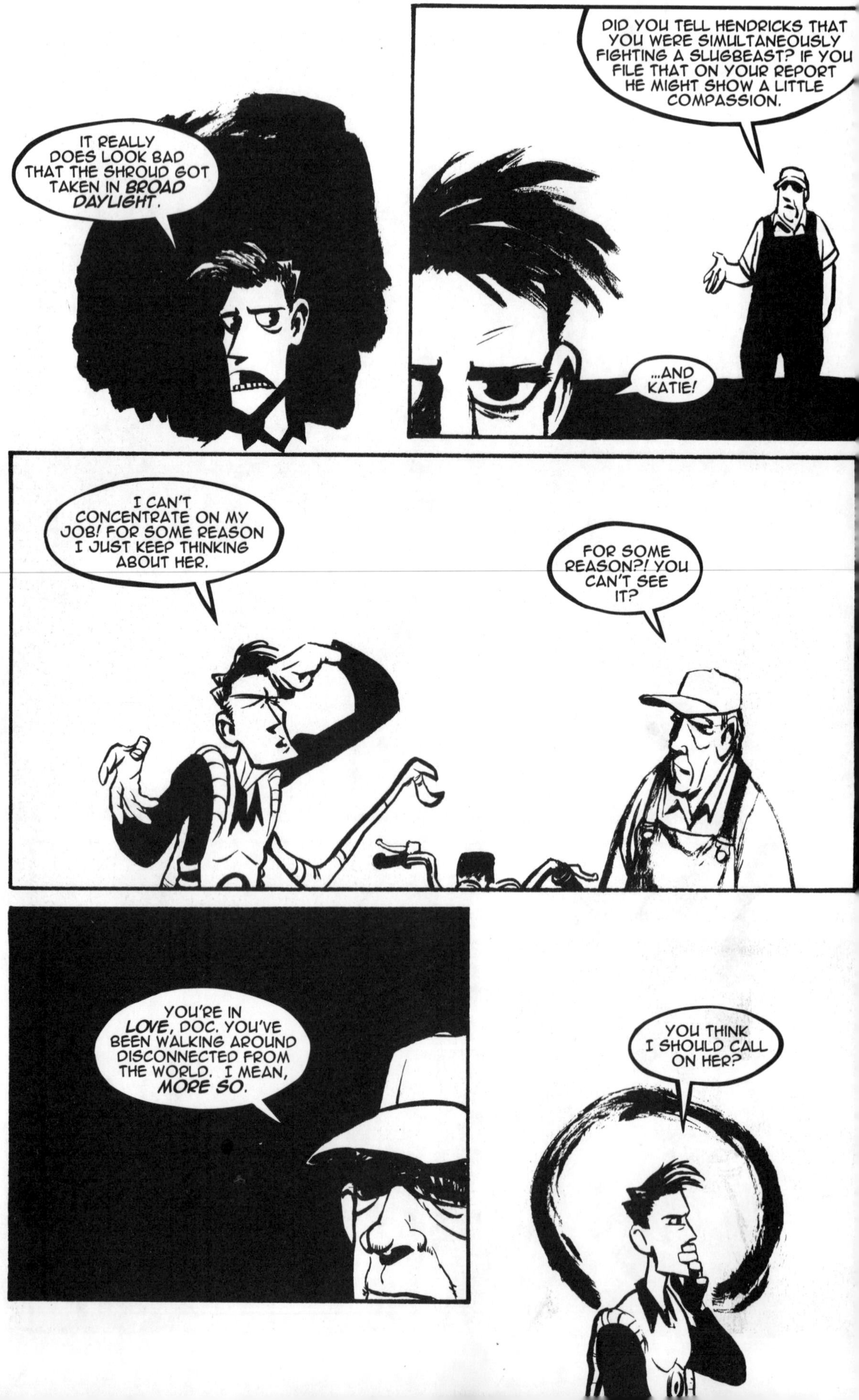
IT REALLY DOES LOOK BAD THAT THE SHROUD GOT TAKEN IN BROAD DAYLIGHT.
DID YOU TELL HENDRICKS THAT YOU WERE SIMULTANEOUSLY FIGHTING A SLUGBEAST? IF YOU FILE THAT ON YOUR REPORT HE MIGHT SHOW A LITTLE COMPASSION.
...AND KATIE!
I CAN'T CONCENTRATE ON MY JOB! FOR SOME REASON I JUST KEEP THINKING ABOUT HER.
FOR SOME REASON?! YOU CAN'T SEE IT?
YOU'RE IN LOVE, DOC. YOU'VE BEEN WALKING AROUND DISCONNECTED FROM THE WORLD. I MEAN, MORE SO.
YOU THINK I SHOULD CALL ON HER?

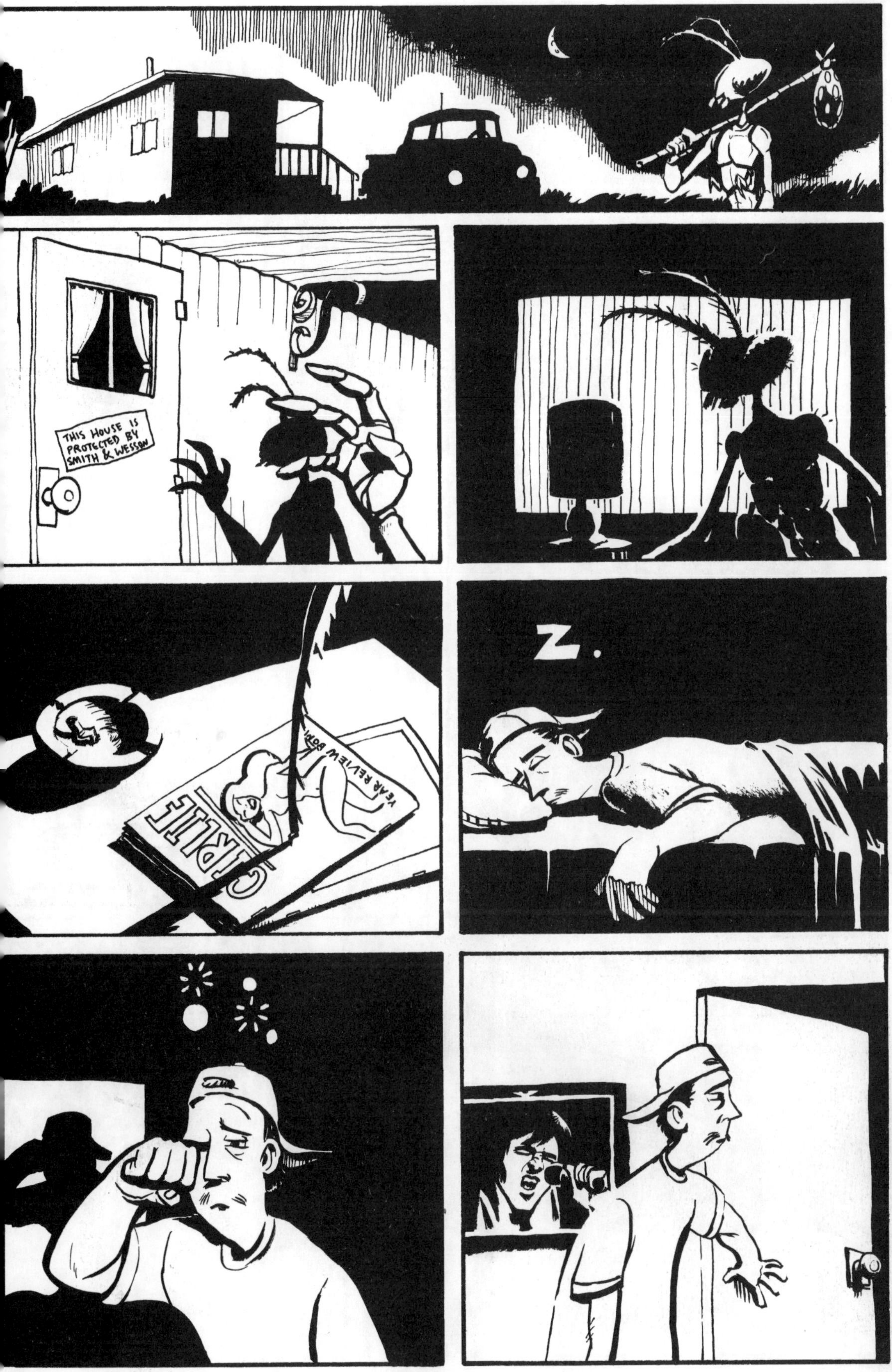
THIS HOUSE IS PROTECTED BY SMITH & WESSON
Z.

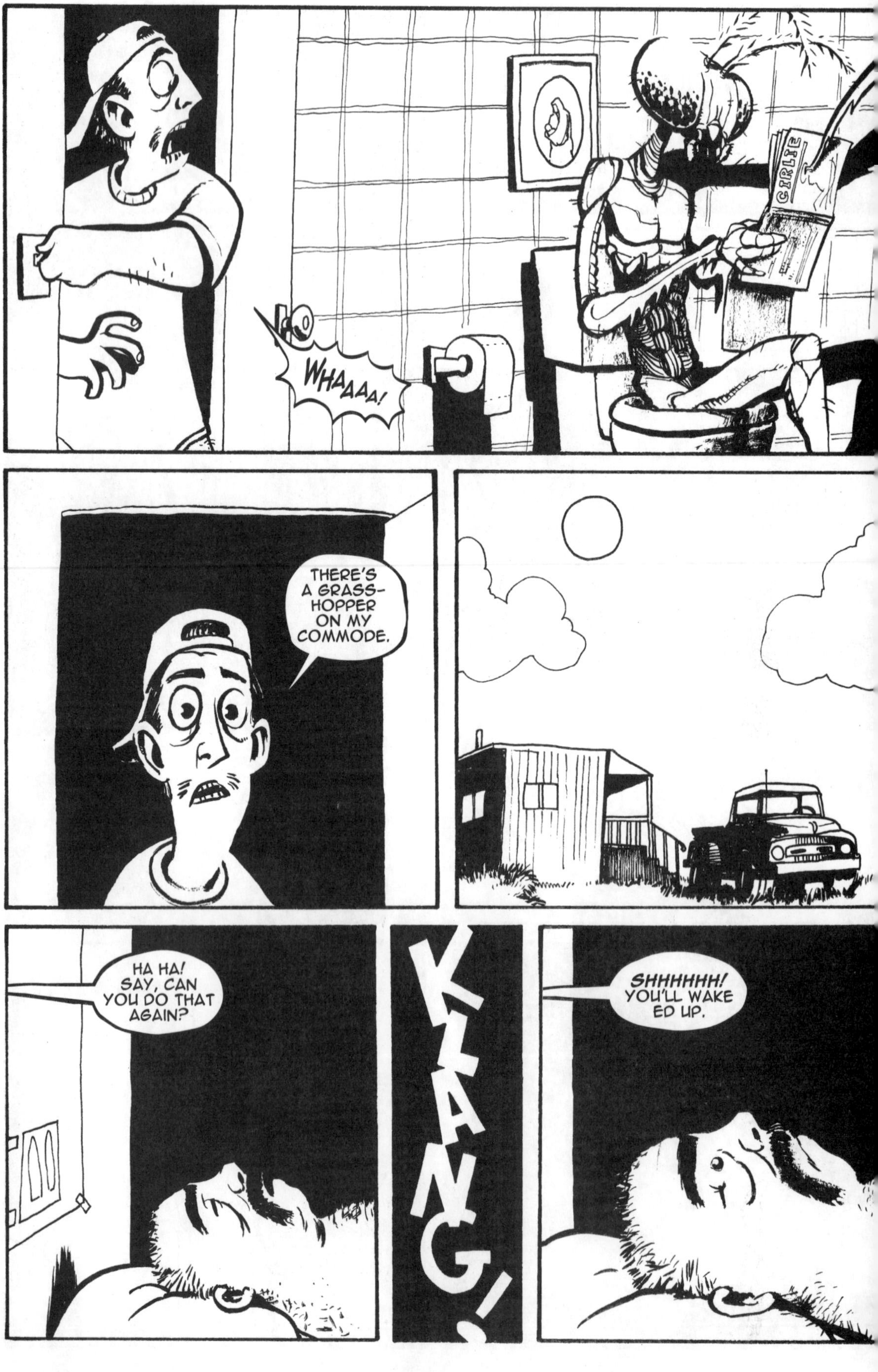

WHAAAA!
GIRLIE
THERE'S A GRASS-HOPPER ON MY COMMODE.
HA HA! SAY, CAN YOU DO THAT AGAIN?
KLANG!
SHHHHHH! YOU'LL WAKE ED UP.

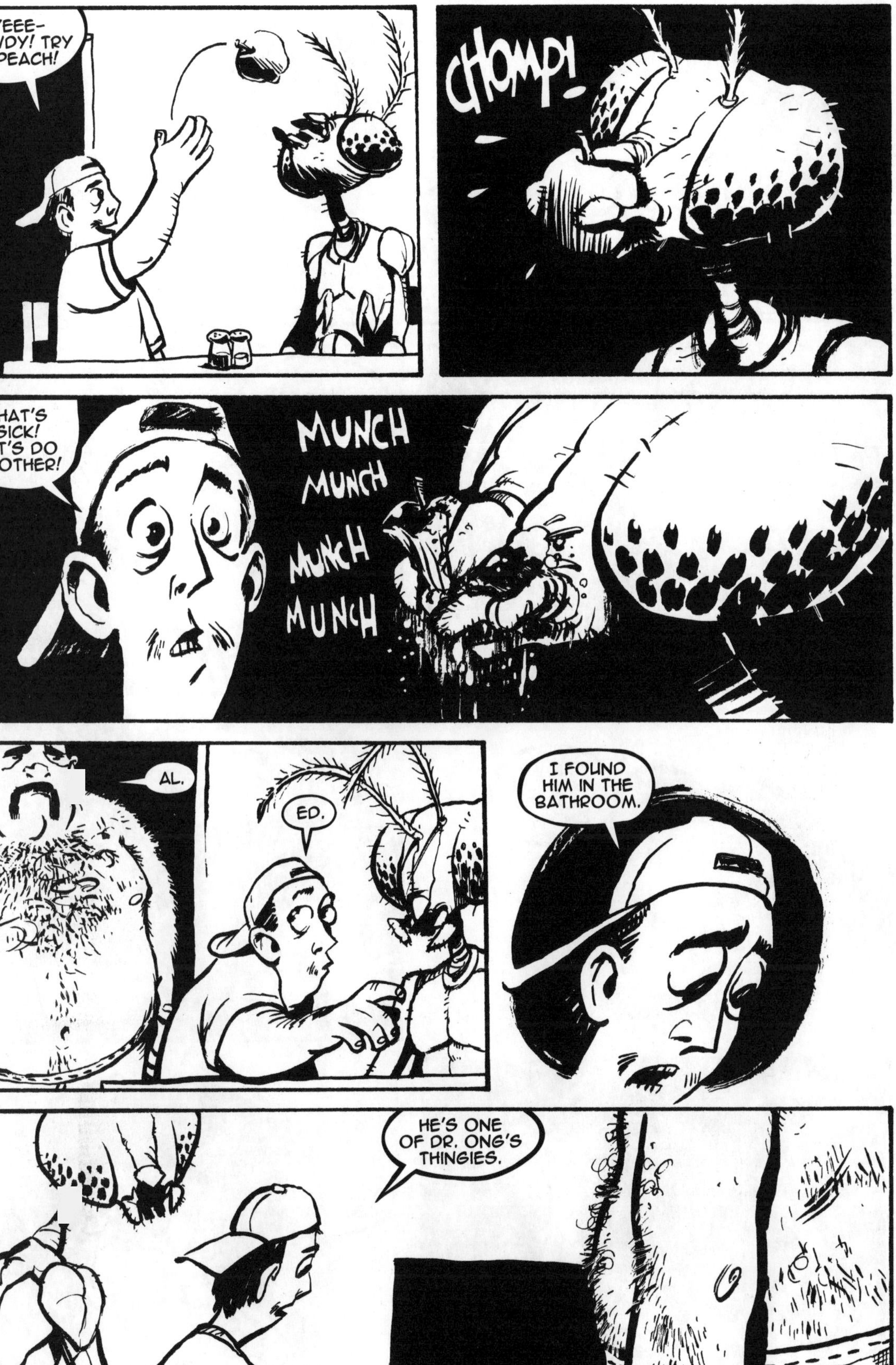
YEEE-HOWDY! TRY A PEACH!
CHOMP!
THAT'S SICK! LET'S DO ANOTHER!
MUNCH
MUNCH
MUNCH
MUNCH
AL.
ED.
I FOUND HIM IN THE BATHROOM.
HE'S ONE OF DR. ONG'S THINGIES.

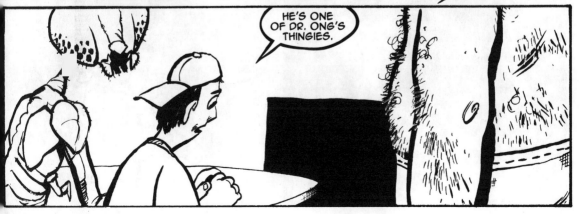

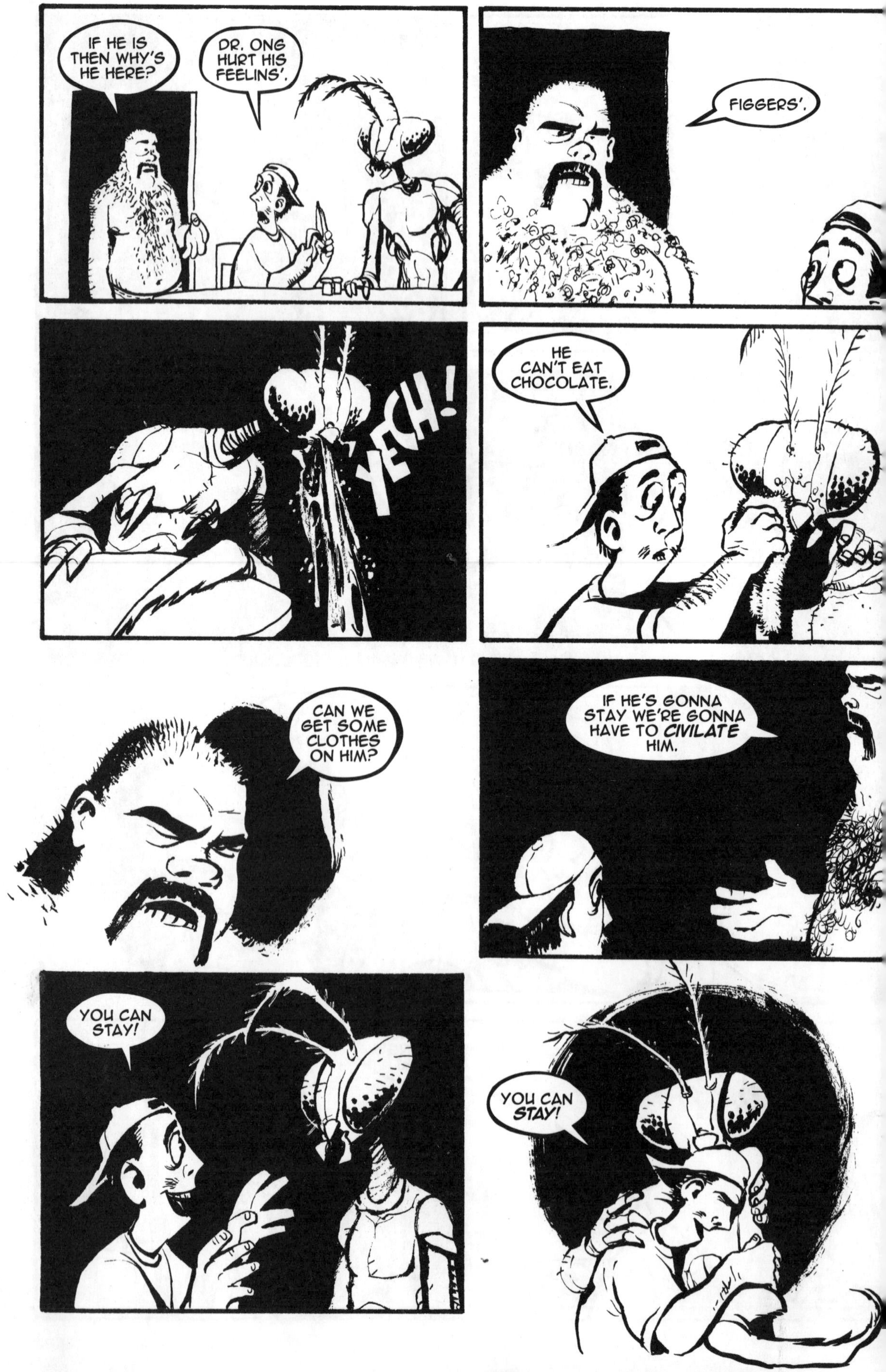
IF HE IS THEN WHY'S HE HERE?
DR. ONG HURT HIS FEELINS'.
FIGGERS'.
YECH!
HE CAN'T EAT CHOCOLATE.
CAN WE GET SOME CLOTHES ON HIM?
IF HE'S GONNA STAY WE'RE GONNA HAVE TO *CIVILATE* HIM.
YOU CAN STAY!
YOU CAN *STAY!*

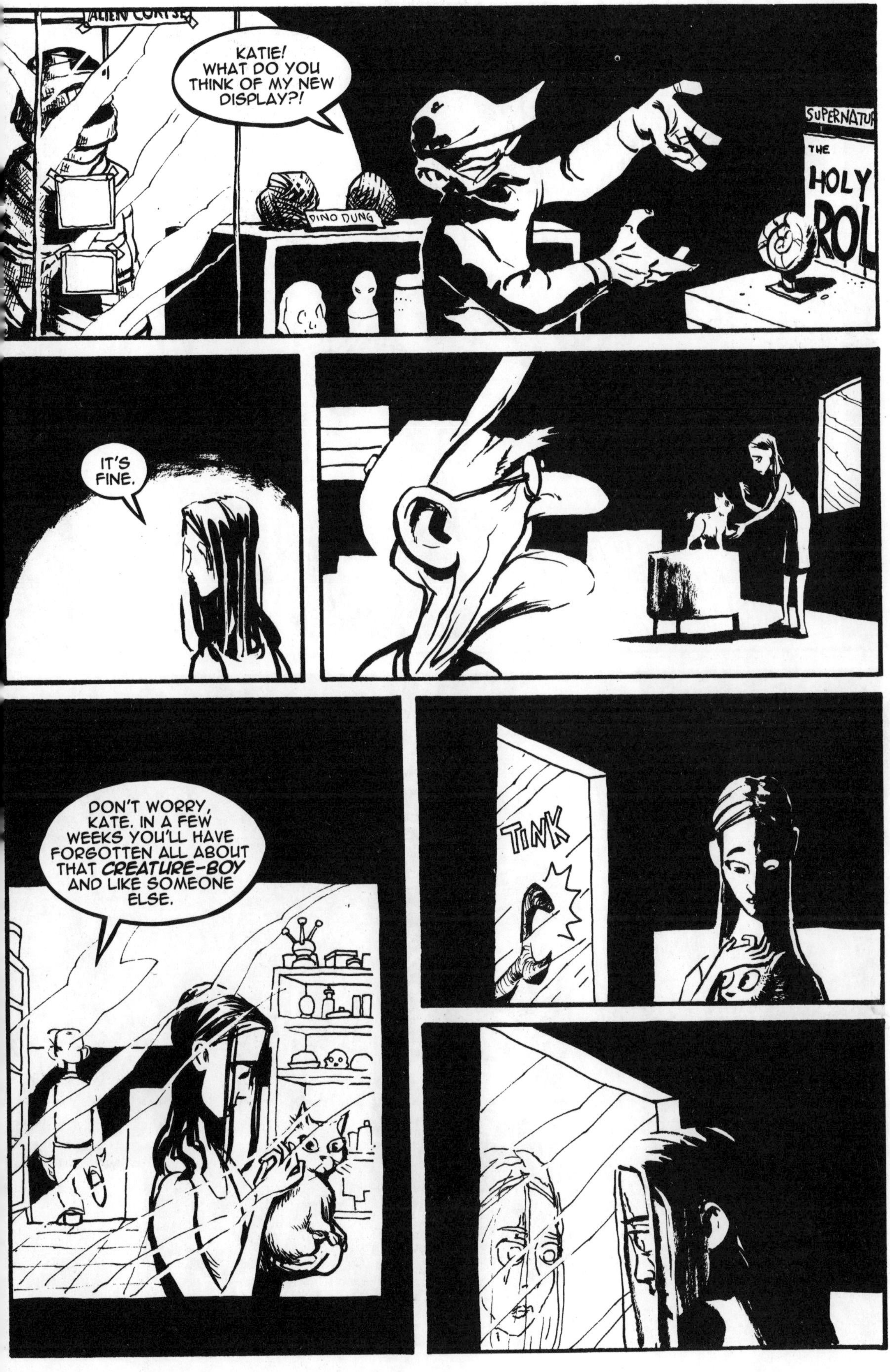
ALIEN CORPSE
KATIE! WHAT DO YOU THINK OF MY NEW DISPLAY?!
DINO DUNG
SUPERNATUR
THE HOLY ROL
IT'S FINE.
DON'T WORRY, KATE. IN A FEW WEEKS YOU'LL HAVE FORGOTTEN ALL ABOUT THAT *CREATURE-BOY* AND LIKE SOMEONE ELSE.
TINK

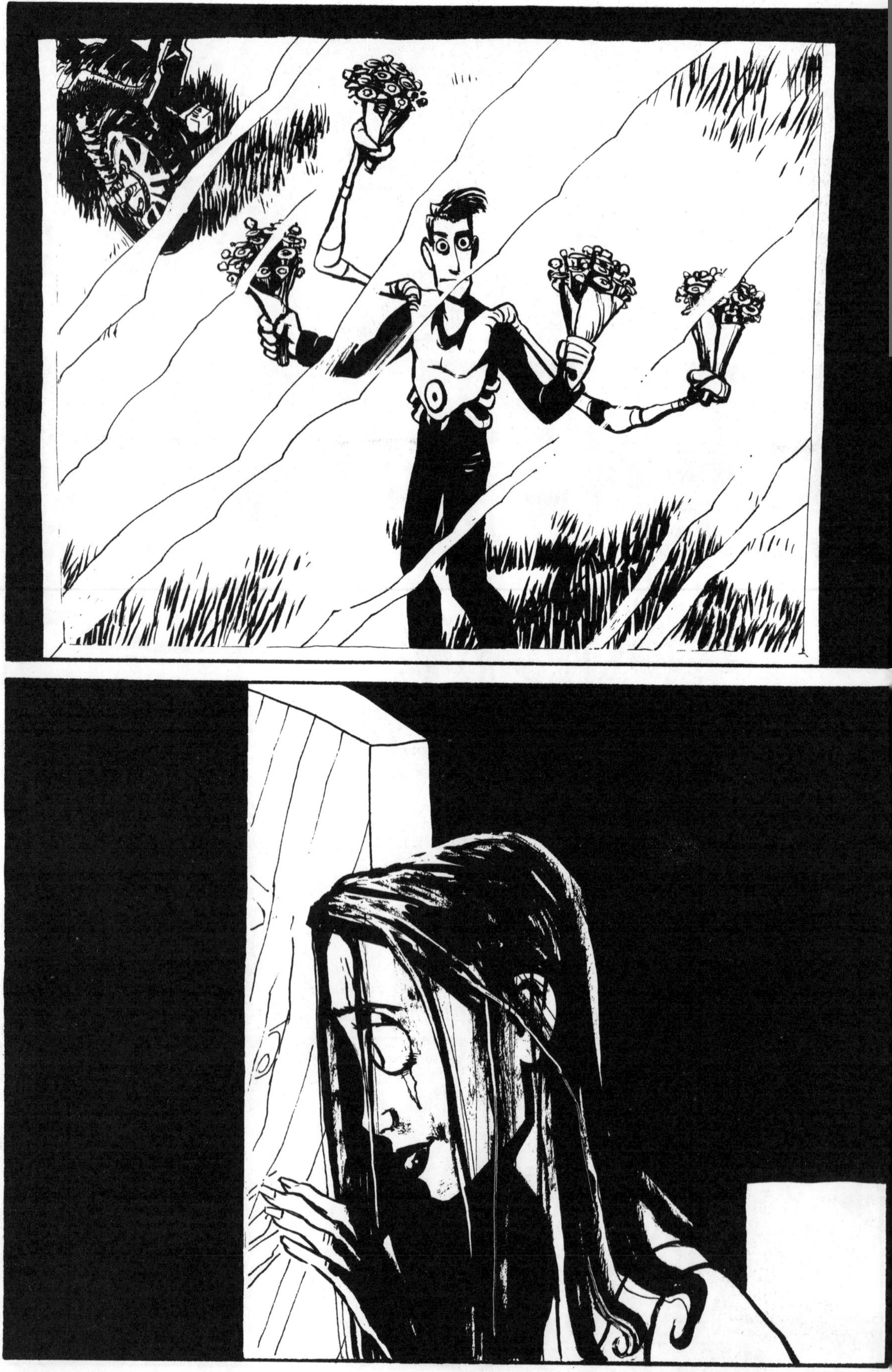

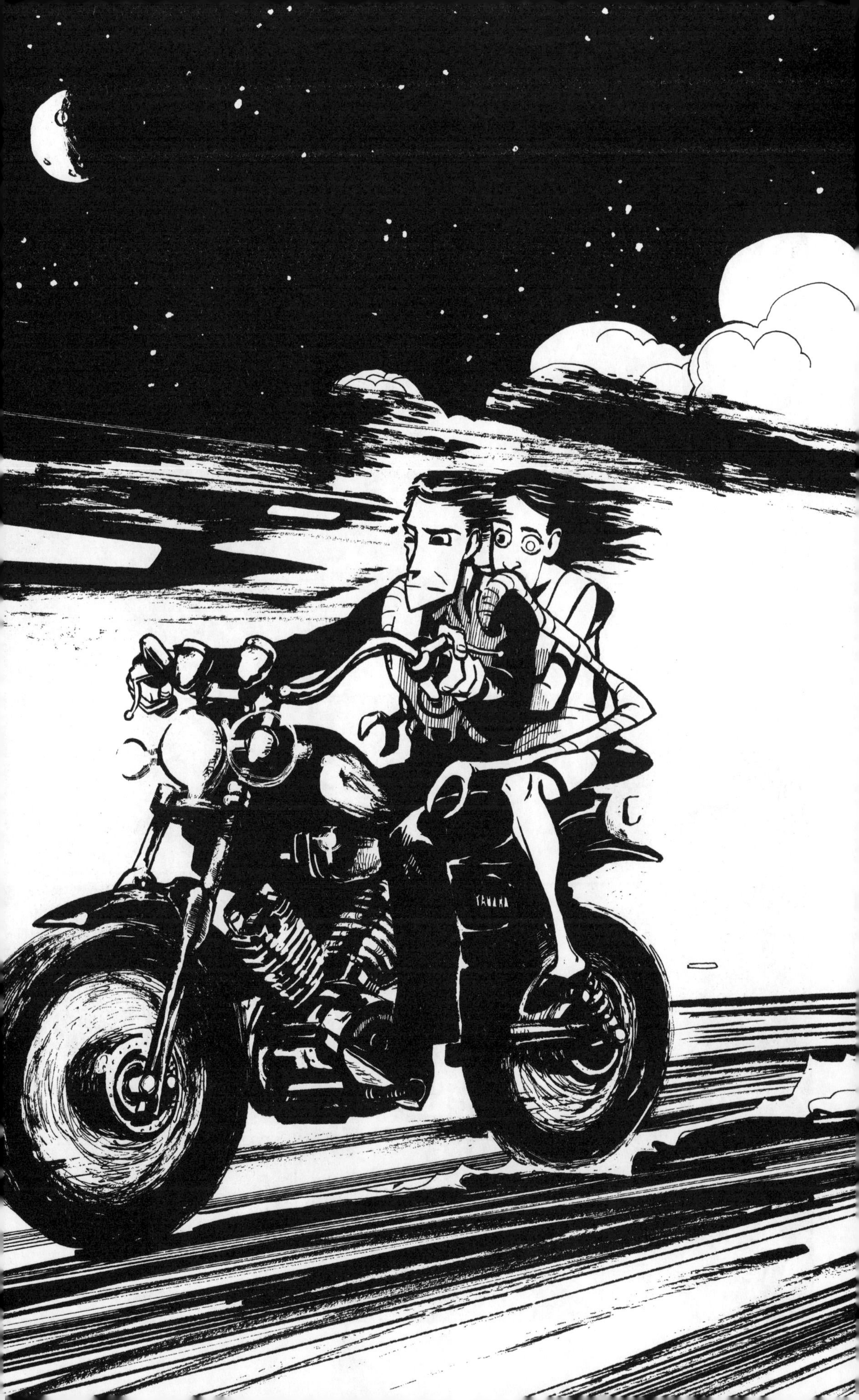

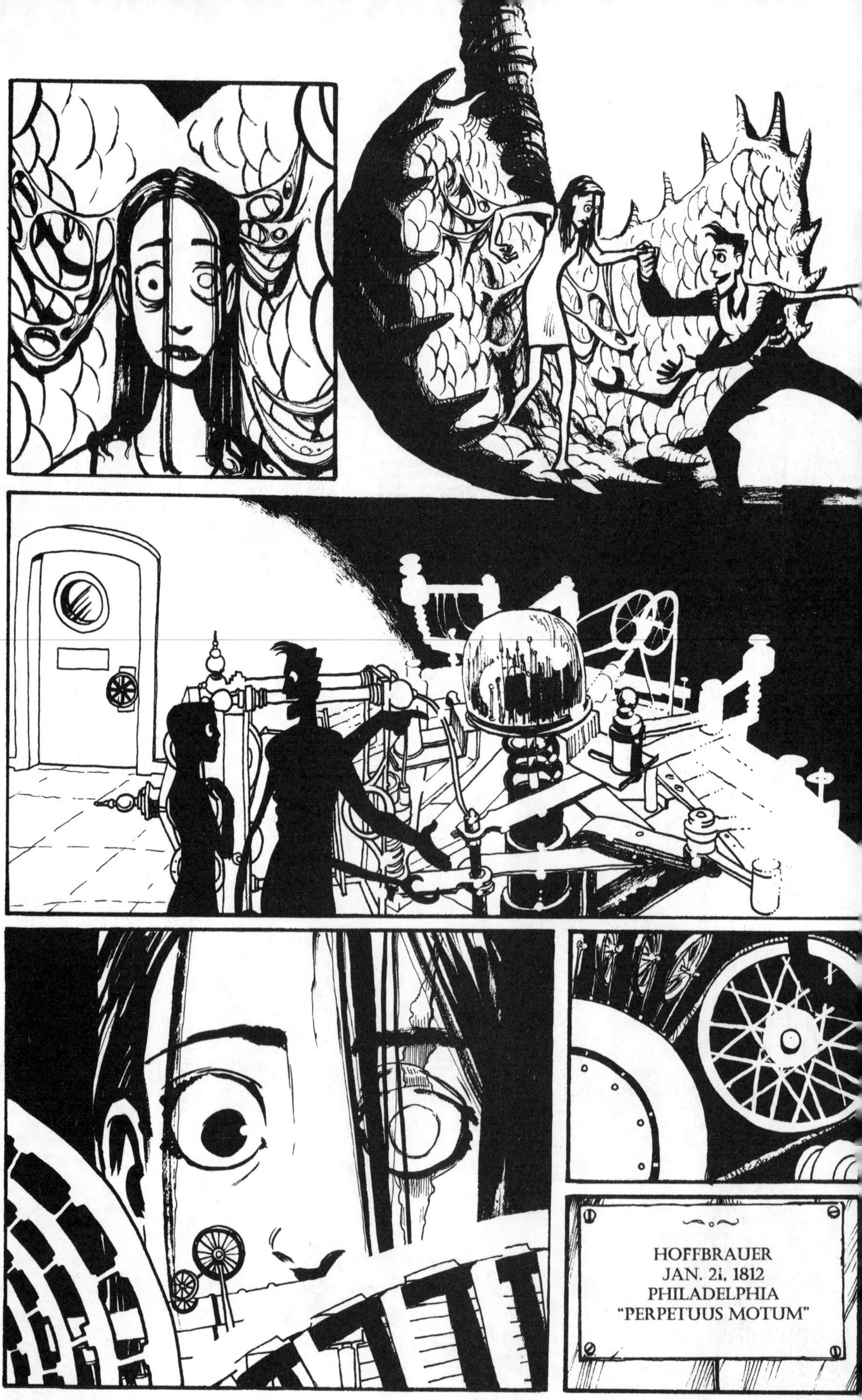
HOFFBRAUER
JAN. 21, 1812
PHILADELPHIA
"PERPETUUS MOTUM"

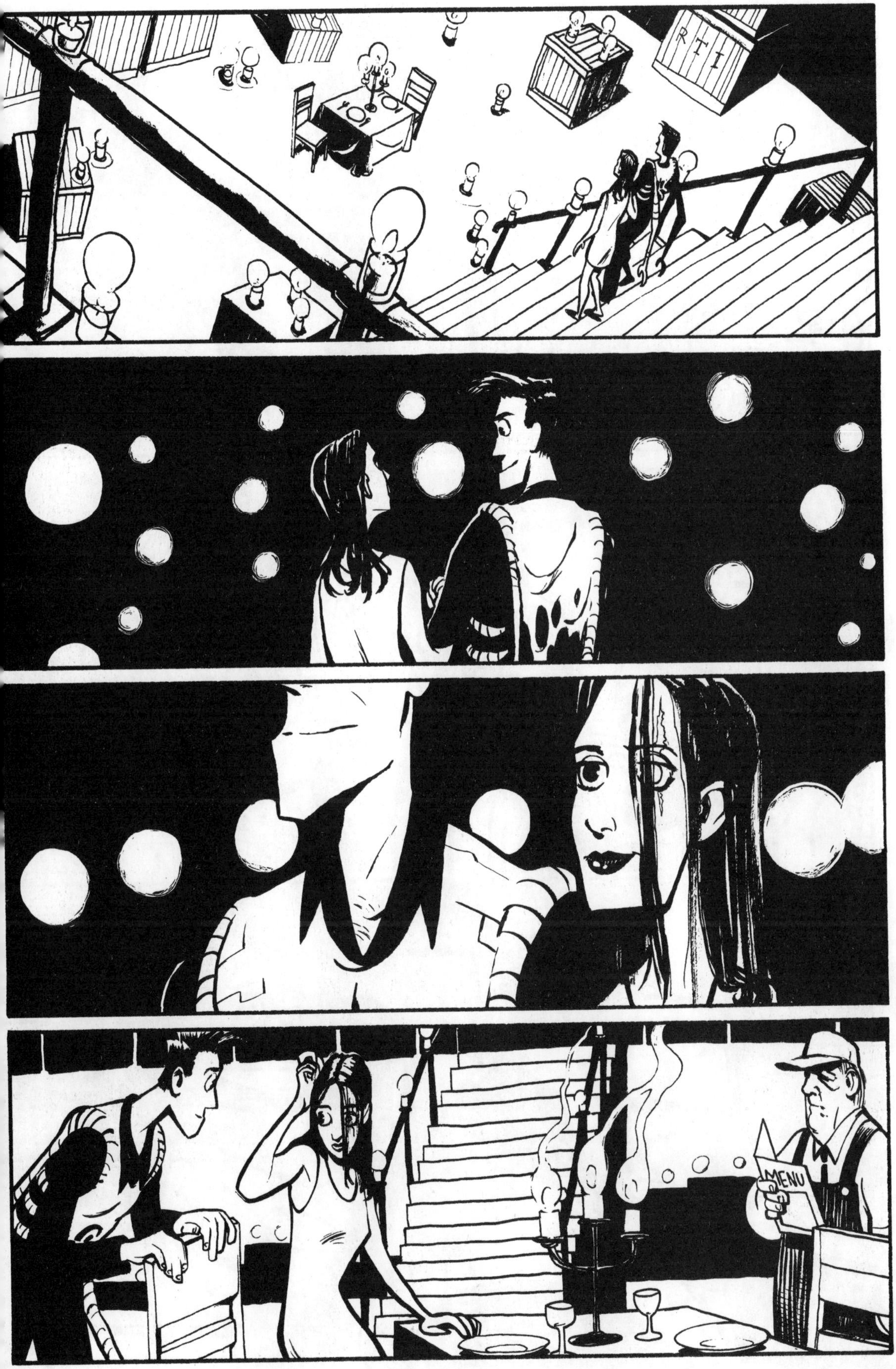
RTI
MENU

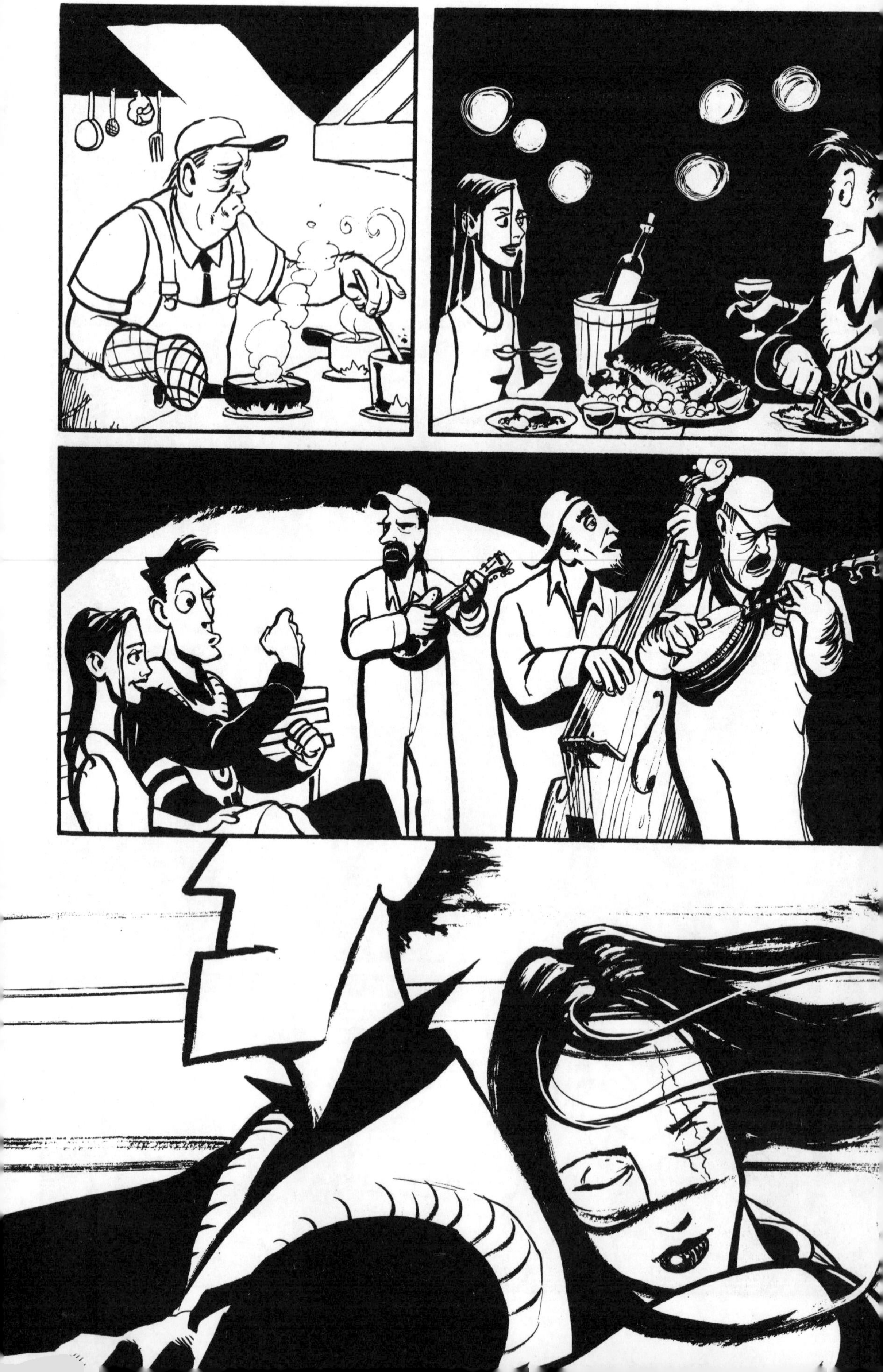

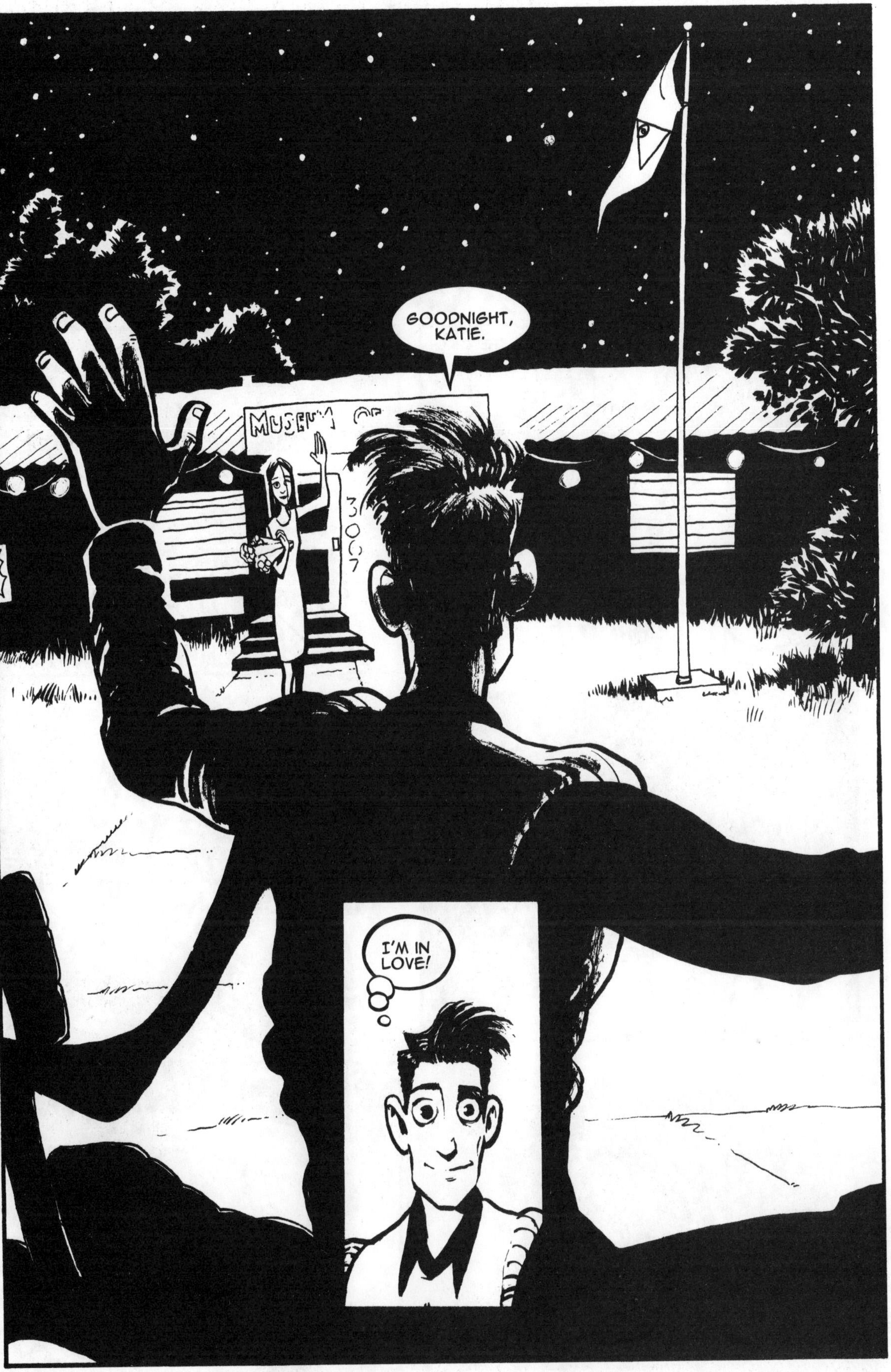
GOODNIGHT, KATIE.
I'M IN LOVE!

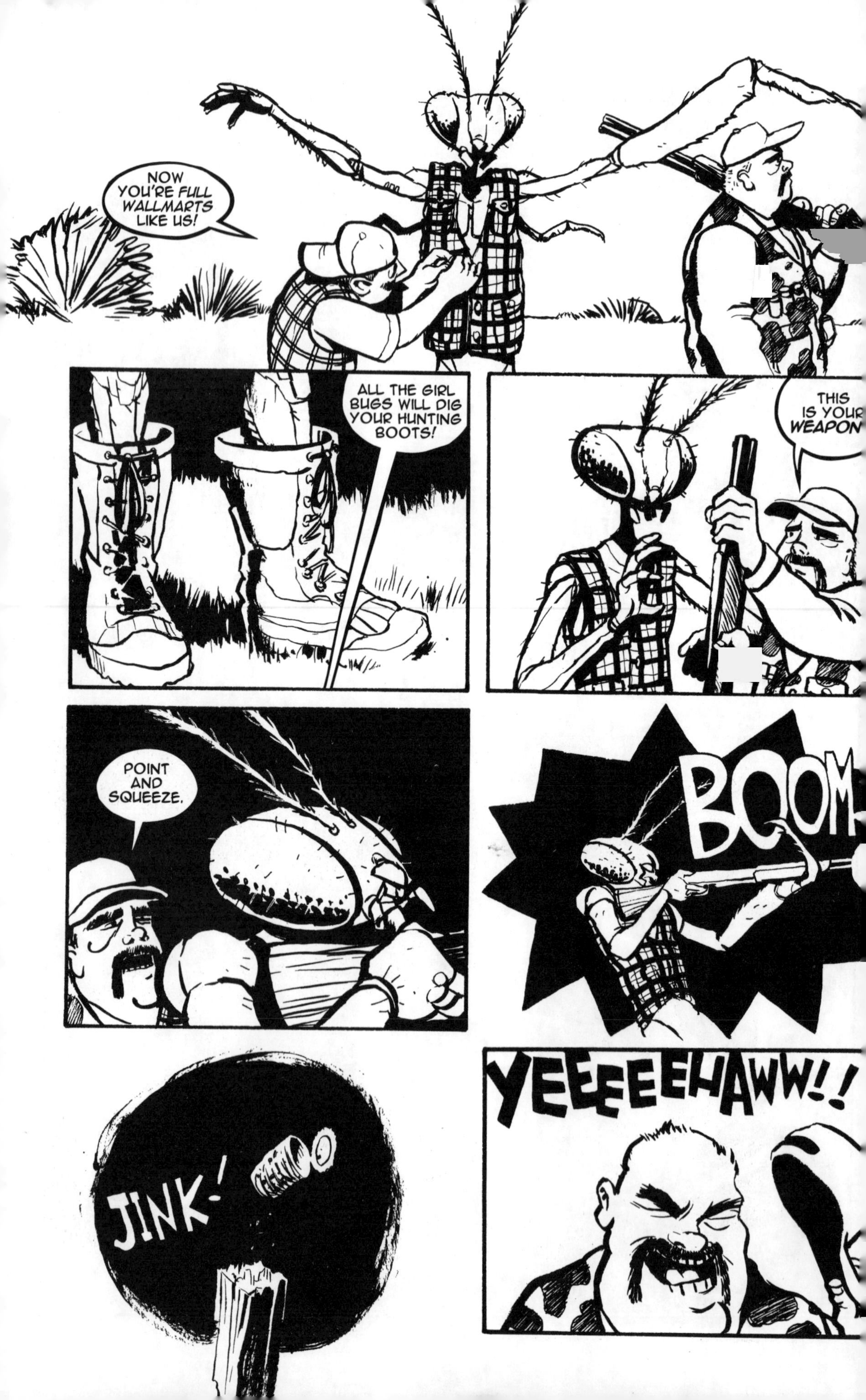
NOW YOU'RE FULL WALLMARTS LIKE US!
ALL THE GIRL BUGS WILL DIG YOUR HUNTING BOOTS!
THIS IS YOUR WEAPON
POINT AND SQUEEZE.
BOOM
JINK!
YEEEEEHAWW!!

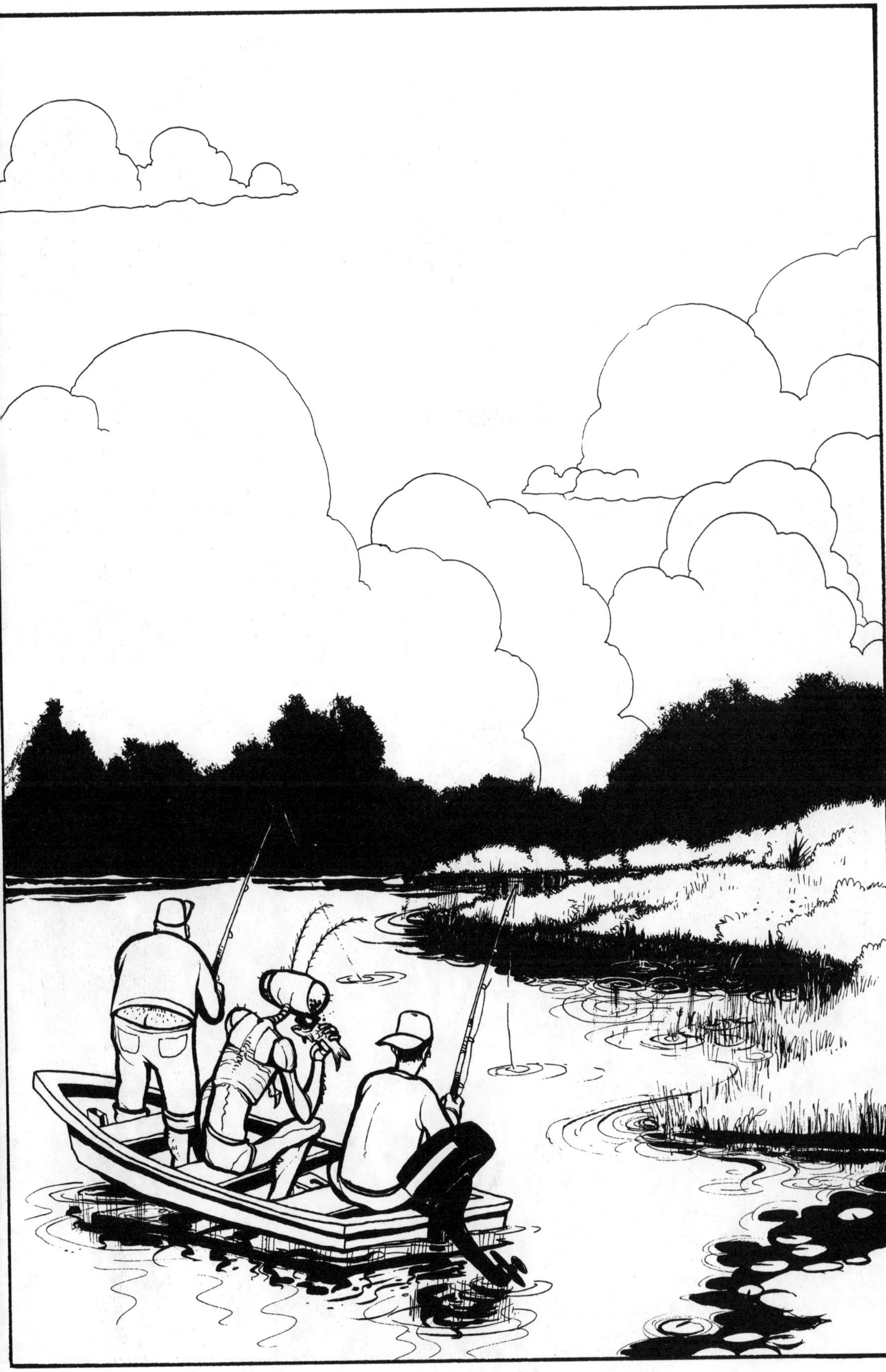

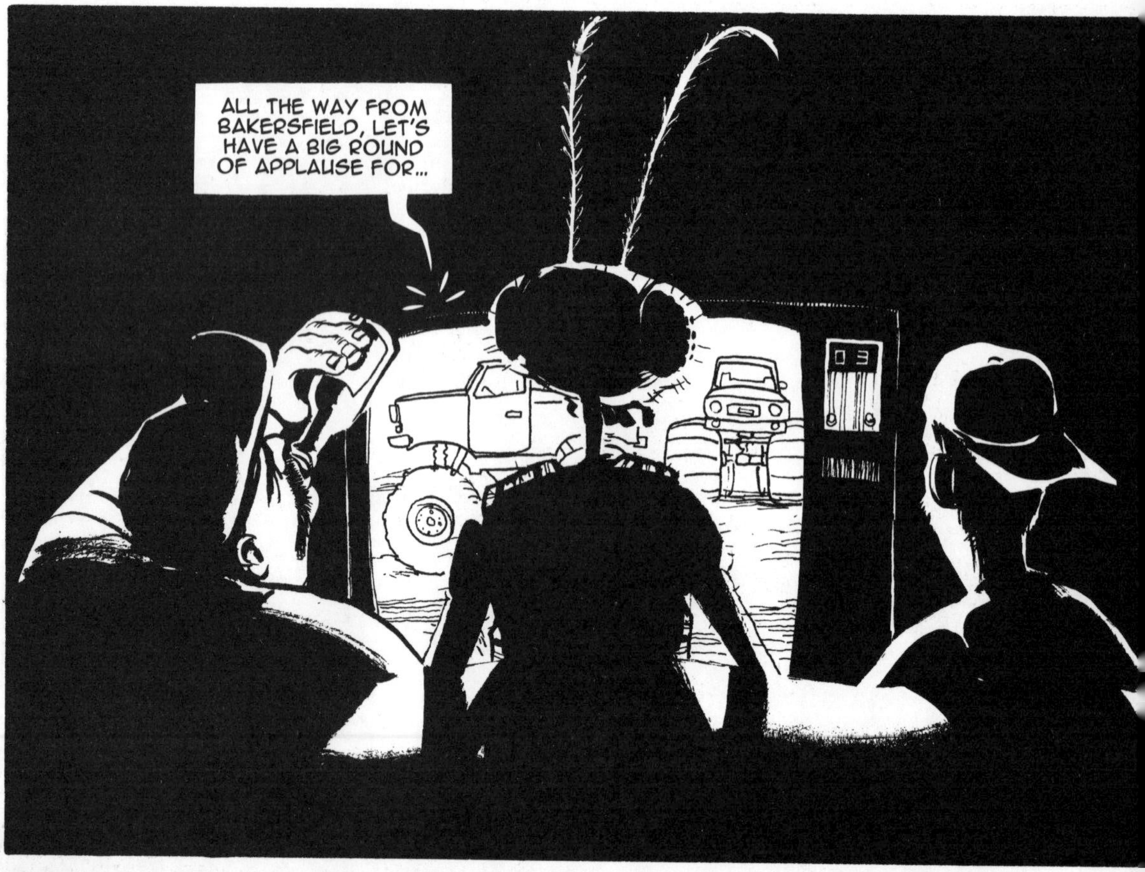
ALL THE WAY FROM BAKERSFIELD, LET'S HAVE A BIG ROUND OF APPLAUSE FOR...

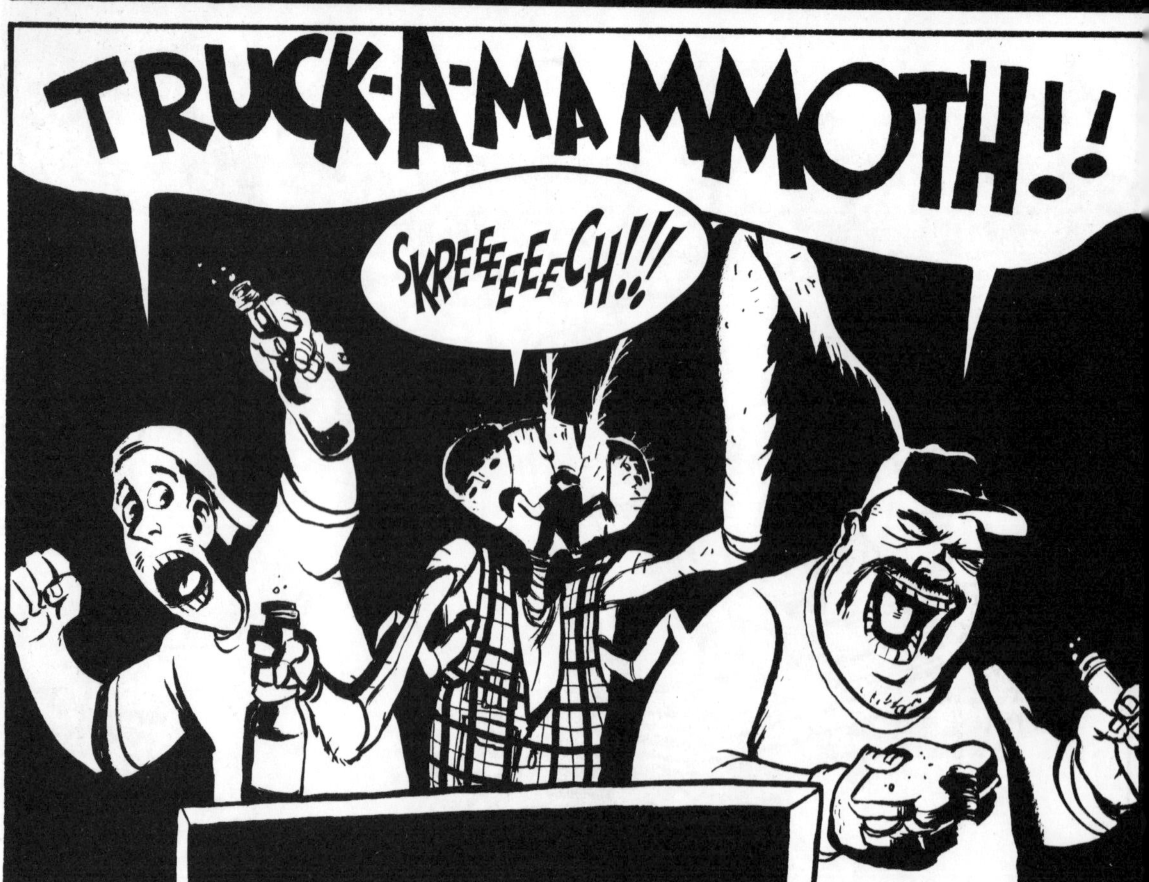
TRUCK-A-MAMMOTH!!
SKREEEEEEECH!!!

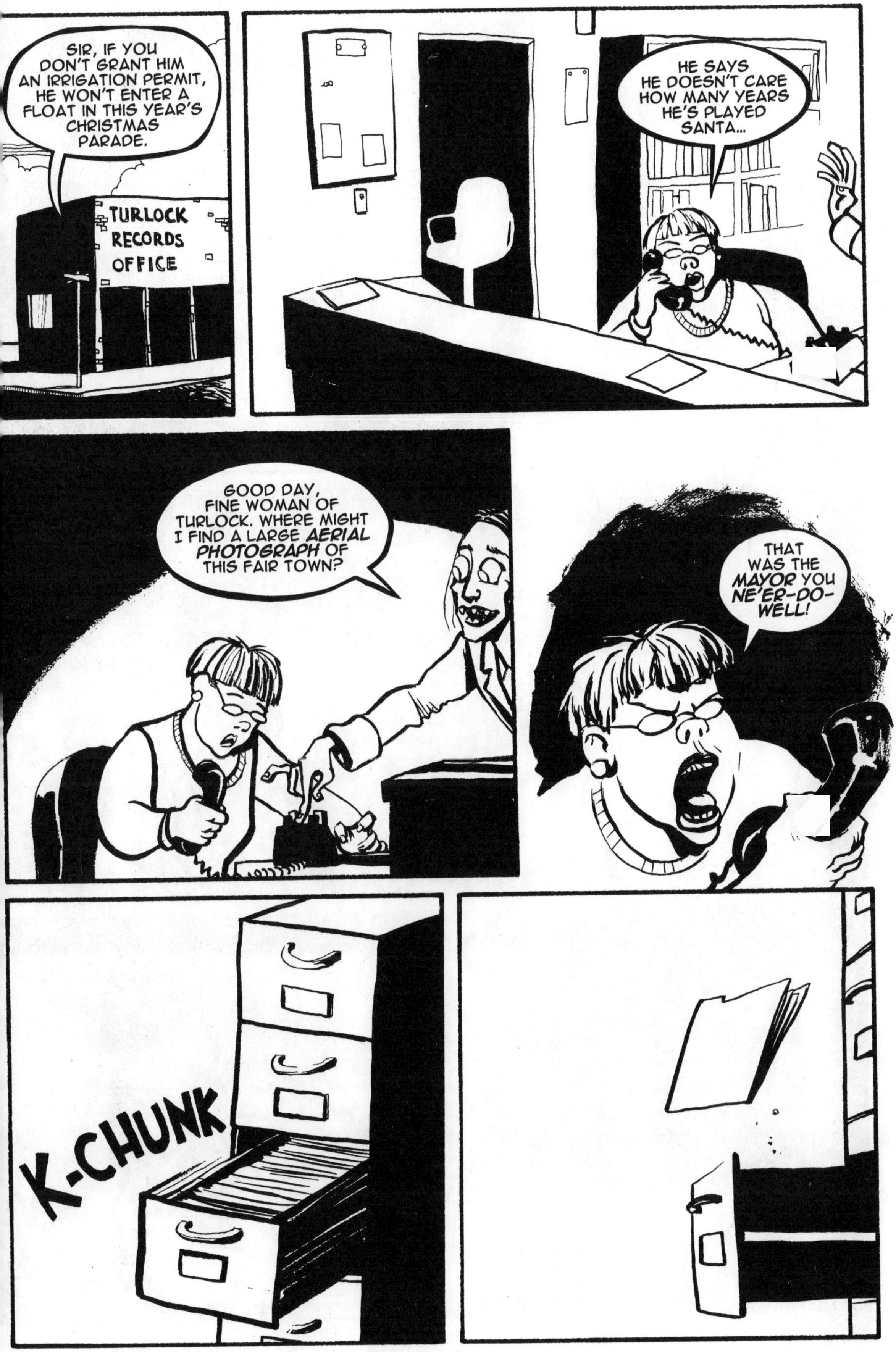
SIR, IF YOU DON'T GRANT HIM AN IRRIGATION PERMIT, HE WON'T ENTER A FLOAT IN THIS YEAR'S CHRISTMAS PARADE.
TURLOCK RECORDS OFFICE
HE SAYS HE DOESN'T CARE HOW MANY YEARS HE'S PLAYED SANTA...
GOOD DAY, FINE WOMAN OF TURLOCK. WHERE MIGHT I FIND A LARGE *AERIAL PHOTOGRAPH* OF THIS FAIR TOWN?
THAT WAS THE *MAYOR* YOU *NE'ER-DO-WELL!*
K-CHUNK

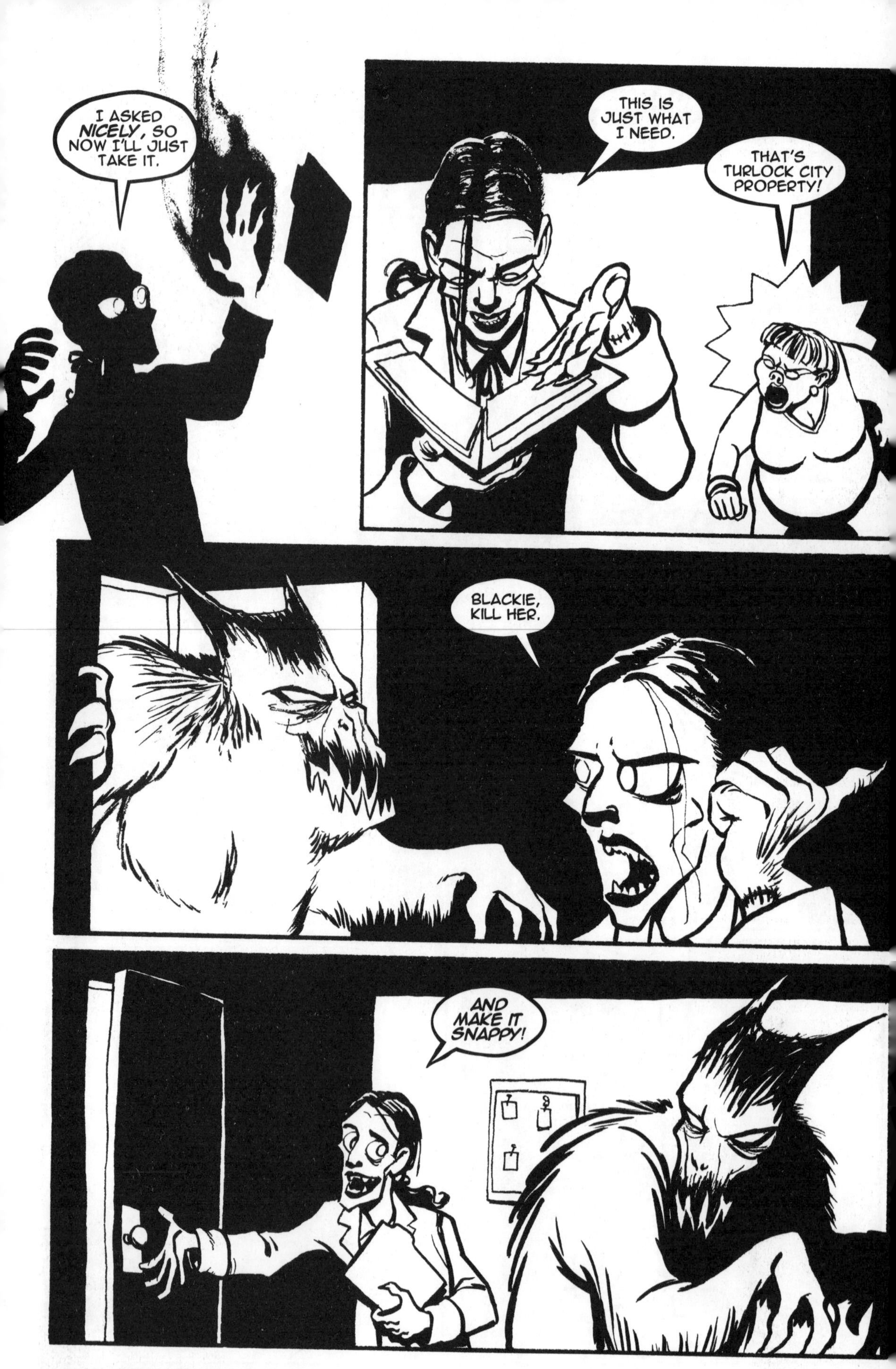
I ASKED NICELY, SO NOW I'LL JUST TAKE IT.
THIS IS JUST WHAT I NEED.
THAT'S TURLOCK CITY PROPERTY!
BLACKIE, KILL HER.
AND MAKE IT SNAPPY!

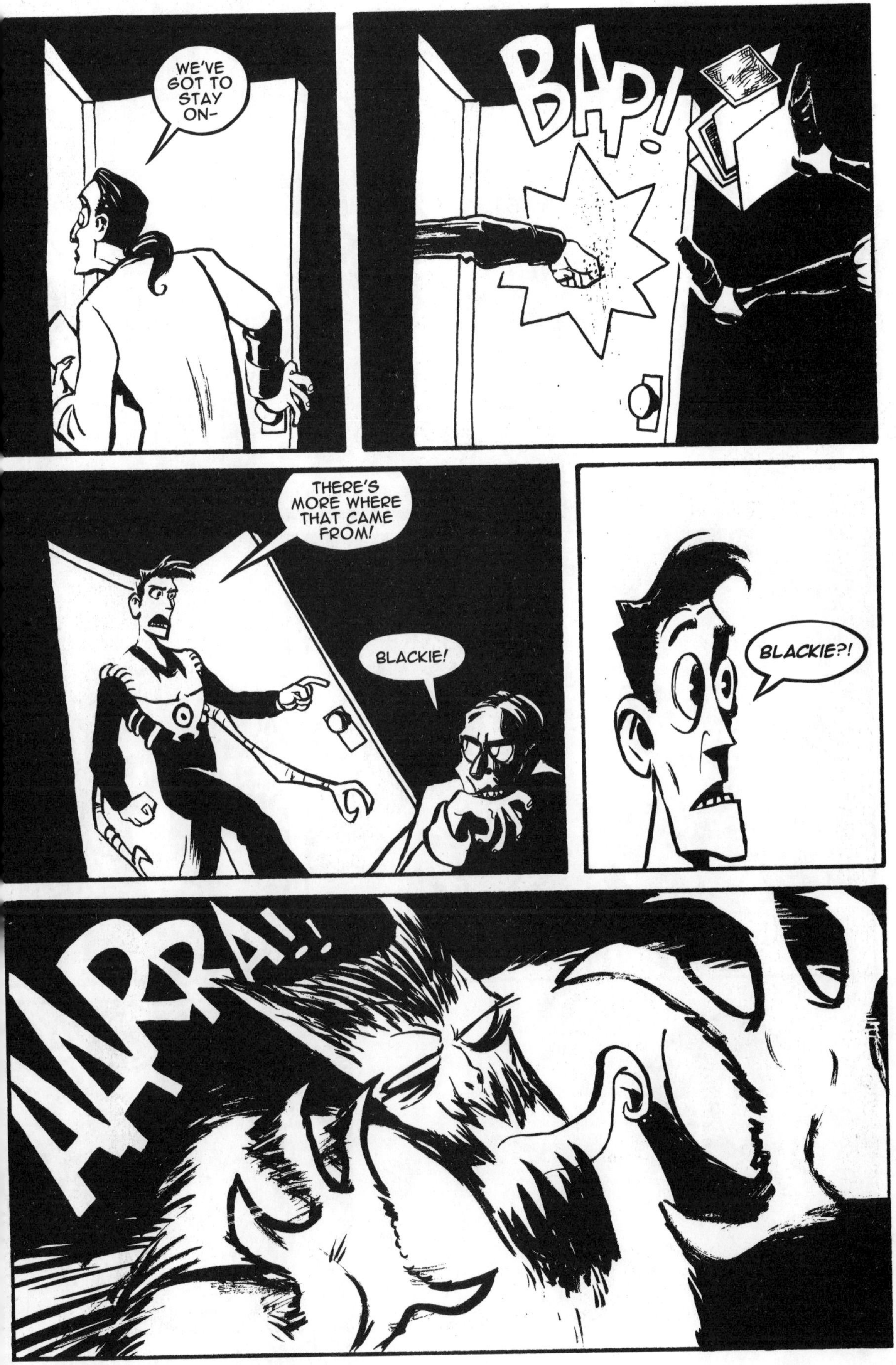
WE'VE GOT TO STAY ON-
BAP!
THERE'S MORE WHERE THAT CAME FROM!
BLACKIE!
BLACKIE?!
AARRA!!

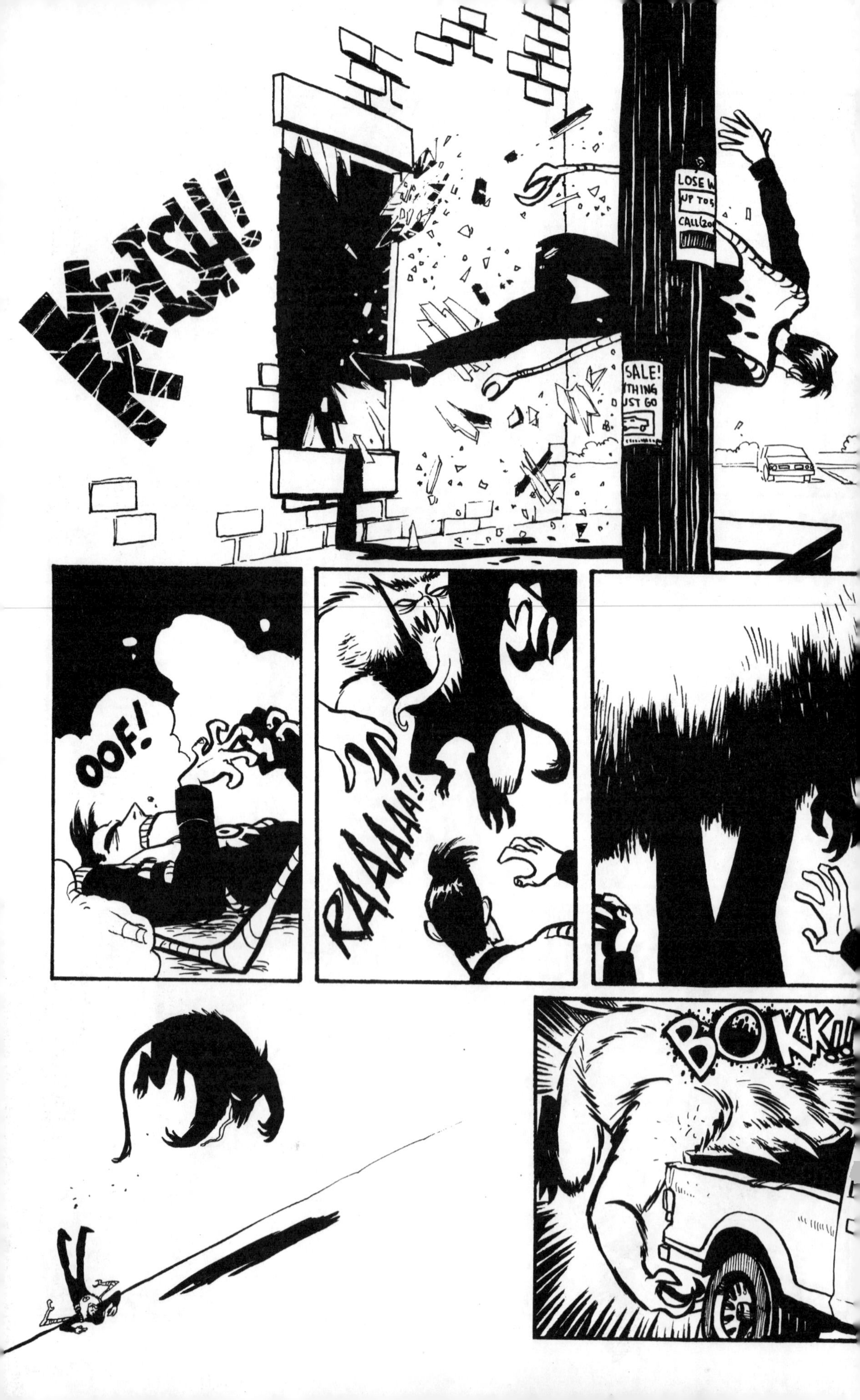
KRASH!
LOSE W
UP TO 5
CALL(20
SALE!
THING
UST GO
OOF!
RAAAAA!!
BOKK!!

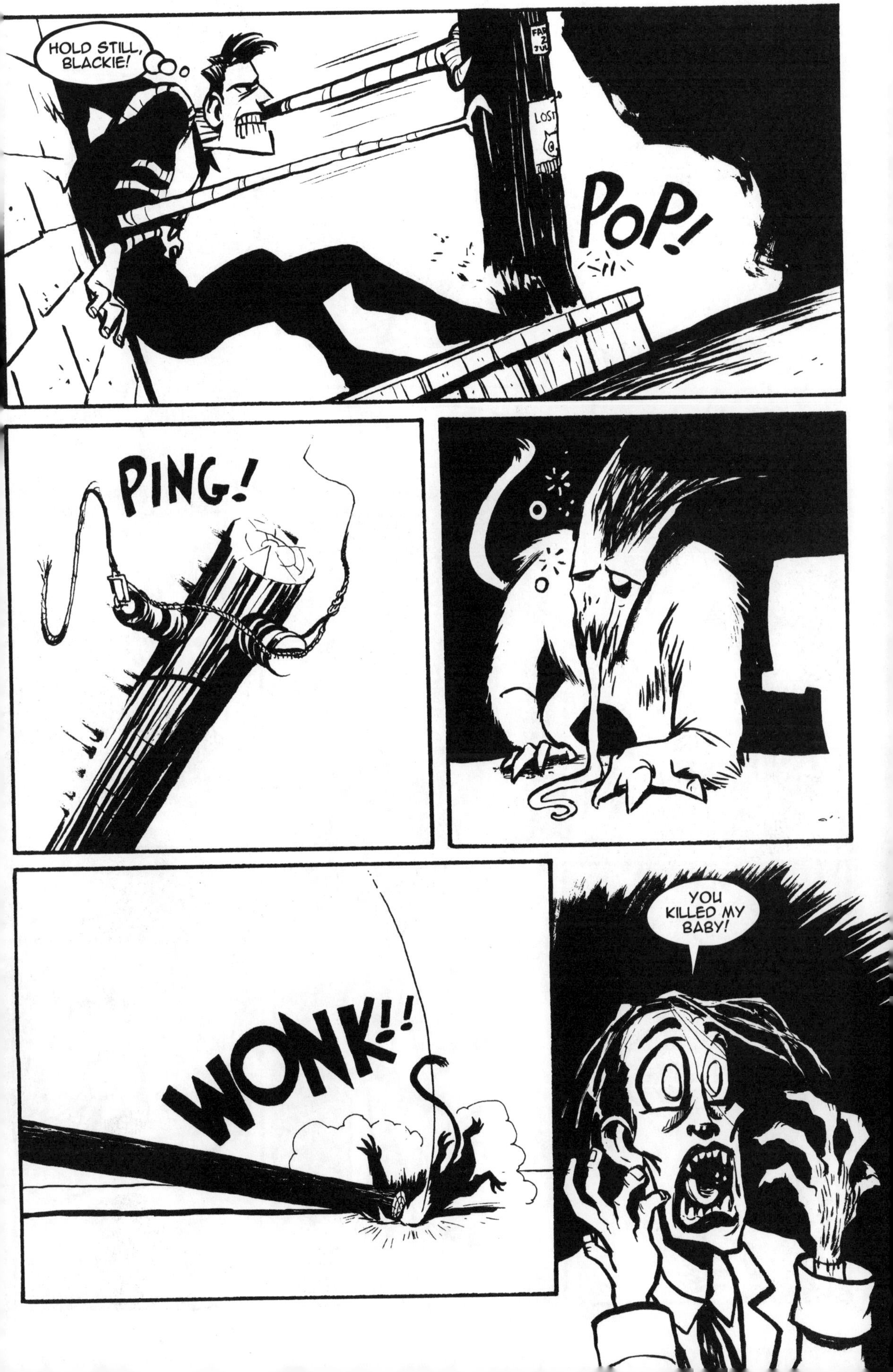
HOLD STILL, BLACKIE!
LOST
POP!
PING!
WONK!!
YOU KILLED MY BABY!

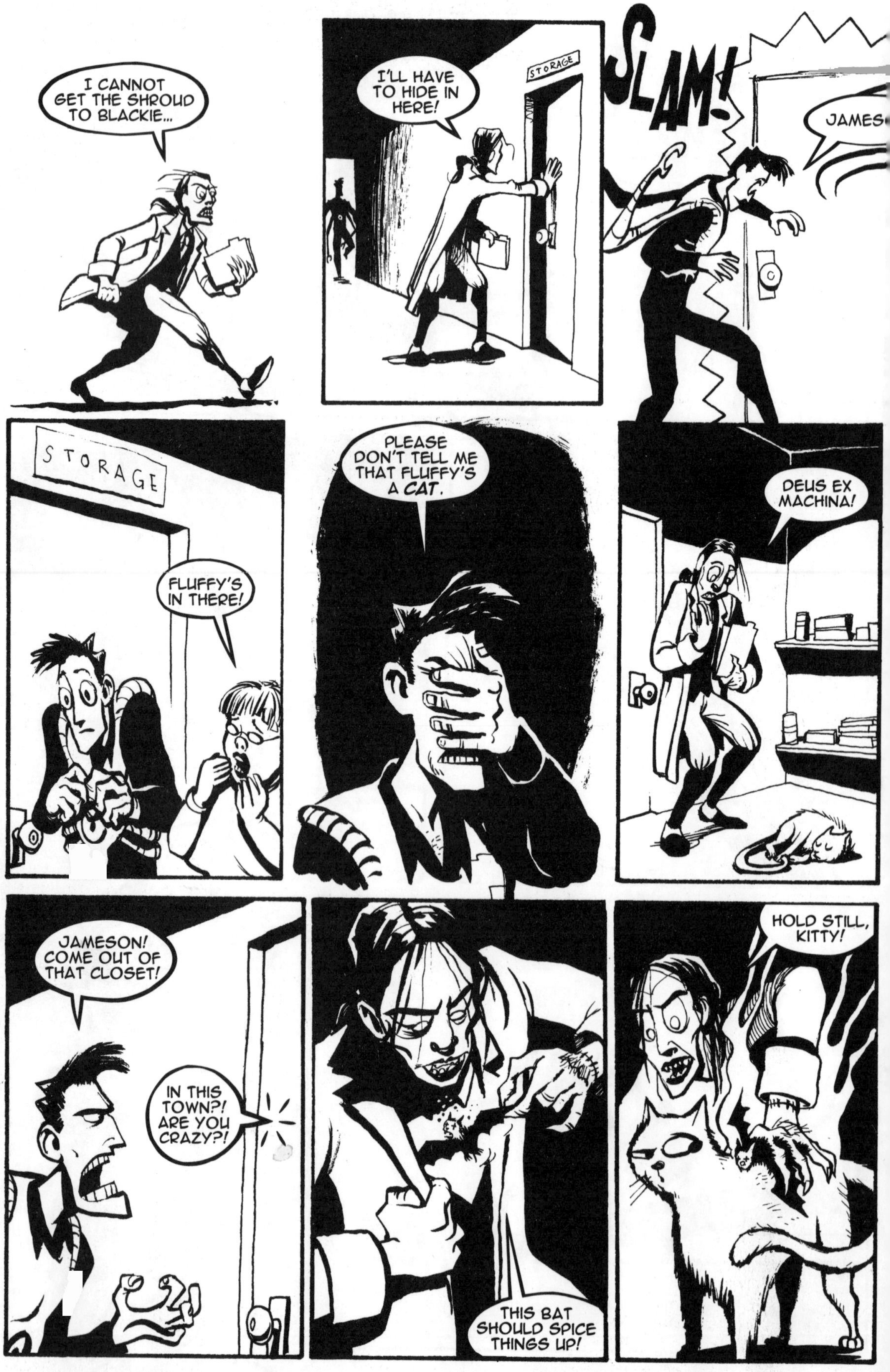
I CANNOT GET THE SHROUD TO BLACKIE...
I'LL HAVE TO HIDE IN HERE!
STORAGE
SLAM!
JAMES
STORAGE
FLUFFY'S IN THERE!
PLEASE DON'T TELL ME THAT FLUFFY'S A *CAT*.
DEUS EX MACHINA!
JAMESON! COME OUT OF THAT CLOSET!
IN THIS TOWN?! ARE YOU CRAZY?!
THIS BAT SHOULD SPICE THINGS UP!
HOLD STILL, KITTY!

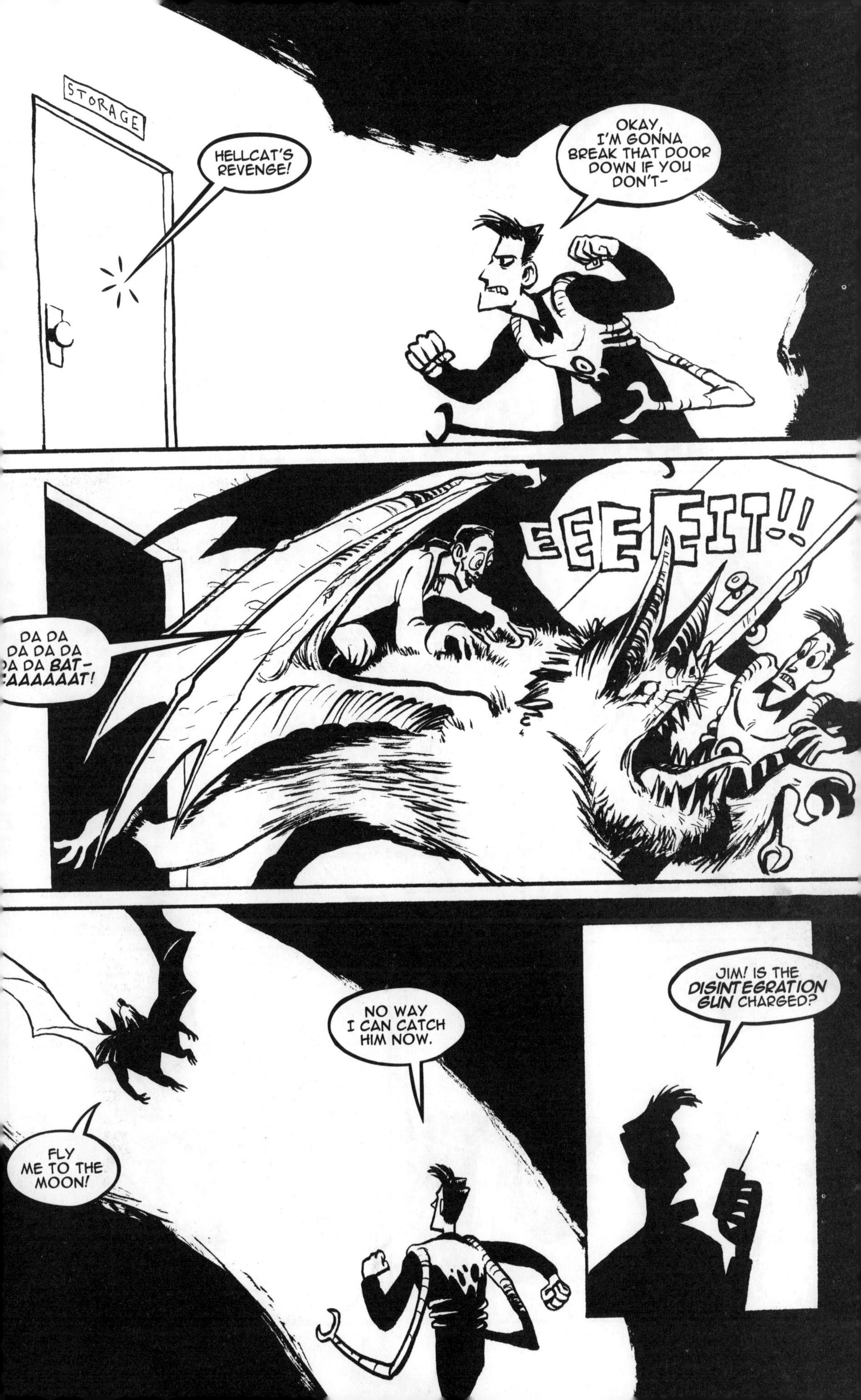
STORAGE
HELLCAT'S REVENGE!
OKAY, I'M GONNA BREAK THAT DOOR DOWN IF YOU DON'T-
EEEEIT!!
DA DA DA DA DA DA DA BAT-CAAAAAAAT!
FLY ME TO THE MOON!
NO WAY I CAN CATCH HIM NOW.
JIM! IS THE DISINTEGRATION GUN CHARGED?

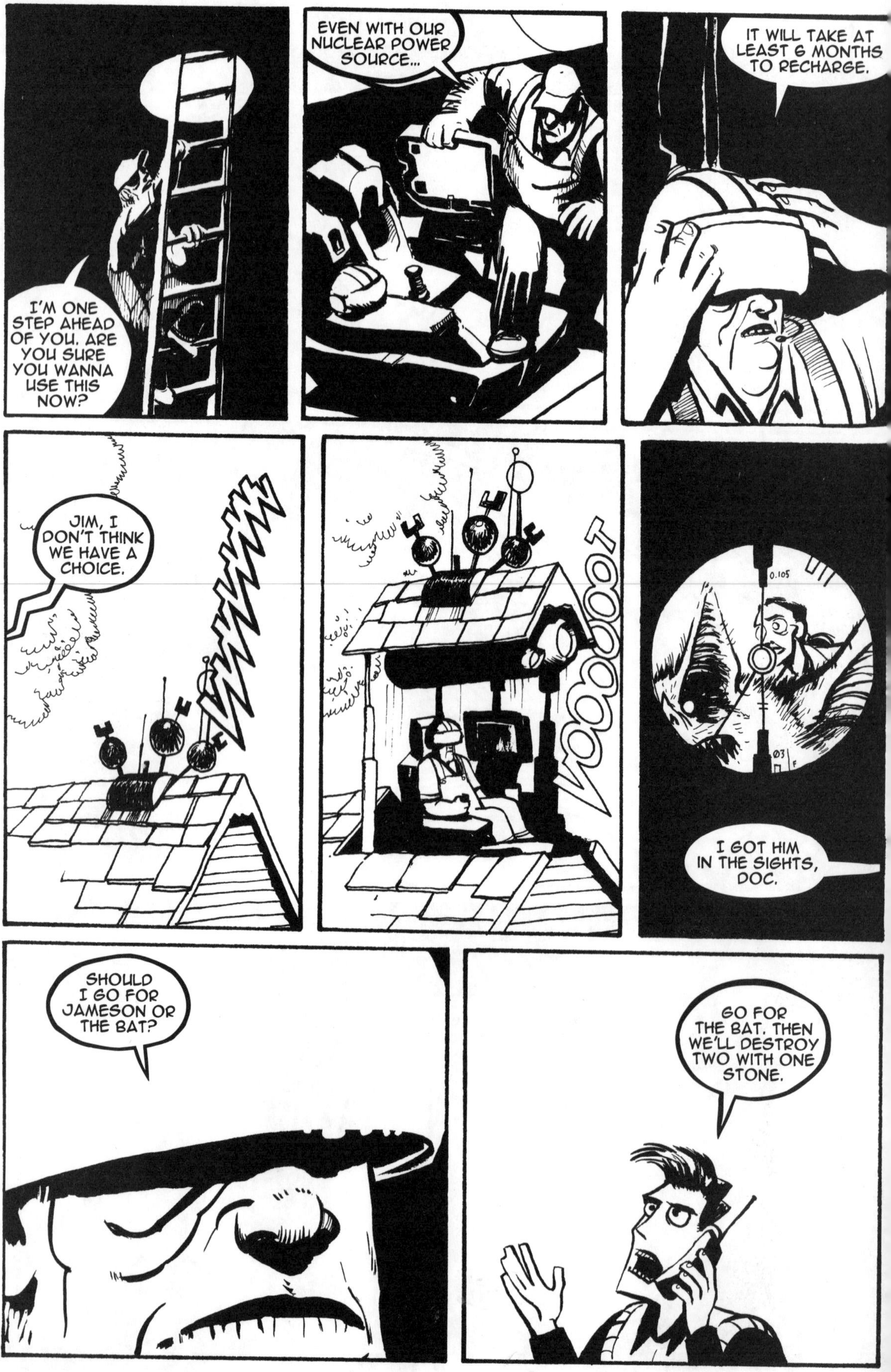
I'M ONE STEP AHEAD OF YOU. ARE YOU SURE YOU WANNA USE THIS NOW?
EVEN WITH OUR NUCLEAR POWER SOURCE...
IT WILL TAKE AT LEAST 6 MONTHS TO RECHARGE.
JIM, I DON'T THINK WE HAVE A CHOICE.
VVVVVVVVVVV
VOOOOOOOT
0.105
I GOT HIM IN THE SIGHTS, DOC.
SHOULD I GO FOR JAMESON OR THE BAT?
GO FOR THE BAT. THEN WE'LL DESTROY TWO WITH ONE STONE.

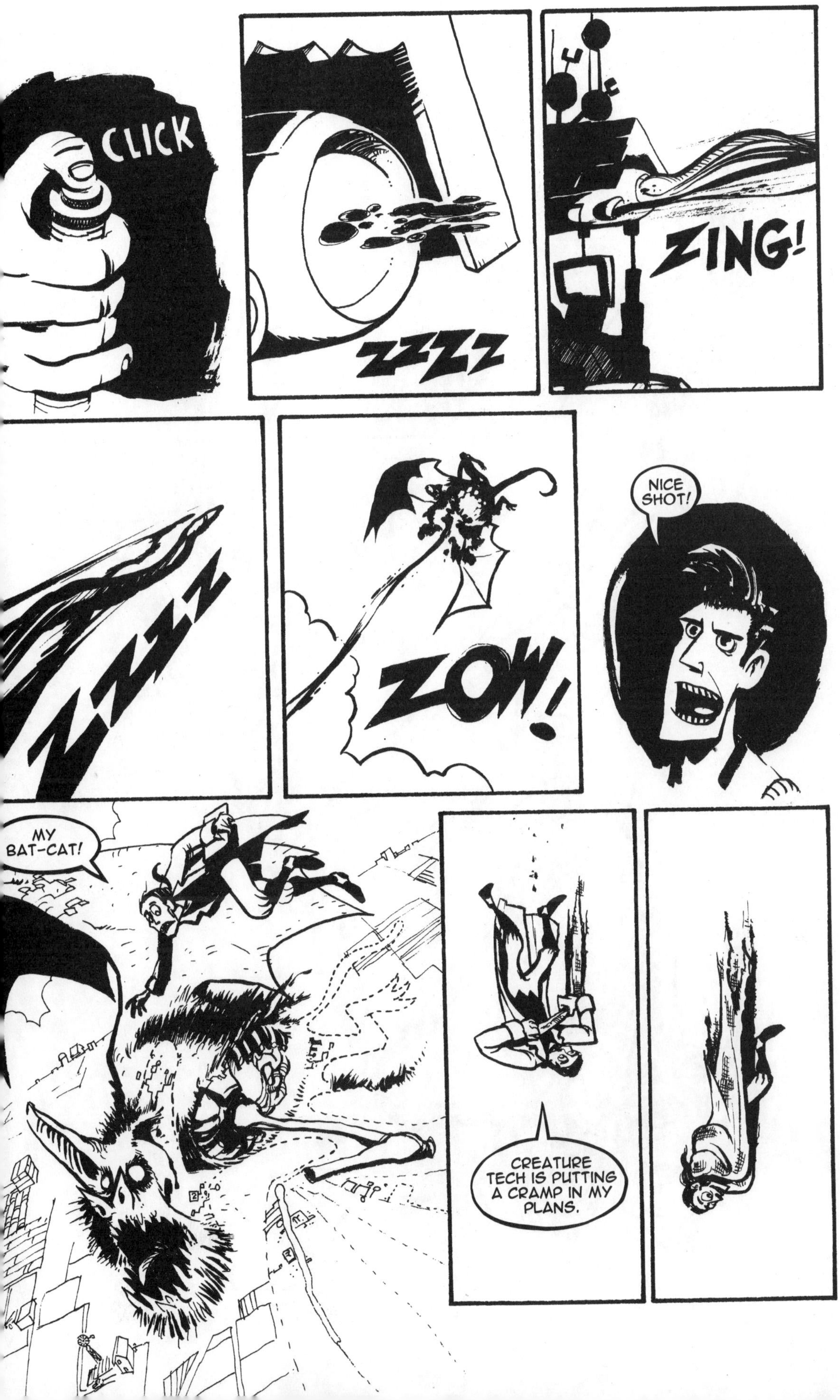
CLICK
ZZZZ
ZING!
ZZZZ
ZOW!
NICE SHOT!
MY BAT-CAT!
CREATURE TECH IS PUTTING A CRAMP IN MY PLANS.

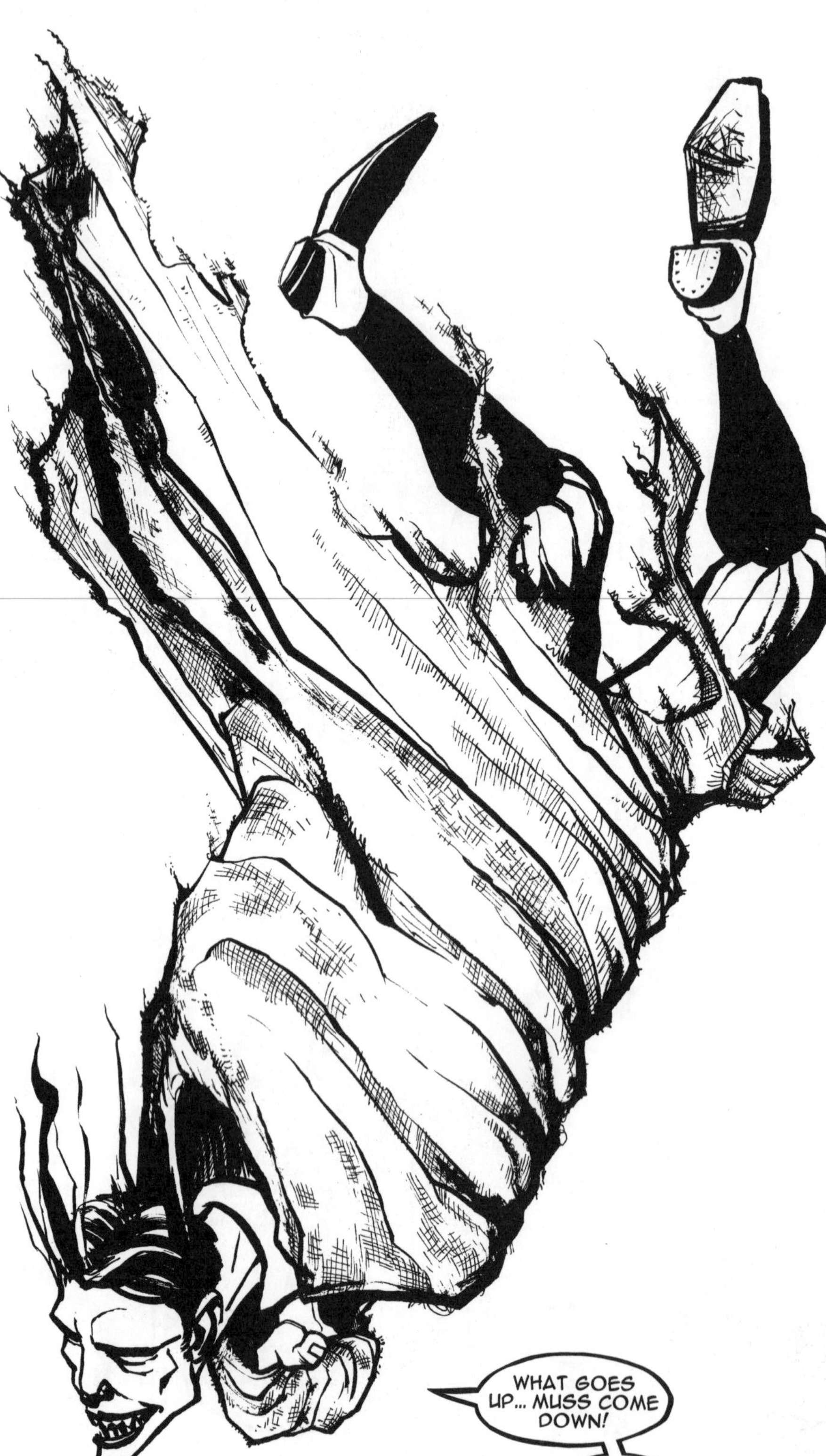
WHAT GOES UP... MUSS COME DOWN!
SPINNIN' WHEEL...

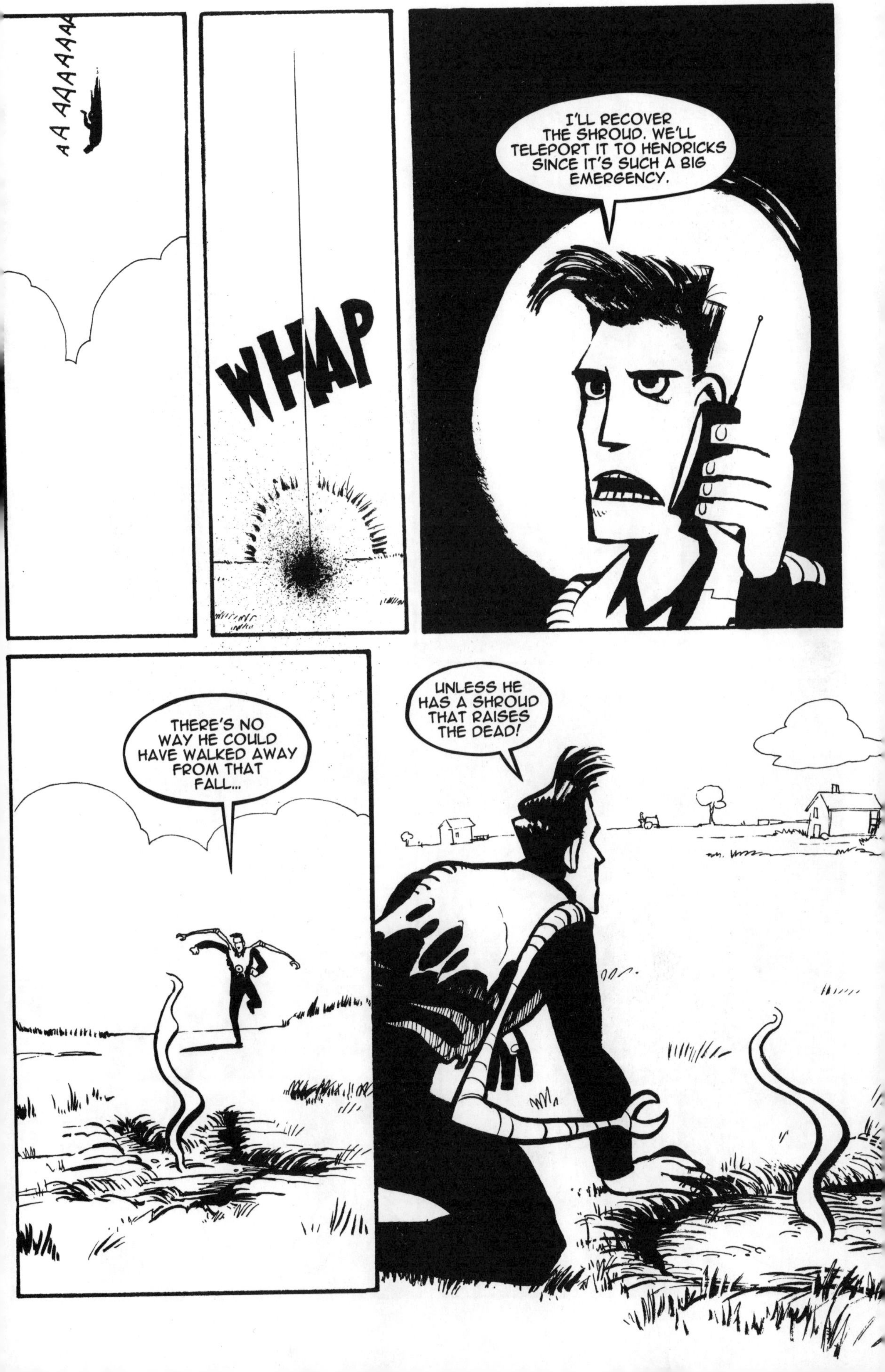
AAAAAAAAA
WHAP
I'LL RECOVER THE SHROUD. WE'LL TELEPORT IT TO HENDRICKS SINCE IT'S SUCH A BIG EMERGENCY.
THERE'S NO WAY HE COULD HAVE WALKED AWAY FROM THAT FALL...
UNLESS HE HAS A SHROUD THAT RAISES THE DEAD!

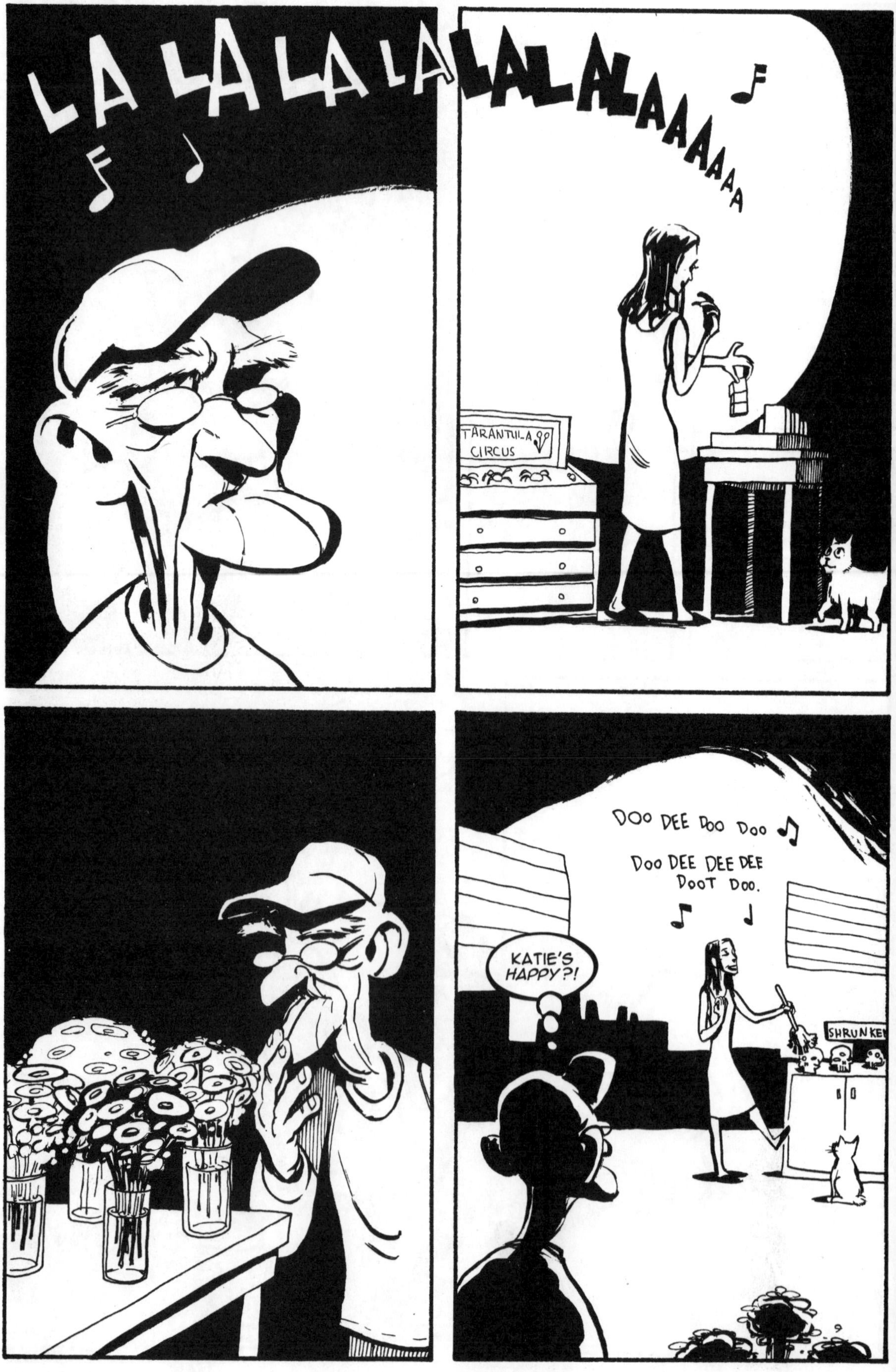
LA LA LA LA LA LALALALAAAAAAAA
TARANTULA CIRCUS
DOO DEE DOO DOO
DOO DEE DEE DEE DOOT DOO.
KATIE'S HAPPY?!
SHRUNKE

HE GOT AWAY.

COME SEE WHAT I'VE FOUND.

THIS IS OUR INVENTORY OF 763 CRATES.

RESEARCH TECH

Crate Number		Warehouse Location	7
			7
693		G7	
694		M2	
695		L5	
696	✓	A	
697		A2	
698		L5	
699		K4	7
700		M4	7
701		B2	7
702	✓	G6	7
703		G6	7
		L5	7
	✓	K3	7
		L5	
7		Ø2	

WE'RE TO STRICTLY ADHERE TO THE NUMERICAL ORDER FOR OPENING THEM.

SO WHY DID HENDRICKS HAVE US JUMP AHEAD TO *CRATE 759* WHICH HAPPENED TO HOUSE THE SHROUD OF TURIN?

I FOUND THIS *INTERNAL MEMO* WHERE CRATES 758 THROUGH 763 WERE BUILT TO CONTAIN *SUPERNATURAL* ARTIFACTS.

SIGNED BY HENDRICKS.

WHAT'S *THIS?*

A NEWS PUBLICATION FROM 1830.

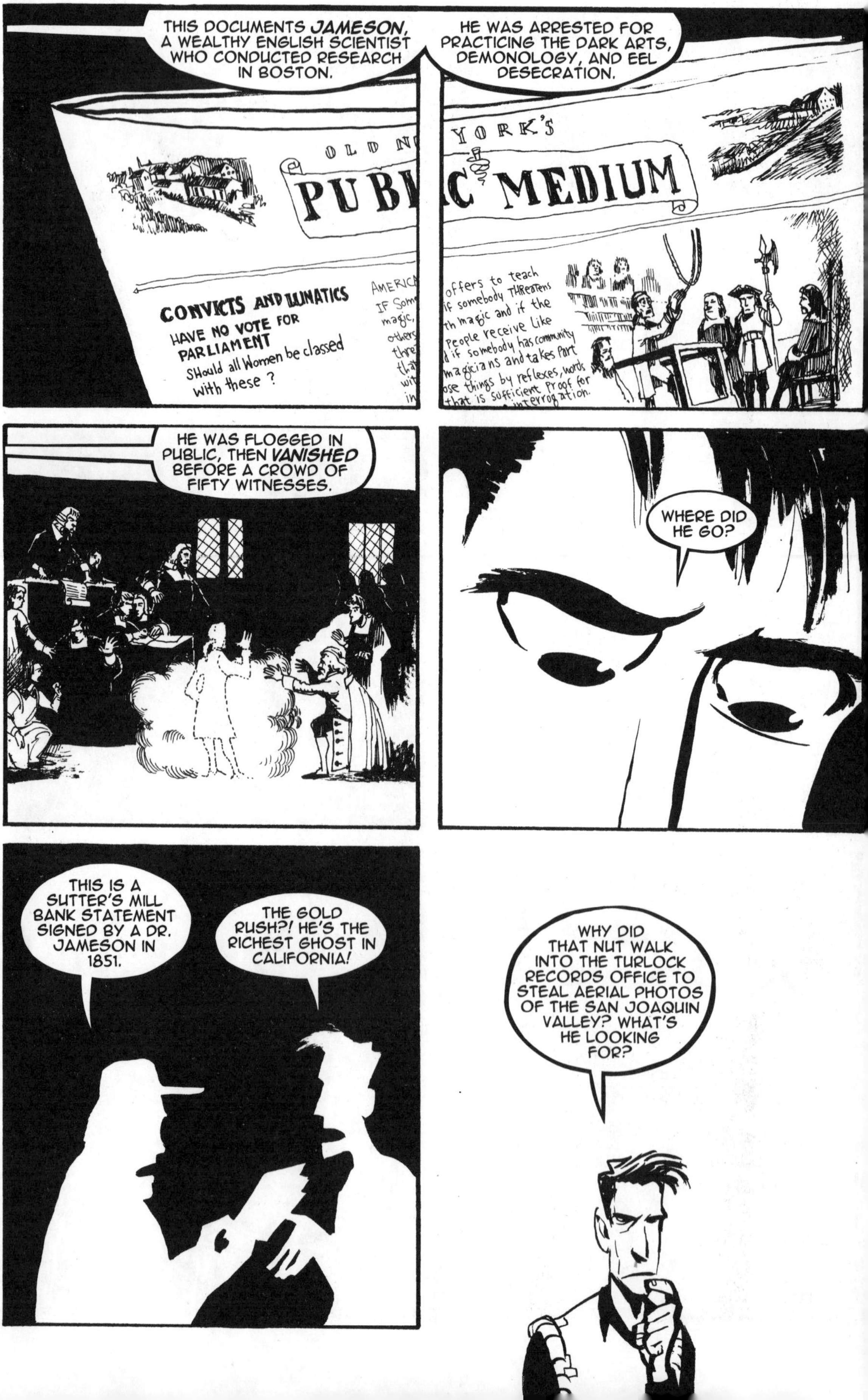

THIS DOCUMENTS JAMESON, A WEALTHY ENGLISH SCIENTIST WHO CONDUCTED RESEARCH IN BOSTON.
HE WAS ARRESTED FOR PRACTICING THE DARK ARTS, DEMONOLOGY, AND EEL DESECRATION.
CONVICTS AND LUNATICS
HAVE NO VOTE FOR PARLIAMENT
SHould all Women be classed with these ?
HE WAS FLOGGED IN PUBLIC, THEN VANISHED BEFORE A CROWD OF FIFTY WITNESSES.
WHERE DID HE GO?
THIS IS A SUTTER'S MILL BANK STATEMENT SIGNED BY A DR. JAMESON IN 1851.
THE GOLD RUSH?! HE'S THE RICHEST GHOST IN CALIFORNIA!
WHY DID THAT NUT WALK INTO THE TURLOCK RECORDS OFFICE TO STEAL AERIAL PHOTOS OF THE SAN JOAQUIN VALLEY? WHAT'S HE LOOKING FOR?

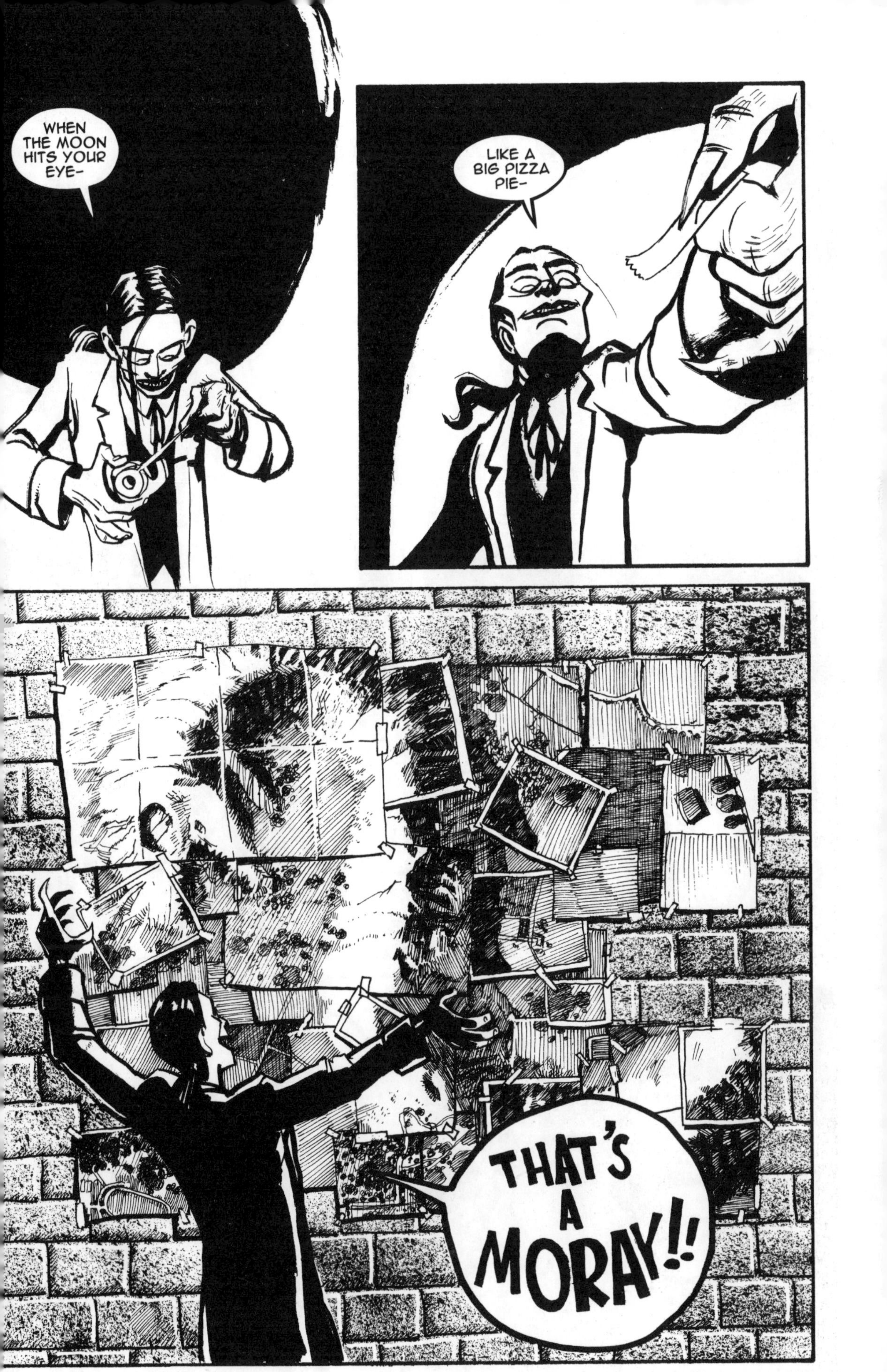
WHEN THE MOON HITS YOUR EYE-
LIKE A BIG PIZZA PIE-
THAT'S A MORAY!!

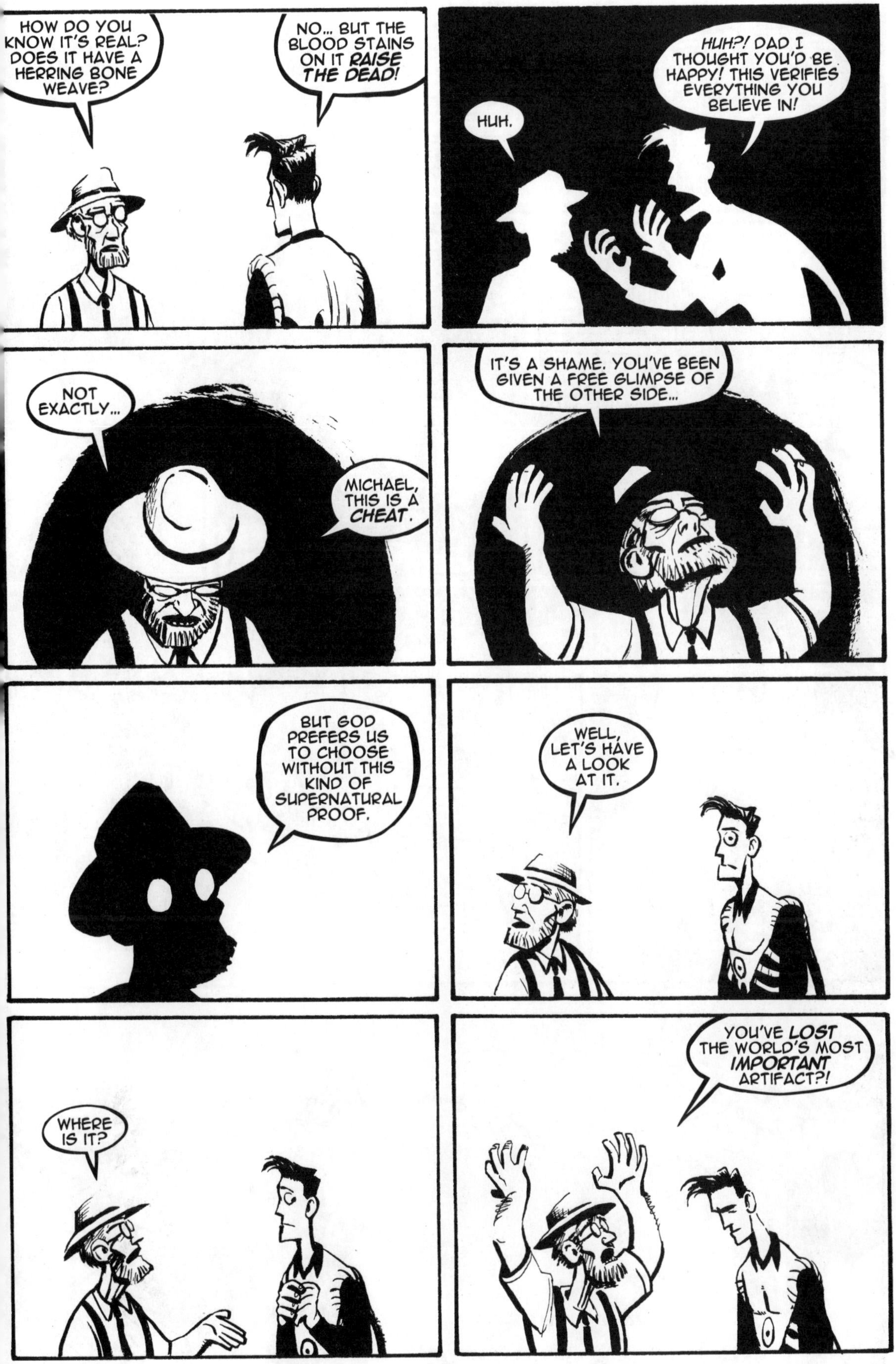
HOW DO YOU KNOW IT'S REAL? DOES IT HAVE A HERRING BONE WEAVE?
NO... BUT THE BLOOD STAINS ON IT *RAISE THE DEAD!*
HUH.
HUH?! DAD I THOUGHT YOU'D BE HAPPY! THIS VERIFIES EVERYTHING YOU BELIEVE IN!
NOT EXACTLY...
MICHAEL, THIS IS A *CHEAT*.
IT'S A SHAME. YOU'VE BEEN GIVEN A FREE GLIMPSE OF THE OTHER SIDE...
BUT GOD PREFERS US TO CHOOSE WITHOUT THIS KIND OF SUPERNATURAL PROOF.
WELL, LET'S HAVE A LOOK AT IT.
WHERE IS IT?
YOU'VE *LOST* THE WORLD'S MOST *IMPORTANT* ARTIFACT?!

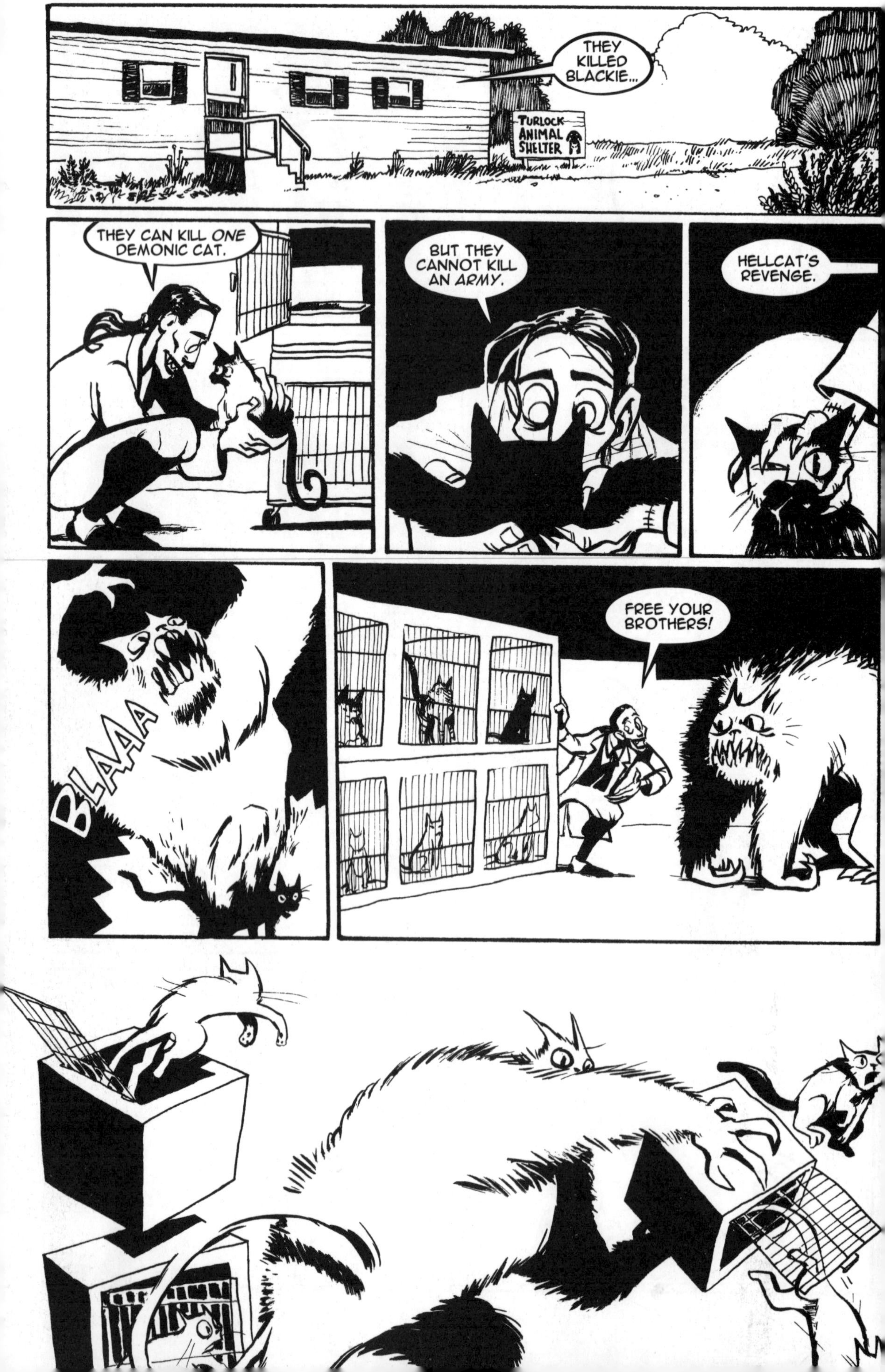
THEY KILLED BLACKIE...
TURLOCK ANIMAL SHELTER
THEY CAN KILL ONE DEMONIC CAT.
BUT THEY CANNOT KILL AN ARMY.
HELLCAT'S REVENGE.
BLAAAA
FREE YOUR BROTHERS!

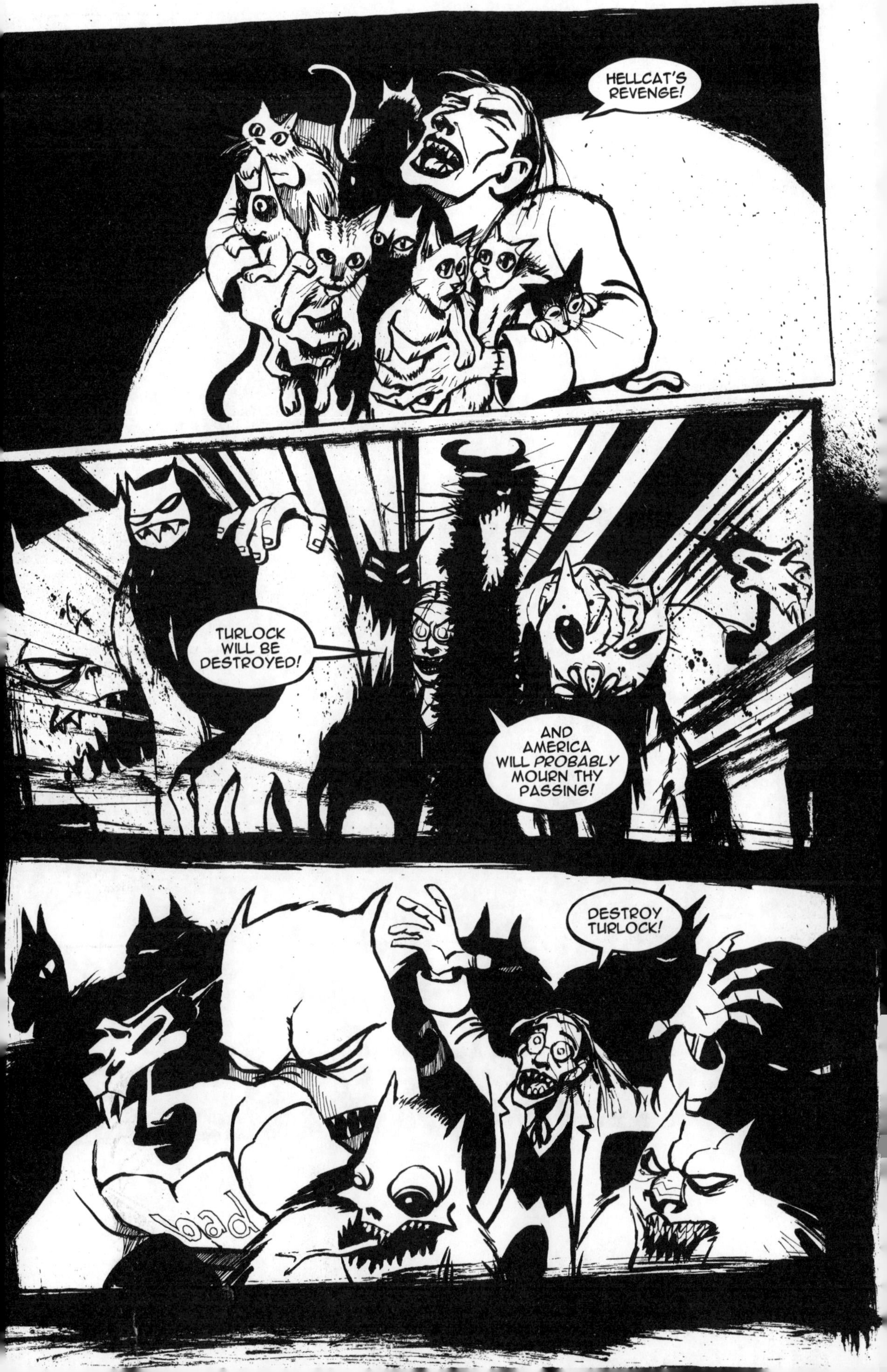
HELLCAT'S REVENGE!
TURLOCK WILL BE DESTROYED!
AND AMERICA WILL PROBABLY MOURN THY PASSING!
DESTROY TURLOCK!

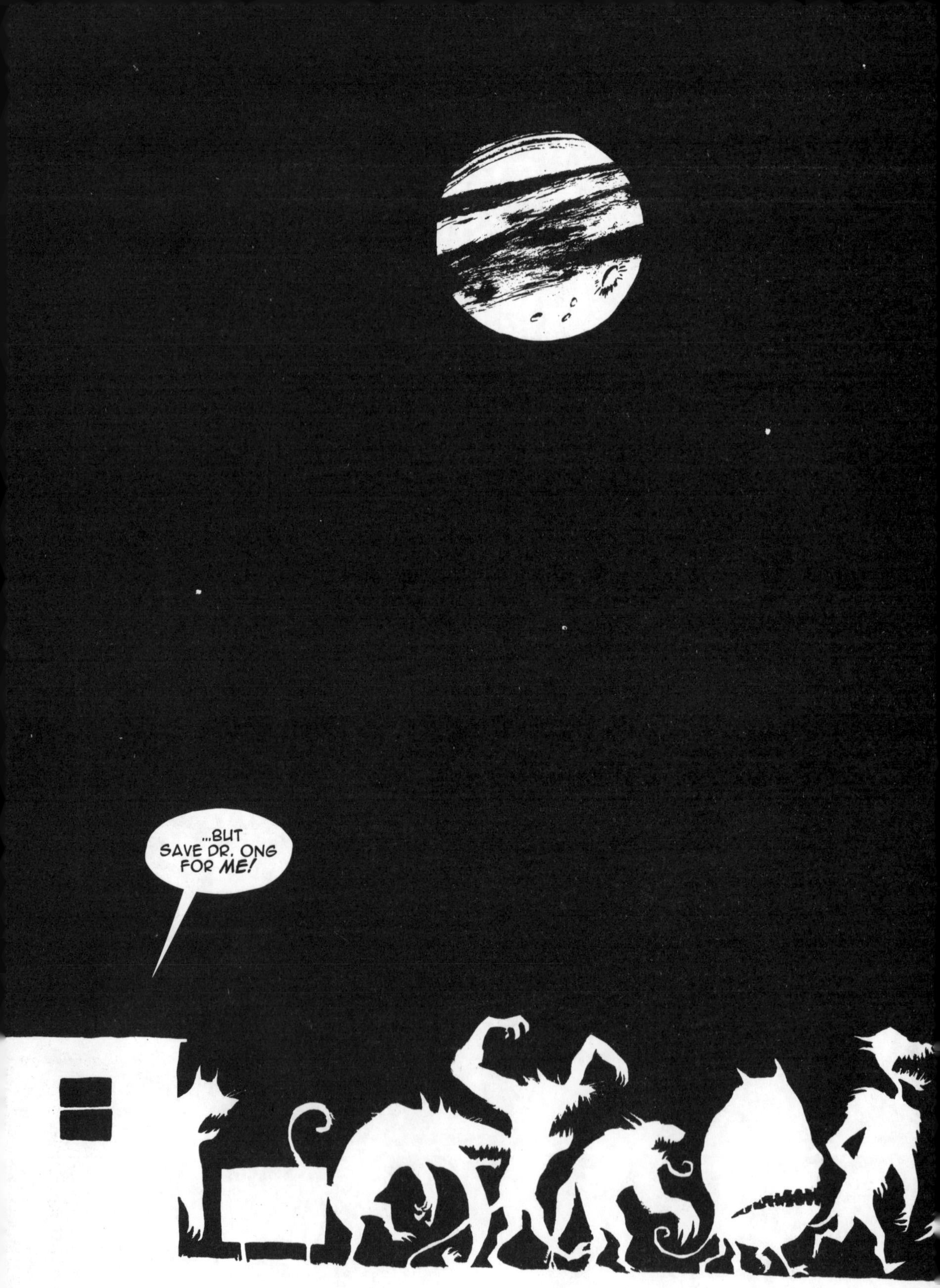
...BUT SAVE DR. ONG FOR ME!

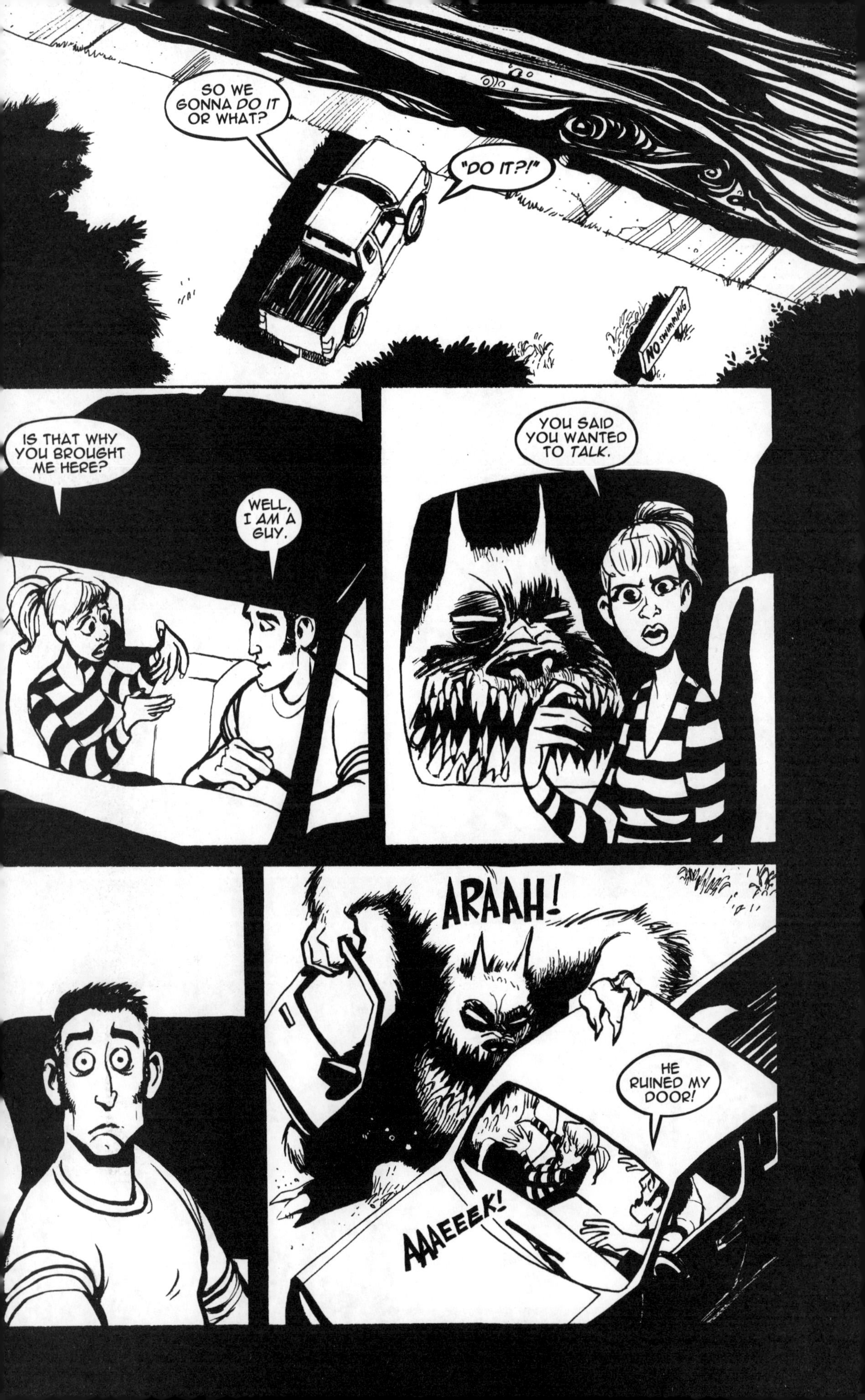

SO WE GONNA *DO IT* OR WHAT?
"DO IT?!"
NO SWIMMING
IS THAT WHY YOU BROUGHT ME HERE?
WELL, I *AM* A GUY.
YOU SAID YOU WANTED TO *TALK*.
ARAAH!
HE RUINED MY DOOR!
AAAEEEK!

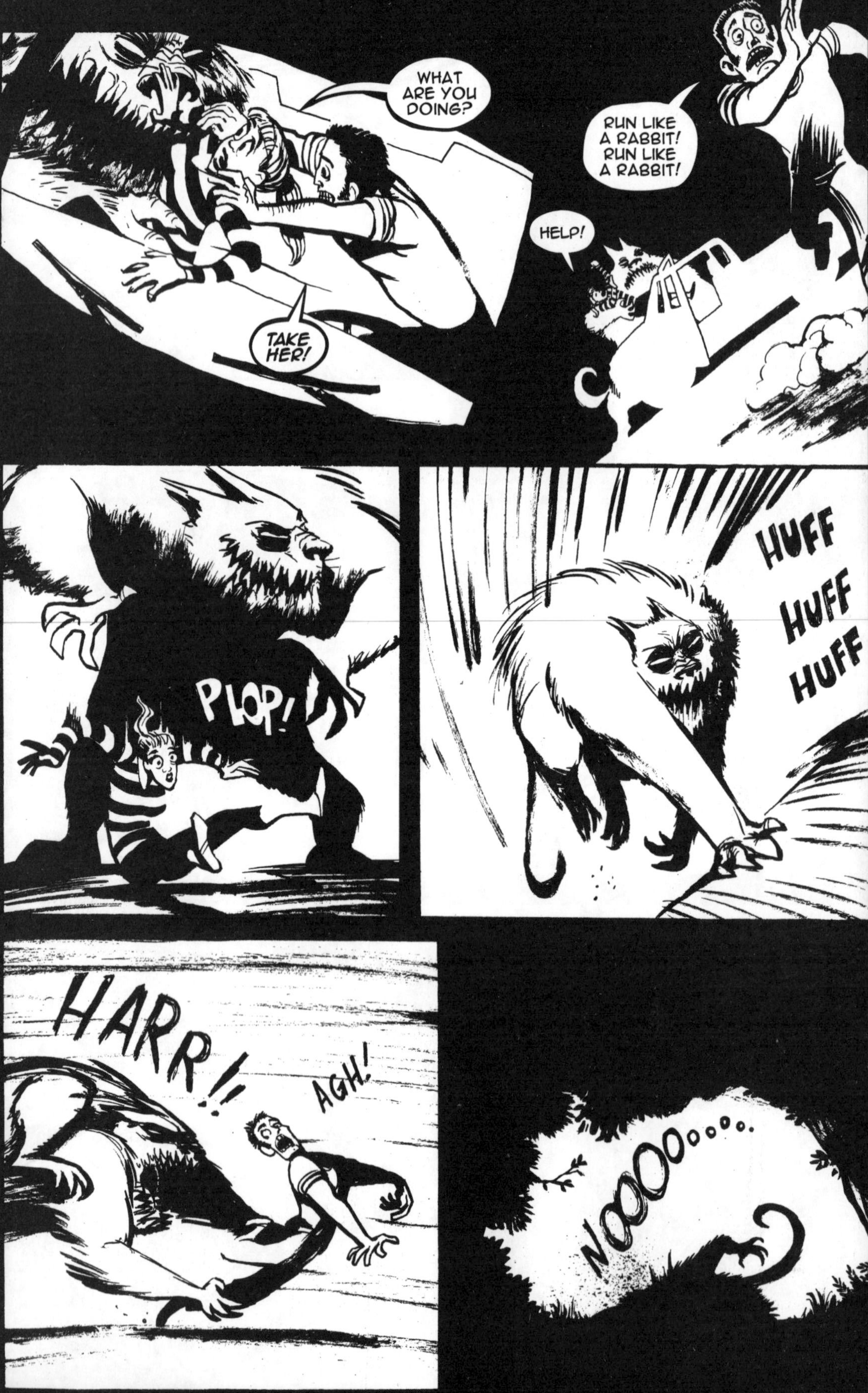
WHAT ARE YOU DOING?
TAKE HER!
RUN LIKE A RABBIT! RUN LIKE A RABBIT!
HELP!
PLOP!
HUFF
HUFF
HUFF
HARR!!
AGH!
NOOOOoooo..

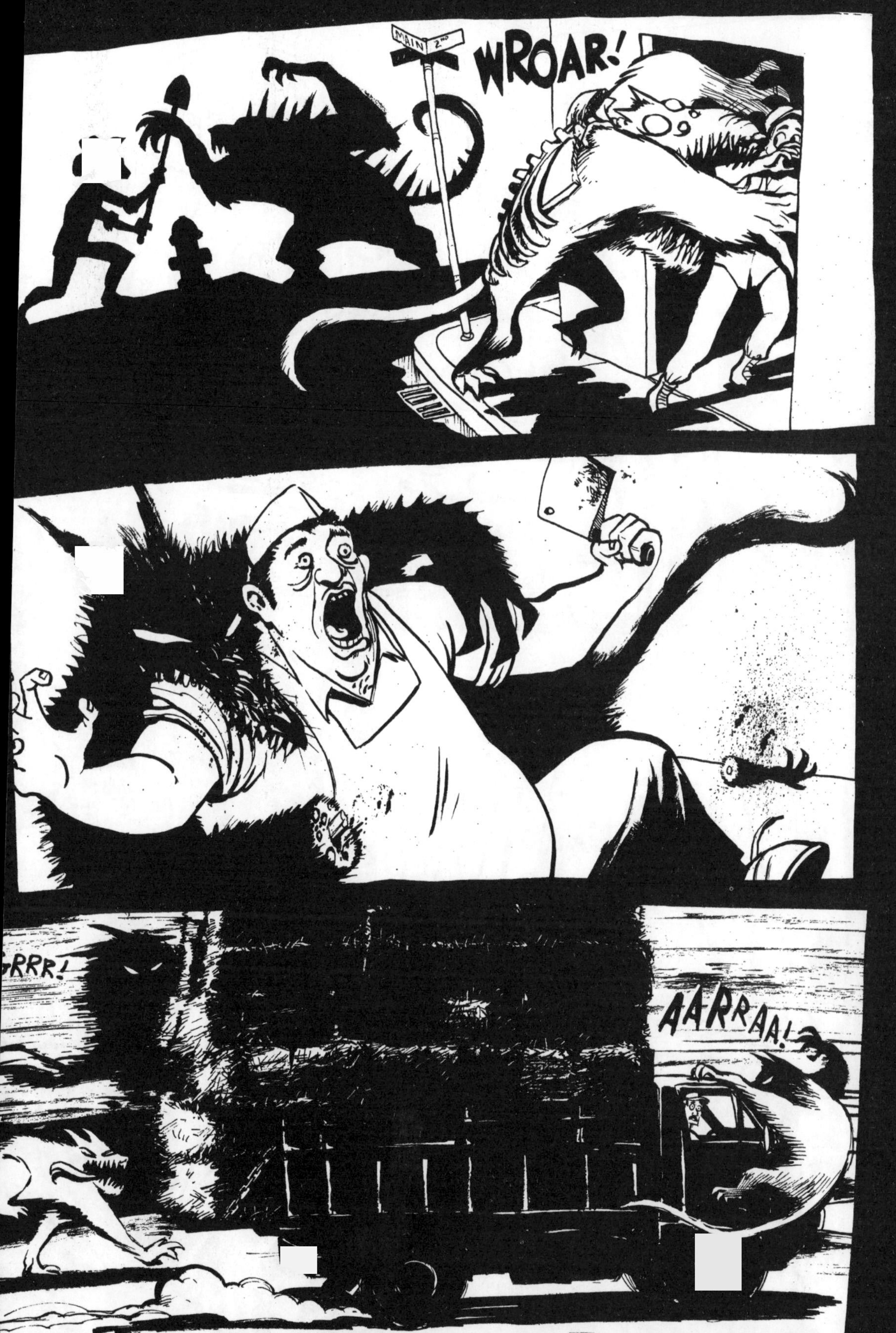
MAIN
2ND
WROAR!
GRRR!
AARRAA!

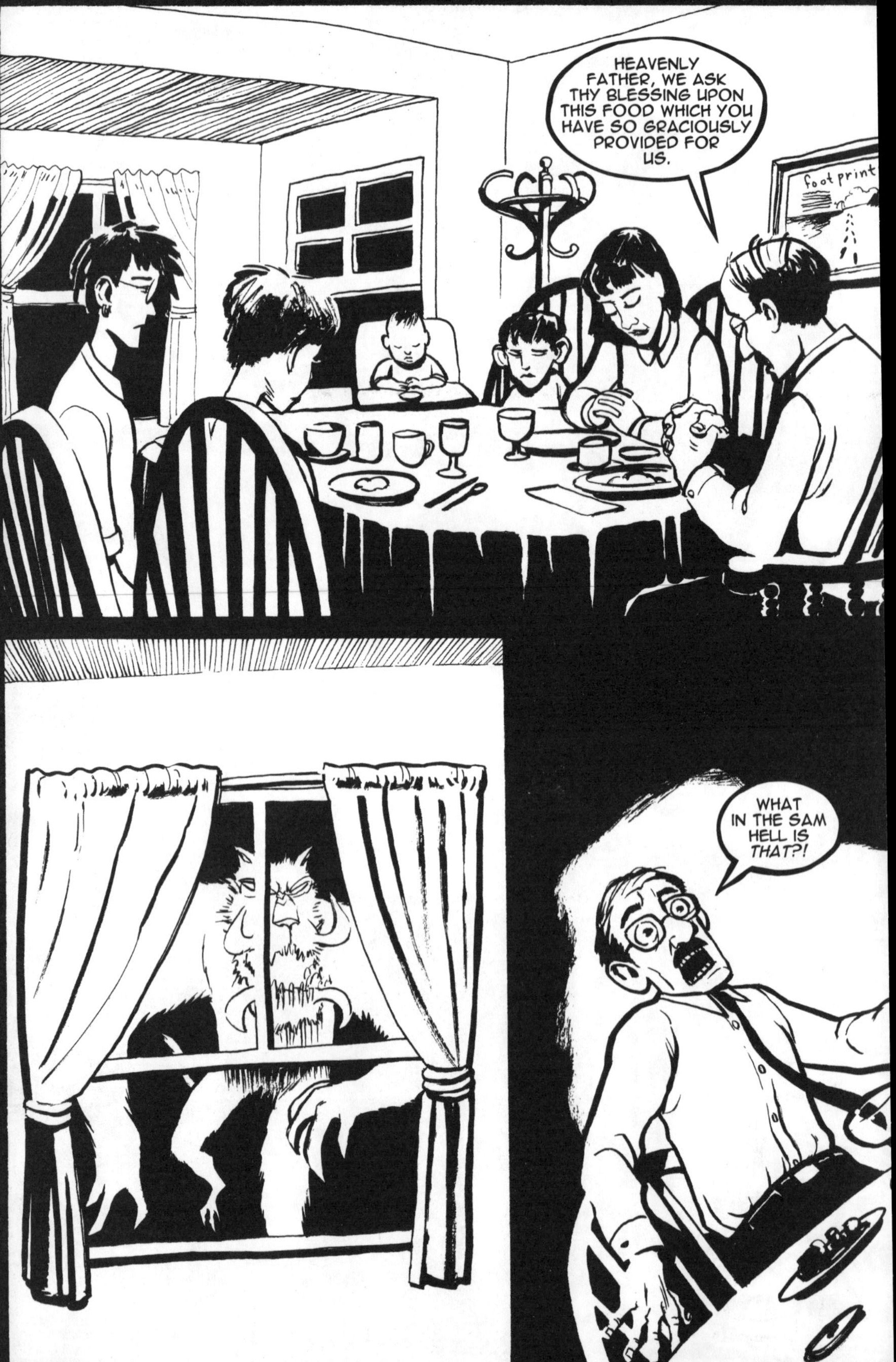
HEAVENLY FATHER, WE ASK THY BLESSING UPON THIS FOOD WHICH YOU HAVE SO GRACIOUSLY PROVIDED FOR US.
foot print
WHAT IN THE SAM HELL IS *THAT?!*

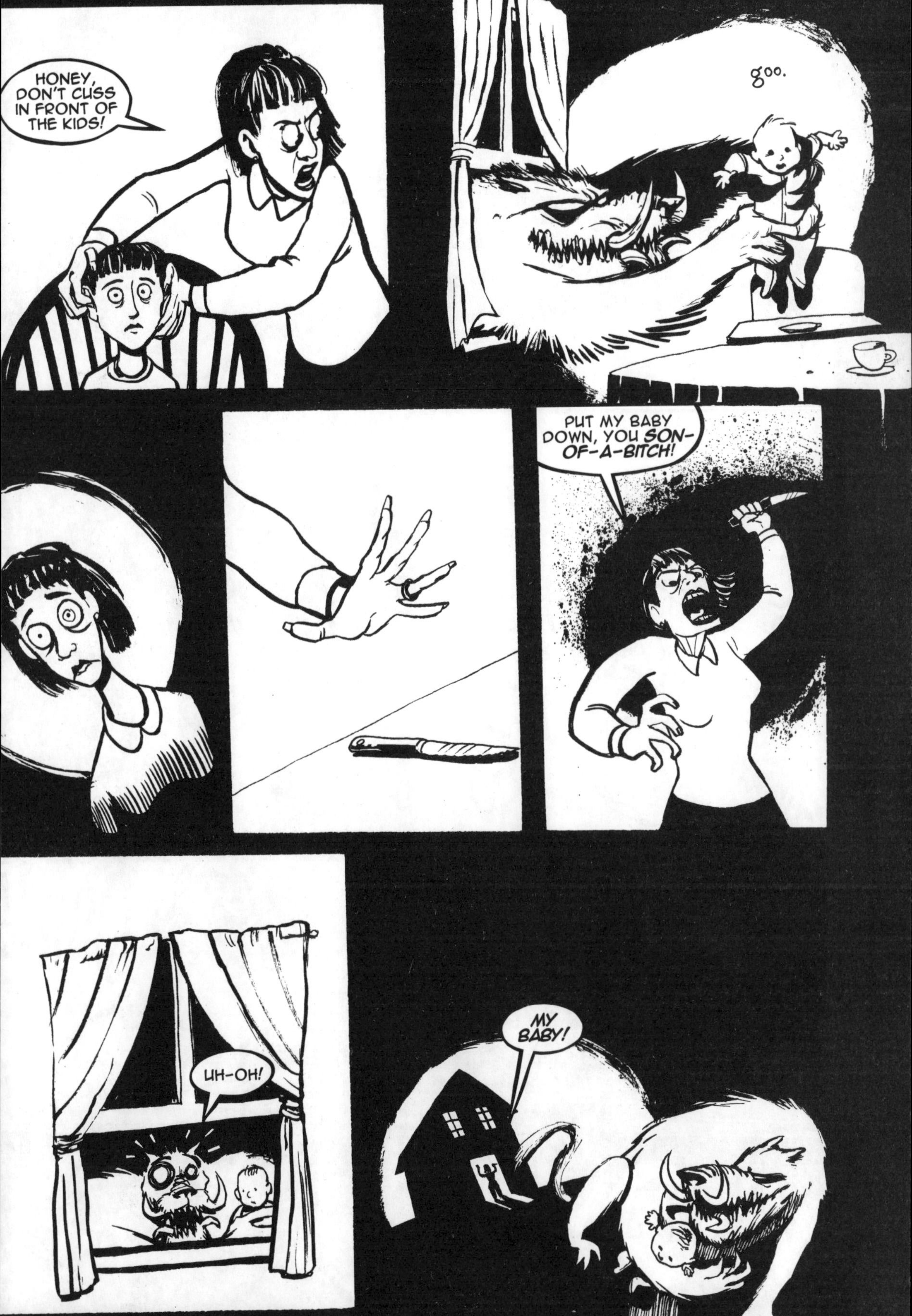
HONEY, DON'T CUSS IN FRONT OF THE KIDS!
goo.
PUT MY BABY DOWN, YOU SON-OF-A-BITCH!
UH-OH!
MY BABY!

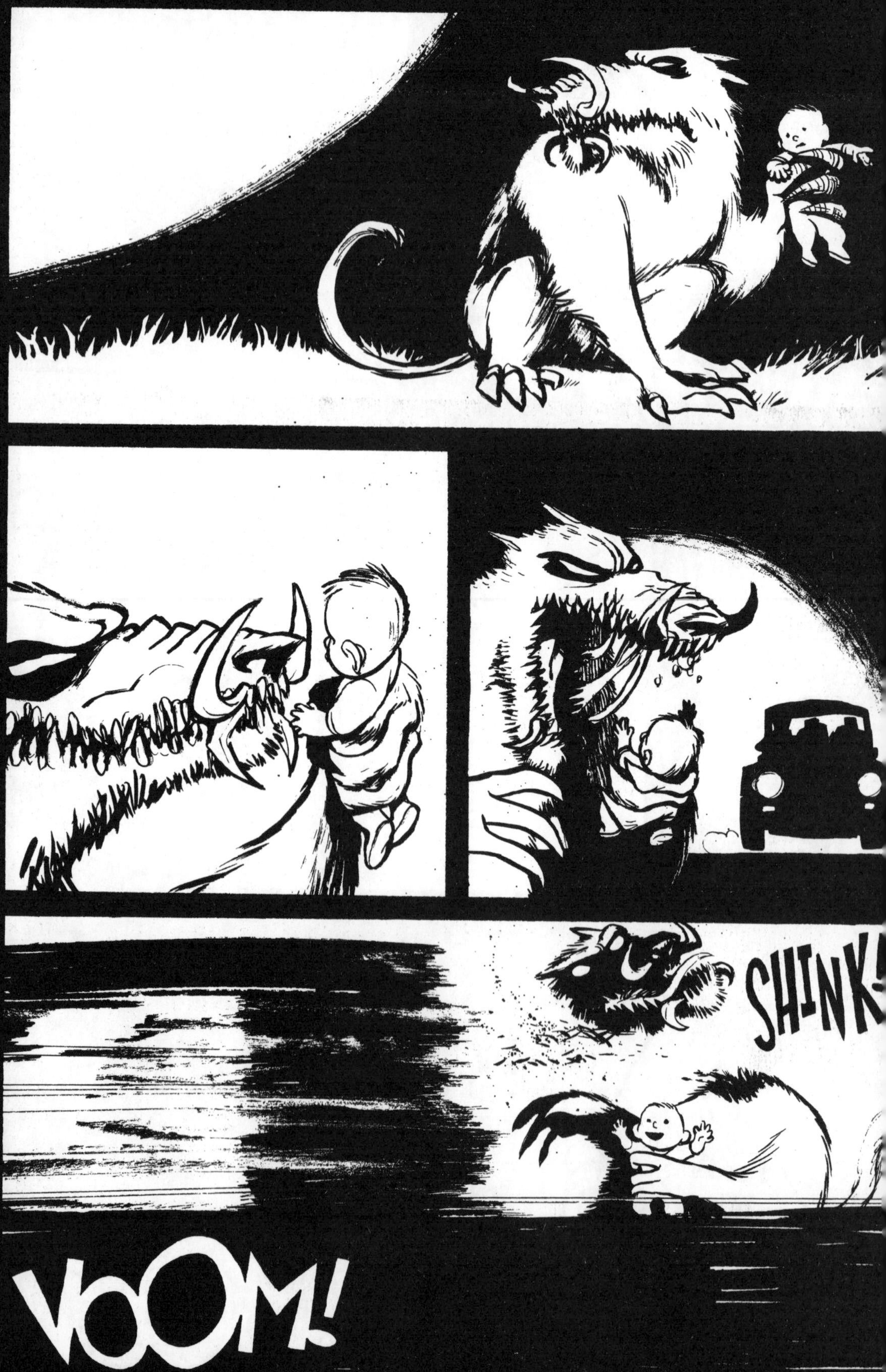
SHINK!
VOOM!

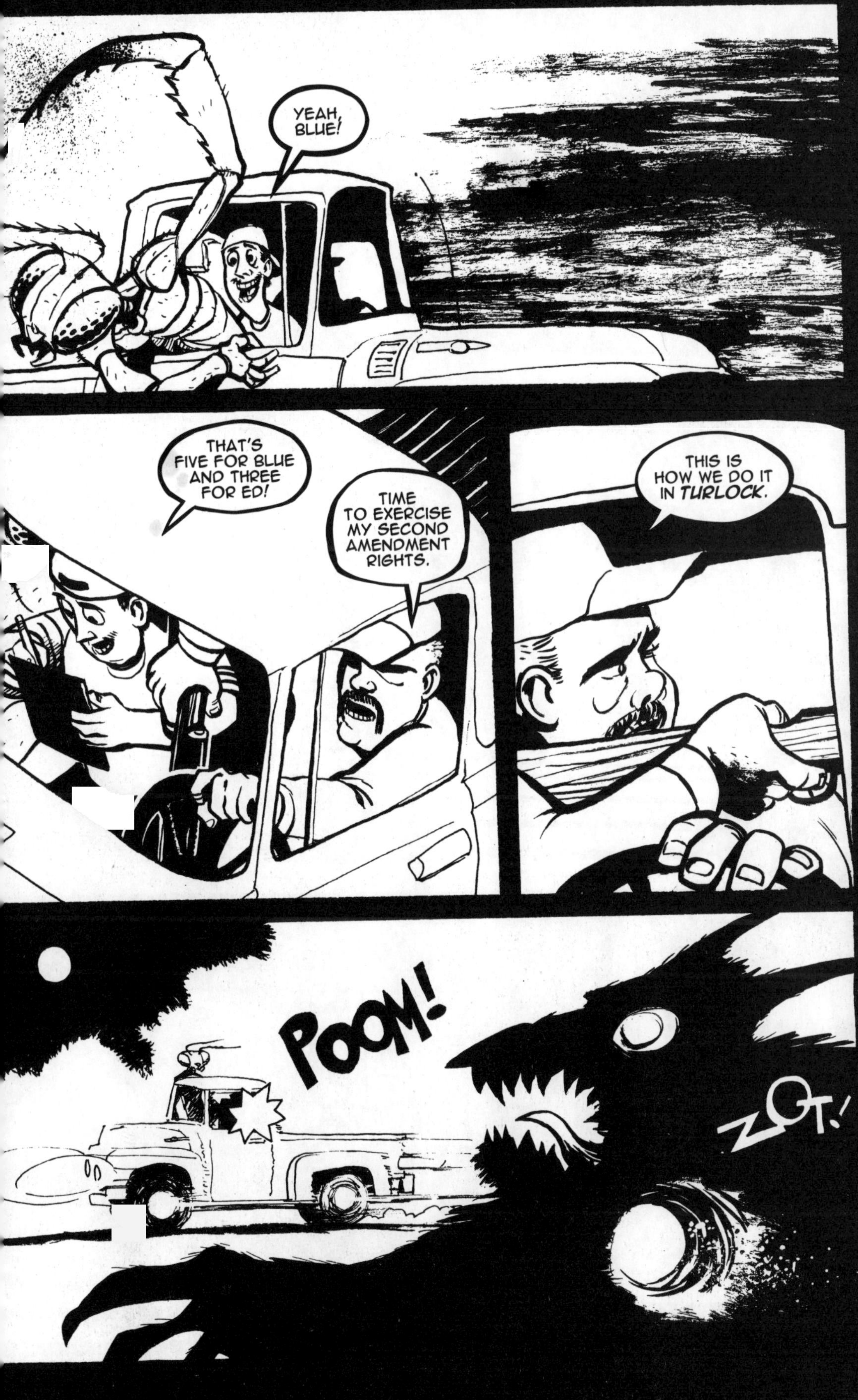
YEAH, BLUE!
THAT'S FIVE FOR BLUE AND THREE FOR ED!
TIME TO EXERCISE MY SECOND AMENDMENT RIGHTS.
THIS IS HOW WE DO IT IN *TURLOCK*.
POOM!
ZOT!

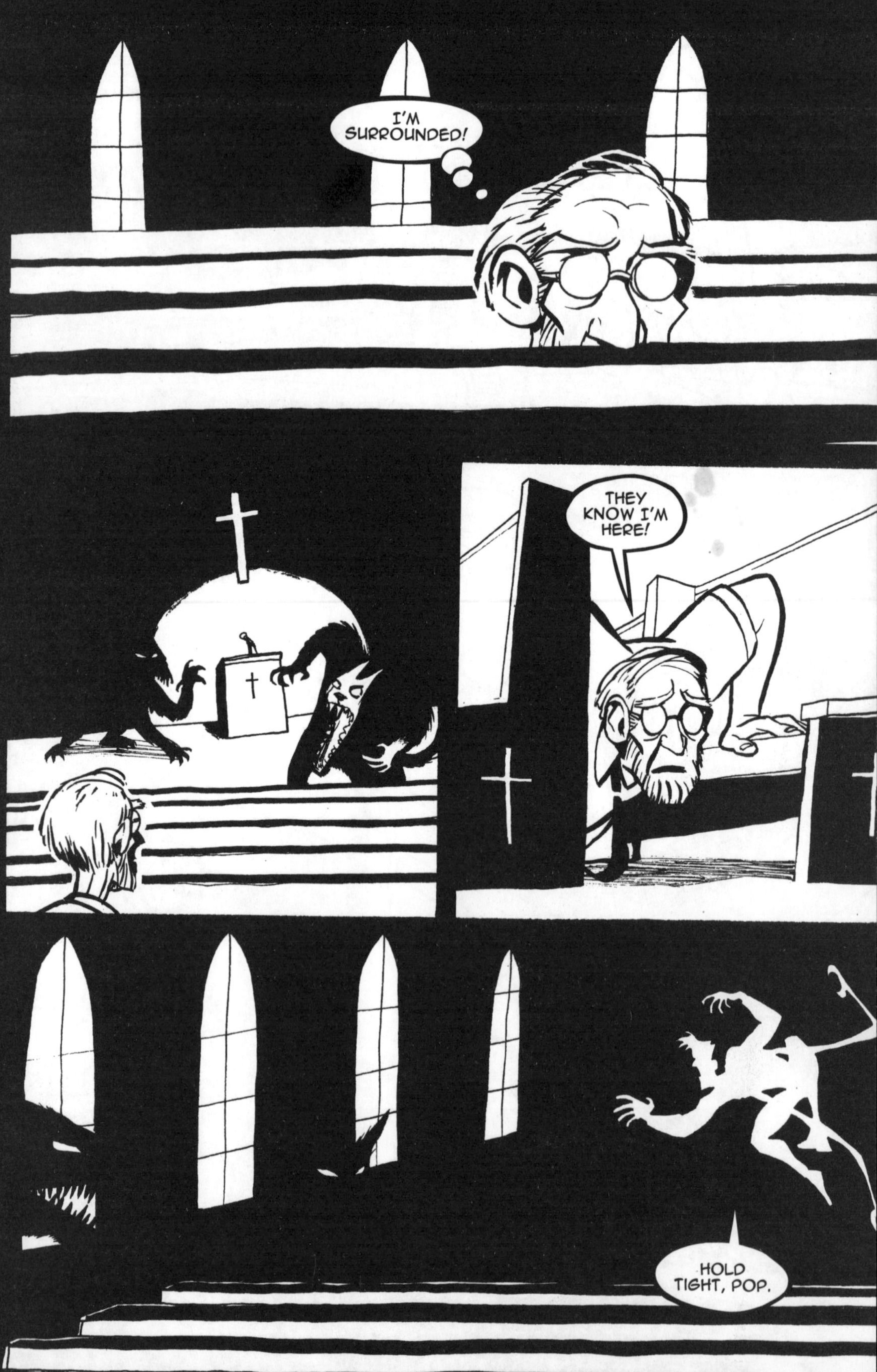
I'M SURROUNDED!
THEY KNOW I'M HERE!
HOLD TIGHT, POP.

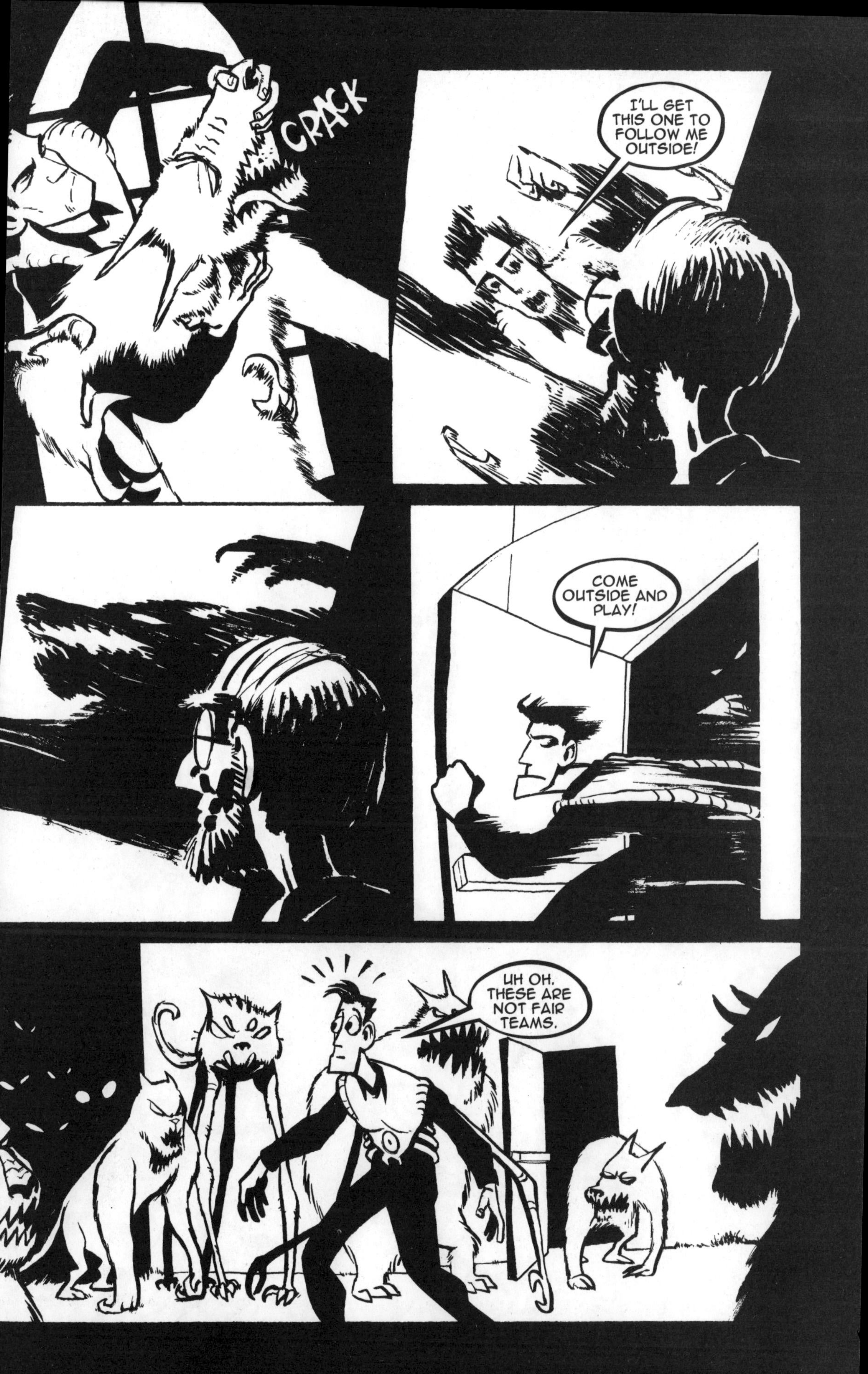

CRACK
I'LL GET THIS ONE TO FOLLOW ME OUTSIDE!
COME OUTSIDE AND PLAY!
UH OH. THESE ARE NOT FAIR TEAMS.

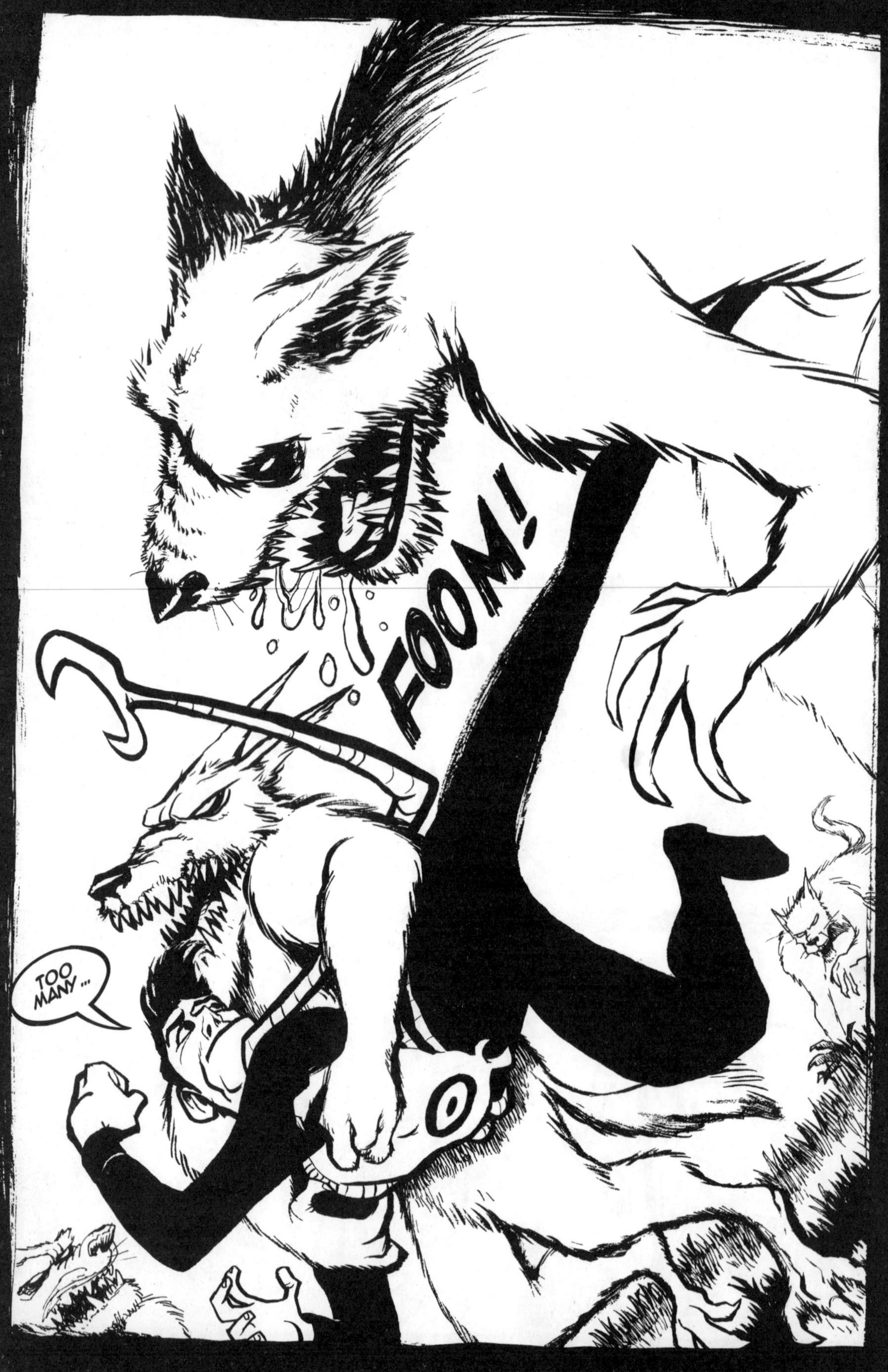
FOOM!
TOO MANY...

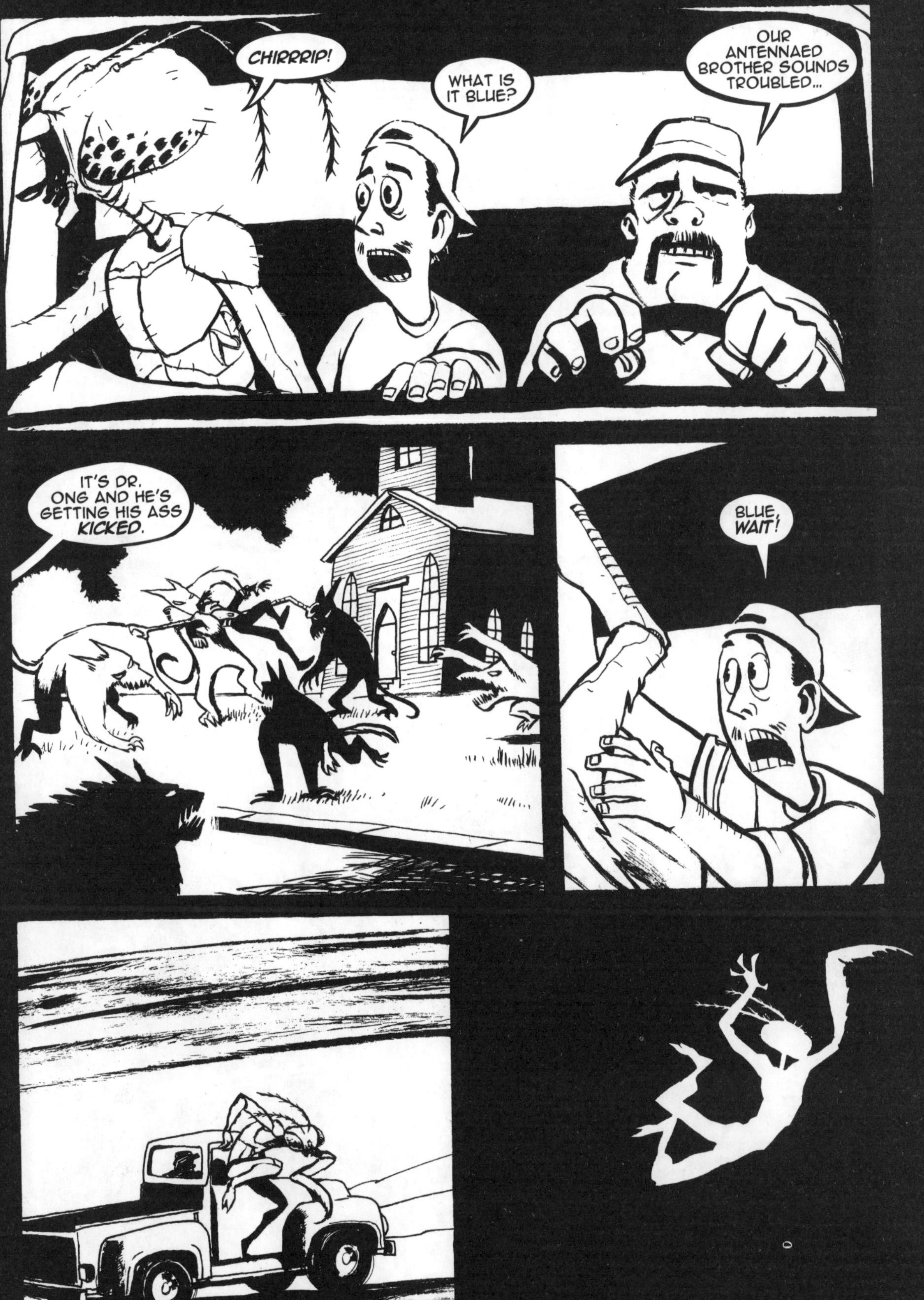
CHIRRRIP!
WHAT IS IT BLUE?
OUR ANTENNAED BROTHER SOUNDS TROUBLED...
IT'S DR. ONG AND HE'S GETTING HIS ASS KICKED.
BLUE, WAIT!

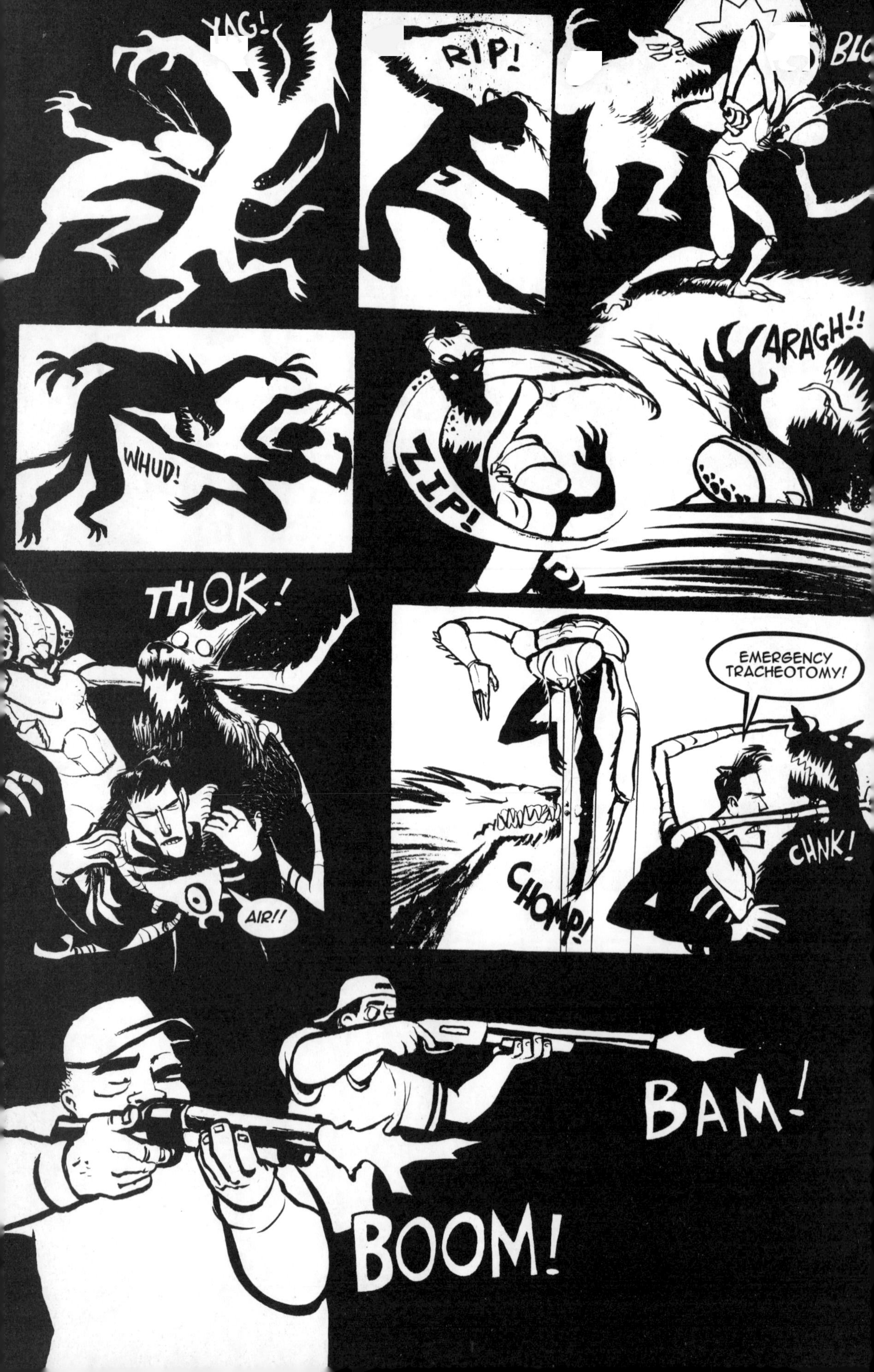
YAG!
RIP!
WHUD!
ZIP!
ARAGH!!
THOK!
AIR!!
EMERGENCY TRACHEOTOMY!
CHOMP!
CHNK!
BAM!
BOOM!

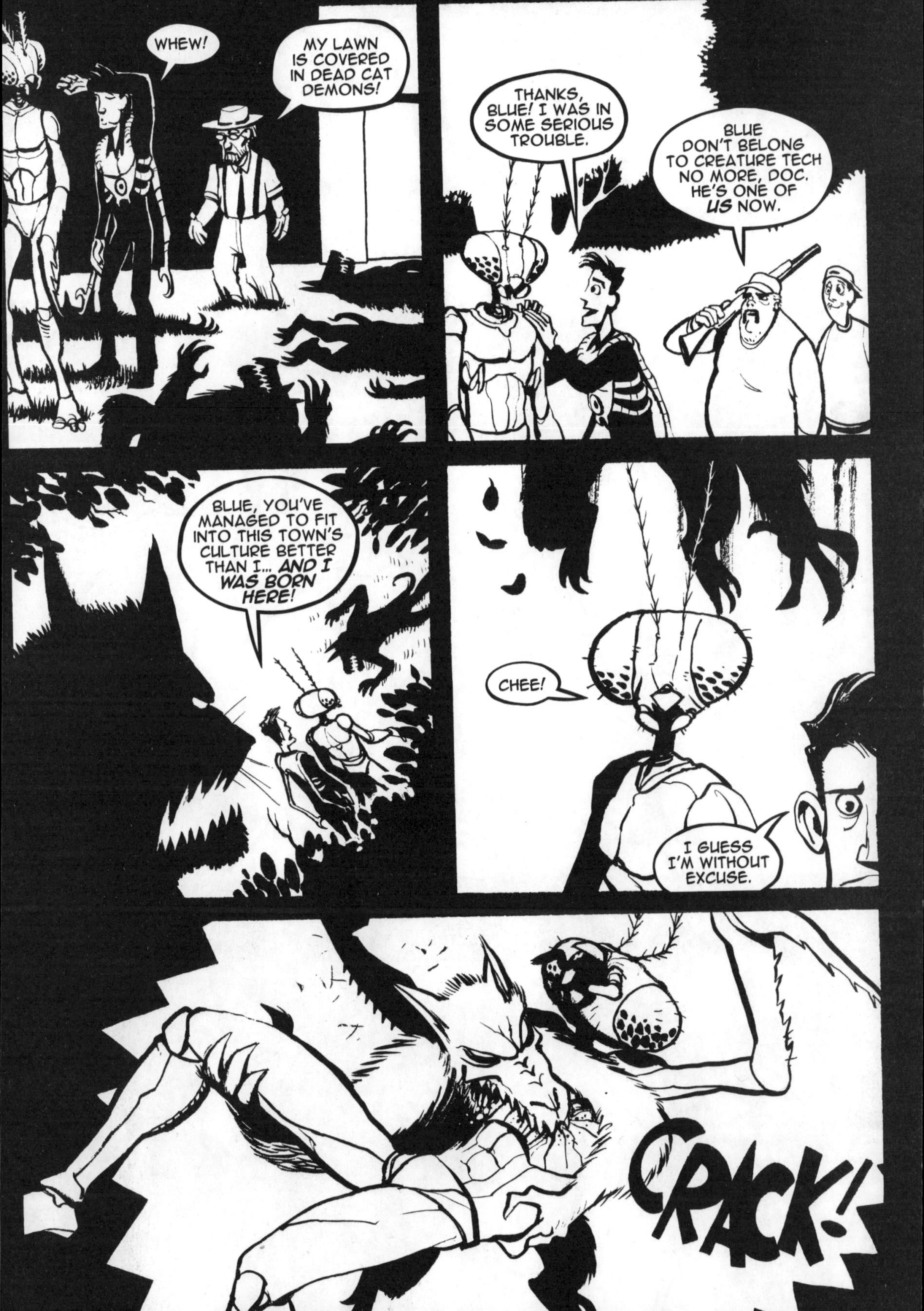
WHEW!
MY LAWN IS COVERED IN DEAD CAT DEMONS!
THANKS, BLUE! I WAS IN SOME SERIOUS TROUBLE.
BLUE DON'T BELONG TO CREATURE TECH NO MORE, DOC. HE'S ONE OF *US* NOW.
BLUE, YOU'VE MANAGED TO FIT INTO THIS TOWN'S CULTURE BETTER THAN I... *AND I WAS BORN HERE!*
CHEE!
I GUESS I'M WITHOUT EXCUSE.
CRACK!

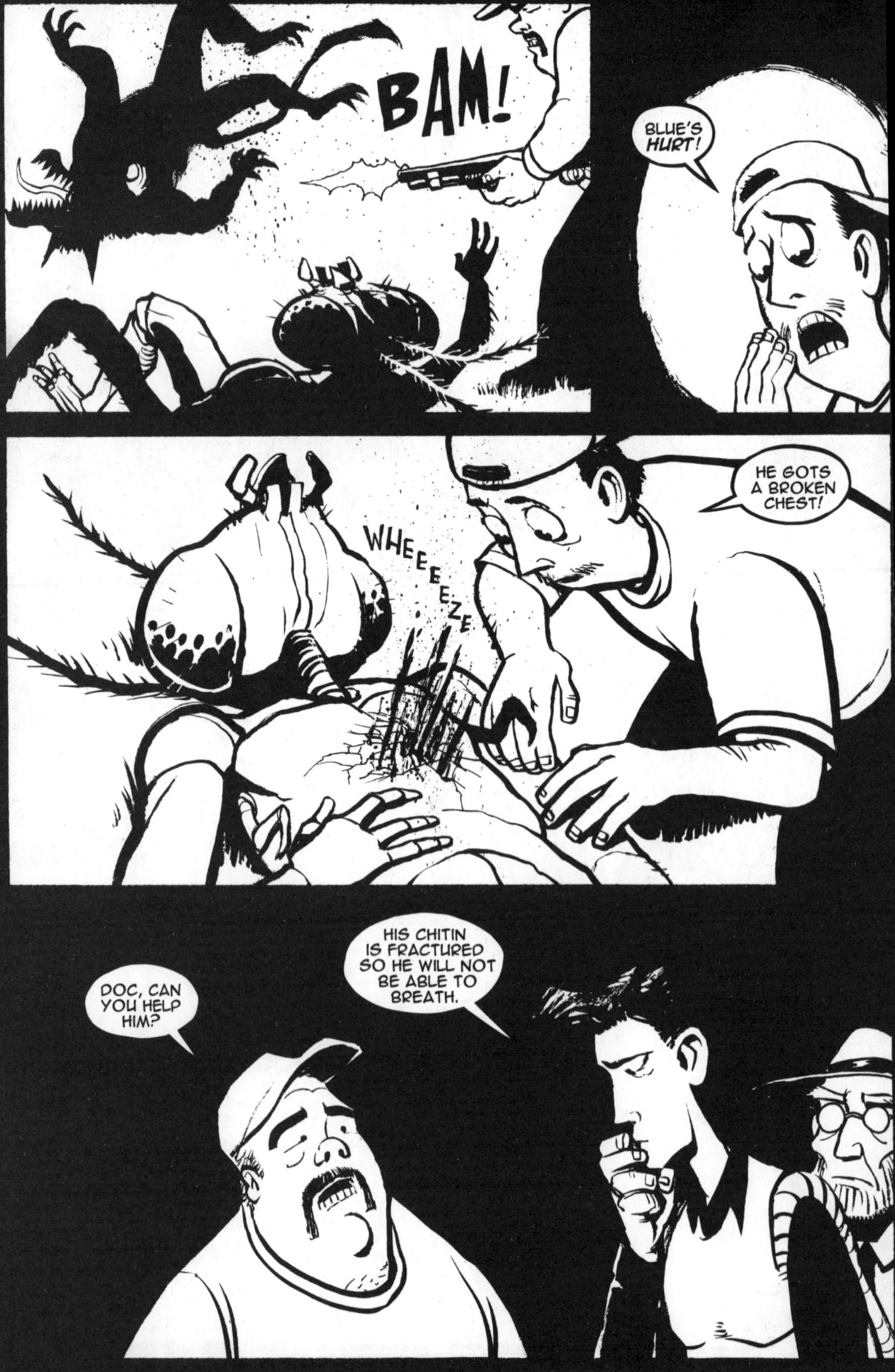
BAM!
BLUE'S *HURT!*
WHEEEEEZE
HE GOTS A BROKEN CHEST!
DOC, CAN YOU HELP HIM?
HIS CHITIN IS FRACTURED SO HE WILL NOT BE ABLE TO BREATH.

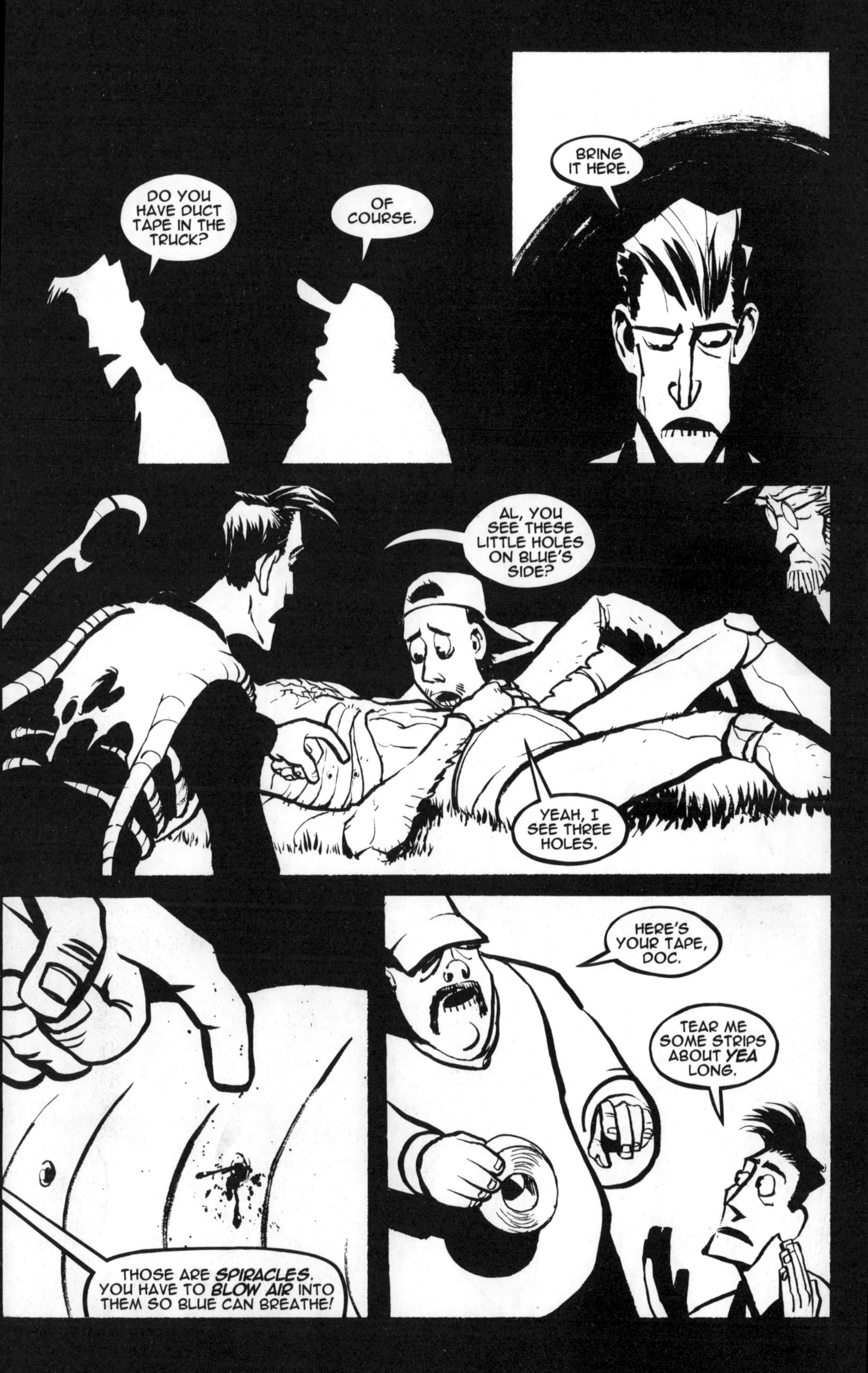
DO YOU HAVE DUCT TAPE IN THE TRUCK?
OF COURSE.
BRING IT HERE.
AL, YOU SEE THESE LITTLE HOLES ON BLUE'S SIDE?
YEAH, I SEE THREE HOLES.
THOSE ARE SPIRACLES. YOU HAVE TO BLOW AIR INTO THEM SO BLUE CAN BREATHE!
HERE'S YOUR TAPE, DOC.
TEAR ME SOME STRIPS ABOUT YEA LONG.

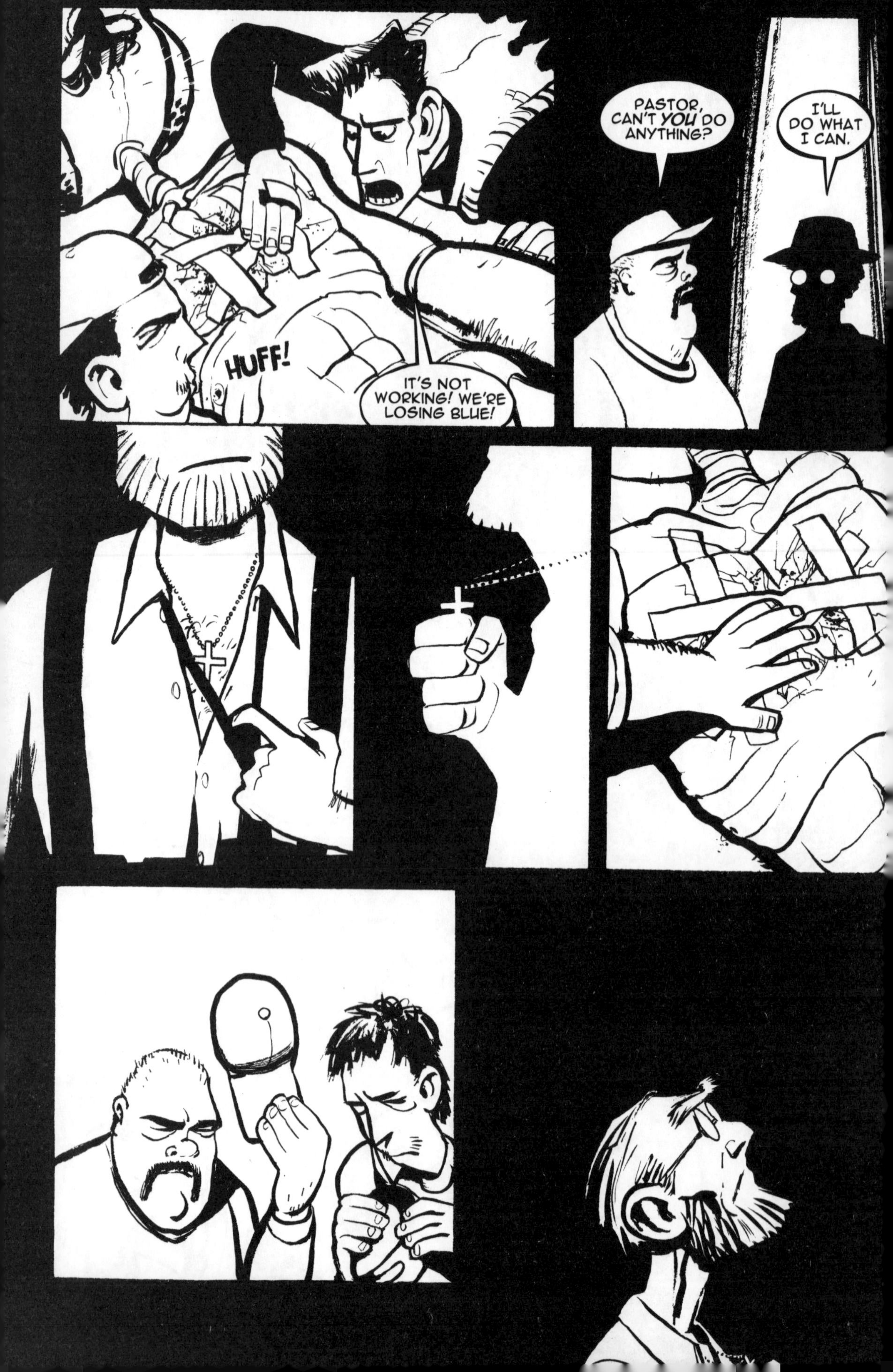
HUFF!
IT'S NOT WORKING! WE'RE LOSING BLUE!
PASTOR, CAN'T YOU DO ANYTHING?
I'LL DO WHAT I CAN.

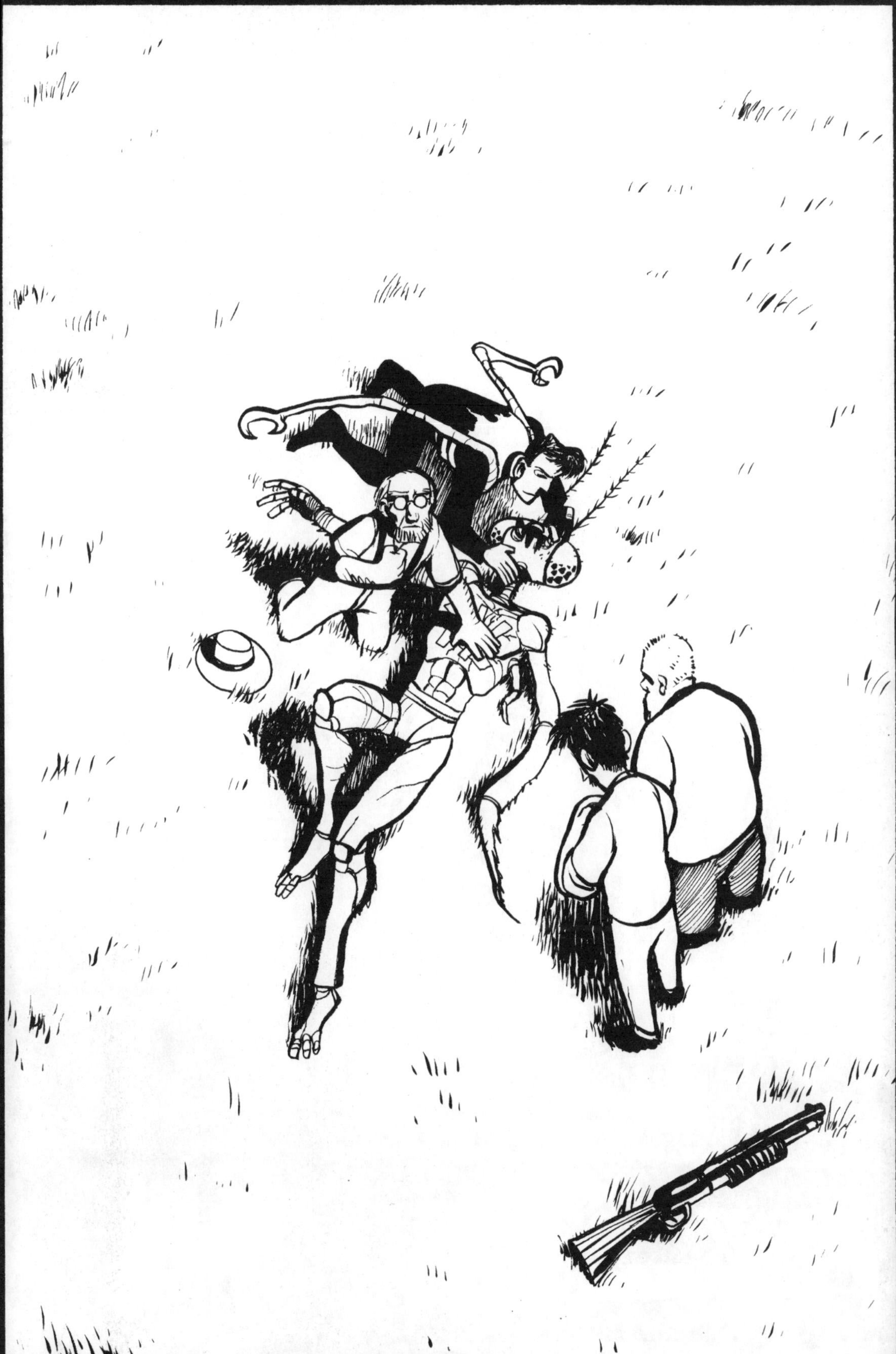

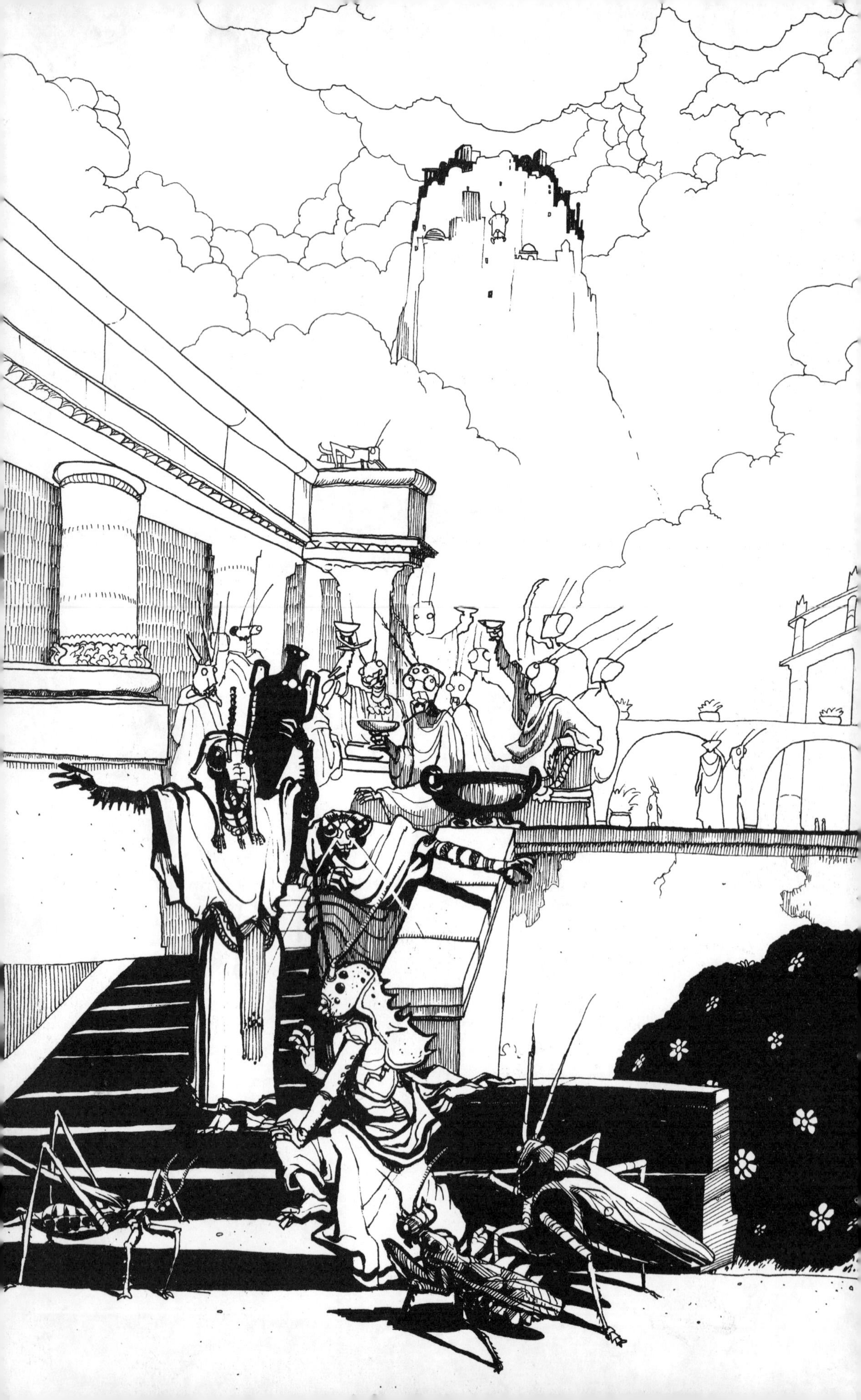

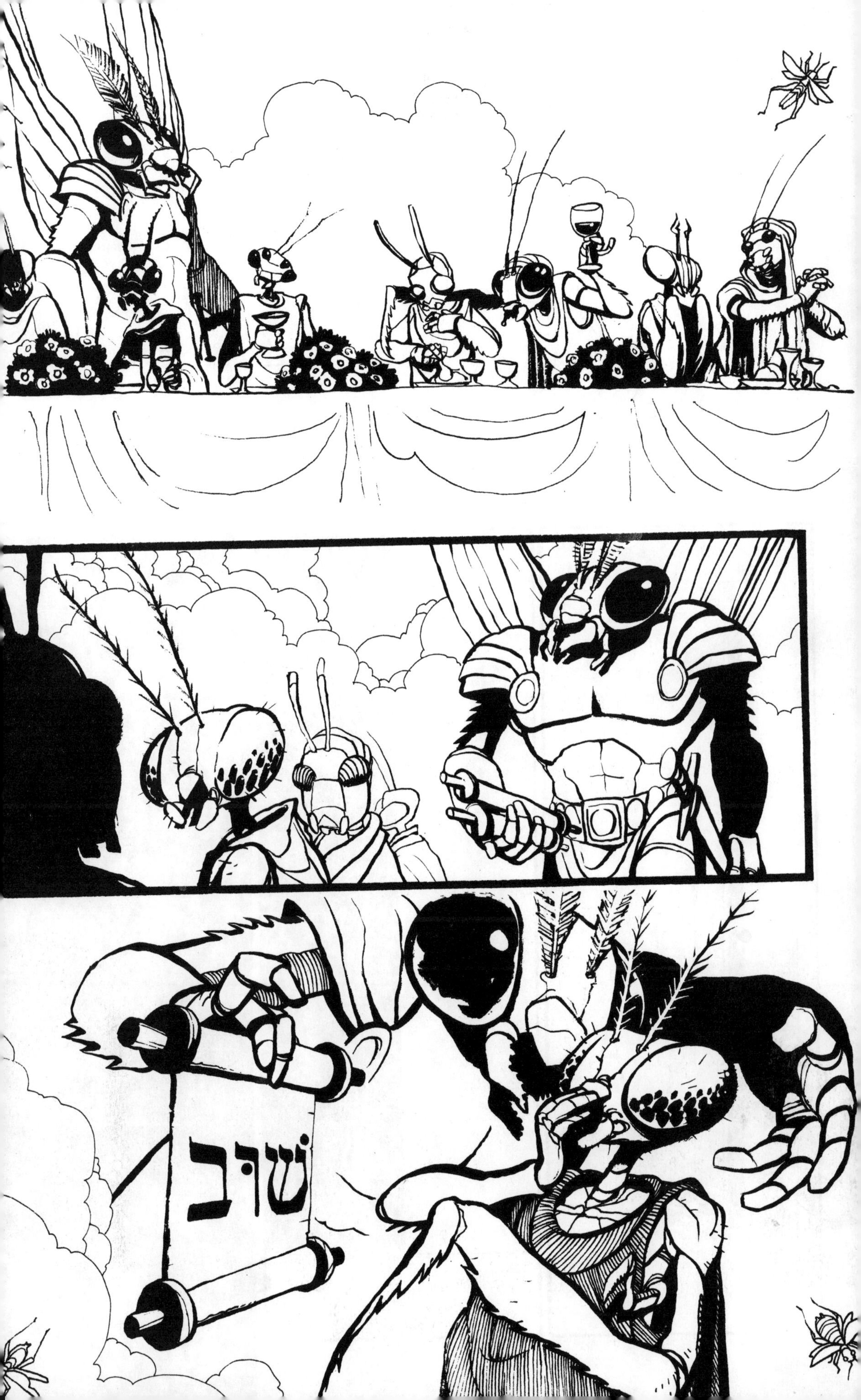

שׁוֹב

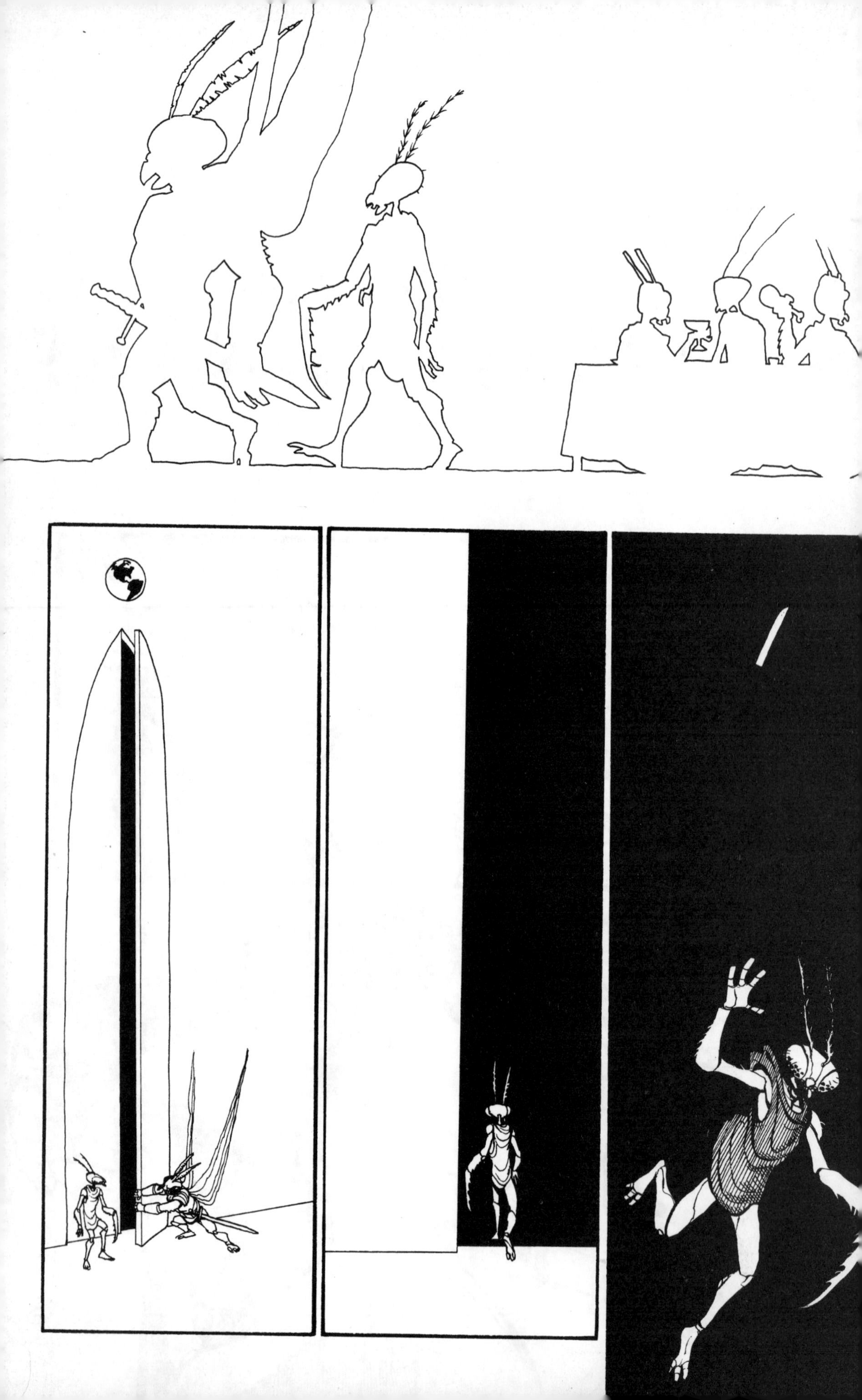

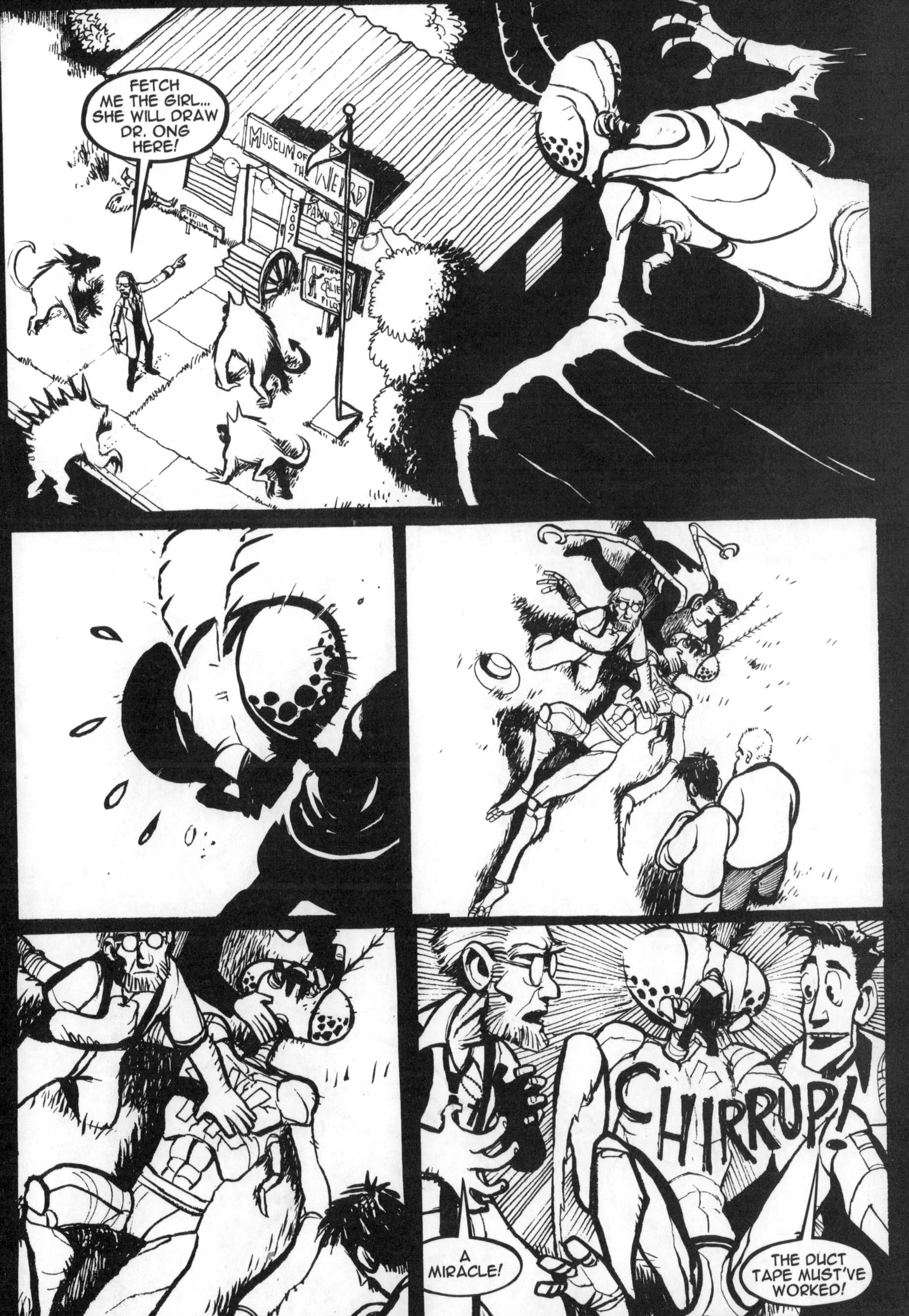
FETCH ME THE GIRL... SHE WILL DRAW DR. ONG HERE!
MUSEUM OF THE WEIRD
PAWN SHOP
CHIRRUP!
A MIRACLE!
THE DUCT TAPE MUST'VE WORKED!

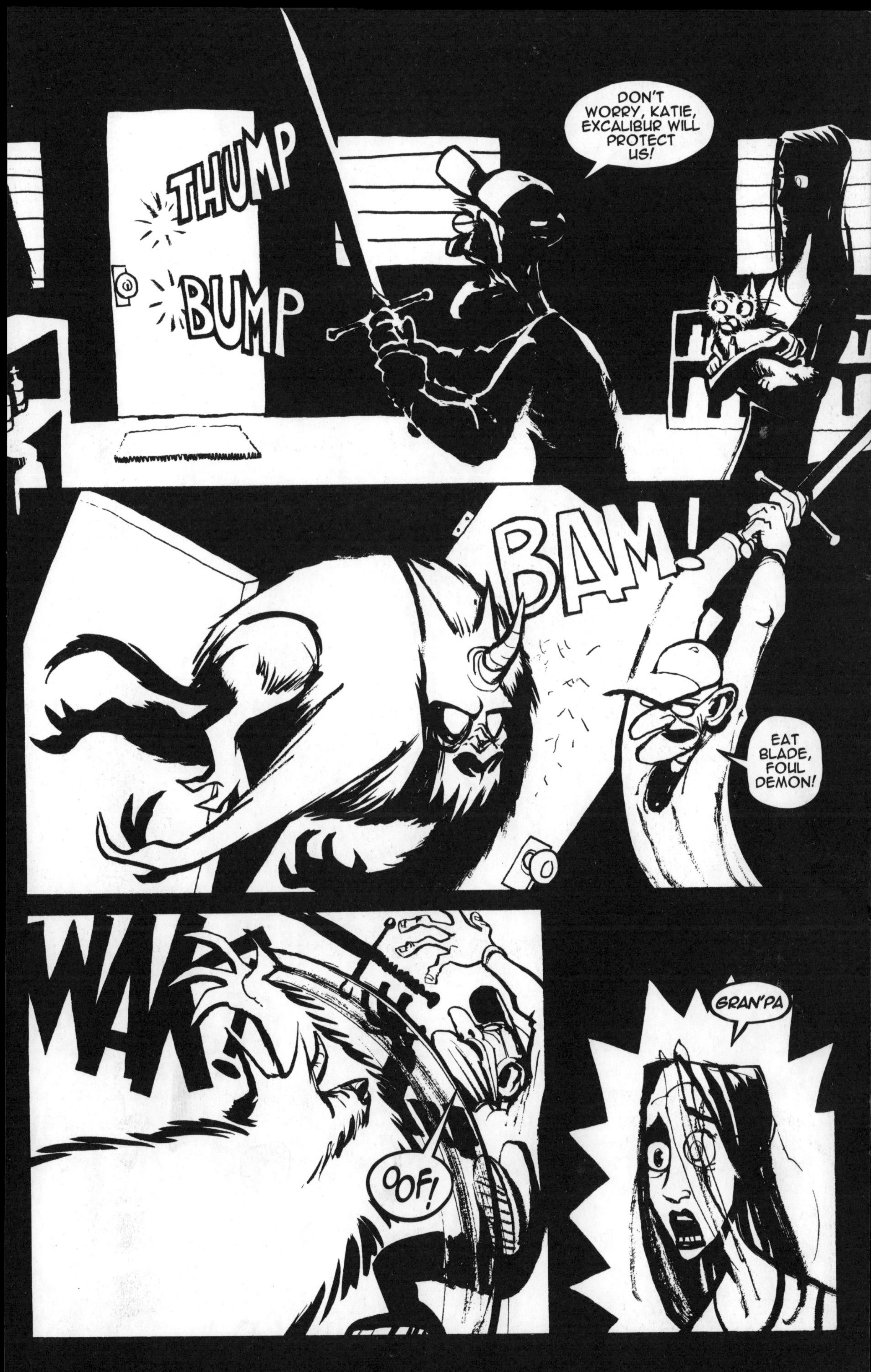

DON'T WORRY, KATIE, EXCALIBUR WILL PROTECT US!
THUMP
BUMP
BAM!
EAT BLADE, FOUL DEMON!
OOF!
GRAN'PA

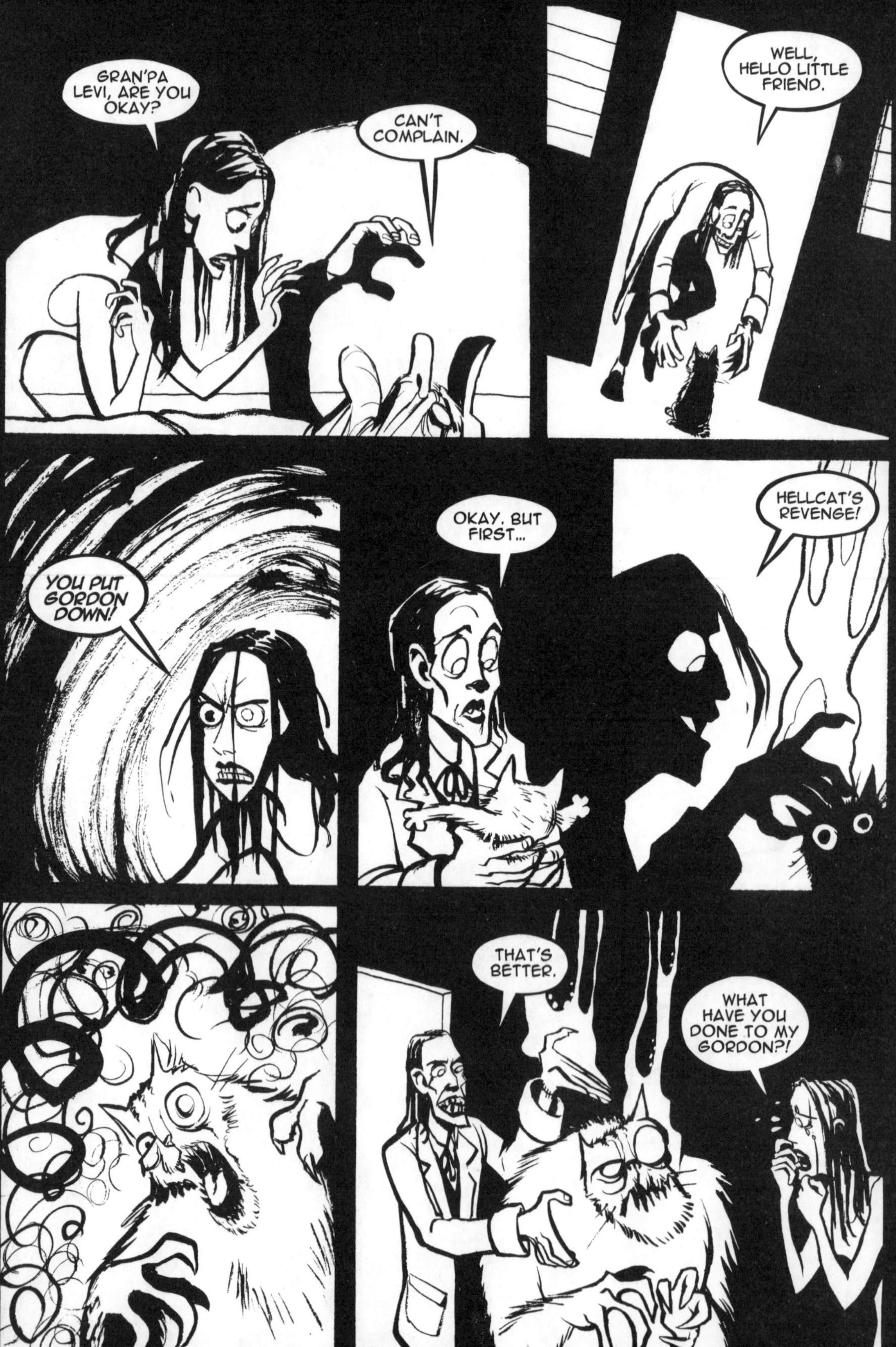
GRAN'PA LEVI, ARE YOU OKAY?
CAN'T COMPLAIN.
WELL, HELLO LITTLE FRIEND.
YOU PUT GORDON DOWN!
OKAY. BUT FIRST...
HELLCAT'S REVENGE!
THAT'S BETTER.
WHAT HAVE YOU DONE TO MY GORDON?!

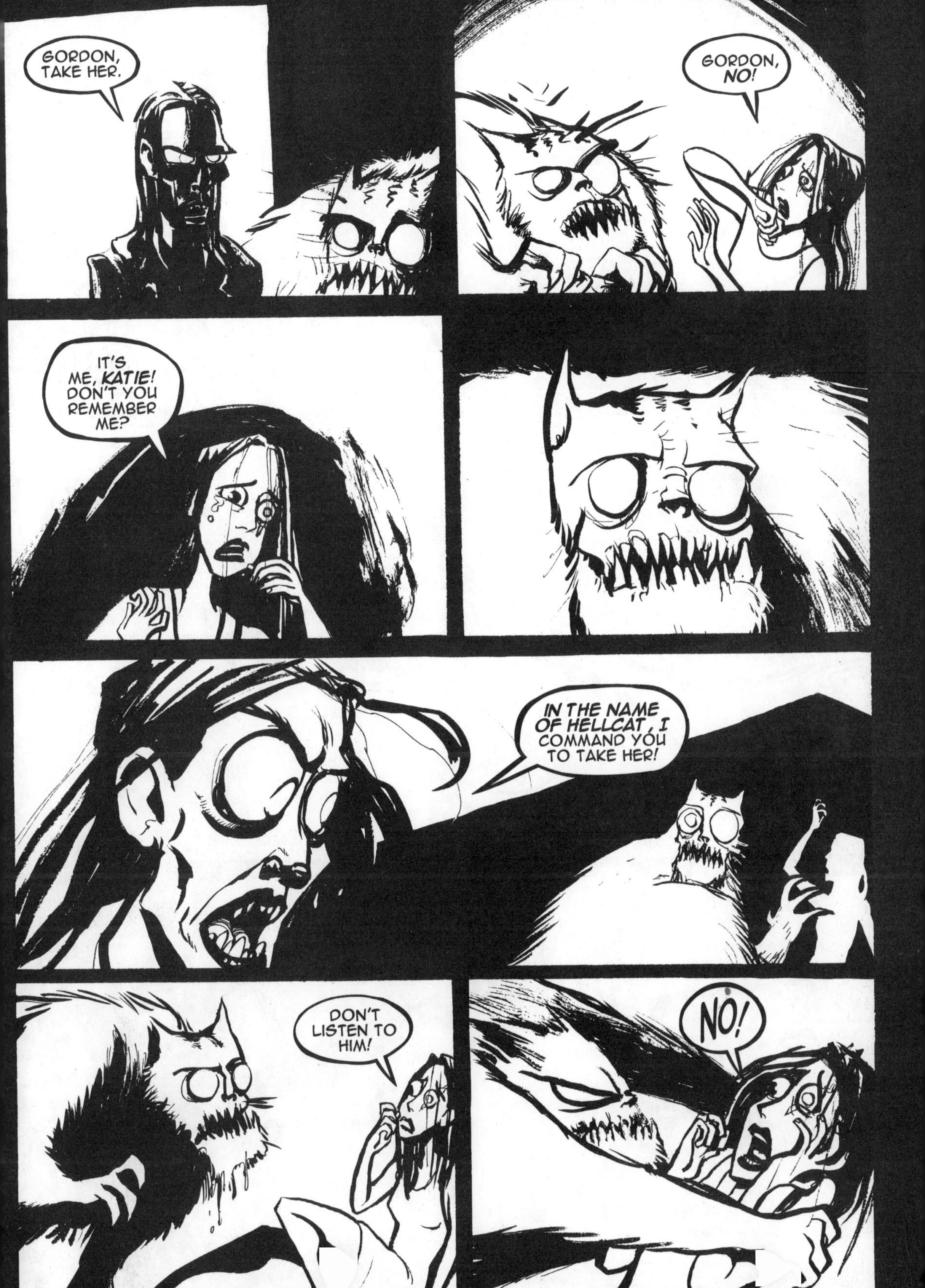
GORDON, TAKE HER.
GORDON, NO!
IT'S ME, KATIE! DON'T YOU REMEMBER ME?
IN THE NAME OF HELLCAT, I COMMAND YOU TO TAKE HER!
DON'T LISTEN TO HIM!
NO!

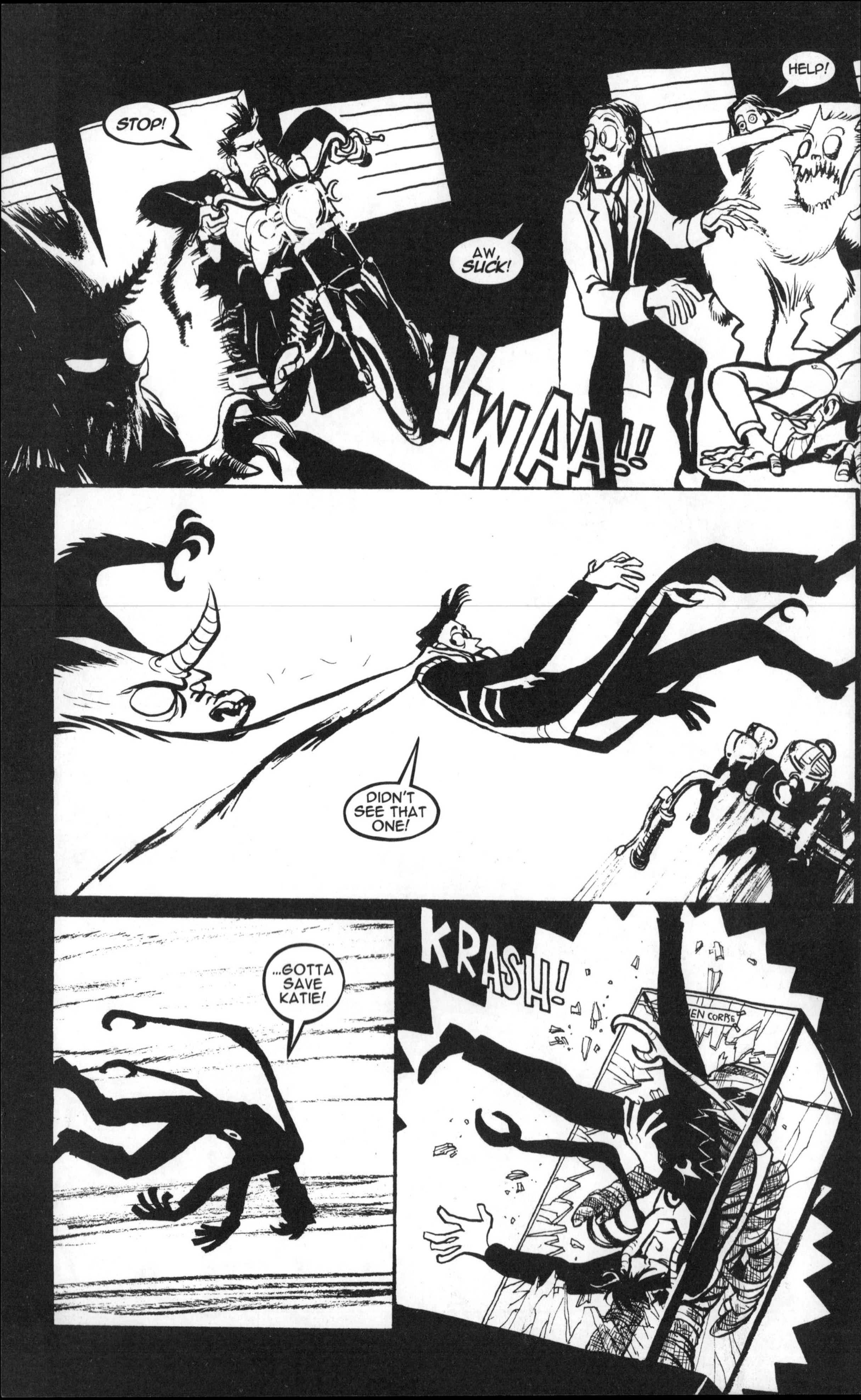
STOP!
AW, SUCK!
HELP!
VWAA!!
DIDN'T SEE THAT ONE!
...GOTTA SAVE KATIE!
KRASH!

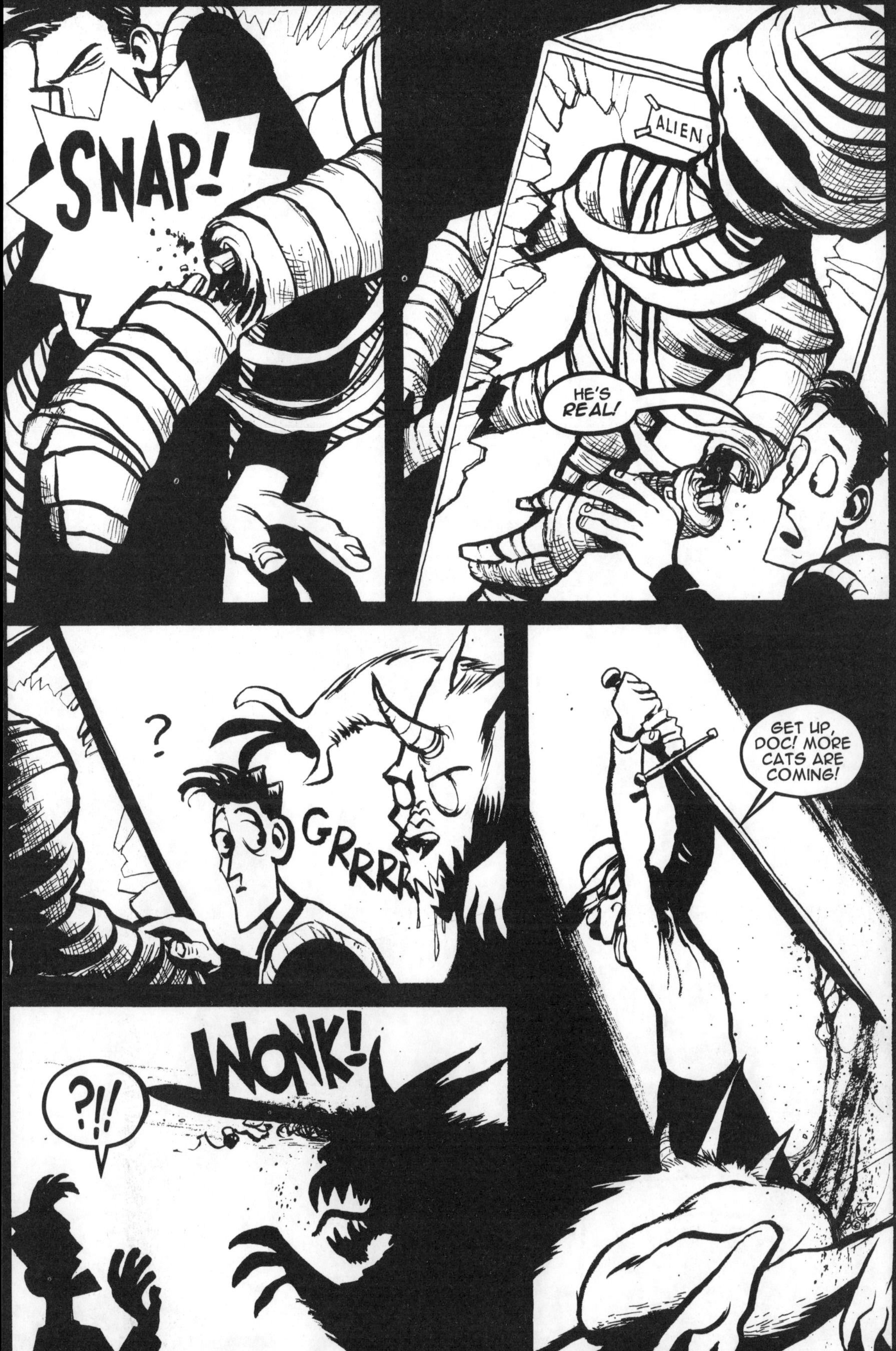
SNAP!
ALIEN
HE'S REAL!
?
GRRRR
GET UP, DOC! MORE CATS ARE COMING!
WONK!
?!!

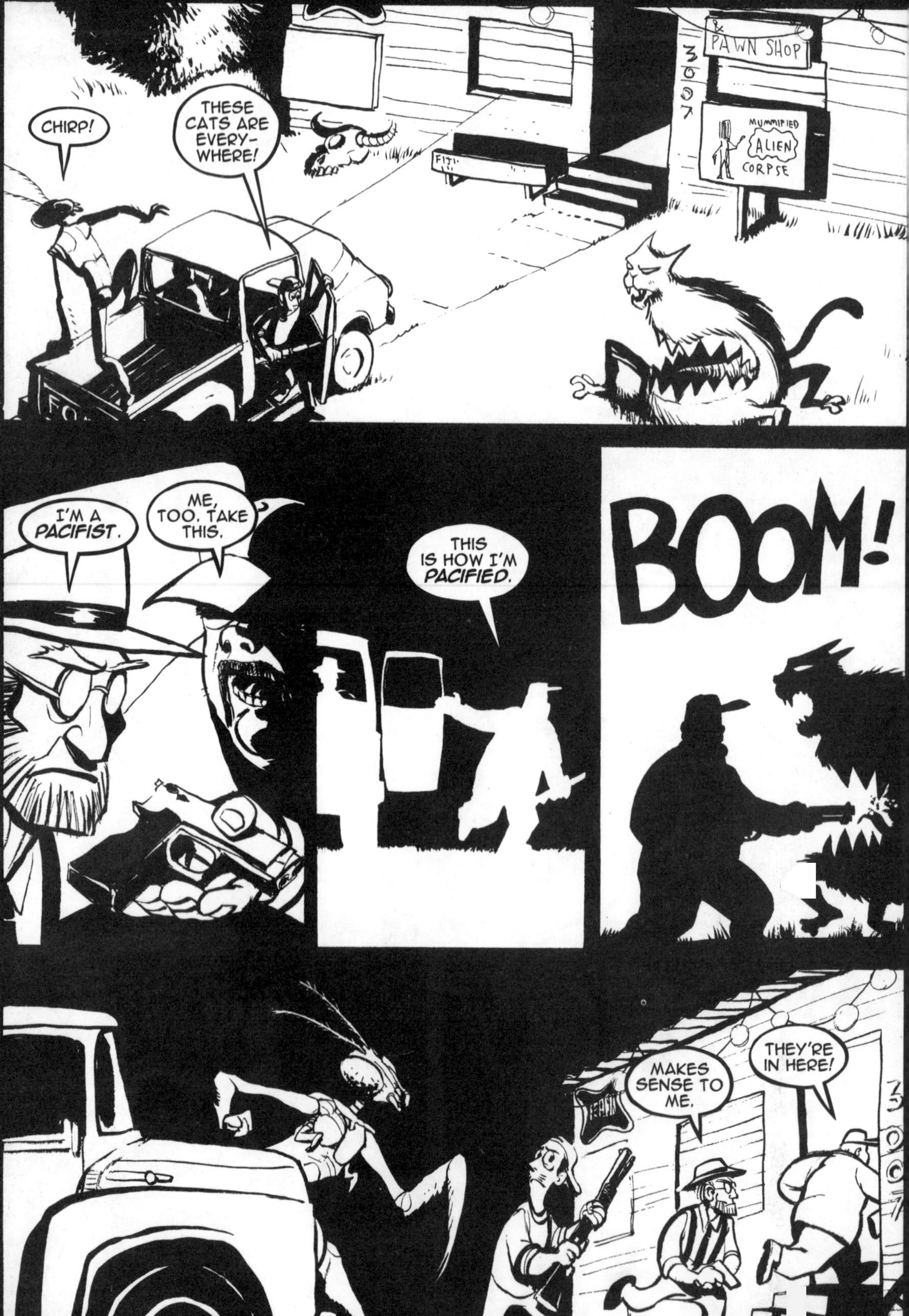
PAWN SHOP
3007
MUMMIFIED ALIEN CORPSE
CHIRP!
THESE CATS ARE EVERY-WHERE!
I'M A PACIFIST.
ME, TOO. TAKE THIS.
THIS IS HOW I'M PACIFIED.
BOOM!
MAKES SENSE TO ME.
THEY'RE IN HERE!

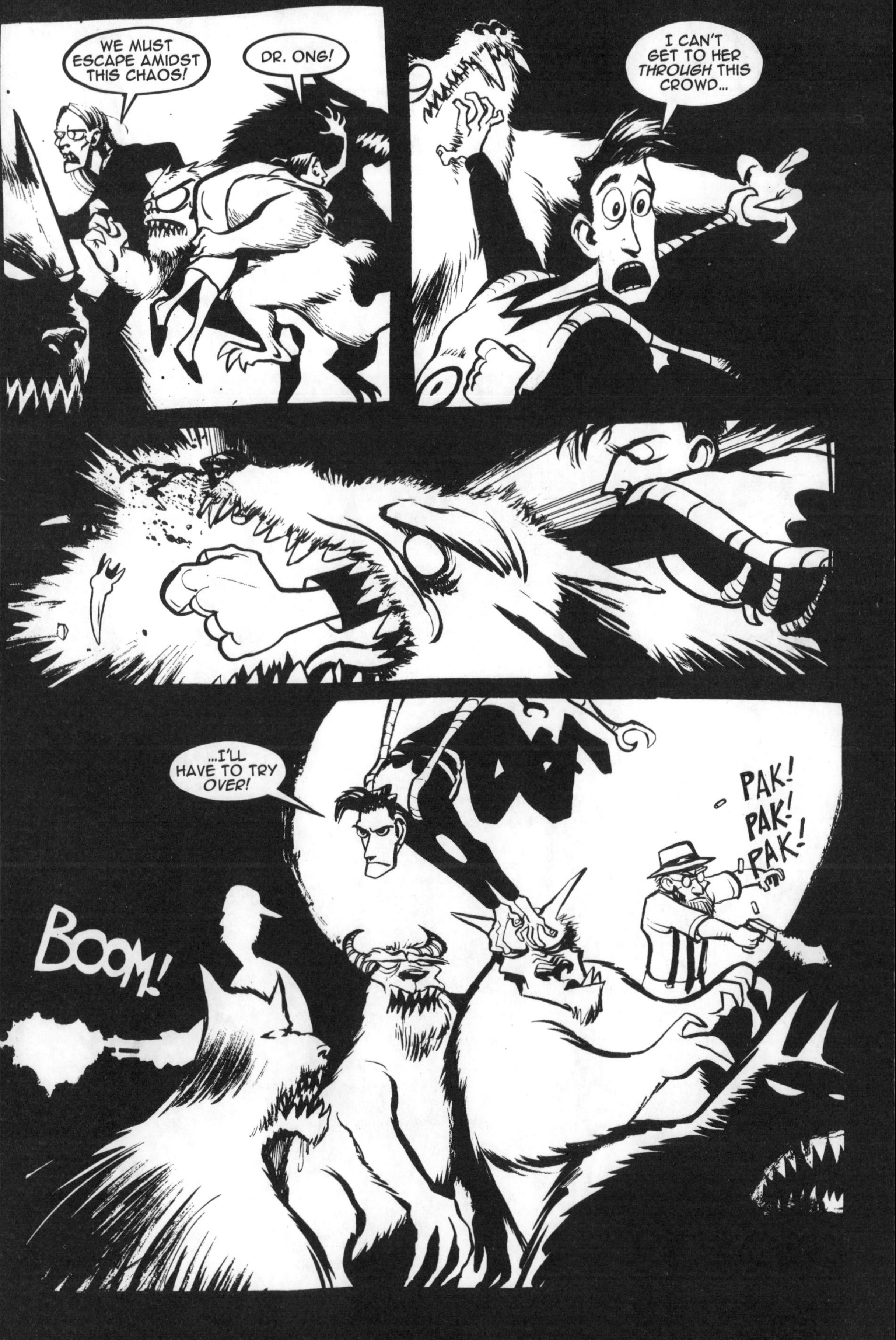

WE MUST ESCAPE AMIDST THIS CHAOS!
DR. ONG!
I CAN'T GET TO HER *THROUGH* THIS CROWD...
...I'LL HAVE TO TRY *OVER*!
PAK! PAK! PAK!
BOOM!

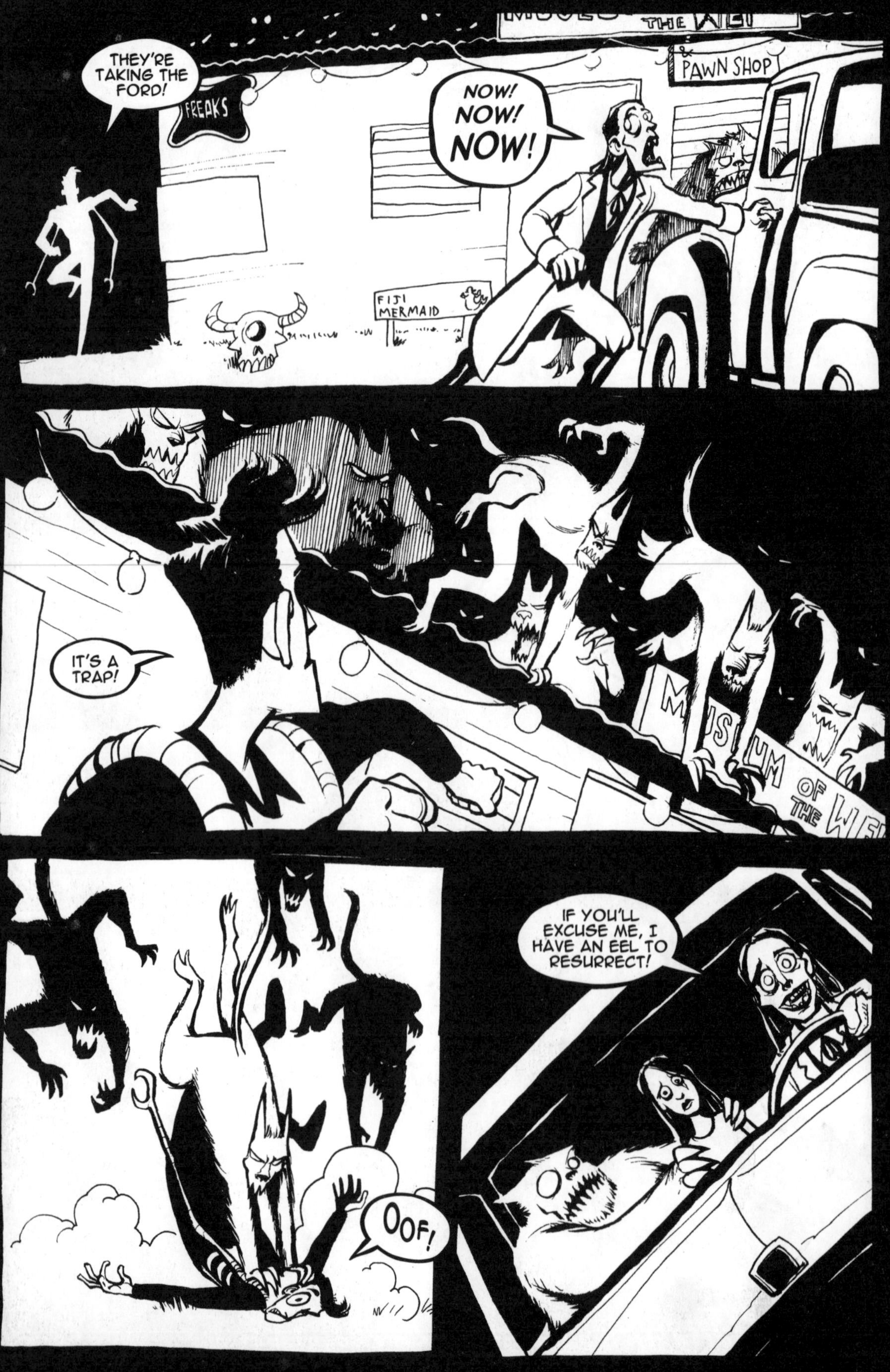
THE W
PAWN SHOP
FREAKS
THEY'RE TAKING THE FORD!
NOW! NOW! NOW!
FIJI MERMAID
IT'S A TRAP!
MUSEUM OF THE WE
OOF!
IF YOU'LL EXCUSE ME, I HAVE AN EEL TO RESURRECT!

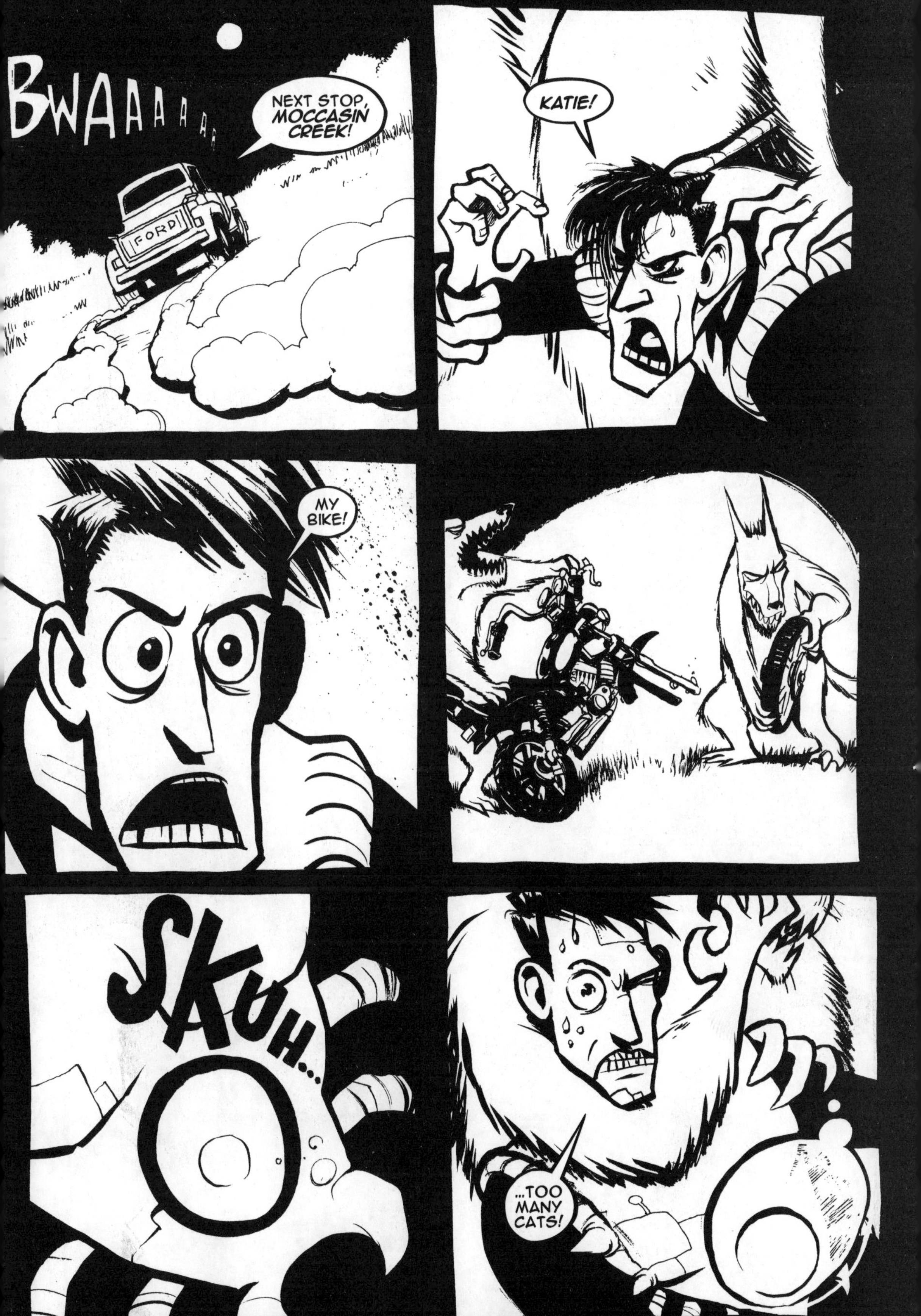
BWAAAAAA
NEXT STOP, MOCCASIN CREEK!
KATIE!
MY BIKE!
SKUH...
...TOO MANY CATS!

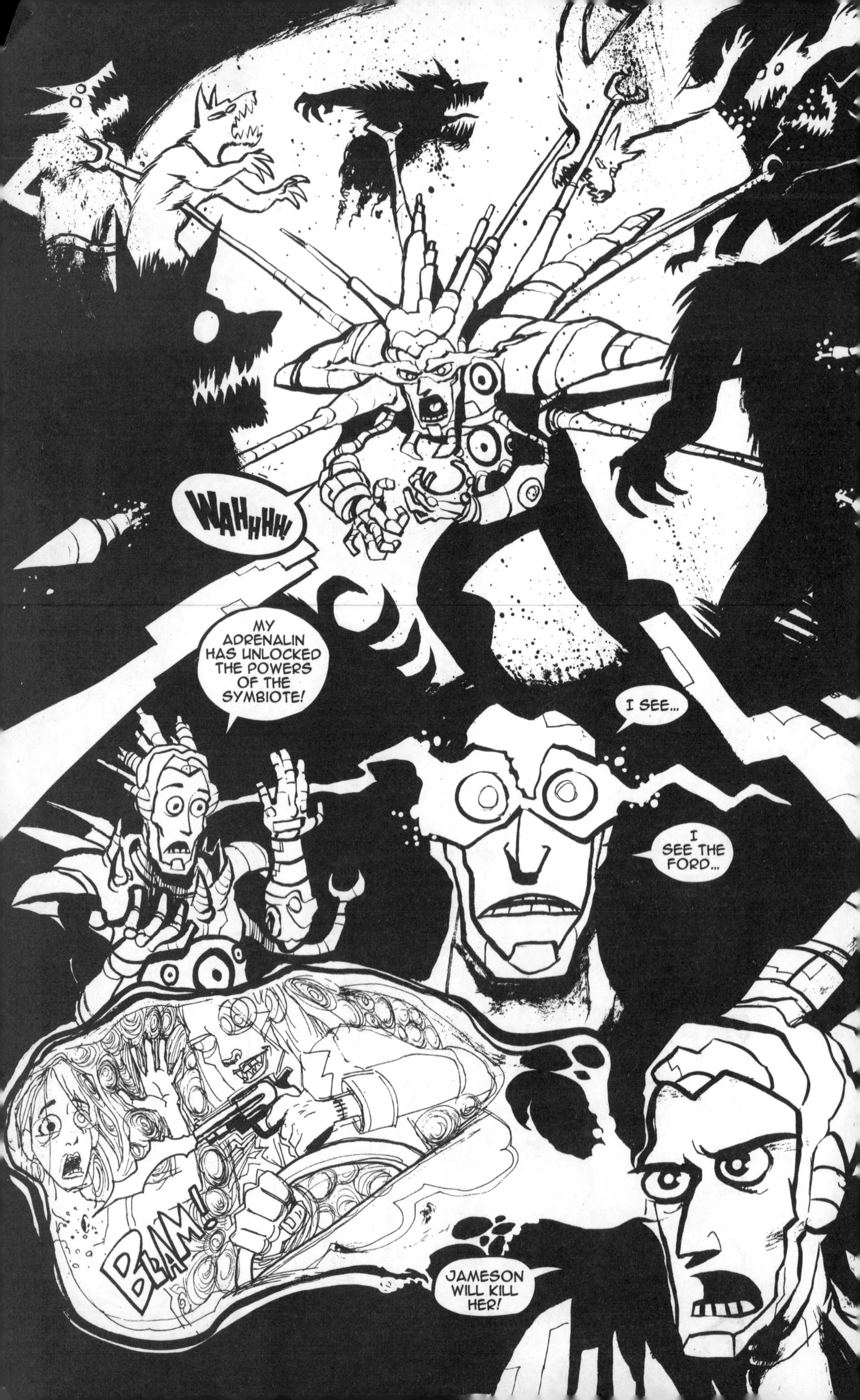
WAHHHH!
MY ADRENALIN HAS UNLOCKED THE POWERS OF THE SYMBIOTE!
I SEE...
I SEE THE FORD...
BBLAM!
JAMESON WILL KILL HER!

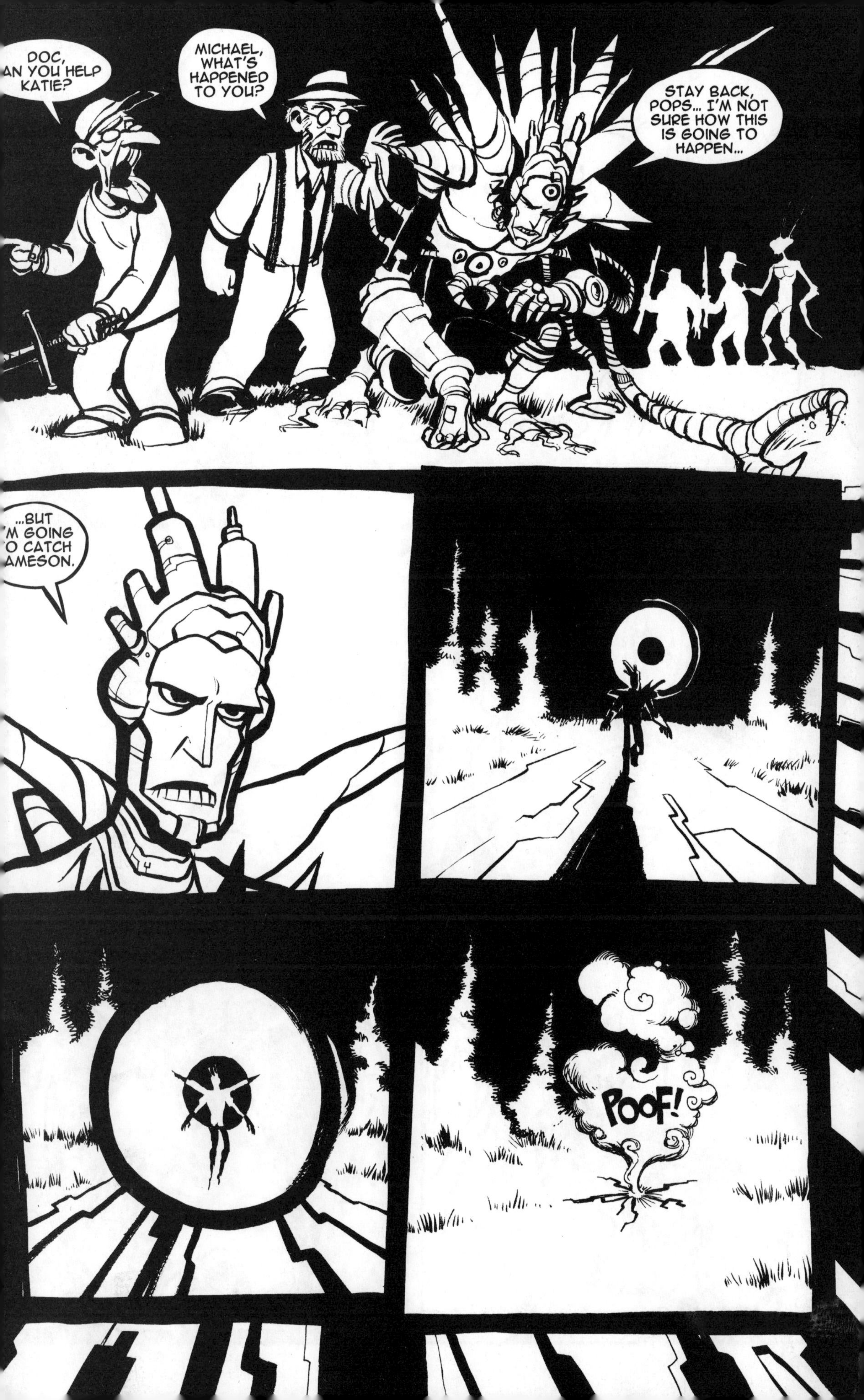
DOC, AN YOU HELP KATIE?
MICHAEL, WHAT'S HAPPENED TO YOU?
STAY BACK, POPS... I'M NOT SURE HOW THIS IS GOING TO HAPPEN...
...BUT 'M GOING 'O CATCH AMESON.
POOF!

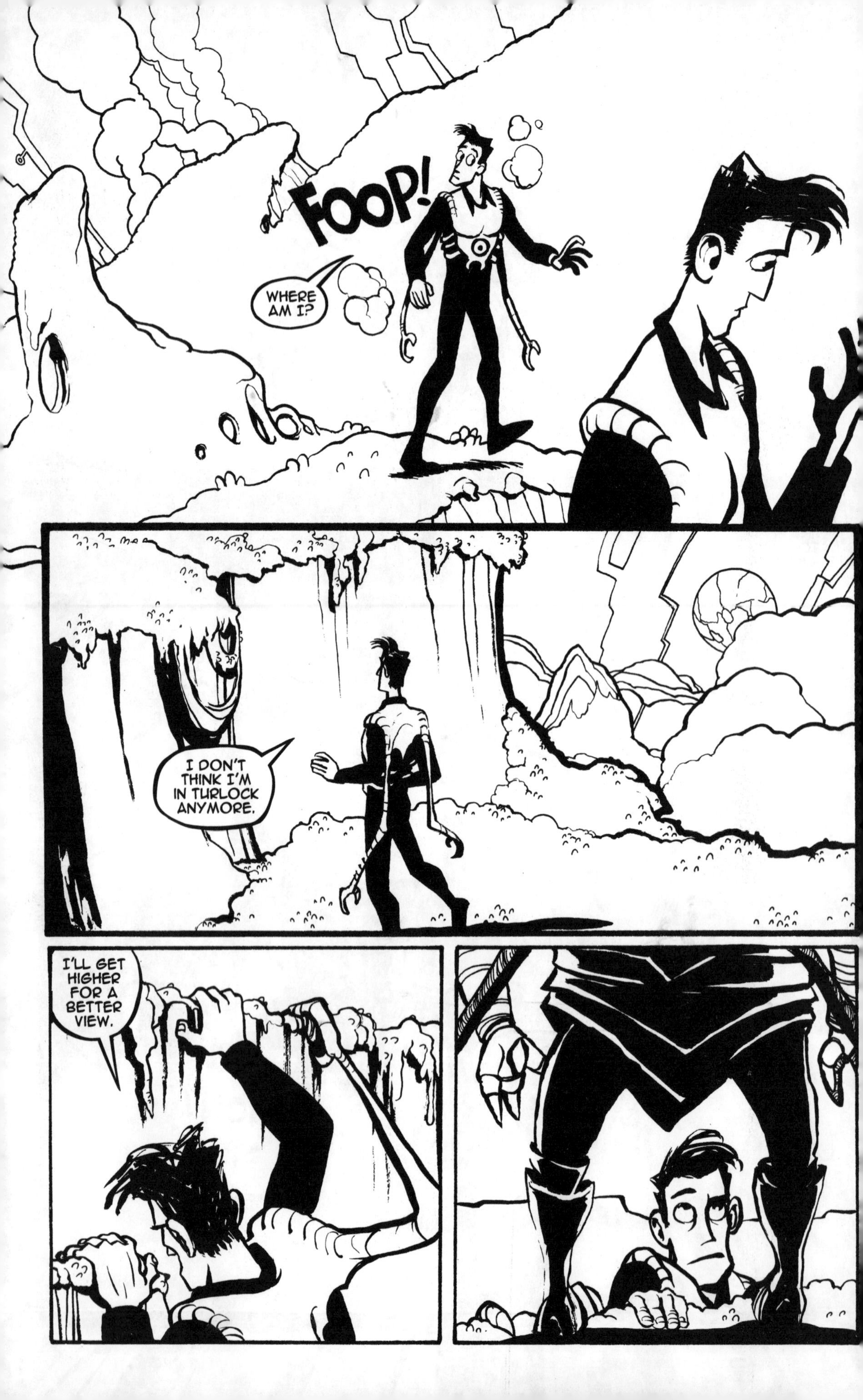
FOOP!
WHERE AM I?
I DON'T THINK I'M IN TURLOCK ANYMORE.
I'LL GET HIGHER FOR A BETTER VIEW.

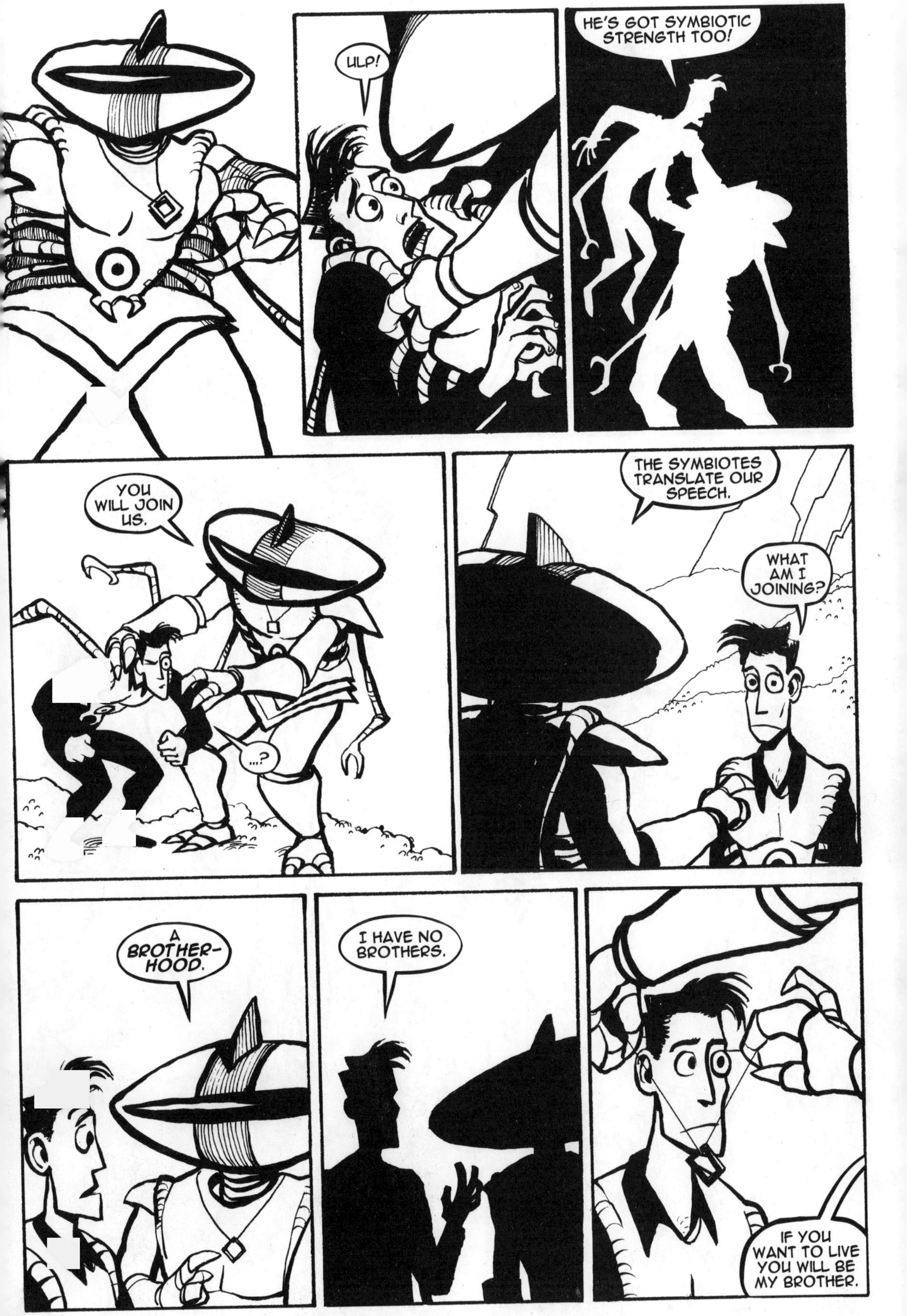
ULP!
HE'S GOT SYMBIOTIC STRENGTH TOO!
YOU WILL JOIN US.
...?
THE SYMBIOTES TRANSLATE OUR SPEECH.
WHAT AM I JOINING?
A BROTHER-HOOD.
I HAVE NO BROTHERS.
IF YOU WANT TO LIVE YOU WILL BE MY BROTHER.

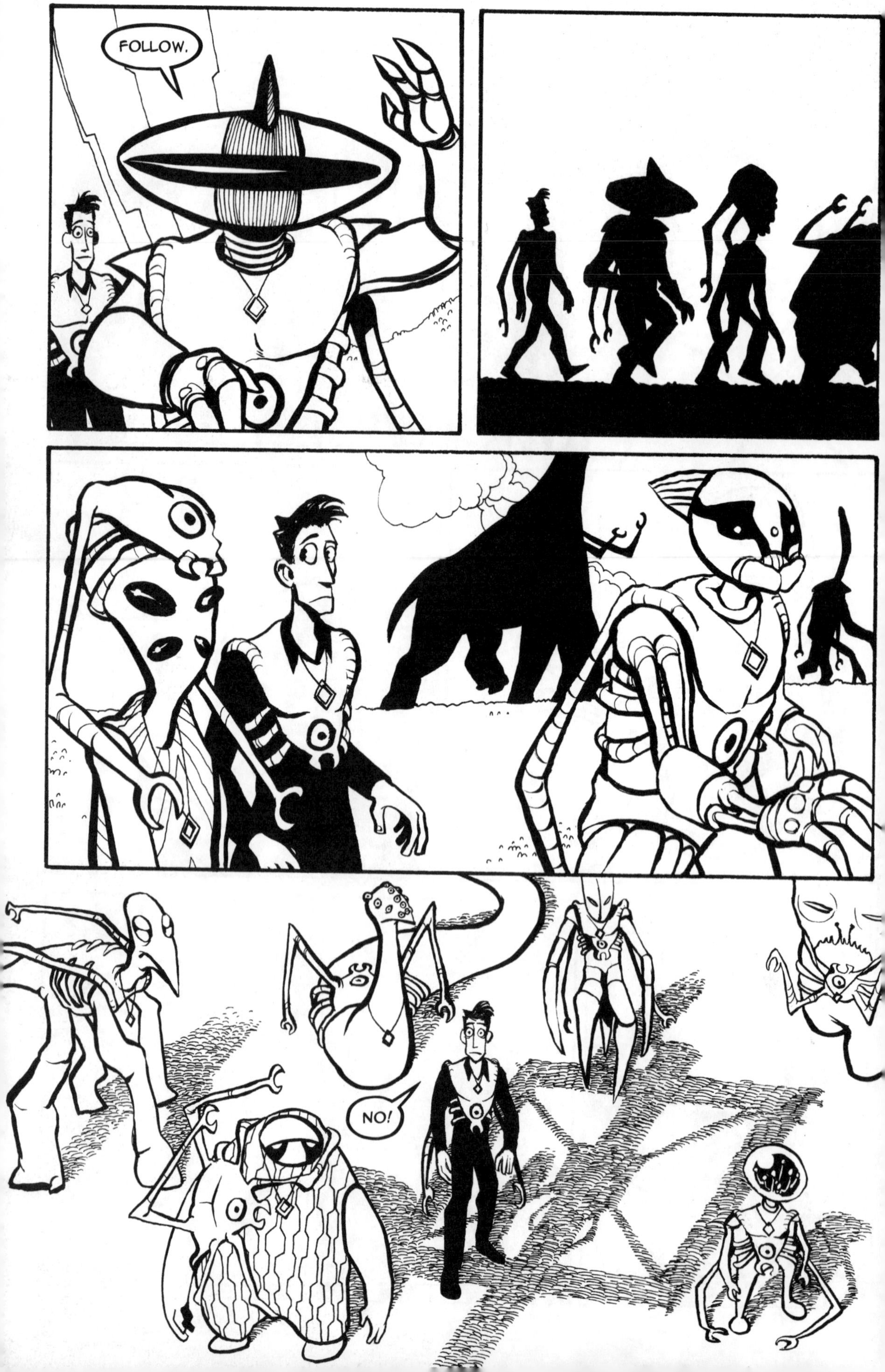
FOLLOW.
NO!

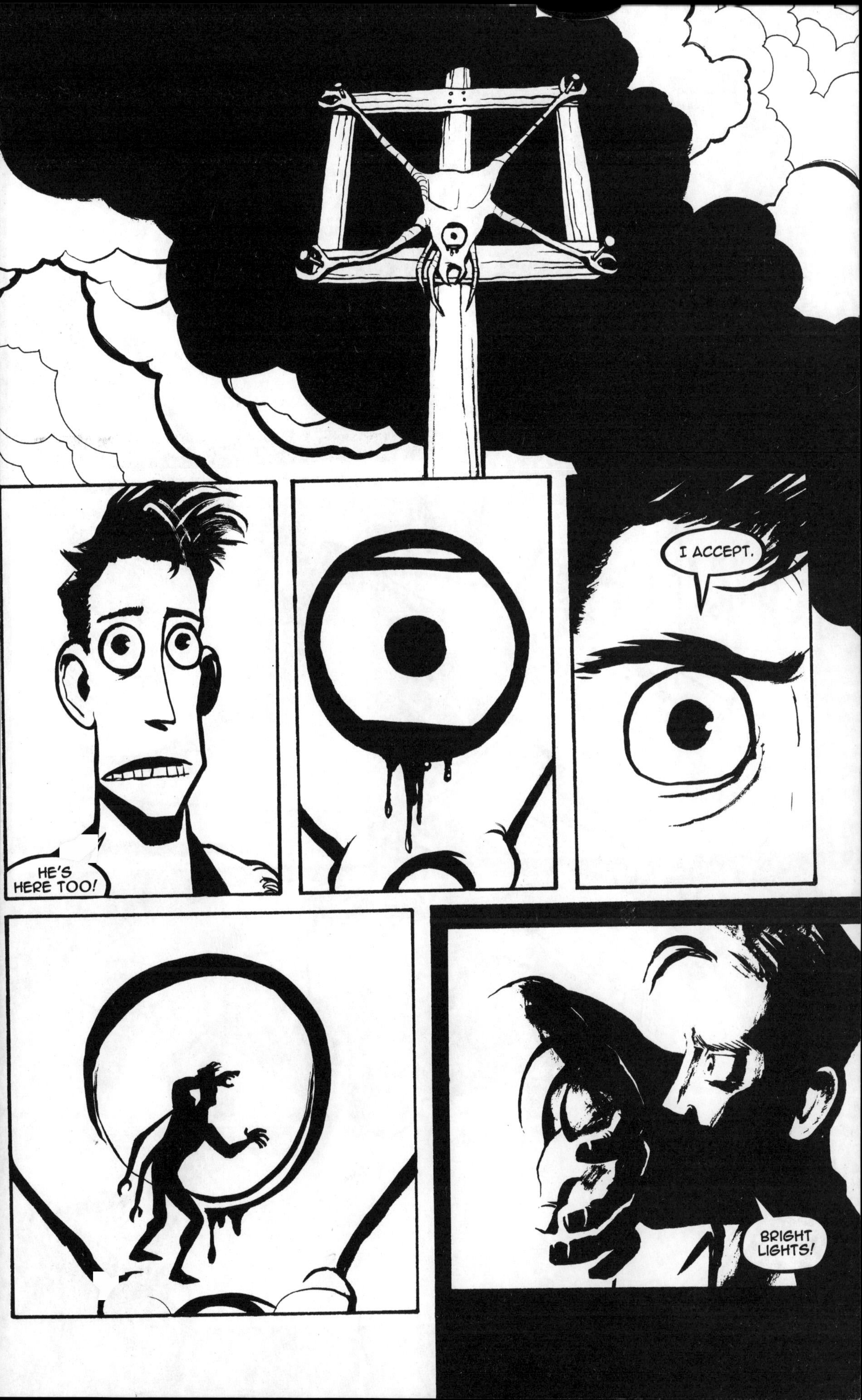
HE'S HERE TOO!
I ACCEPT.
BRIGHT LIGHTS!

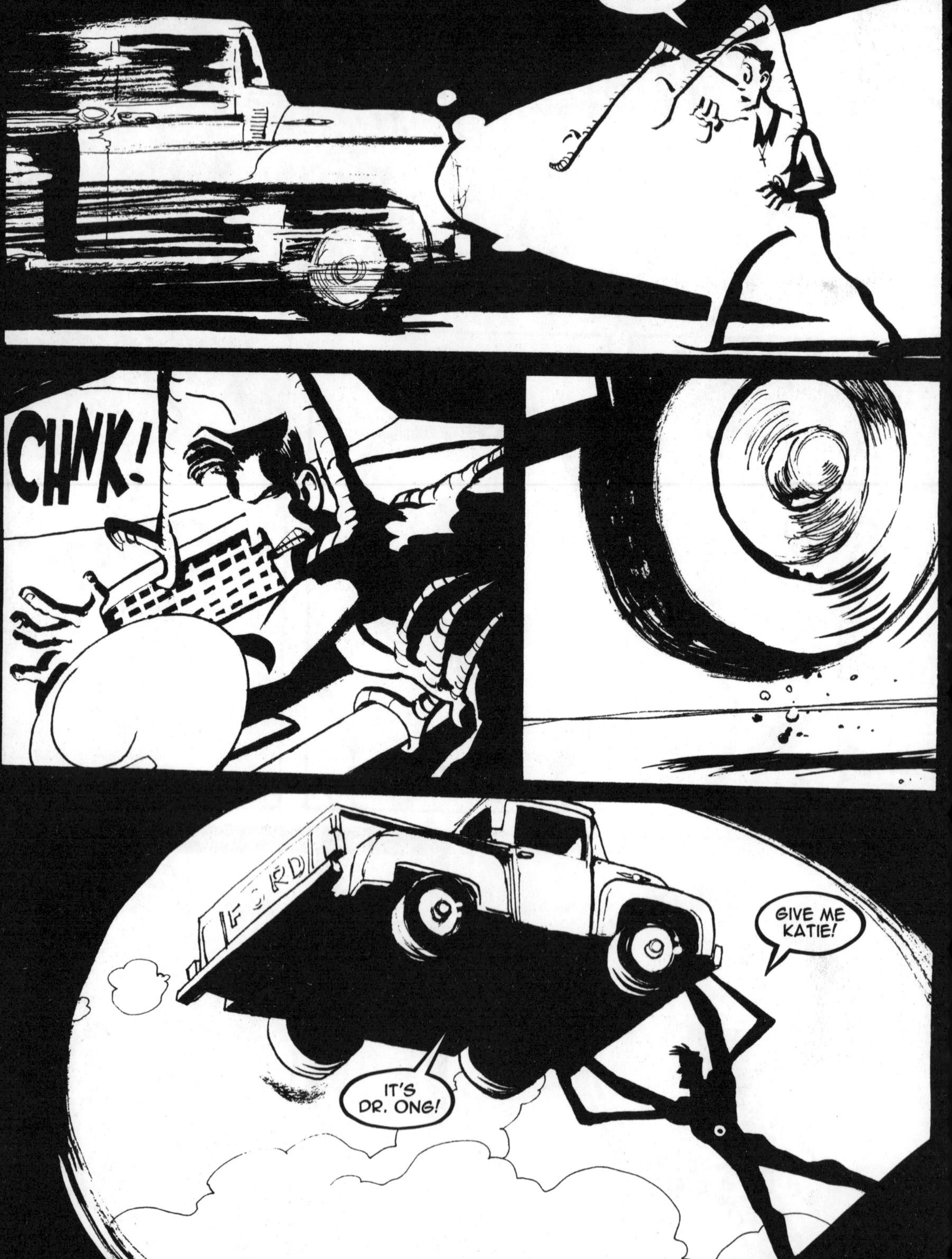
KATIE?
CHNK!
GIVE ME KATIE!
IT'S DR. ONG!

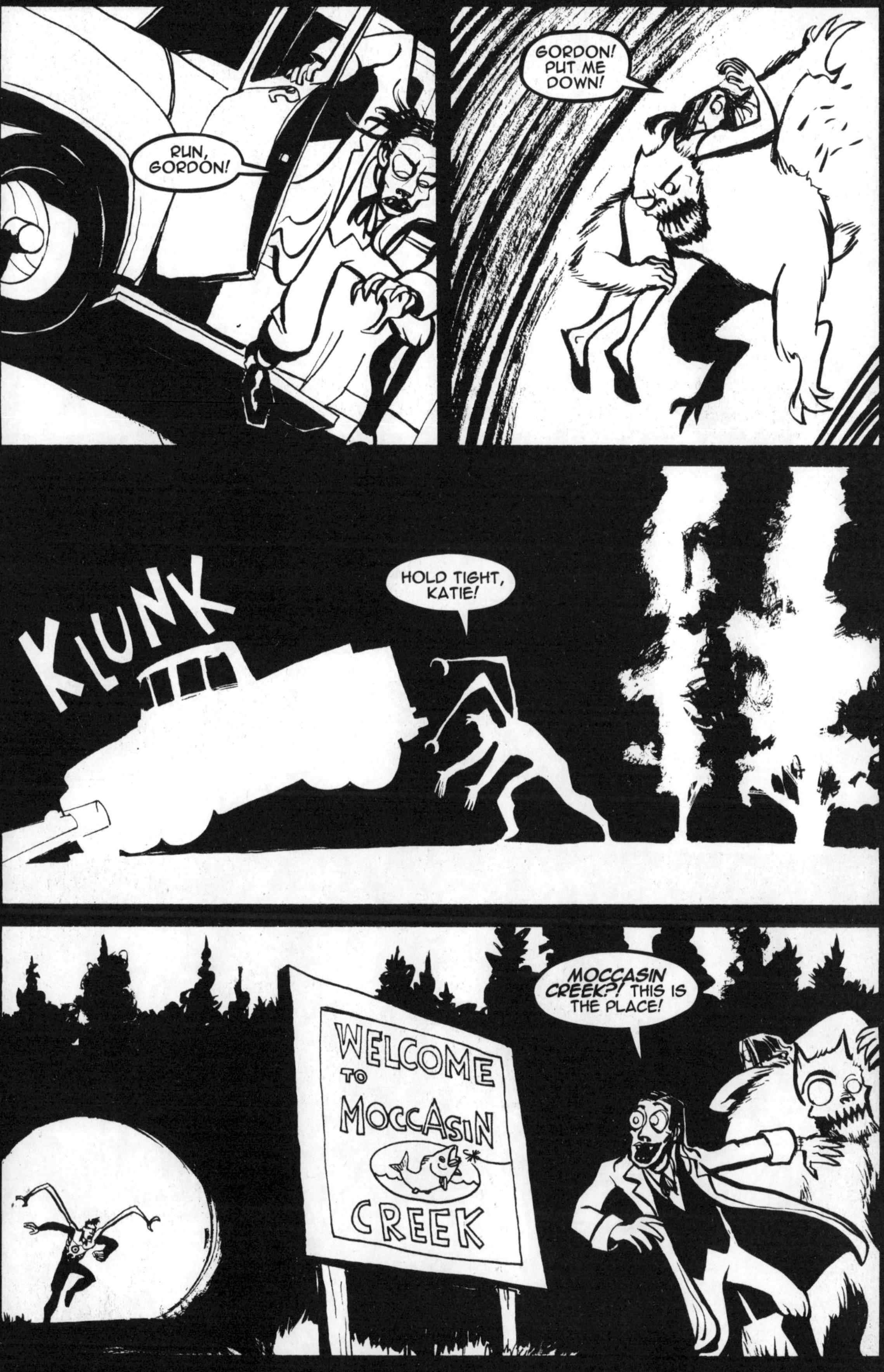
RUN, GORDON!
GORDON! PUT ME DOWN!
KLUNK
HOLD TIGHT, KATIE!
WELCOME TO MOCCASIN CREEK
MOCCASIN CREEK?! THIS IS THE PLACE!

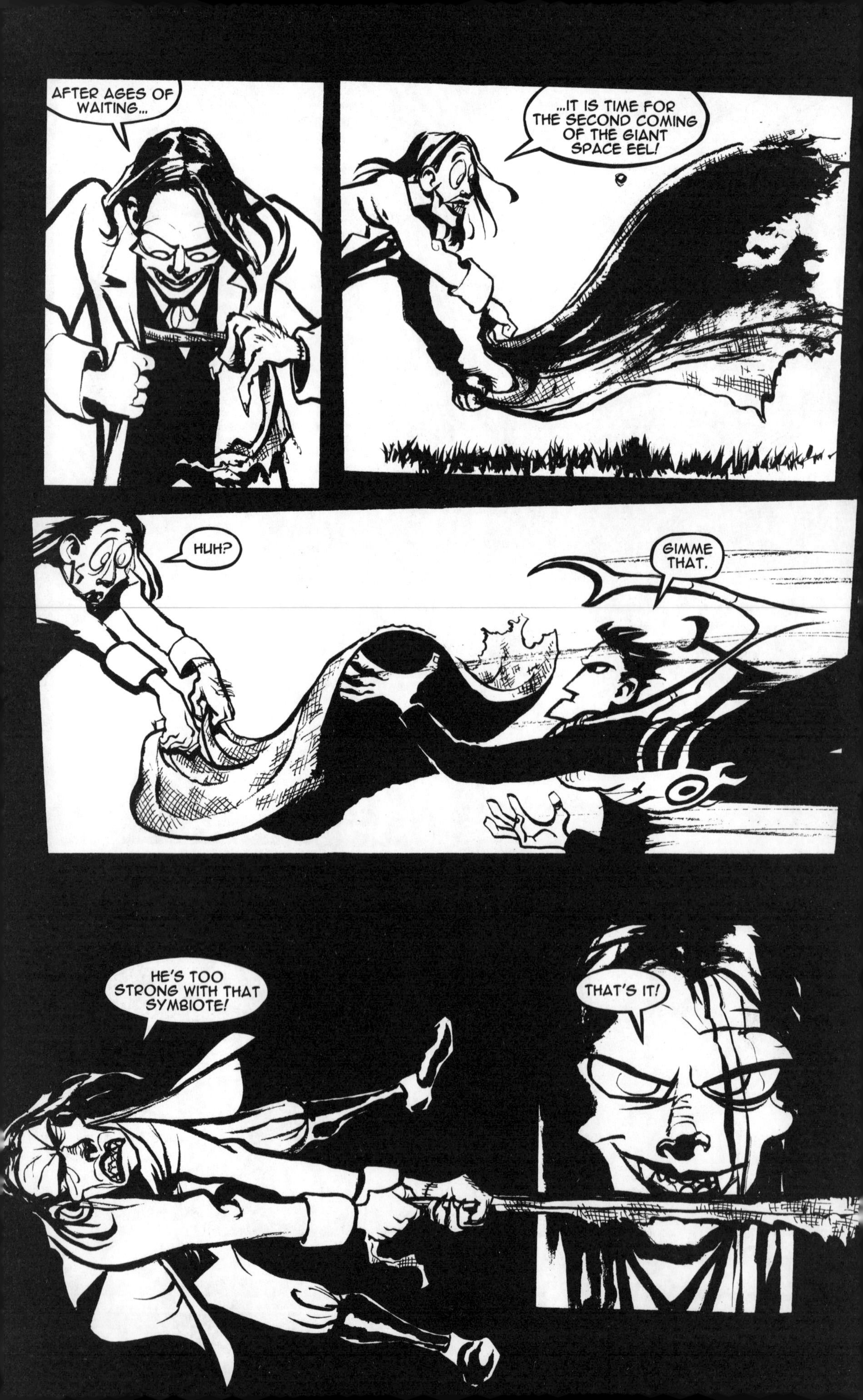
AFTER AGES OF WAITING...
...IT IS TIME FOR THE SECOND COMING OF THE GIANT SPACE EEL!
HUH?
GIMME THAT.
HE'S TOO STRONG WITH THAT SYMBIOTE!
THAT'S IT!

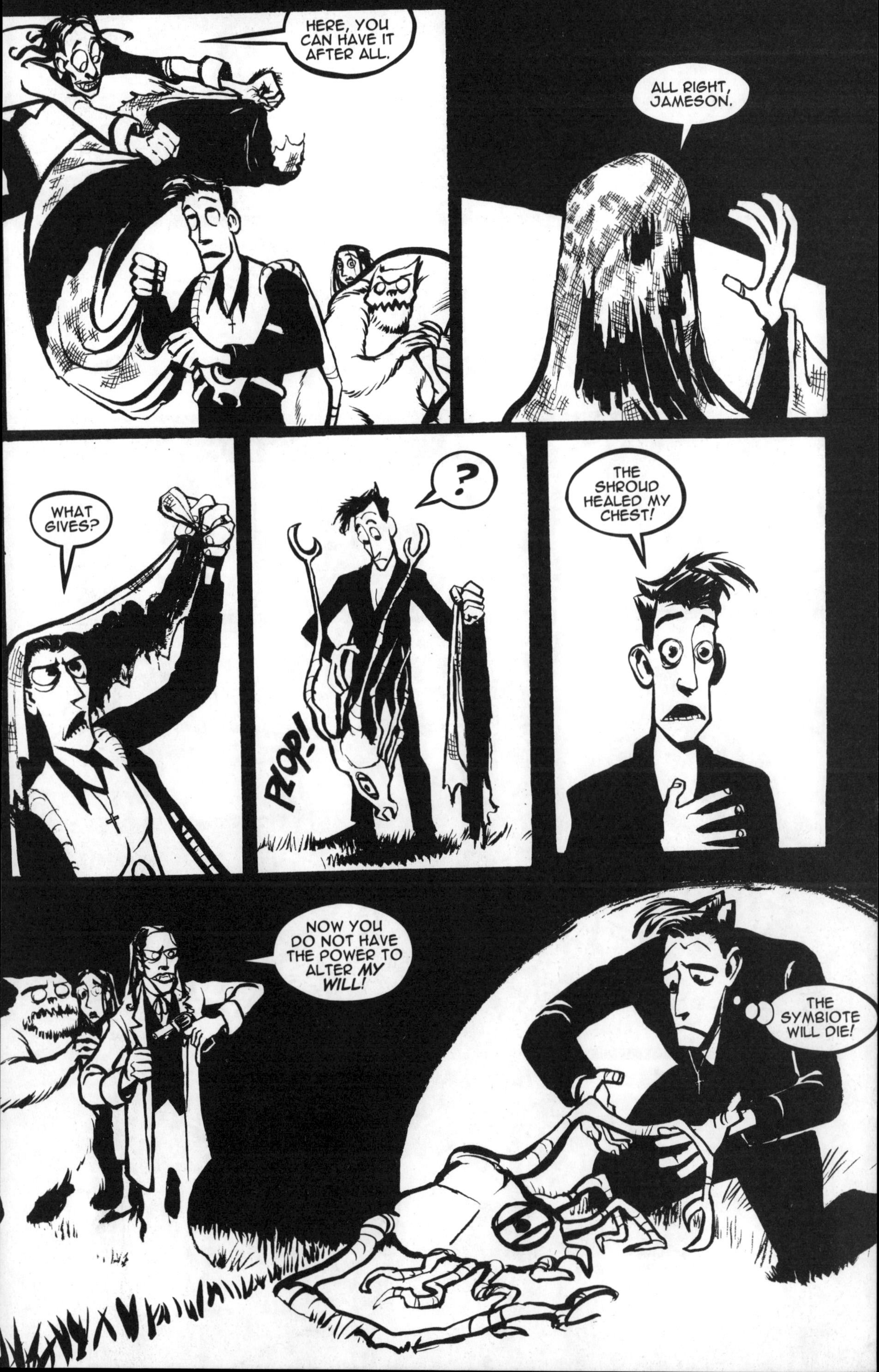
HERE, YOU CAN HAVE IT AFTER ALL.
ALL RIGHT, JAMESON.
WHAT GIVES?
?
PLOP!
THE SHROUD HEALED MY CHEST!
NOW YOU DO NOT HAVE THE POWER TO ALTER MY WILL!
THE SYMBIOTE WILL DIE!

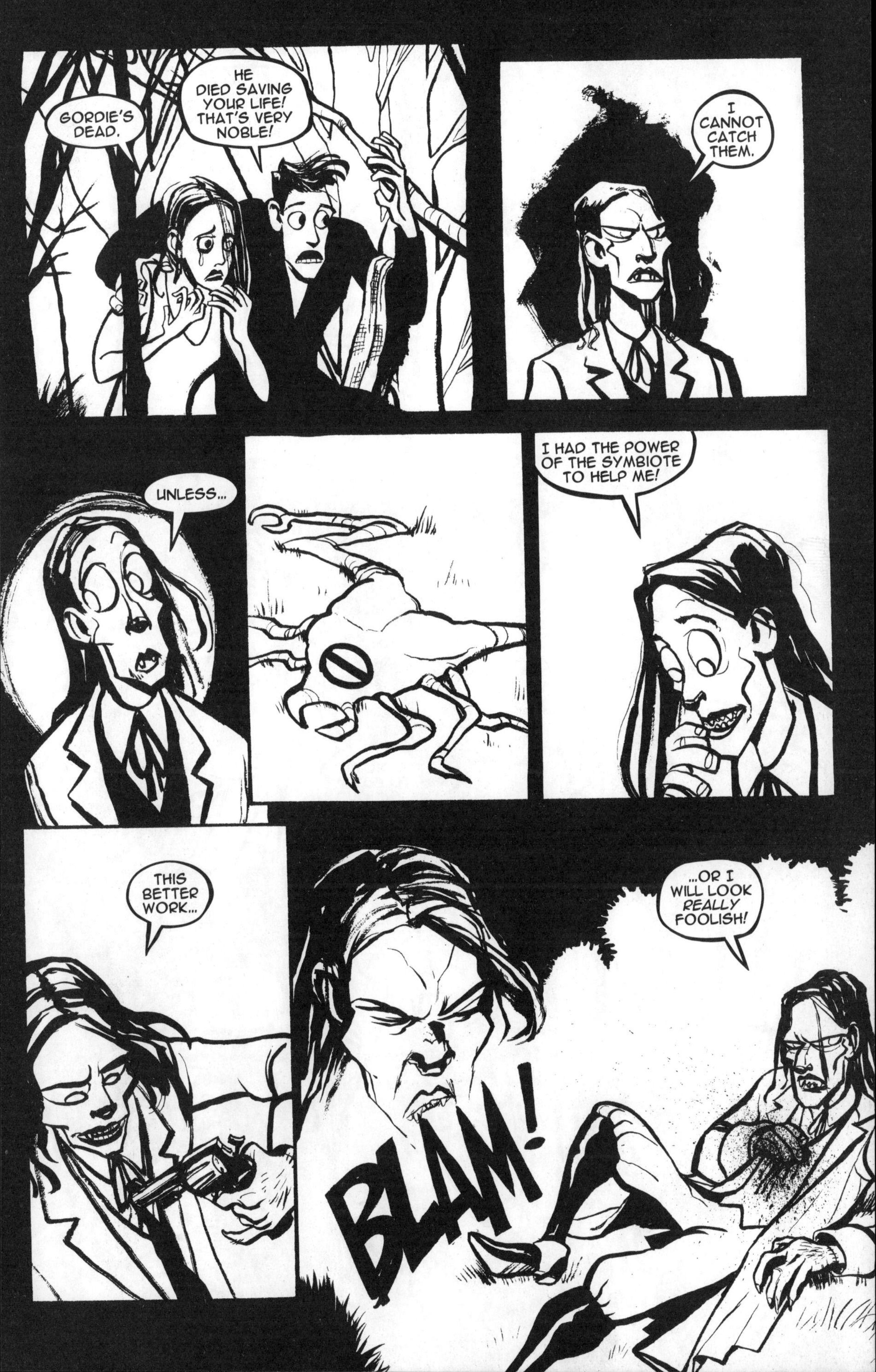
GORDIE'S DEAD.
HE DIED SAVING YOUR LIFE! THAT'S VERY NOBLE!
I CANNOT CATCH THEM.
UNLESS...
I HAD THE POWER OF THE SYMBIOTE TO HELP ME!
THIS BETTER WORK...
BLAM!
...OR I WILL LOOK *REALLY* FOOLISH!

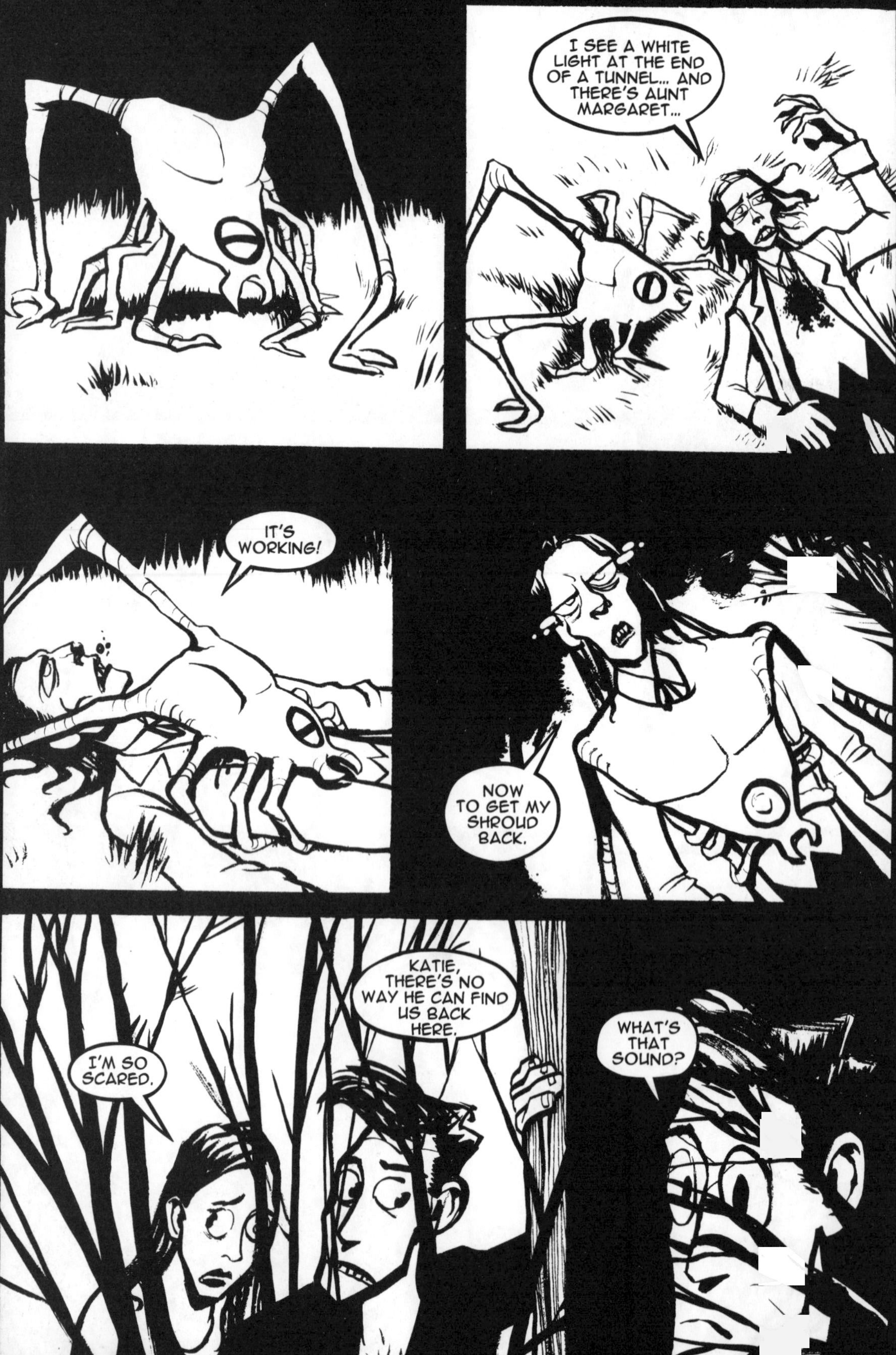
I SEE A WHITE LIGHT AT THE END OF A TUNNEL... AND THERE'S AUNT MARGARET...
IT'S WORKING!
NOW TO GET MY SHROUD BACK.
I'M SO SCARED.
KATIE, THERE'S NO WAY HE CAN FIND US BACK HERE.
WHAT'S THAT SOUND?

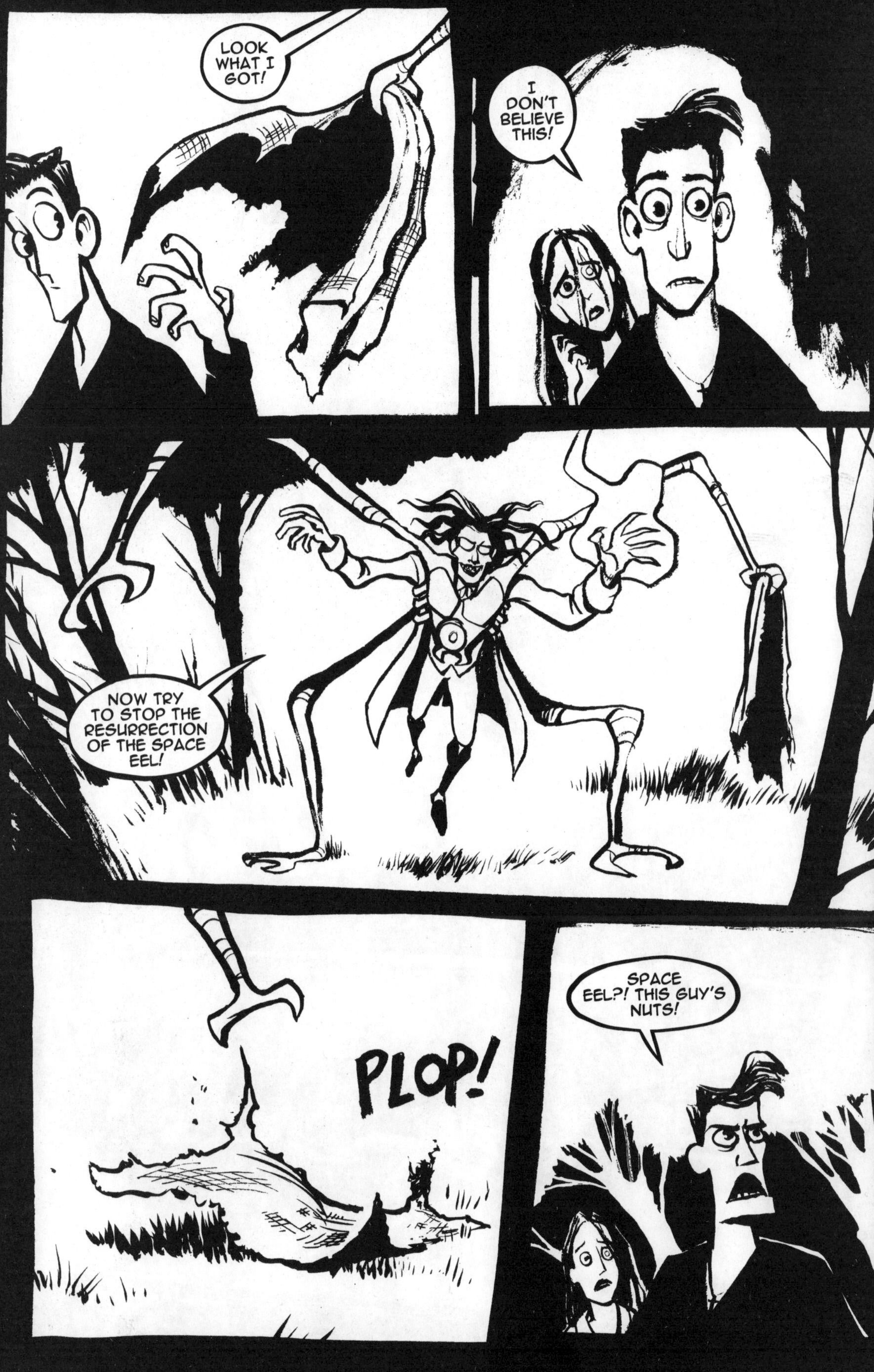
LOOK WHAT I GOT!
I DON'T BELIEVE THIS!
NOW TRY TO STOP THE RESURRECTION OF THE SPACE EEL!
PLOP!
SPACE EEL?! THIS GUY'S NUTS!

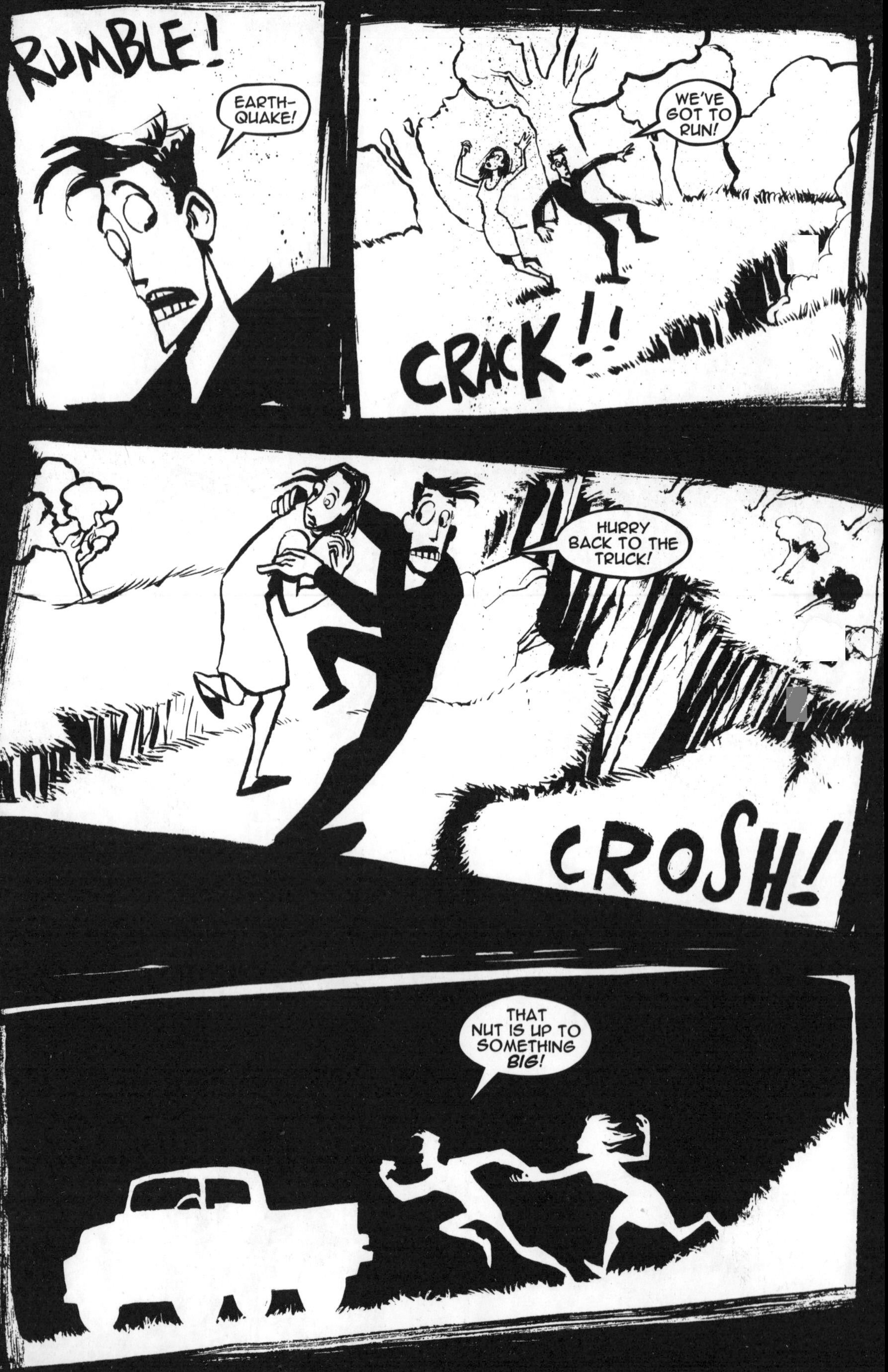
RUMBLE!
EARTH-QUAKE!
WE'VE GOT TO RUN!
CRACK!!
HURRY BACK TO THE TRUCK!
CROSH!
THAT NUT IS UP TO SOMETHING BIG!

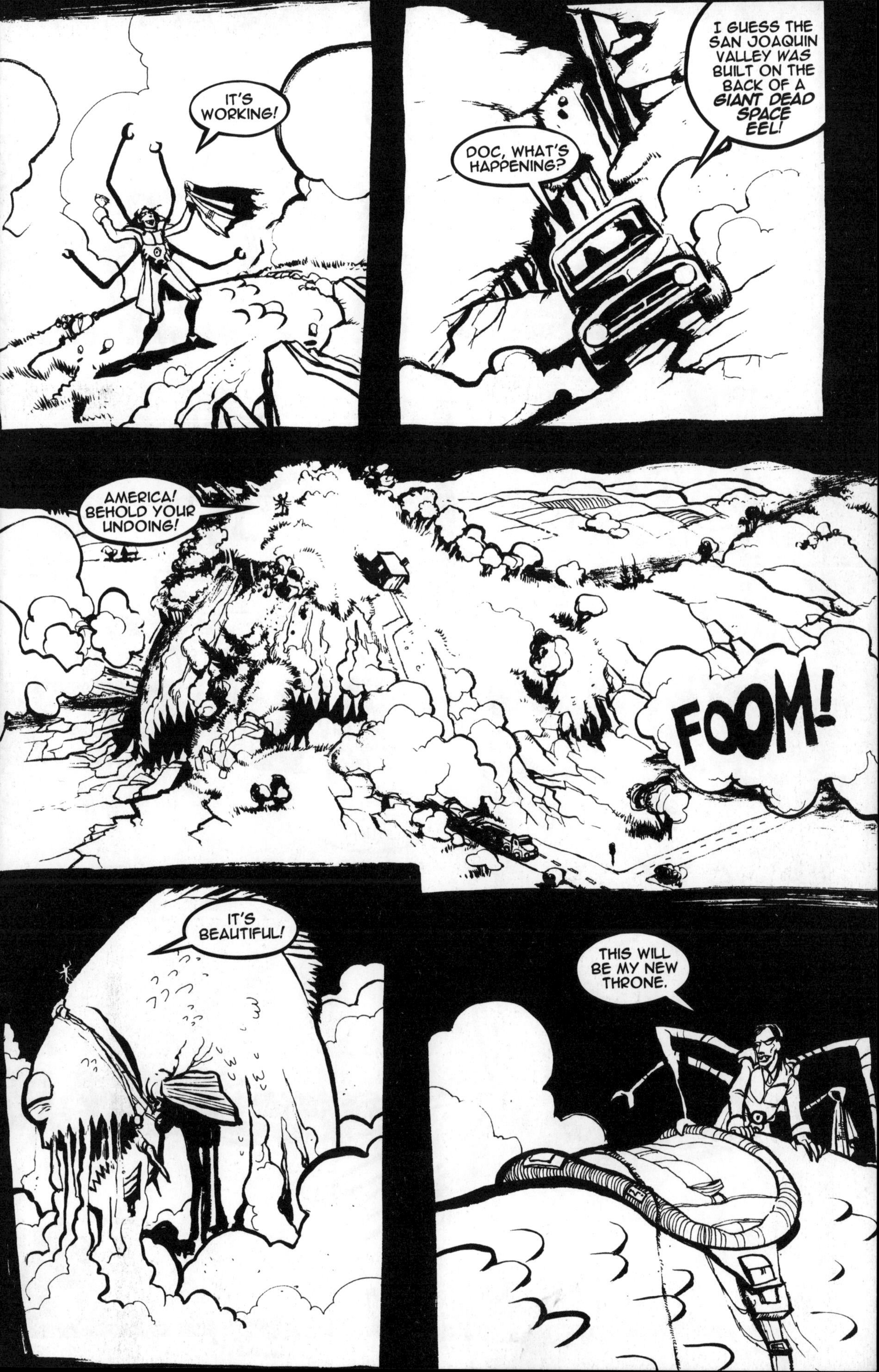
IT'S WORKING!
DOC, WHAT'S HAPPENING?
I GUESS THE SAN JOAQUIN VALLEY WAS BUILT ON THE BACK OF A GIANT DEAD SPACE EEL!
AMERICA! BEHOLD YOUR UNDOING!
FOOM!
IT'S BEAUTIFUL!
THIS WILL BE MY NEW THRONE.

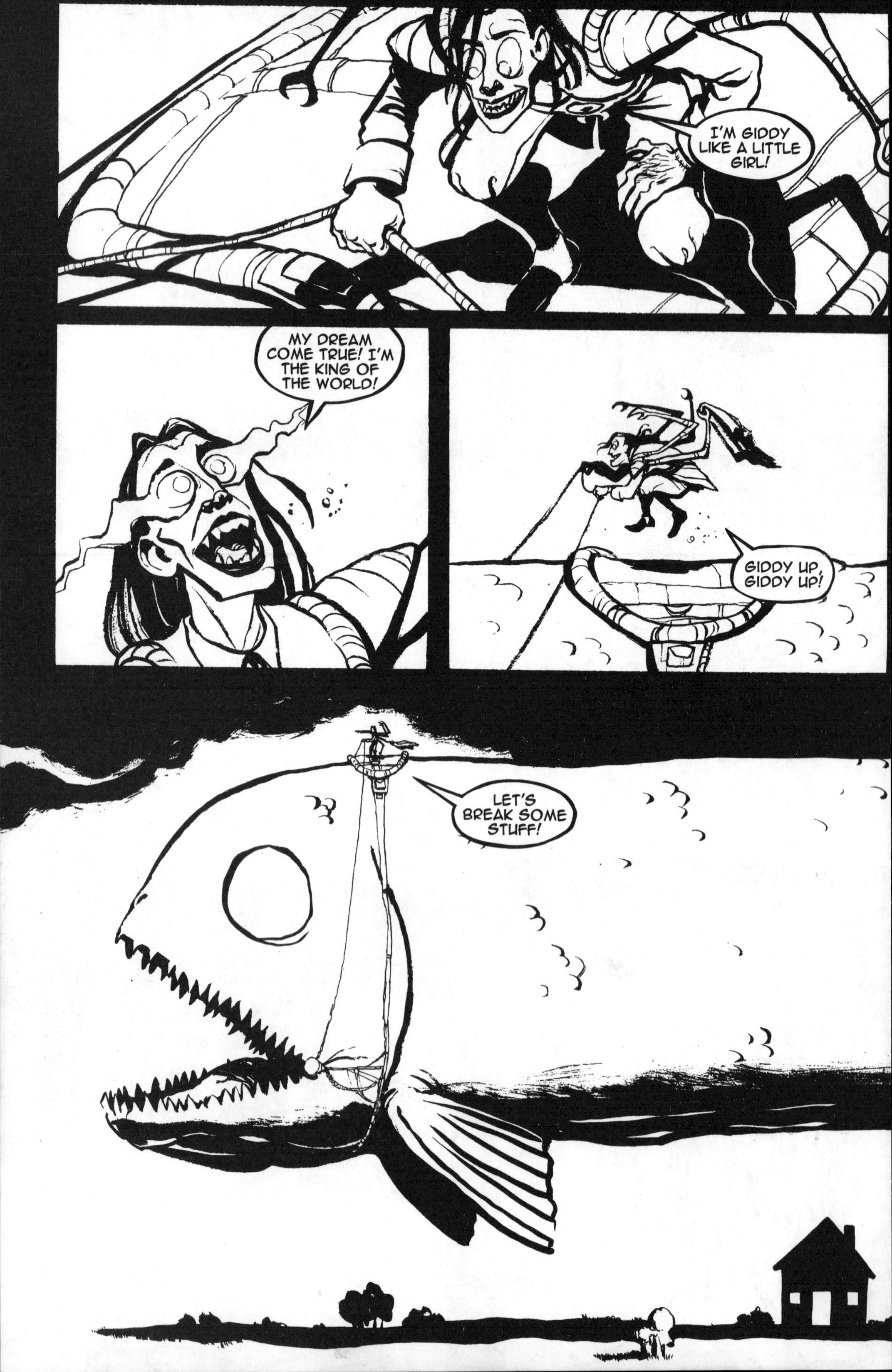
I'M GIDDY LIKE A LITTLE GIRL!
MY DREAM COME TRUE! I'M THE KING OF THE WORLD!
GIDDY UP, GIDDY UP!
LET'S BREAK SOME STUFF!

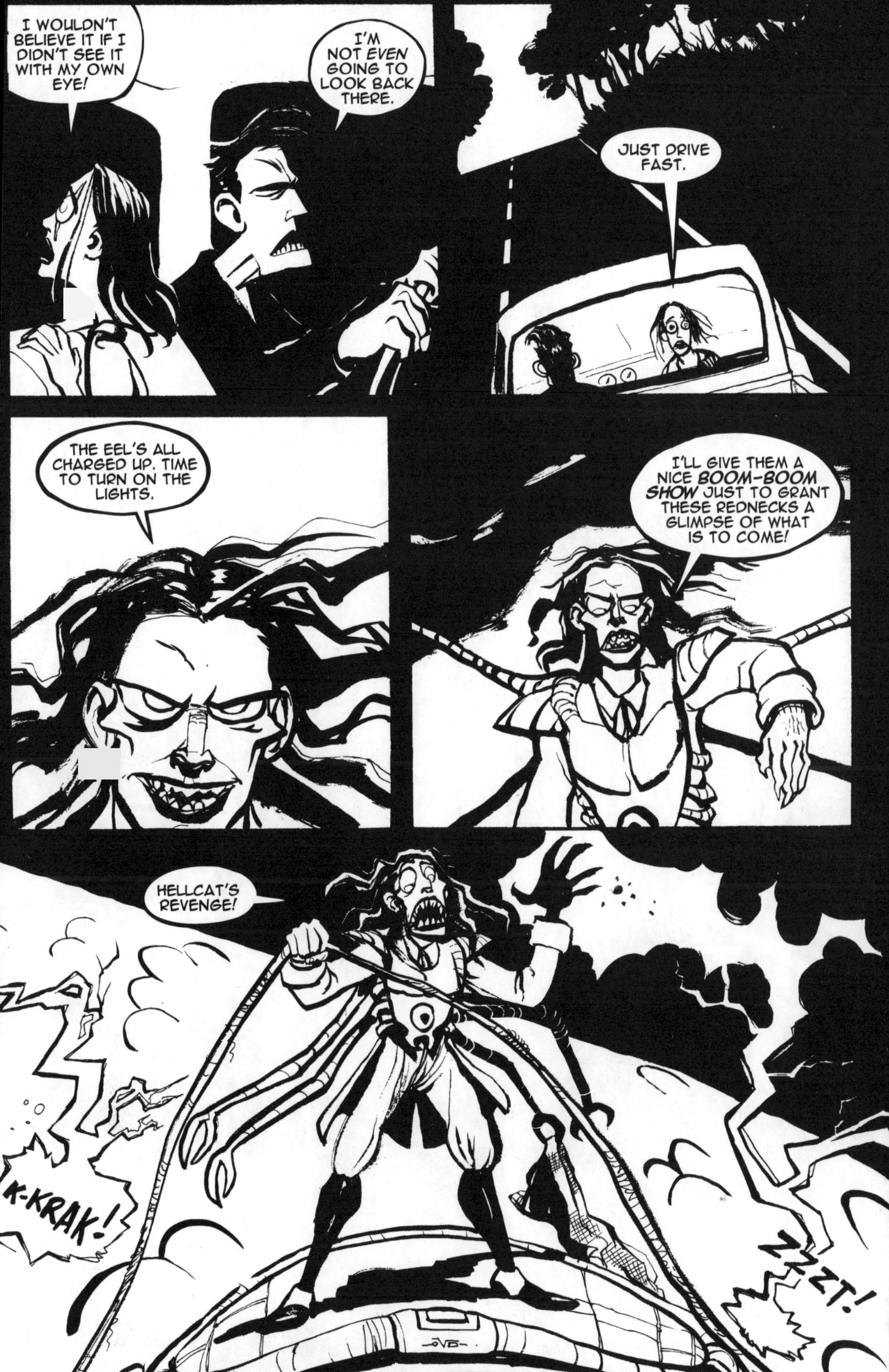

I WOULDN'T BELIEVE IT IF I DIDN'T SEE IT WITH MY OWN EYE!
I'M NOT *EVEN* GOING TO LOOK BACK THERE.
JUST DRIVE FAST.
THE EEL'S ALL CHARGED UP. TIME TO TURN ON THE LIGHTS.
I'LL GIVE THEM A NICE **BOOM-BOOM SHOW** JUST TO GRANT THESE REDNECKS A GLIMPSE OF WHAT IS TO COME!
HELLCAT'S REVENGE!
K-KRAK!
ZZZZT!

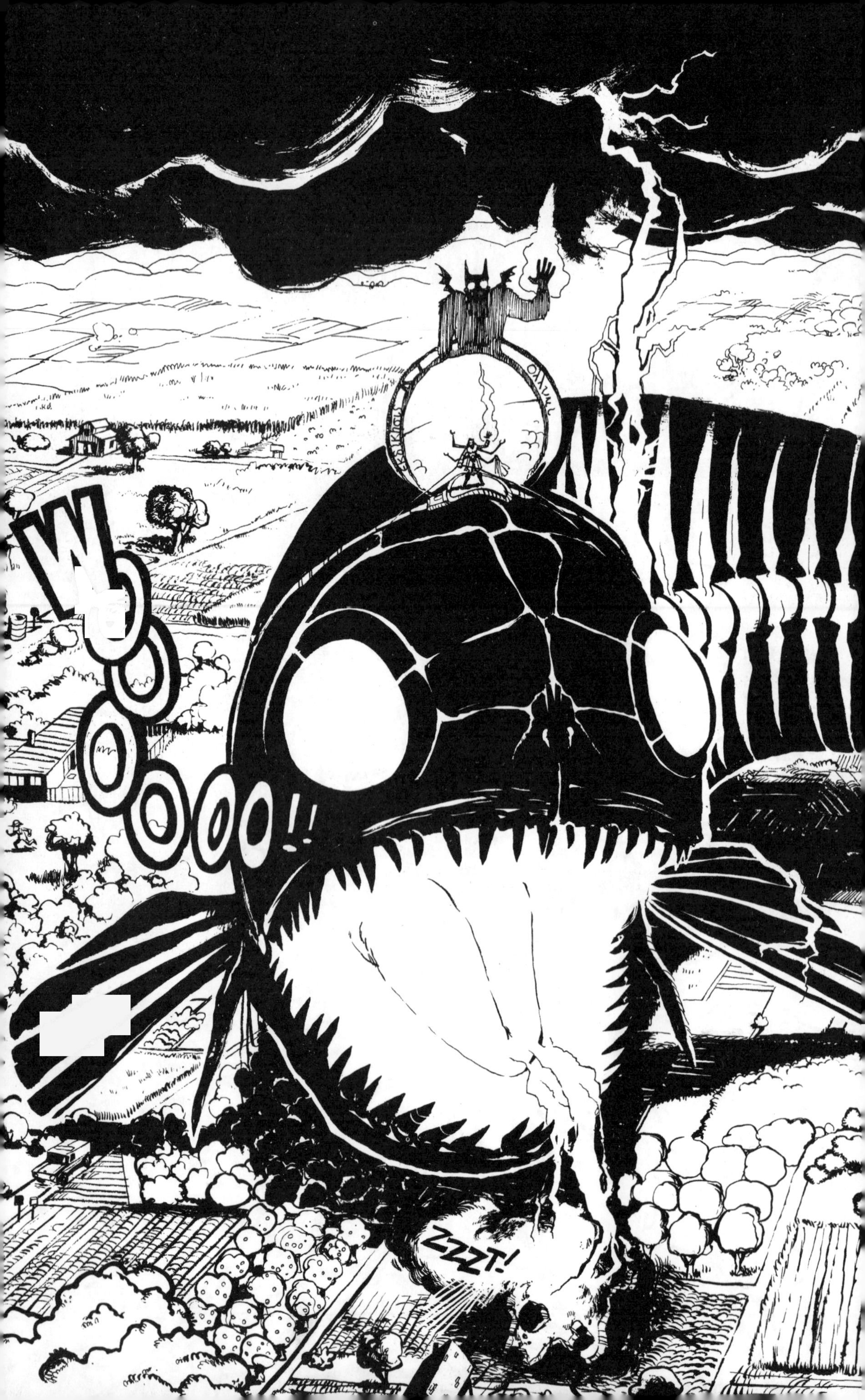
WOOOOOOO!!
ZZZZT!

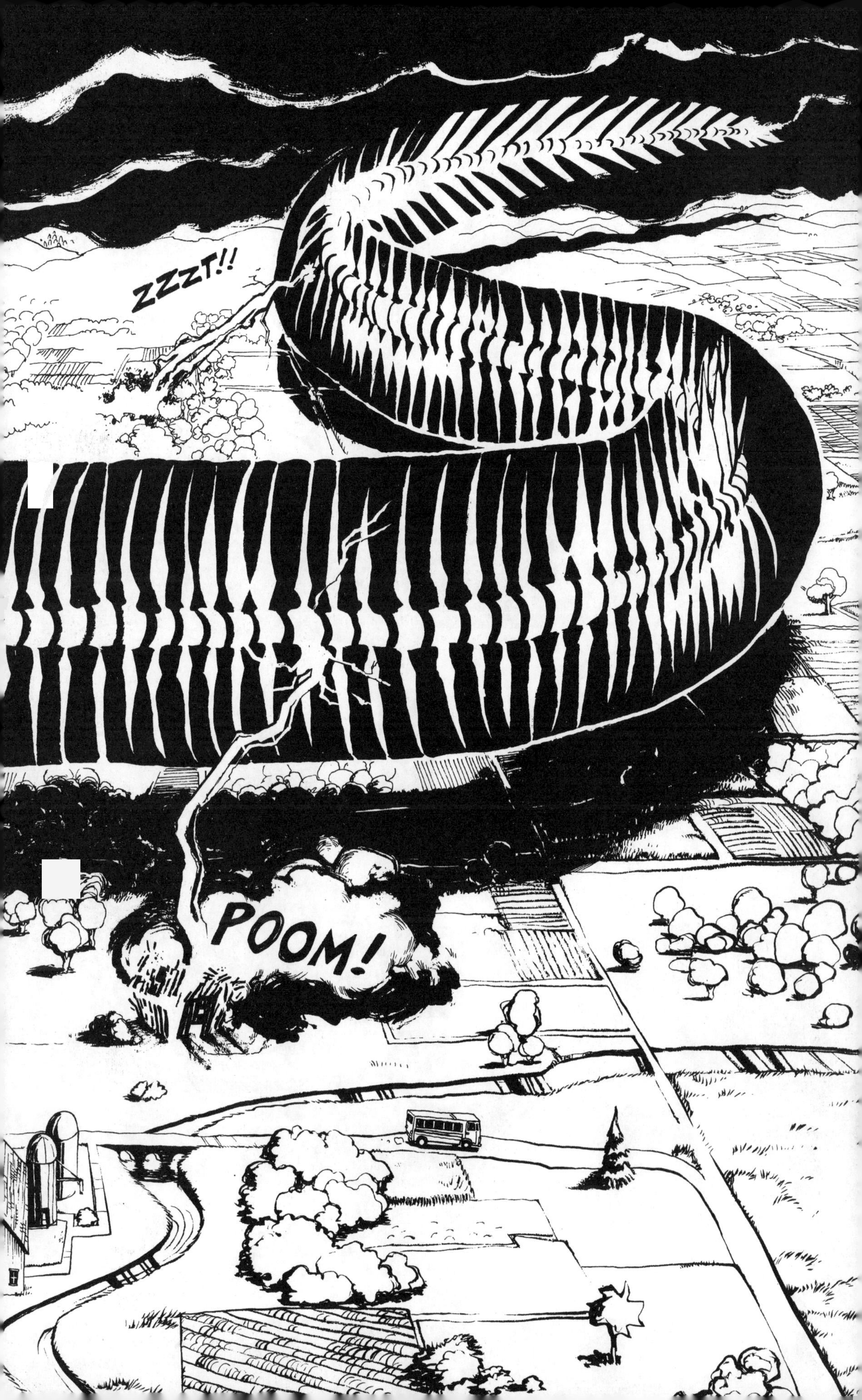
ZZZT!!
POOM!

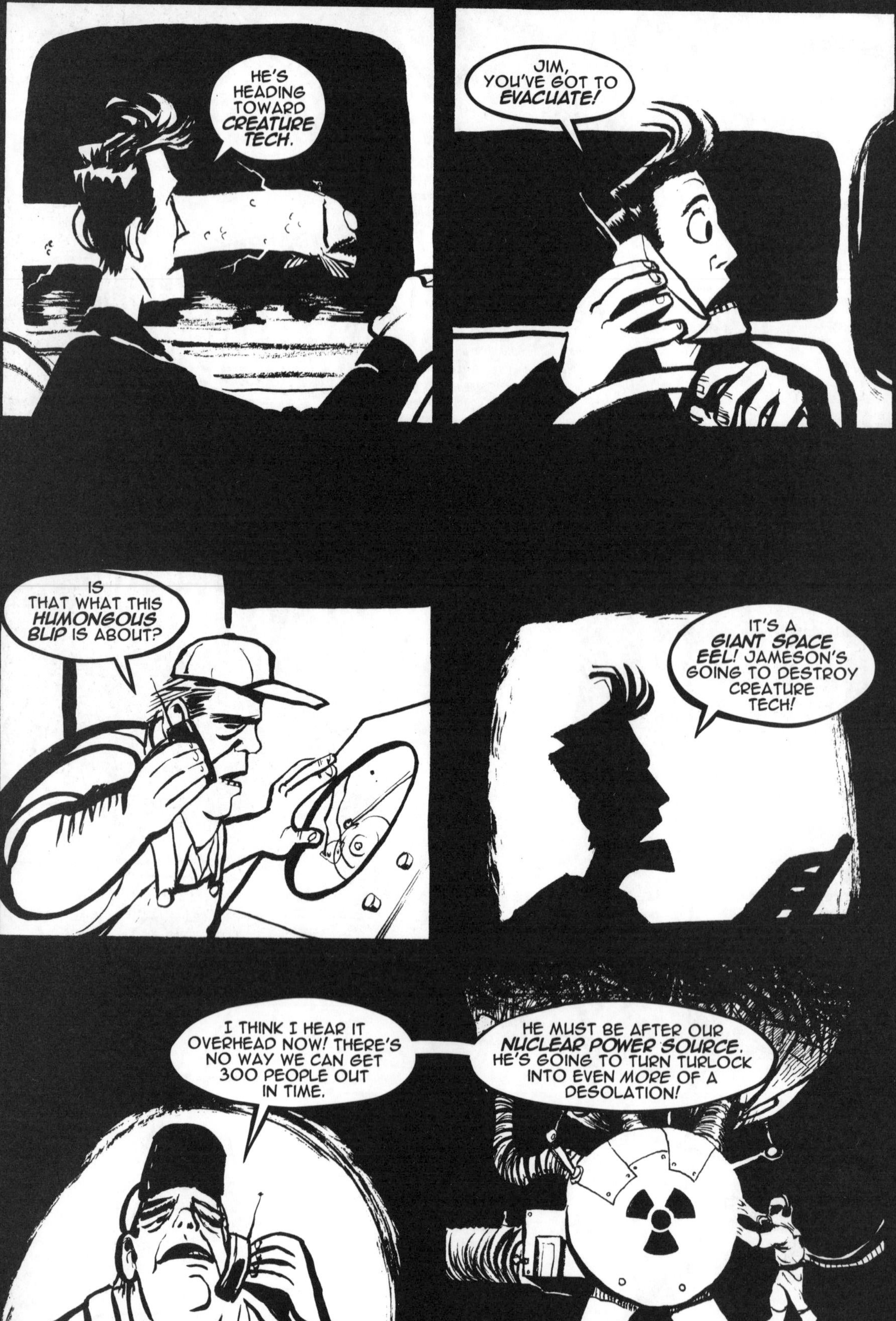
HE'S HEADING TOWARD *CREATURE* TECH.
JIM, YOU'VE GOT TO *EVACUATE!*
IS THAT WHAT THIS *HUMONGOUS BLIP* IS ABOUT?
IT'S A *GIANT SPACE EEL!* JAMESON'S GOING TO DESTROY CREATURE TECH!
I THINK I HEAR IT OVERHEAD NOW! THERE'S NO WAY WE CAN GET 300 PEOPLE OUT IN TIME.
HE MUST BE AFTER OUR *NUCLEAR POWER SOURCE*. HE'S GOING TO TURN TURLOCK INTO EVEN *MORE* OF A DESOLATION!

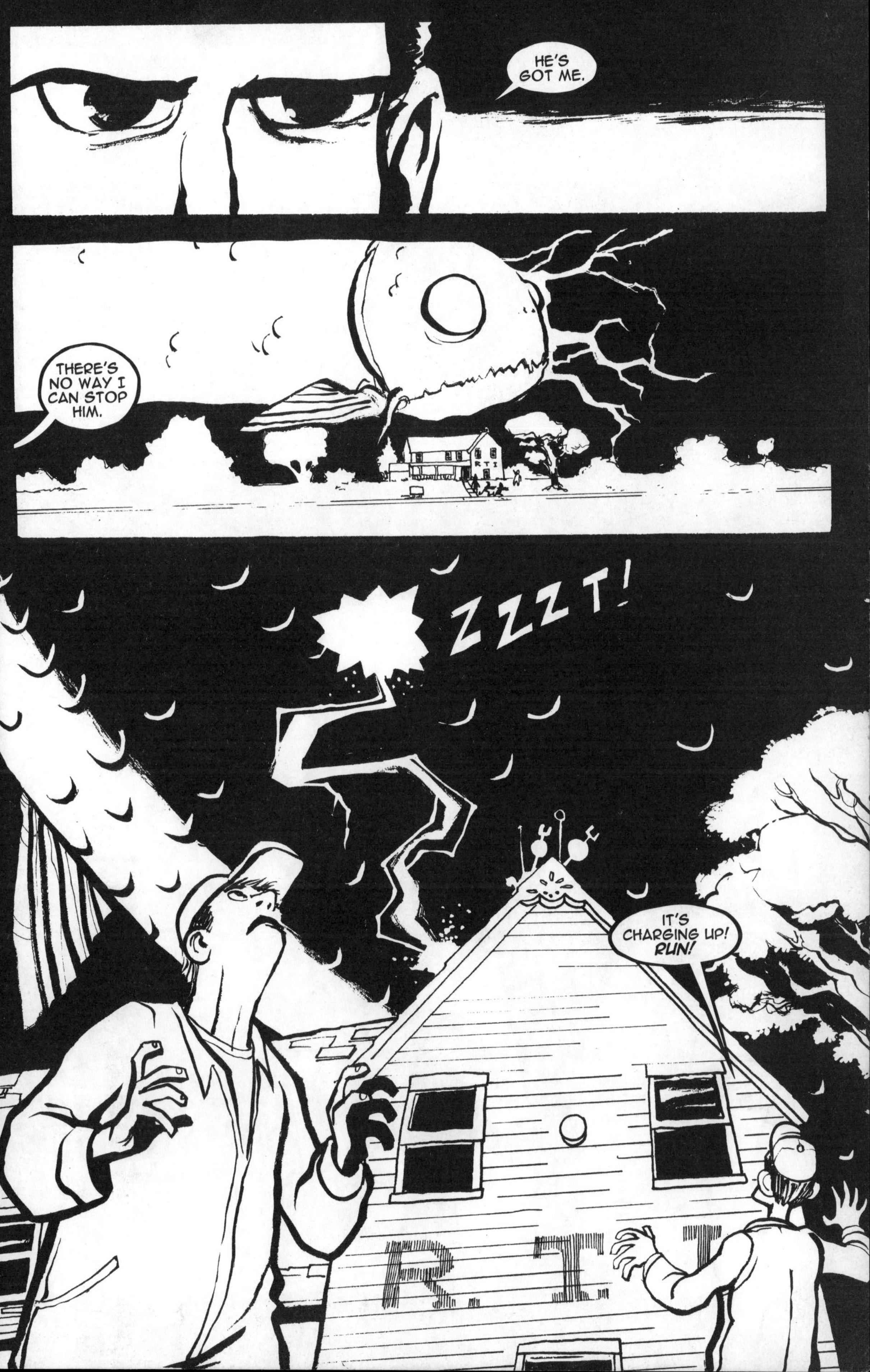
HE'S GOT ME.
THERE'S NO WAY I CAN STOP HIM.
ZZZT!
IT'S CHARGING UP! RUN!

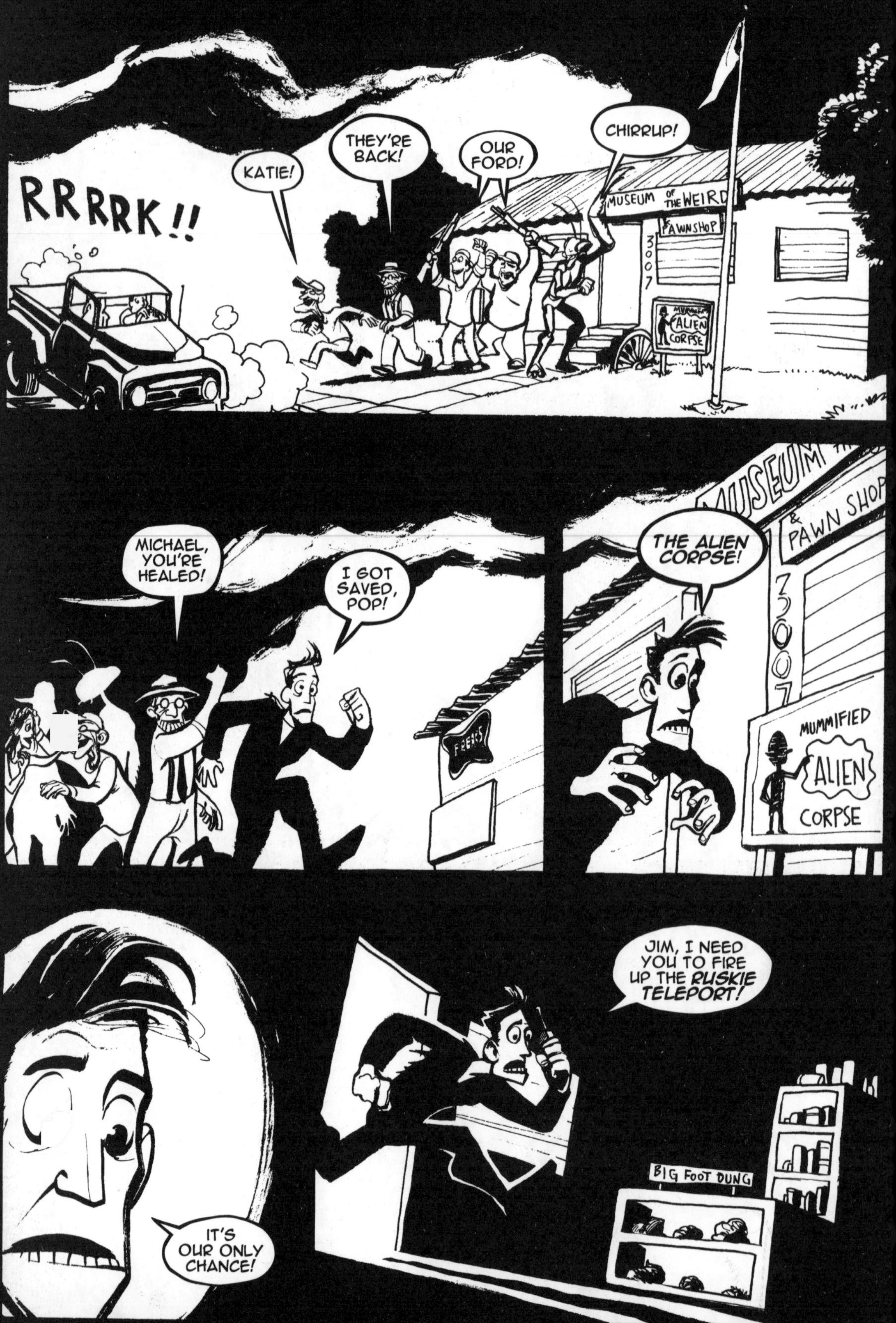
RRRRK!!
KATIE!
THEY'RE BACK!
OUR FORD!
CHIRRUP!
MUSEUM OF THE WEIRD
PAWNSHOP
3007
ALIEN CORPSE
MICHAEL, YOU'RE HEALED!
I GOT SAVED, POP!
MUSEUM
& PAWN SHOP
THE ALIEN CORPSE!
3007
MUMMIFIED ALIEN CORPSE
JIM, I NEED YOU TO FIRE UP THE RUSKIE TELEPORT!
BIG FOOT DUNG
IT'S OUR ONLY CHANCE!

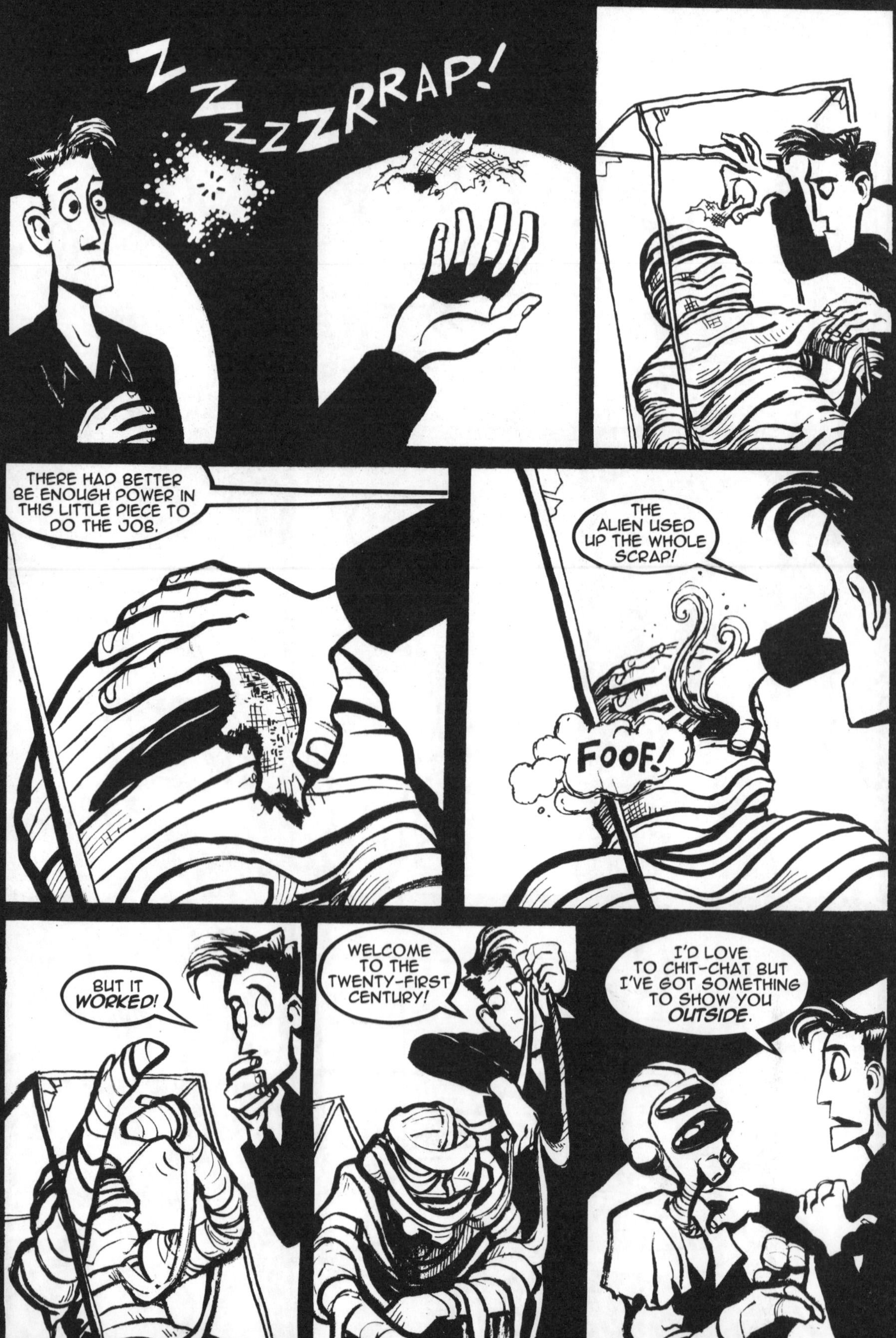
ZZZZZZRRAP!
THERE HAD BETTER BE ENOUGH POWER IN THIS LITTLE PIECE TO DO THE JOB.
THE ALIEN USED UP THE WHOLE SCRAP!
FOOF!
BUT IT WORKED!
WELCOME TO THE TWENTY-FIRST CENTURY!
I'D LOVE TO CHIT-CHAT BUT I'VE GOT SOMETHING TO SHOW YOU OUTSIDE.

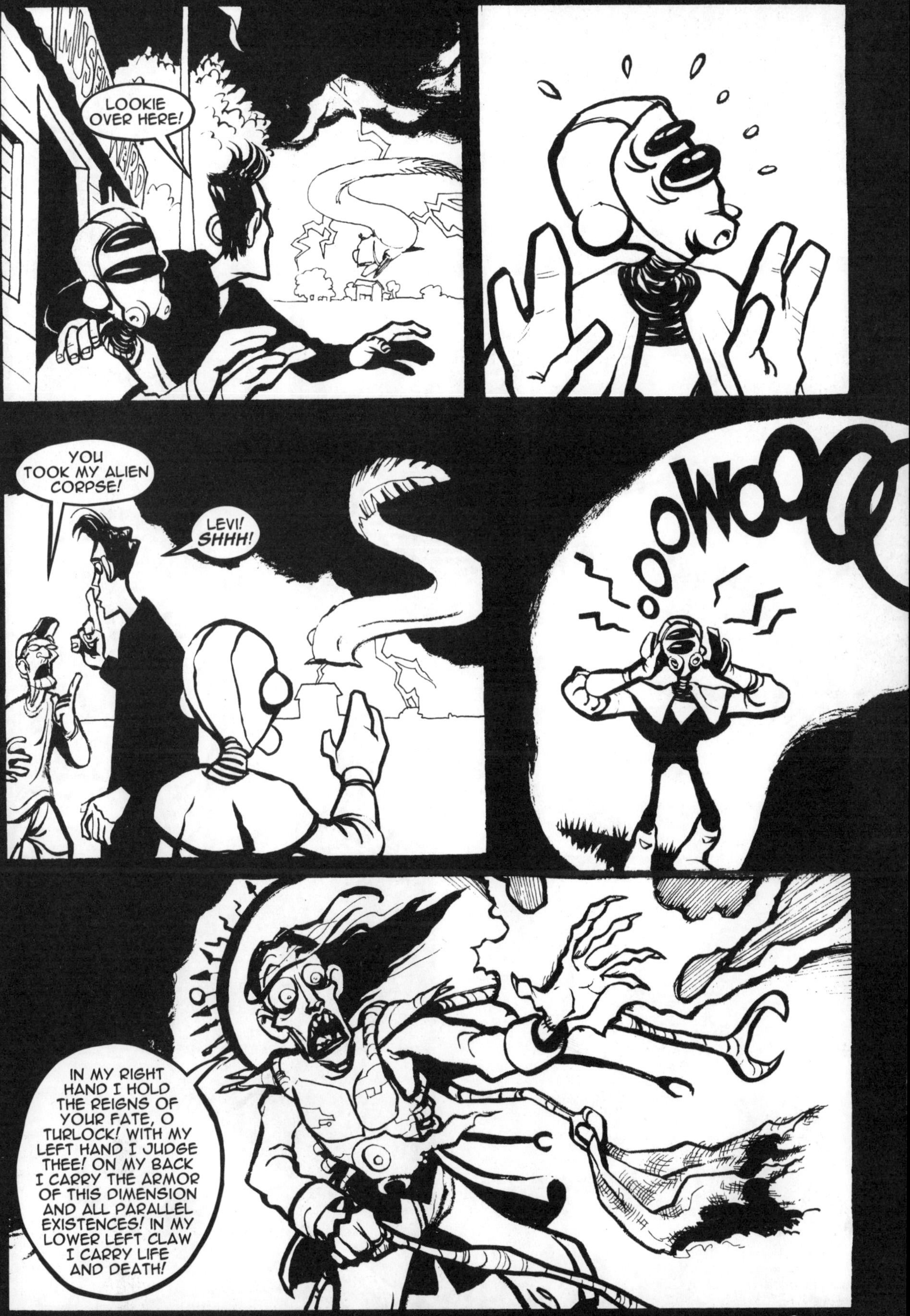
MUSEUM
NERD
LOOKIE OVER HERE!
YOU TOOK MY ALIEN CORPSE!
LEVI! SHHH!
OOWOOO
IN MY RIGHT HAND I HOLD THE REIGNS OF YOUR FATE, O TURLOCK! WITH MY LEFT HAND I JUDGE THEE! ON MY BACK I CARRY THE ARMOR OF THIS DIMENSION AND ALL PARALLEL EXISTENCES! IN MY LOWER LEFT CLAW I CARRY LIFE AND DEATH!
OOOWWOOOOOOOOWOOOOOWWWOOOOOOOOOOOOOOO

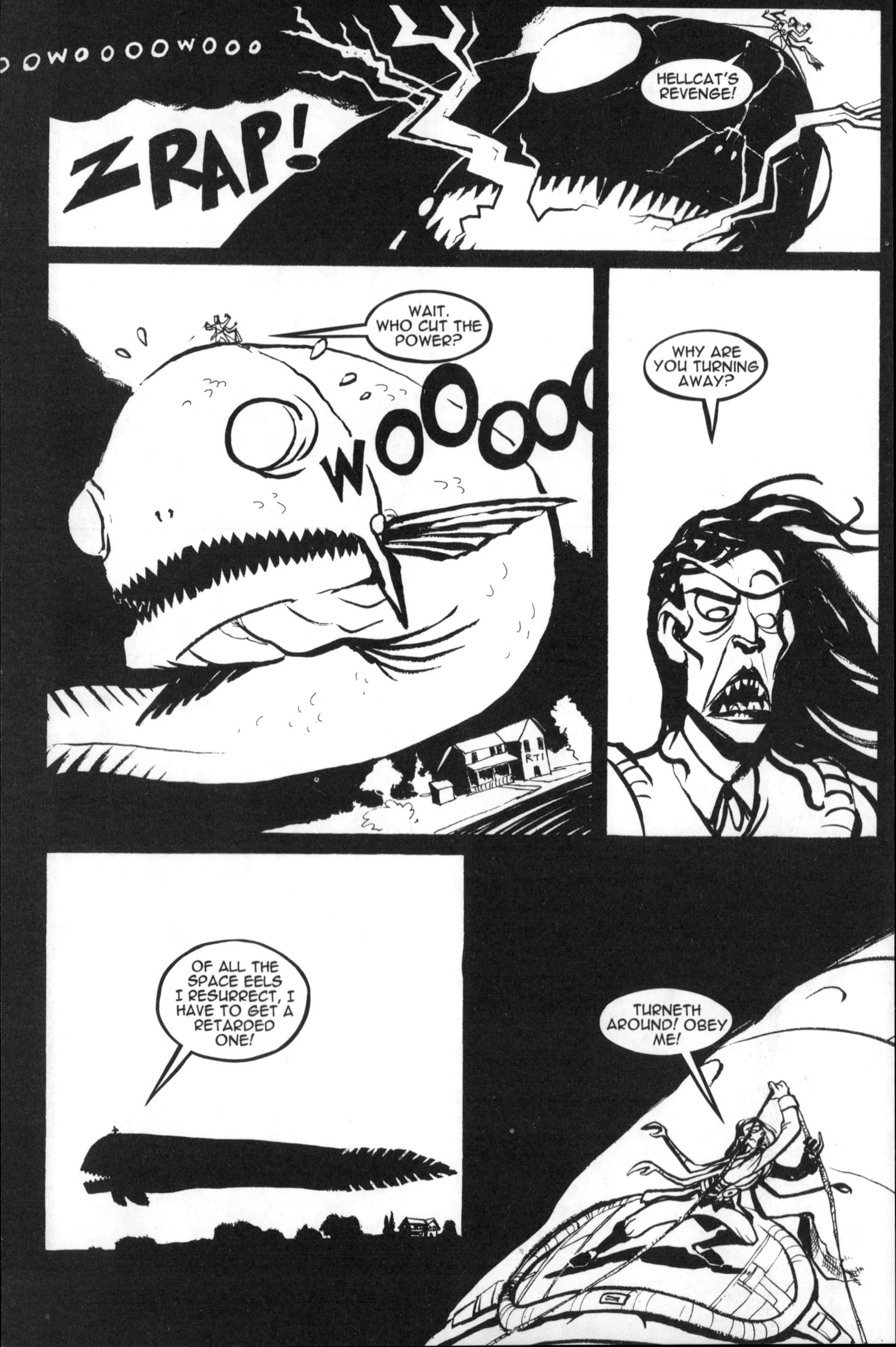
OWOOOOOWOOO
ZRAP!
HELLCAT'S REVENGE!
WAIT. WHO CUT THE POWER?
WOOOOO
WHY ARE YOU TURNING AWAY?
OF ALL THE SPACE EELS I RESURRECT, I HAVE TO GET A RETARDED ONE!
TURNETH AROUND! OBEY ME!

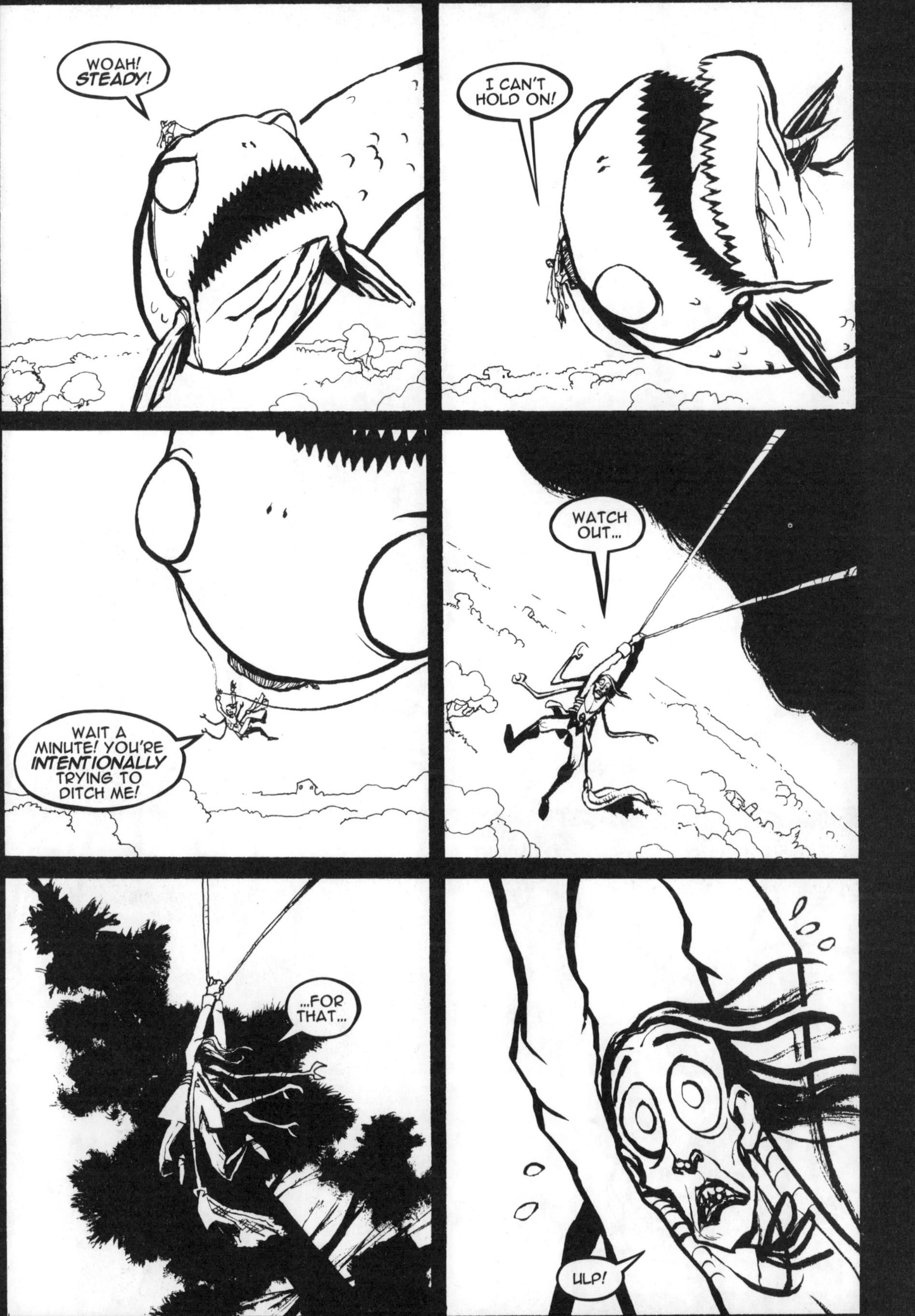
WOAH! STEADY!
I CAN'T HOLD ON!
WAIT A MINUTE! YOU'RE INTENTIONALLY TRYING TO DITCH ME!
WATCH OUT...
...FOR THAT...
ULP!

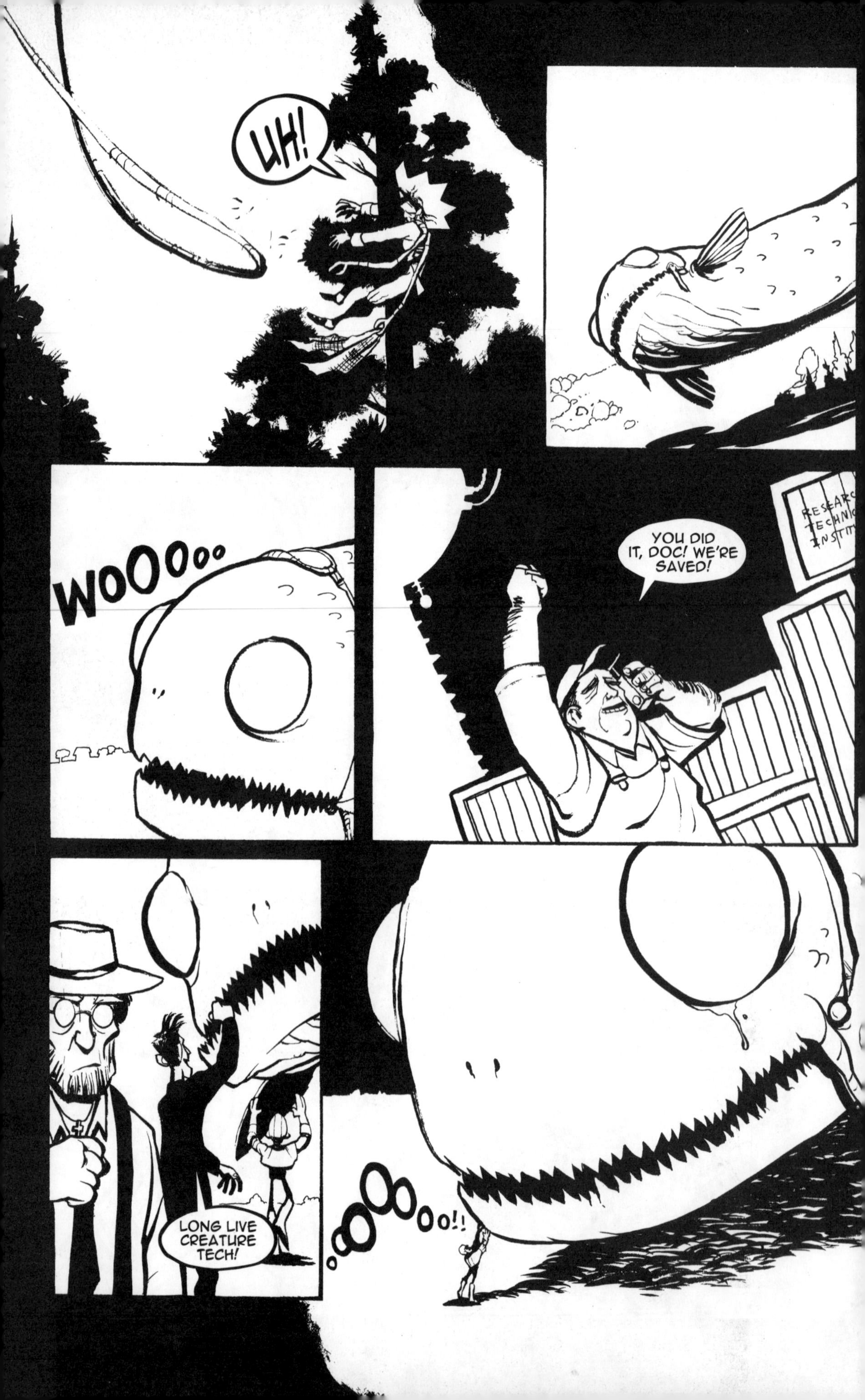
UH!
WOOOoo
YOU DID IT, DOC! WE'RE SAVED!
LONG LIVE CREATURE TECH!
oOOOOoo!!

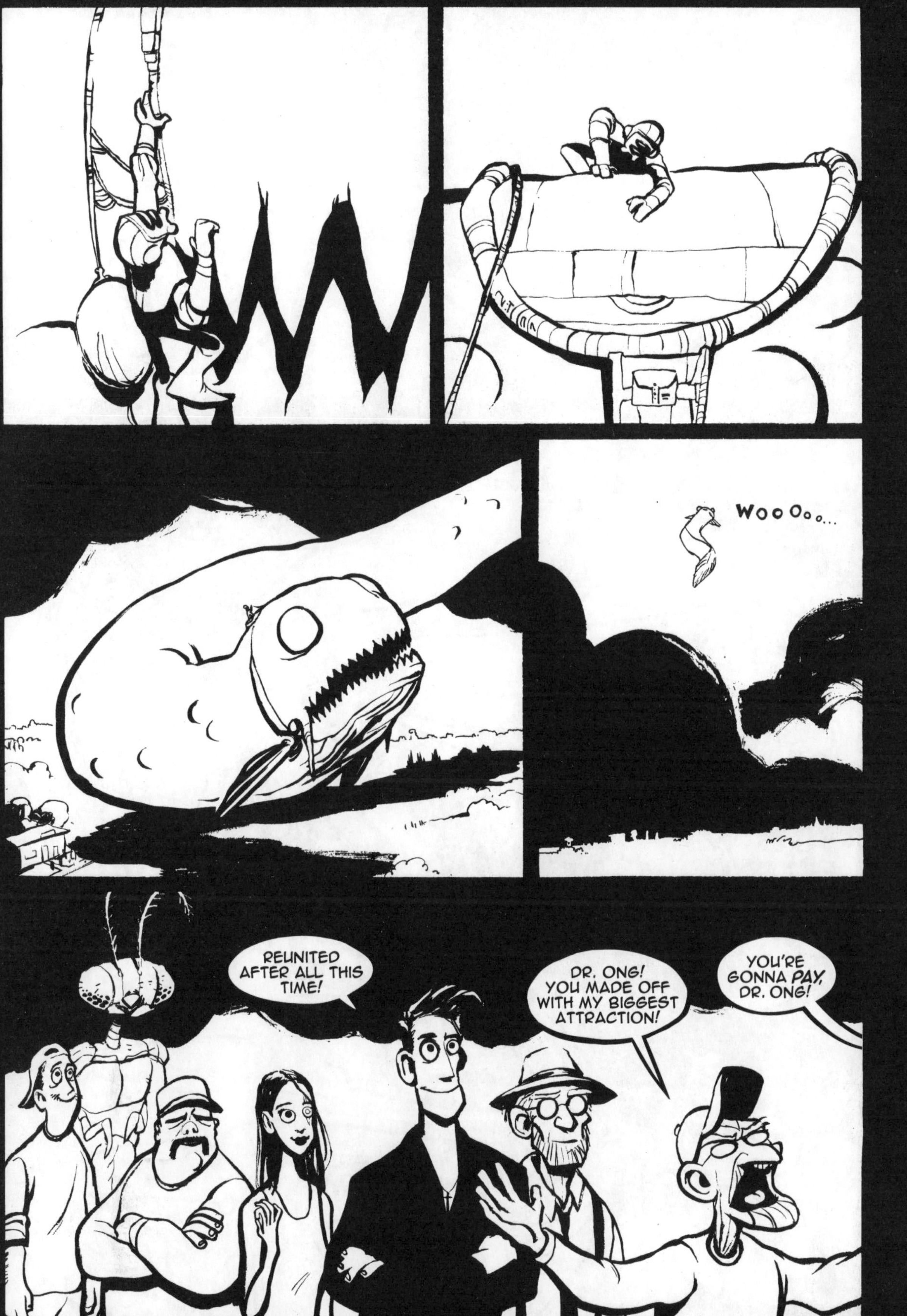
WOOOoo...
REUNITED AFTER ALL THIS TIME!
DR. ONG! YOU MADE OFF WITH MY BIGGEST ATTRACTION!
YOU'RE GONNA PAY, DR. ONG!

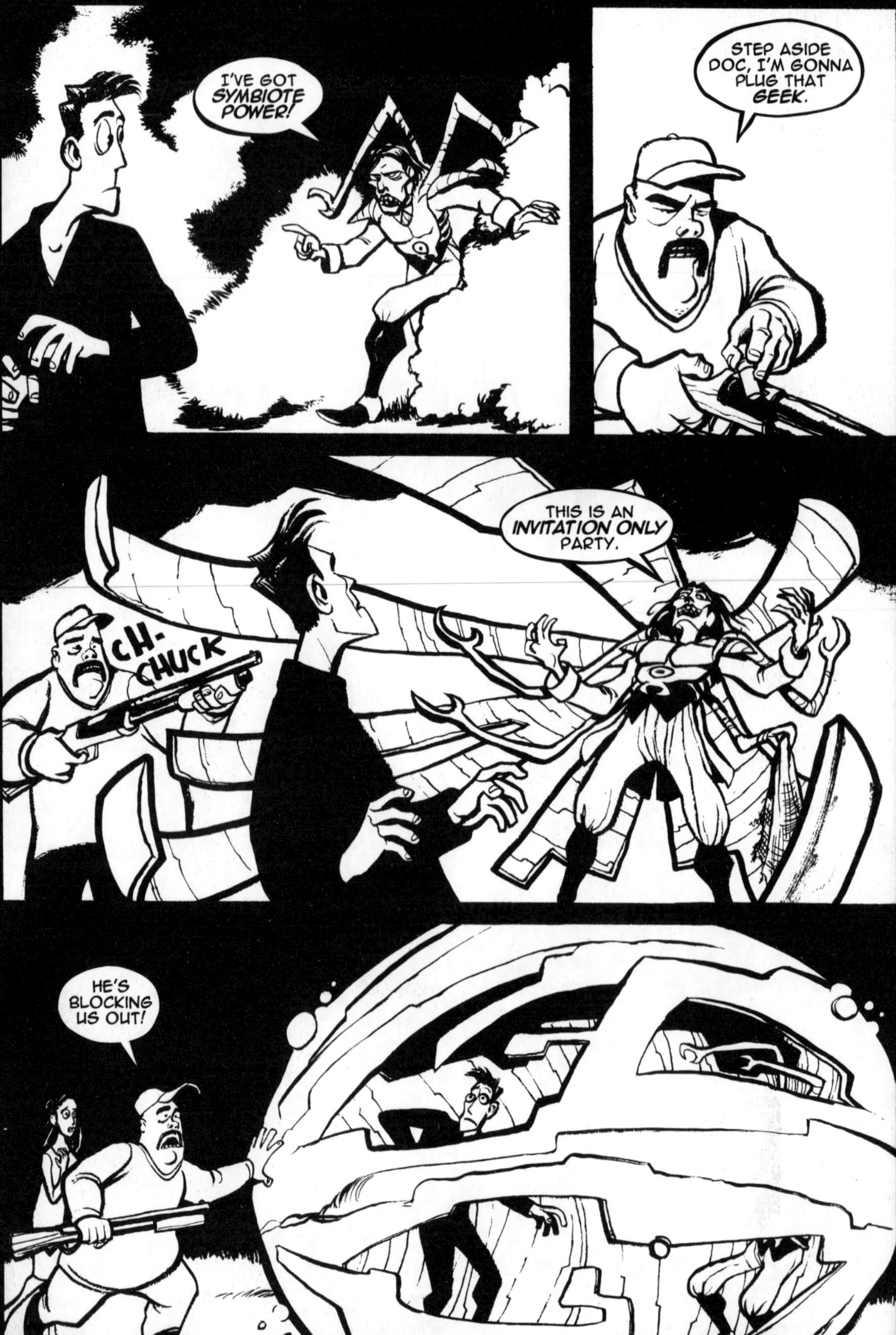
I'VE GOT SYMBIOTE POWER!
STEP ASIDE DOC, I'M GONNA PLUG THAT GEEK.
THIS IS AN INVITATION ONLY PARTY.
CH-CHUCK
HE'S BLOCKING US OUT!

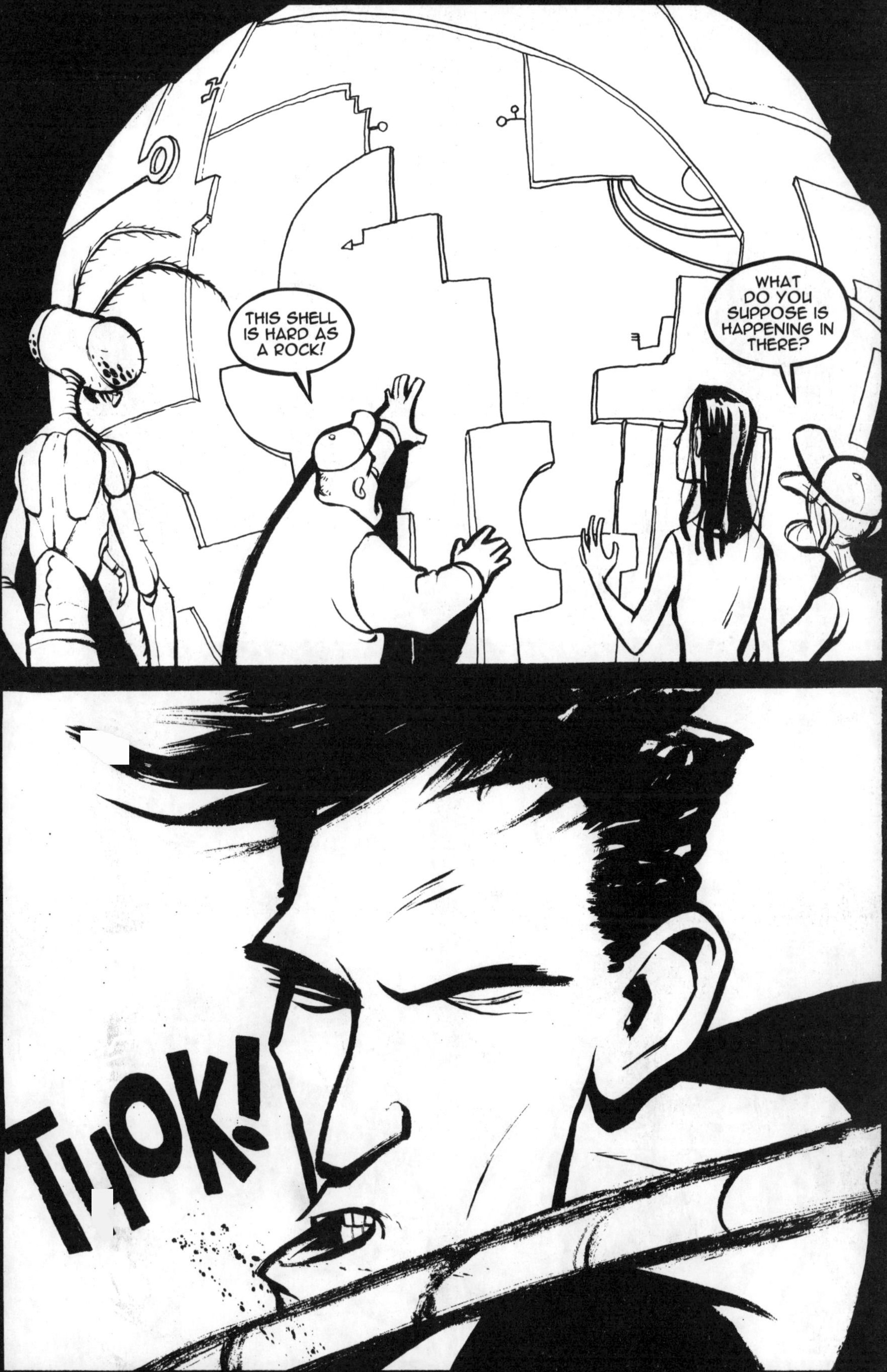
THIS SHELL IS HARD AS A ROCK!
WHAT DO YOU SUPPOSE IS HAPPENING IN THERE?
THOK!

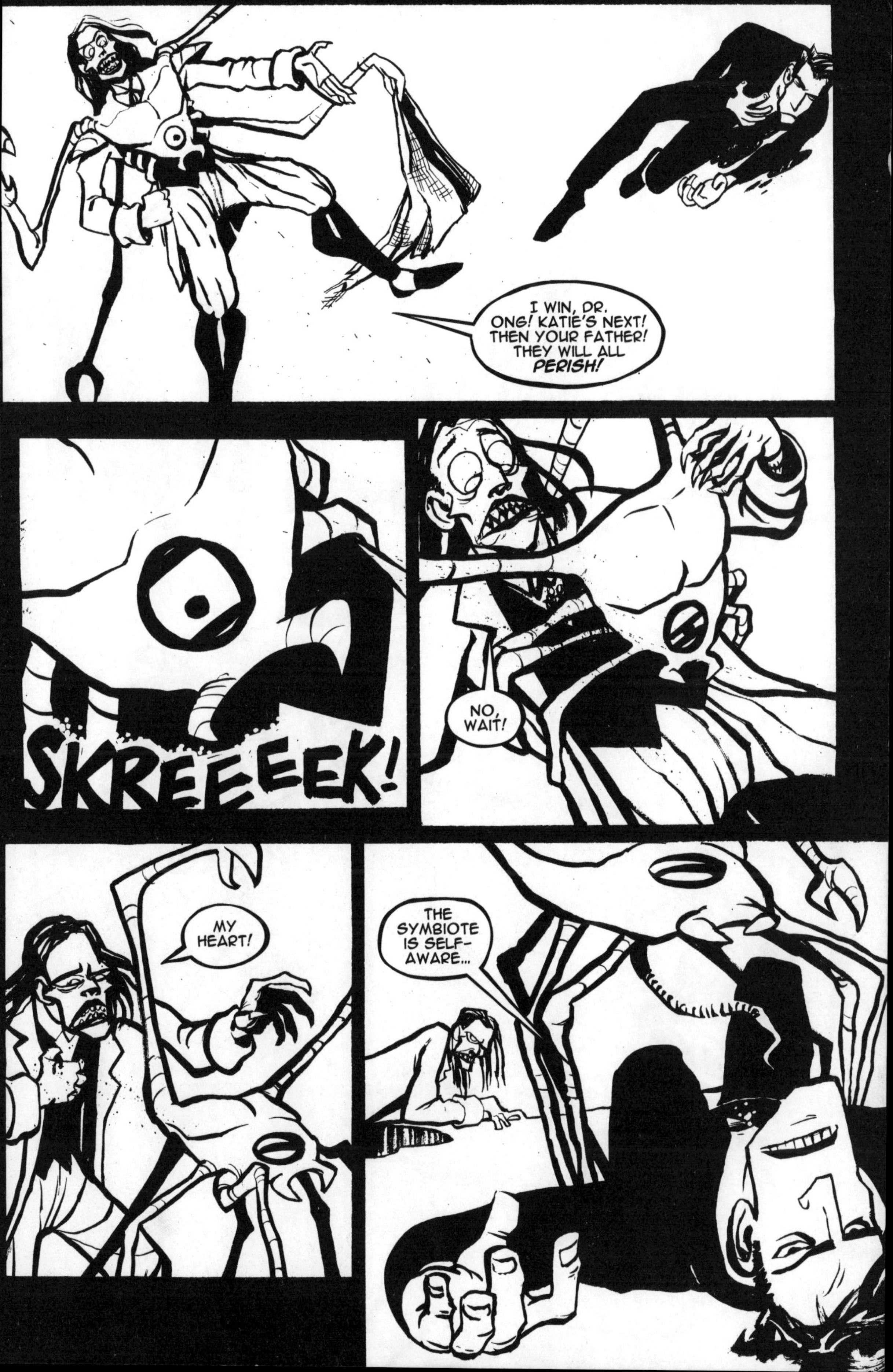
I WIN, DR. ONG! KATIE'S NEXT! THEN YOUR FATHER! THEY WILL ALL *PERISH!*
SKREEEEK!
NO, WAIT!
MY HEART!
THE SYMBIOTE IS SELF-AWARE...

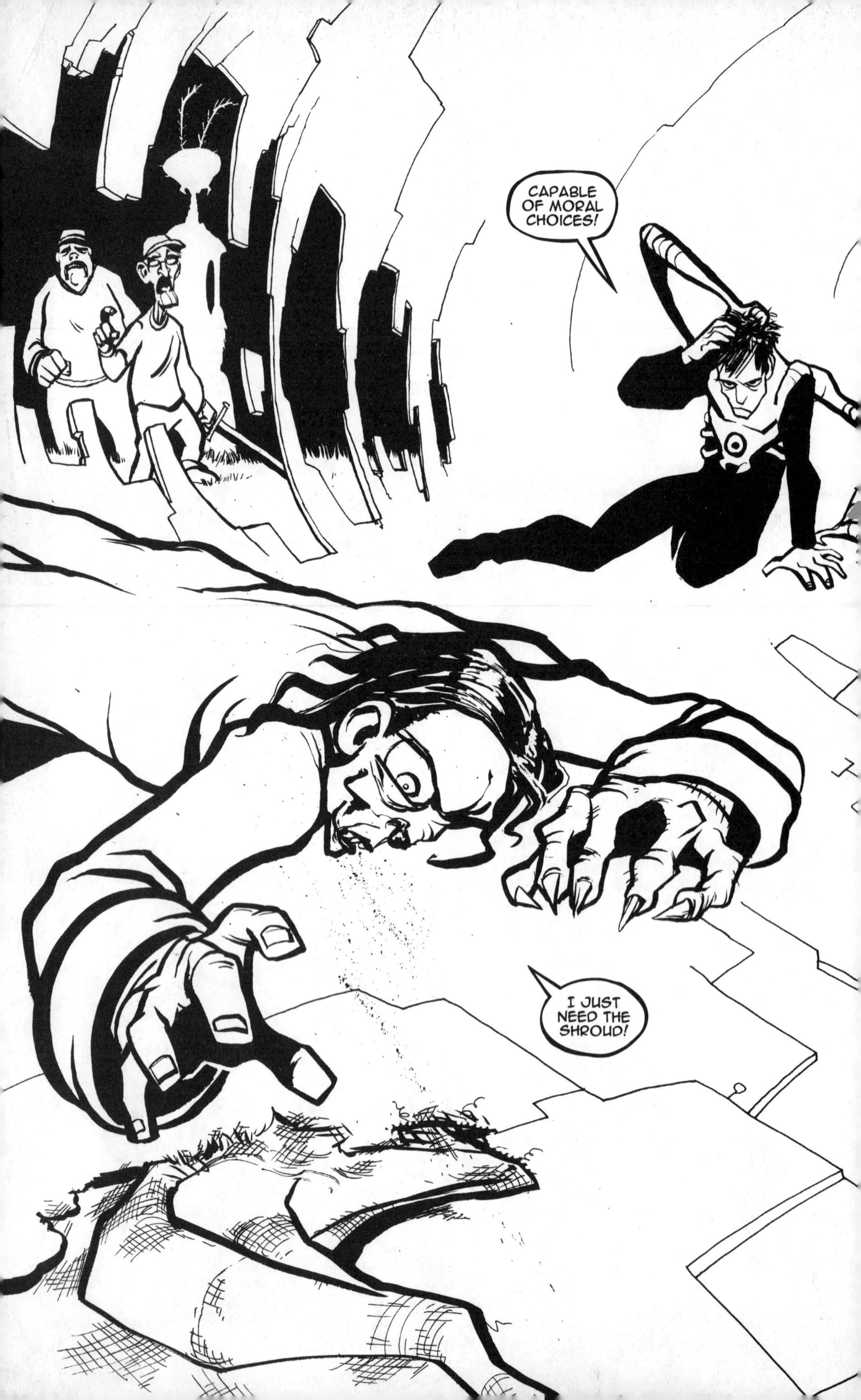
CAPABLE OF MORAL CHOICES!
I JUST NEED THE SHROUD!

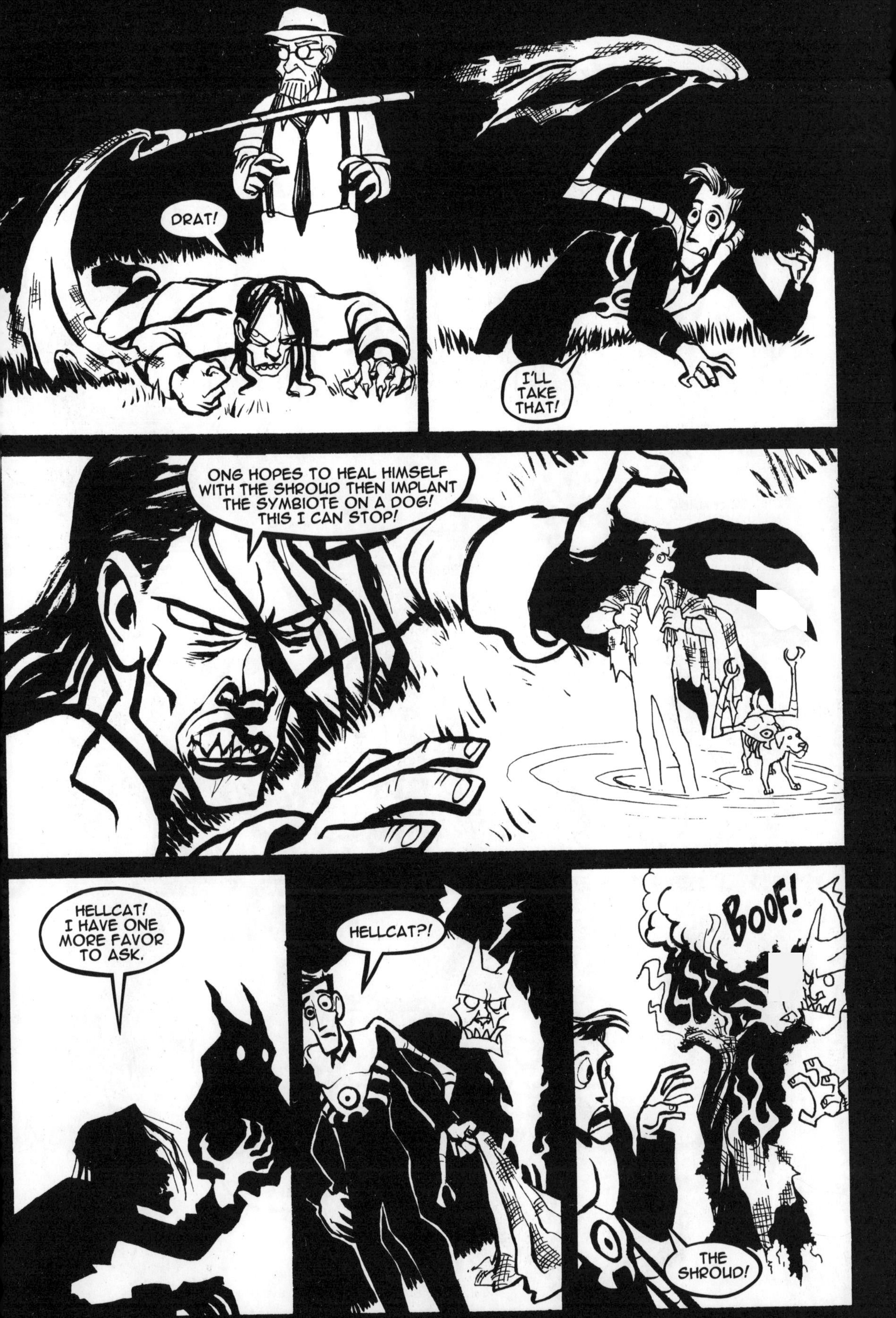
DRAT!
I'LL TAKE THAT!
ONG HOPES TO HEAL HIMSELF WITH THE SHROUD THEN IMPLANT THE SYMBIOTE ON A DOG! THIS I CAN STOP!
HELLCAT! I HAVE ONE MORE FAVOR TO ASK.
HELLCAT?!
BOOF!
THE SHROUD!

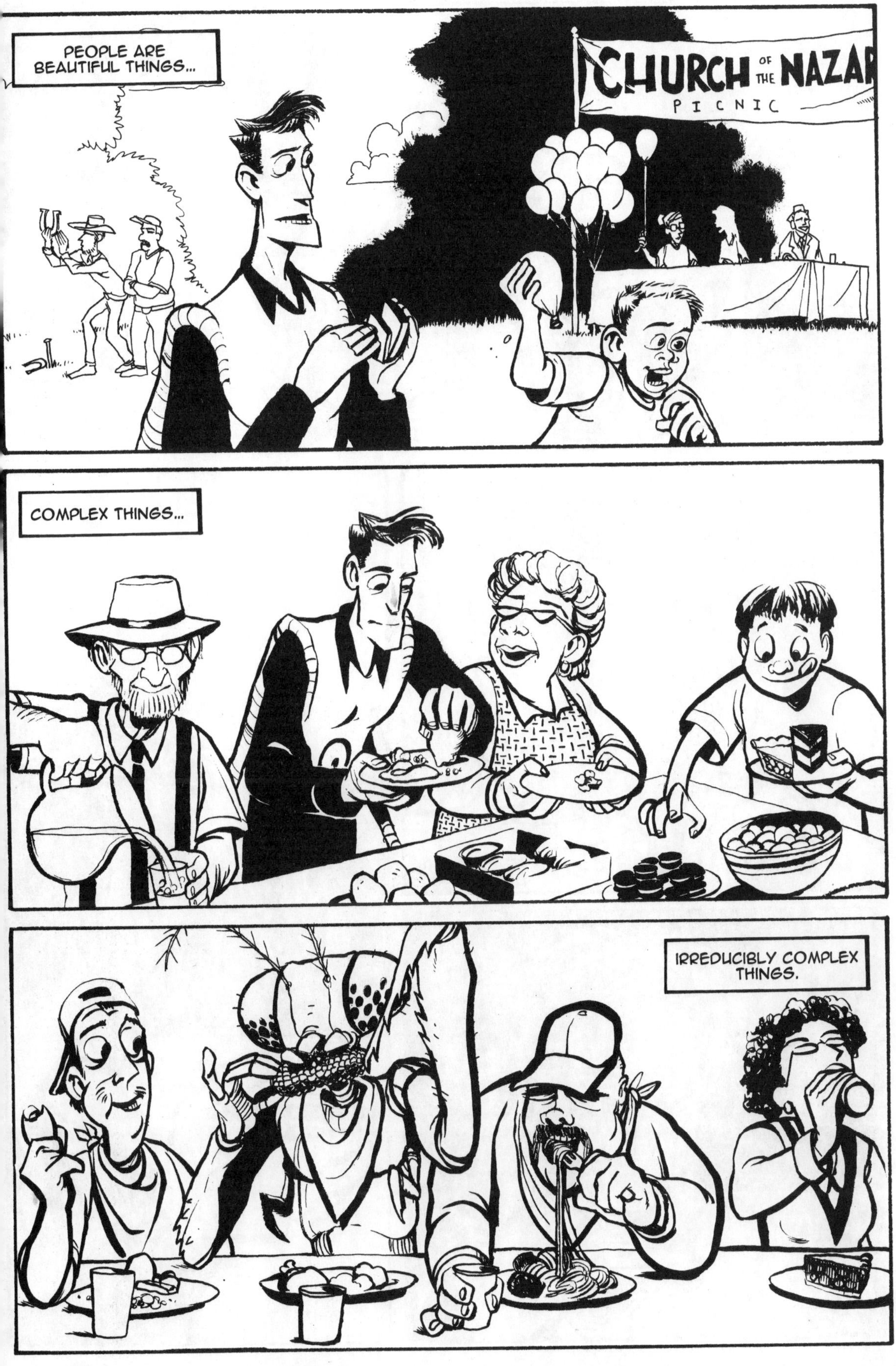
PEOPLE ARE BEAUTIFUL THINGS...
CHURCH OF THE NAZAR
PICNIC
COMPLEX THINGS...
IRREDUCIBLY COMPLEX THINGS.

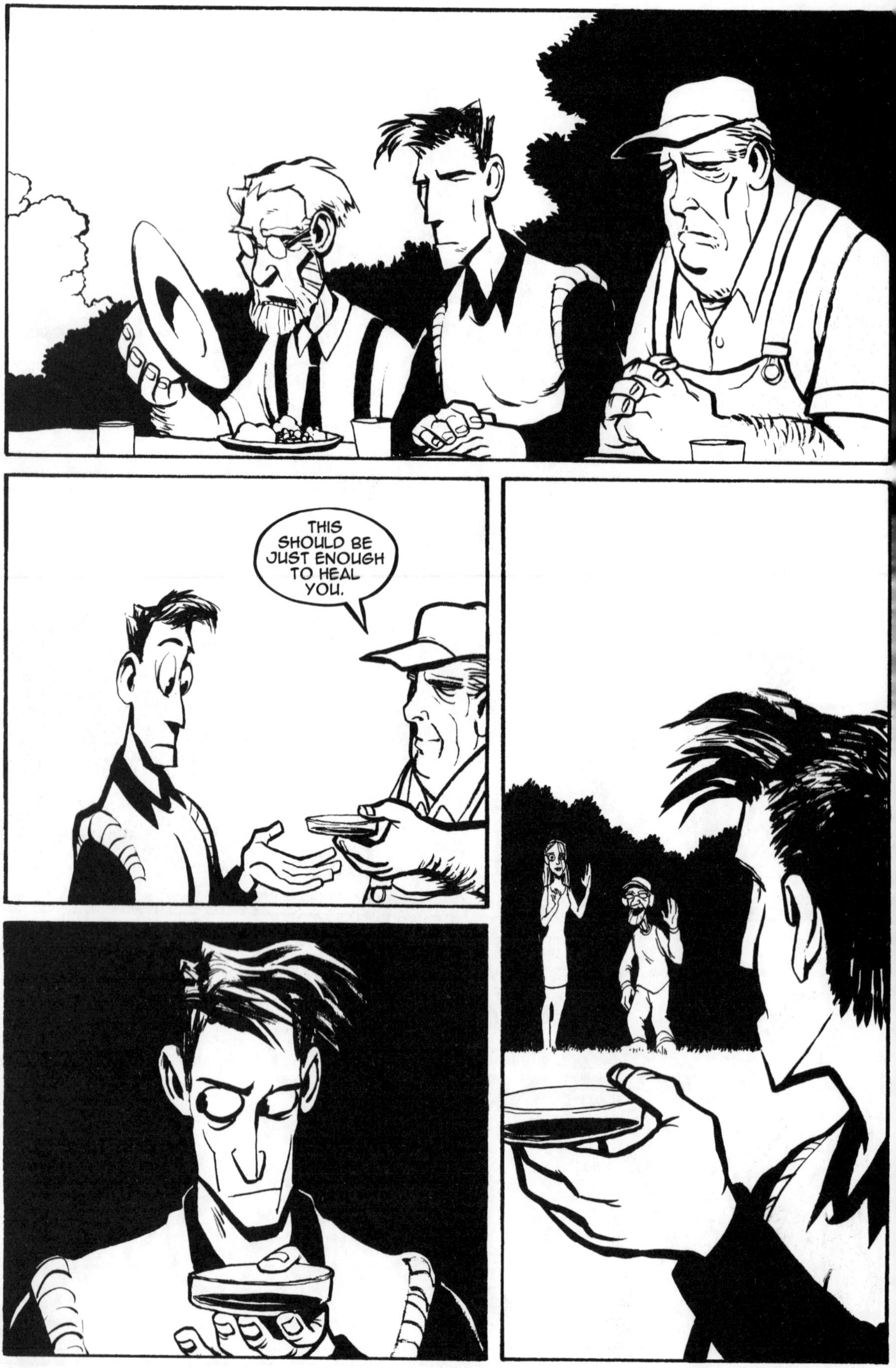
THIS SHOULD BE JUST ENOUGH TO HEAL YOU.

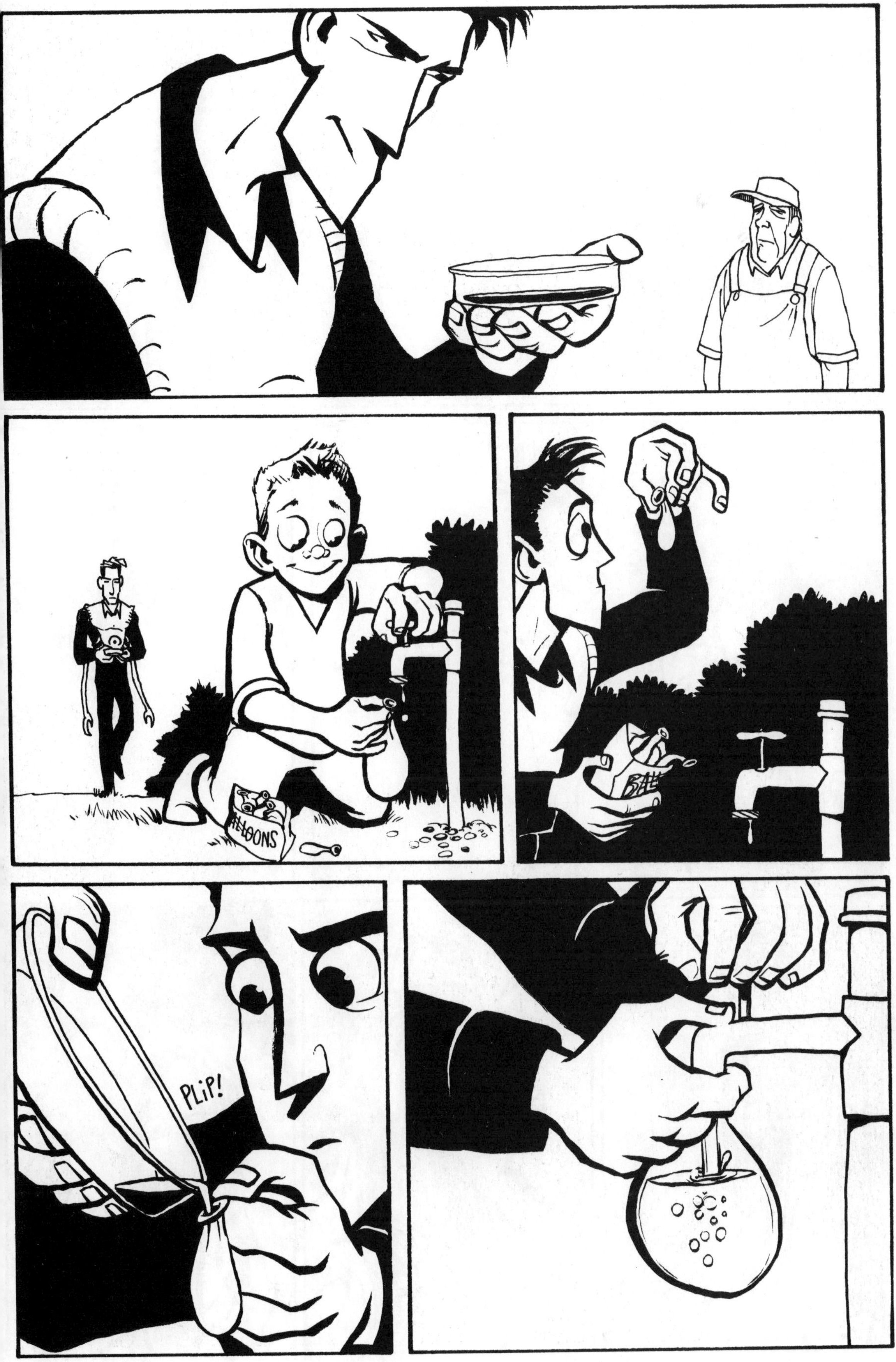
PLIP!

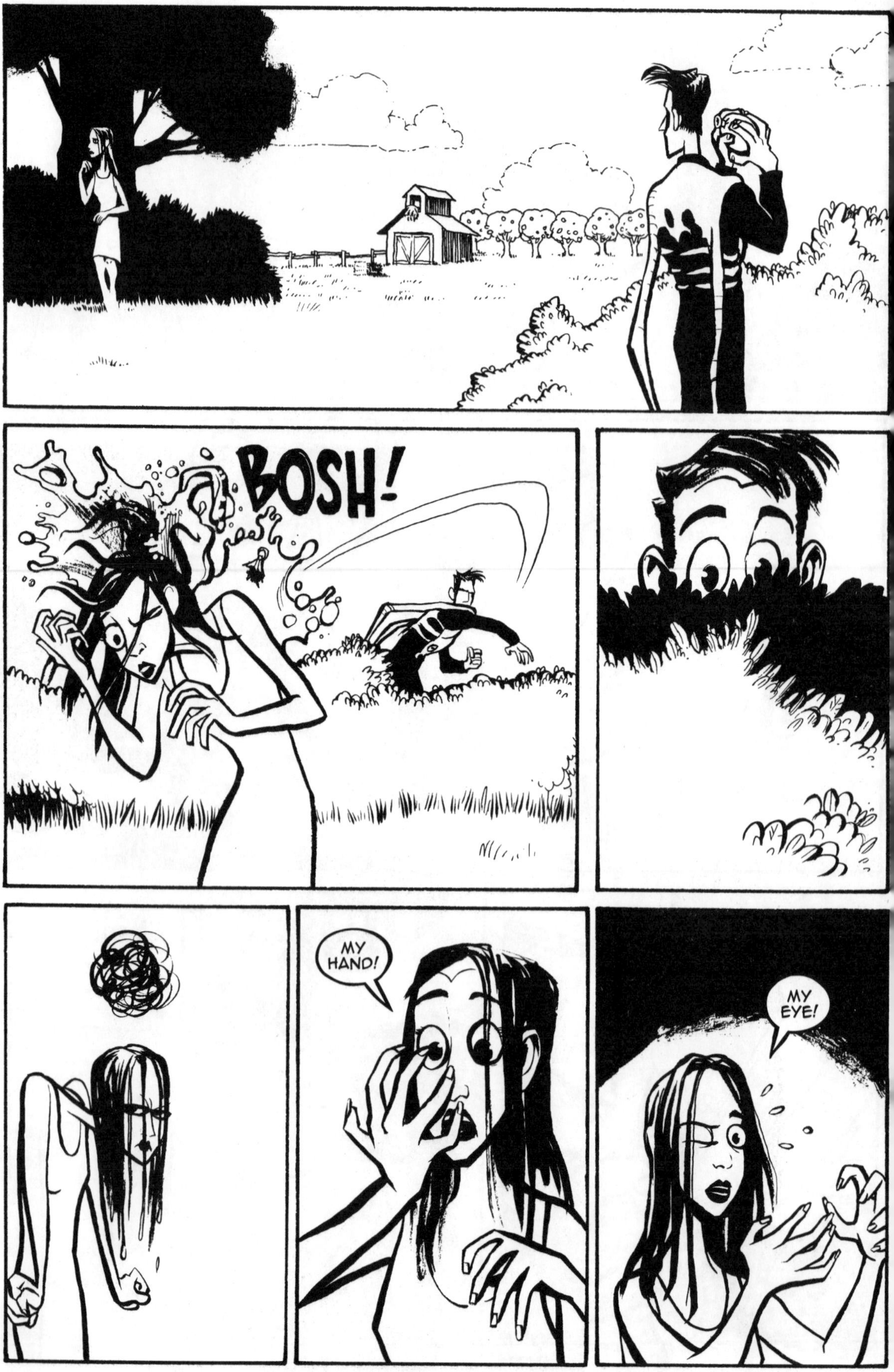
BOSH!
MY HAND!
MY EYE!

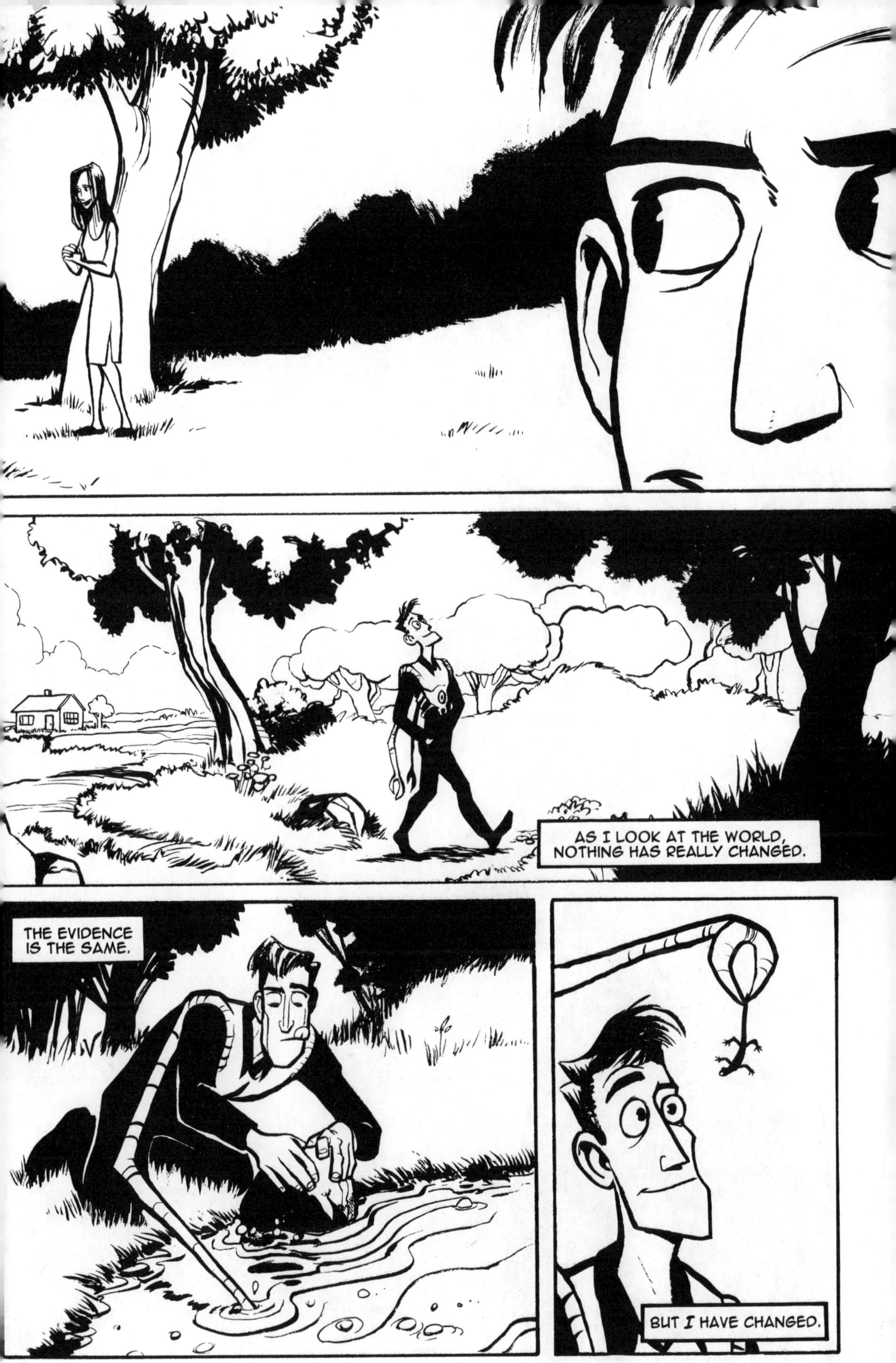
AS I LOOK AT THE WORLD, NOTHING HAS REALLY CHANGED.
THE EVIDENCE IS THE SAME.
BUT I HAVE CHANGED.

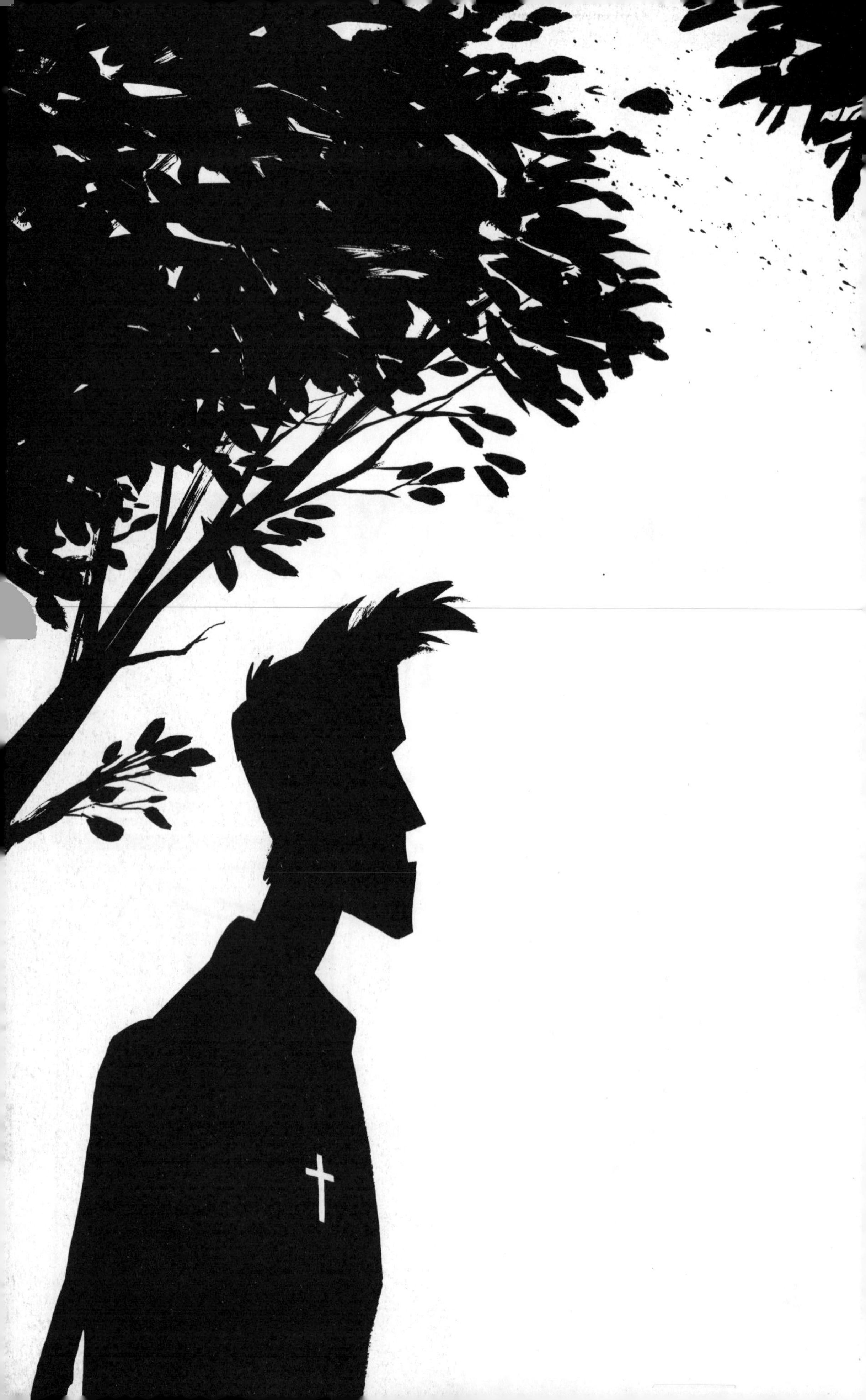

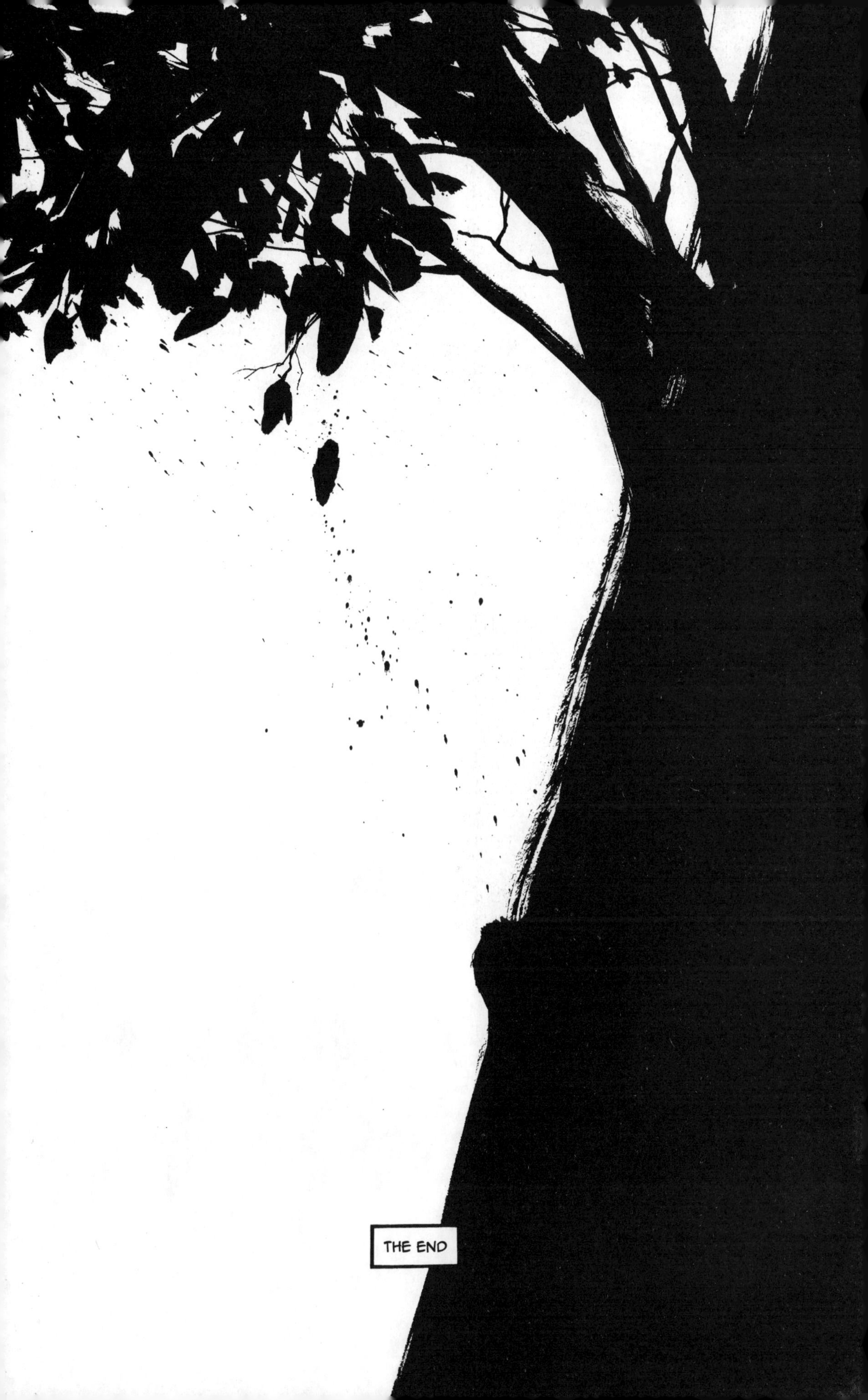
THE END

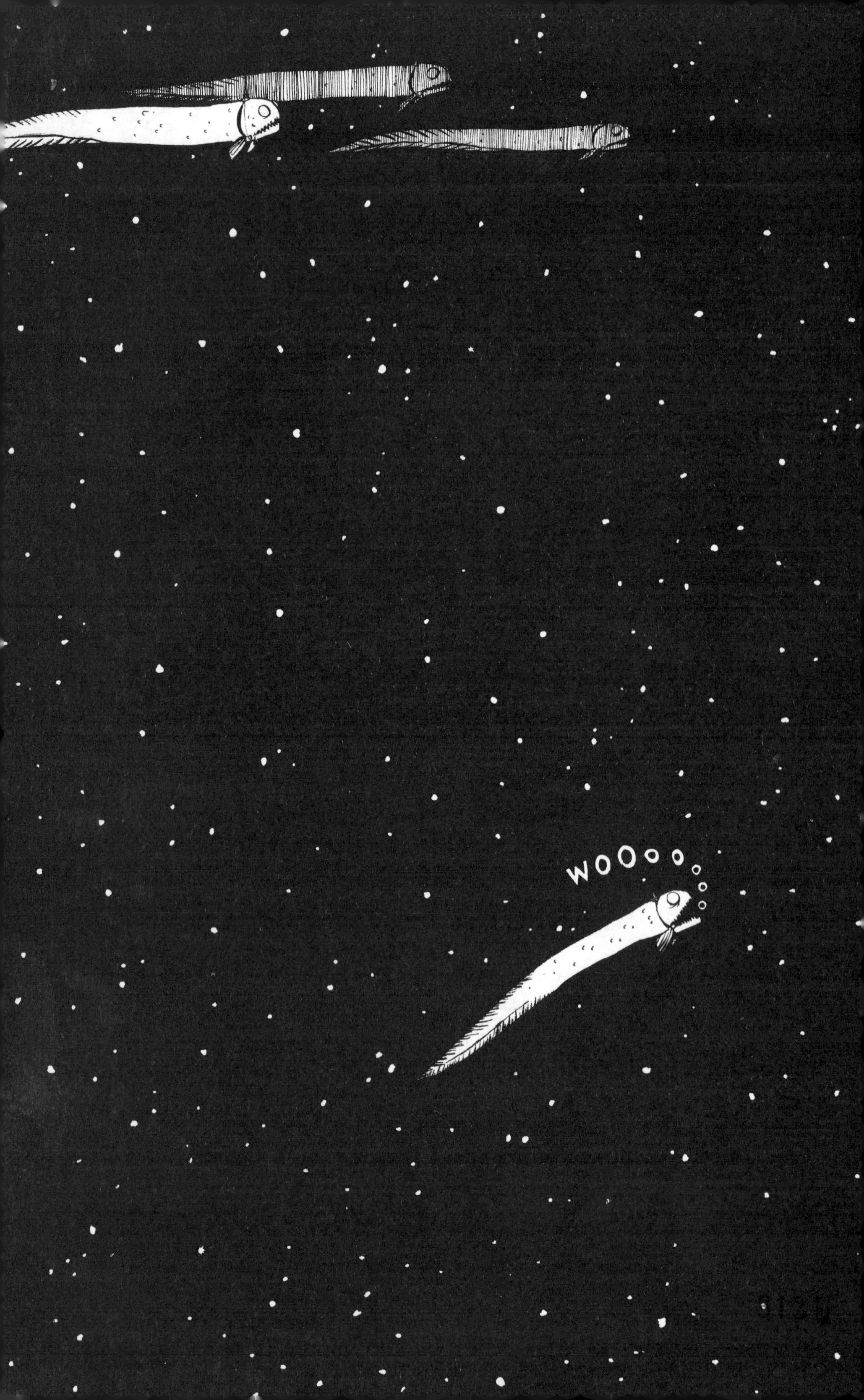
WOOooooo